THE AMALFI SECRET

THE AMALFI SECRET

DEAN REINEKING
CATHERINE REINEKING

STONEBROOK PUBLISHING

Stonebrook Publishing
Saint Louis, Missouri

A STONEBROOK PUBLISHING BOOK

©2025, Dean Reineking and Catherine Reineking

All rights reserved. Published in the United States by Stonebrook Publishing, a division of Stonebrook Enterprises, LLC, Saint Louis, Missouri. No part of this book may be reproduced, scanned, or distributed in any printed or electronic form without written permission from the author.

Scripture texts in this work are taken from the *New American Bible, revised edition* © 2010, 1991, 1986, 1970 Confraternity of Christian Doctrine, Washington, D.C. and are used by permission of the copyright owner.

All Rights Reserved. No part of the New American Bible may be reproduced in any form without permission in writing from the copyright owner.

This book is a work of fiction. Names, characters, businesses, organizations, places, events and incidents either are the product of the authors' imaginations or are used fictitiously. Any resemblance to actual persons, living or dead, events, or locales is entirely coincidental.

Please do not participate in or encourage piracy of copyrighted materials in violation of the author's rights.

Library of Congress Control Number: 2025907229

Paperback ISBN: 978-1-955711-37-1
eBook ISBN: 978-1-955711-38-8

www.stonebrookpublishing.net
PRINTED IN THE UNITED STATES OF AMERICA

"Take no part in the fruitless works of darkness; rather, expose them."

Ephesians 5:11

PREFACE

JANUARY 2025

Gabe sat in his favorite chair. The weight of two decades of memories pressed heavily on his mind. He'd just watched the second inauguration of Donald Trump, a moment that encapsulated the tumultuous journey of the past twenty years. The backdrop for the inauguration was a wall of former presidents stretching from Bill Clinton to the present. Each had taken their turn standing guard over history. And each represented the peaceful transition of power.

At center stage stood Trump. His visage was bold and confident, no challenge too big, no accomplishment out of reach. He proclaimed the golden age of America, greater than ever before. He said America would be a nation like no other, full of compassion, courage, and exceptionalism. He promised American power would stop all wars and bring a new spirit of unity to a world that was angry, violent, and totally unpredictable. His range of assurances was far-reaching.

As Carrie Underwood belted out a flawless acapella version of "America the Beautiful," Gabe grappled with a whirlwind of thoughts. He couldn't help but draw parallels between Trump's grandiose claims and the messianic visions of old. Trump promised everything. He laid out a bold vision, *but what does it mean?* Gabe wondered.

Reverend Franklin Graham went so far as to pray, "Father, when Donald Trump's enemies thought he was down and out, you and you alone saved his life and raised him up with strength and power by your mighty hand." The tone implied a mandate not only from the American people but also from Almighty God himself.

Gabe's gaze shifted to a portrait hanging next to the TV. It was Anna, her stunning beauty undiminished by the passage of time. A deep foreboding tore at his heart. She had opened his eyes to so many dark secrets, secrets that had shaped their work and lives. He missed everything about her.

Gabe pondered the future. Would America become the shining beacon of hope that Donald Trump promised? The past twenty years had been a rollercoaster; the future remained uncertain. Yet, amidst it all, Gabe found solace in the memory of Anna. The work they'd undertaken together was a bittersweet comfort. However, she'd often said, even in the darkest of times, there was always light and hope. He flicked off the TV, picked up his backpack, and walked out the door.

1

POST-SEPTEMBER 11, 2001

The lone fisherman realized the time was approaching. It was nearly eleven o'clock. Pulling his woolen cap down against the chill of the autumn night, he chuckled as he mused about the interesting character who'd approached him at the docks that afternoon.

Who am I to ask questions? he thought. After all, he'd been pulling in only small catches lately. Seemed like an awfully simple, if mildly inconvenient, task for the amount of cash the stranger had offered.

As he maneuvered his small, wooden rig along the coastline, the lights of the Amalfi Hotel emerged from the blackness. He guided his boat into position and scanned his surroundings. No one else was fishing the waters below the hotel. He was alone.

When he cut the engine, he could see a party in progress on one of the balconies. It appeared to be in full swing with loud, raucous voices. He unfolded his fishing net and hoped they'd be too drunk to notice him.

He checked his watch again and surveyed the rest of the hotel. Many of the windows were already dark. A lone person was standing on the balcony one floor above the party. He was leaning on the banister and watching the boisterous activity below.

The fisherman continued to unfold his net as he awaited the exact moment. Suddenly, he heard a woman shout above the din.

"Look! Look out there!"

"Where?" the others questioned as they crowded the balcony rail.

"Right there!" said a redhead who pointed in his direction. "Can you see him? Check it out; he looks like something straight out of *Old Man and the Sea*. Wave and see if you can get his attention."

The fisherman tried to ignore them.

Three floors above the party, another man stood hidden in the shadows. He'd been there for the better part of an hour.

"Come to bed, John," his wife whispered sleepily. "We might as well try to get some rest despite the noise." Francesca Roslo was already in bed and felt very tired.

The man stepped in from the balcony. "They're just having a little fun, the excitement of a big trip and all. Just imagine if we were that young again. We certainly wouldn't be thinking about sleep right now." His soothing words masked his apprehension. He knew the time was close. He stepped back out on the balcony and ducked into the shadows to watch the activity below.

More partygoers had gathered along the rail to catch a glimpse of the fisherman untangling his nets. One of them, a skinny teenager, climbed up on the stone ledge and nearly lost his balance. The fisherman heard a collective gasp as an older gentleman pulled him back from the edge.

The fisherman acted as if he hadn't noticed and checked his watch again. It was time. He laid down his nets and picked up a flashlight. He pointed it up toward the hotel windows and flashed it not once, not twice, but three distinct times.

A cheer went up from the balcony. "He sees us!" the redhead shouted, followed by congratulatory backslaps all around.

The man in the shadows had also seen the three flashes. Concerned, John Roslo stepped back inside his hotel room. He walked to the bed and sat beside his wife, gently stroking her face.

"Fran, I know you're tired, but I'm not ready for bed. It's a beautiful night. I'm going to take a stroll down to the water."

"Please don't be out too late, dear," she pleaded. "It's been a long day, and we both need some sleep."

"You go ahead and sleep. I'll join you when I get back from my walk."

He bent down, whispered a few words in her ear, and kissed her on the cheek. Comforted, she rolled over and exhaled a deep sigh.

Roslo straightened himself and crossed the room to the bureau where he kept his attaché case. He quietly unlocked it and pulled out an old journal. He slipped the journal into the breast pocket of his jacket and relocked the case. He paused a moment and heard Francesca's breathing slow to a rhythmic pattern. She was already asleep. Everything was ready.

He tiptoed to the door, turned off the light, and stepped into the dimly lit corridor. A figure emerged from the shadows as he turned to lock the door. Before Roslo could react, the sting of a needle pierced the side of his neck. In an instant, the stranger vanished up the staircase.

Panicked, John Roslo grasped the door handle, re-entered his room, and stumbled into the bathroom. He closed the door behind him. As tremendous pressure squeezed his chest, a distinct numbness traveled through his body. He splashed water on his face, then doubled over as he felt his throat constrict.

Roslo grabbed his journal but was already losing his fine motor skills. The journal crashed to the floor. He realized what was happening and struggled to fight the leaden feeling that crept into his right arm.

I haven't much time, he thought as he gasped for breath. With great effort, he raised his hand to the mirror. As he groped for the hot water knob, the paralysis reached his heart. The last thing he saw was his own contorted face in the mirror.

In the bedroom, Francesca slept peacefully, lulled by the sounds of the sea. Hours later, she rolled over in the early morning chill and reached for the familiar warmth of the man she had loved for sixty years. But he wasn't there.

Two floors below, Gabe Roslo had finally entered deep sleep after tossing and turning for most of the night. The party on the balcony below had wound down, and the only sound was the pulse of the sea. A nearly full moon cast a glow on the wall and added to the serenity.

Gabe had arrived the previous evening at the invitation of his grandparents, John and Francesca Roslo. He hadn't seen them in over a year and looked forward to this reunion in Italy. As a Canadian climbing guide, Gabe also anticipated the challenging peaks Italy would provide. During the long twenty-two-hour journey from western Canada, warm memories of his youth had filtered through his mind. He loved his grandparents, especially his grandfather, who had been like a father to him.

Suddenly, the phone rang, tearing him from his sleep. Gabe squinted as he picked up his watch from the bedside table—5:45. *It must be a mistake,* he thought. He rubbed the sleep from his eyes and reached for the phone.

"Gabe, it's me, Gram. Please come quickly. Something's wrong with your grandfather. I think he's…" Unable to finish her words, she broke into sobs.

"I'll be right there."

Gabe jumped from the bed. He grabbed an old T-shirt, stumbled into a pair of sweatpants, and ran for the stairs. In seconds, he was in their room, where his grandmother was weeping in the open doorway. Just beyond, he saw his grandfather on the floor in the bathroom.

Gabe rushed in and crouched down beside him. He fought to maintain composure and instinctively felt for a pulse. It was futile. One touch of his grandfather's cold, stiff arm confirmed what his grandmother had been unable to say. His grandfather was gone and had probably been dead for most of the night.

He put his arms around his grandmother, gently supporting her as the tears flowed. Neither of them said a word. After a few moments, he led her to the nearest chair and helped her sit down. He crouched down beside her and placed a protective arm around her.

"Gram, I'm so very sorry," he repeated several times while she rested her head against his shoulder.

"We knew this would come someday," she whispered to him. "Just not right now."

A flurry of thoughts raced through Gabe's mind—what to do when someone dies in a foreign country, who to notify, what to do first. He knew he'd have to deal with all those details, but right now, the most important thing was helping his grandmother. Gabe stood and handed her some tissues.

He went back into the bathroom and could see that his grandfather had cut his head—from the fall, he guessed. Gabe grabbed a towel, gently lifted him off the floor, and moved him to the bed. He placed the towel under his head and pulled the blankets across his chest.

Gabe took a few steps back and looked at his grandmother. She smiled slightly and moved to the edge of the bed, where she sat down and lovingly caressed the head of the man she'd loved for so many years.

"Gram, I'm going to call the innkeeper," he said. He searched his mental register for the name of the man he'd briefly met when he arrived the night before.

"Lorenzo?" she asked, "Yes, please do. He and your grandfather were such good friends. He'll know what to do."

Gabe dialed the main desk but got no answer. The Amalfi Hotel was a family business, and it was still very early.

"I need to go upstairs and find him," Gabe said. "Why don't you come to my room and lie down for a few minutes?"

"Oh, my sweet Gabe," she replied, composing herself, "your grandfather and I have been together so long. I need some time with him. Go find Lorenzo, and I'll stay with my John."

Gabe hesitated and watched his grandmother. She was slight of stature and frail to look at, but he knew from experience that she had an inner strength that would get her through almost any trial.

That was the kind of love he'd wanted for Sarah and himself, a love that would last until death. *But that will never happen now,* he thought. He shook off the mental lapse, turned, and bounded up the stairs, three at a time.

The terrace café of the Amalfi Hotel was nearly the highest point of the building, surpassed only by the level above with the office and a three-car parking garage. The hotel was originally a residence built into a cliff that overlooked the Mediterranean on the outskirts of Amalfi. Gabe would have been drawn in by the breathtaking views any other time, but at the moment, he had only one goal: to find Lorenzo Bonelli.

He spotted Signore Bonelli behind the serving counter in the dining room. His back was to Gabe, and he was squeezing juice for the morning's breakfast.

"Excuse me, Signore Bonelli," Gabe called as he zigzagged through the tables.

Momentarily startled, Lorenzo turned around. "I'm sorry, we don't serve breakfast until 7:00," he began before he recognized Gabe, "but for John's grandson, I can have a cappuccino ready in two minutes."

Lorenzo Bonelli was smiling broadly, but then he noticed the look on Gabe's face. "What is it, young man? Is something wrong?" he asked.

"My grandfather—he passed away last night."

Gabe saw the puzzled look on Lorenzo's face and tried again. "He died."

Lorenzo gasped, closed his eyes, and whispered, "Gesù, Maria, Giuseppe, resto suo anima. Where is Francesca? Is she all right?" he asked as he hastily removed his apron and washed the juice from his hands.

"Yes, for the moment. She's with my grandfather now. She found him in the bathroom a few minutes ago, but I think he's been dead for a few hours."

"Let's go to him," Lorenzo said, already heading for the staircase.

Gabe was astonished at the speed by which Lorenzo descended the four flights of stairs. Despite his age, it was obvious that years of climbing the stairs of the Amalfi Hotel had kept him in excellent physical condition.

"I don't want you to worry, Gabriel," Lorenzo said as they reached the bottom of the staircase. "Your grandfather is…was…one of my closest friends, and Francesca is like family. You take care of her. I'll take care of the rest."

He pushed open the door. "Francesca, I'm here."

Gabe stood in the doorway and watched as the two embraced. His grandfather had only mentioned Lorenzo in passing, but he was obviously a close family friend. Then Gabe was struck by a thought as he absorbed that bittersweet moment. *How could he love his grandfather so much yet know so little about him?* Gabe was grateful that his grandfather had invited him to Italy, but he was also sad. Now, there would be things he would *never* know about him.

Lorenzo and Francesca stood silently and looked at John's body on the bed. Gabe stepped back into the bathroom to be alone for a moment. He closed the door and fumbled for the light switch. In the darkness, he stumbled against something on the floor. When he found the switch, he flicked on the light to see what he'd kicked. It was an old book that had slid under the skirt of the vanity.

He picked it up and thumbed through it. The pages were damp and certain ones had been torn out. With yellowed pages and a cracked leather binding, he was almost certain it was an antique. The pages were filled with handwritten script. *Is this some type of journal or maybe a diary?* he thought.

He stepped back into the room. "Gram, I found this on the floor in the bathroom. Did you drop it?"

"May I see that?" Lorenzo asked, intercepting it before Gabe could hand it to his grandmother. "It looks very old. Perhaps it belonged to John."

"I don't know," Francesca replied. "It might have been John's, but I've never seen it before. He was always reading, you know. He probably had it in his attaché case, but I learned long ago not to ask what he was up to."

She smiled and thought back on all the years she'd kept her questions to herself in support of John and his work for the National Security Agency. They'd agreed long ago on a "don't ask, don't tell" policy as it related to his work—well, most of the time, anyway.

Eyeing the book, Lorenzo made an offer. "Perhaps you'd like me to keep John's things for you, Francesca. I have a safe upstairs in my private residence."

"That would be so kind of you, Lorenzo," she said.

"Don't worry, my dear. I'll take care of everything. I'll arrange to have John moved to a funeral home here in Amalfi until we can get him home to the States." He then turned to Gabe and added, "When you gather your grandfather's things, please bring them to me, and we'll lock them in the safe."

Lorenzo looked back at Francesca, "You and Gabe are welcome to stay as my guests as long as you wish. I'll provide anything you need. Is there anything more I can do right now?"

Francesca thought for a moment. "Yes, there is. Would you please call my cousins in Ravello?"

Lorenzo agreed, bowed slightly, and promised to return with coffee and breakfast after making the call. He handed the book back to Gabe and pulled the door shut. Gabe briefly looked at the book and then set it on a table in the corner.

Fifteen minutes later, Lorenzo reappeared with a tray and carried it to the balcony. He set it on the table and arranged two place settings.

"It's all set," he said. "I've called your cousins. They're on the way, and the funeral director should be here within the hour. There's something else I need to take care of, but here's your breakfast. Is there anything else you need right now, Francesca?"

"No, thank you so much, Lorenzo. We'll be fine for now."

Lorenzo bowed again and departed.

Gabe helped his grandmother to the balcony and into a chair, then sat beside her. He downed a cup of coffee while his grandmother picked at a pastry. There was a long silence. At last, he asked her who he needed to call stateside. She thought for a long moment.

While Gabe waited for a response, he saw Lorenzo return and go into the bathroom with a caddy of cleaning supplies.

"Please get in touch with Zachary Beckett," she finally said in response to Gabe's question. "He goes by Zach. He worked for your grandfather before John retired. He's still at the NSA and will want to know about John. The number for his private line is in our travel documents on the top shelf in the armoire. John always carried a list for emergencies, you know. I think you should contact Zach right away. Lorenzo should be able to help you connect the call."

Gabe stepped back into the room to retrieve the travel documents. He quickly found the list. "Always be prepared," his grandfather had told him many times. "It works in Boy Scouts, and it works in life."

Gabe took the phone numbers and went to the bathroom where Lorenzo was cleaning. The door was slightly ajar. He rapped once and pushed it open.

"Lorenzo, could you…?" he began before stopping cold. Lorenzo was frozen in place, standing in front of the sink and staring at the mirror.

What Gabe saw made his blood run cold. Scrawled in the steamed-up mirror were the letters

**T H B S T
I S H R
S A**

The end of the last letter trailed down the mirror as if the writer hadn't the strength to remove his hand before it fell.

"What the hell is that?" Gabe demanded in a harsh whisper. His words snapped Lorenzo from his trancelike state.

Lorenzo struggled for words and turned slowly to face him. "I... I don't know what it means. I bent down to clean the blood from the floor and left the hot water running. The mirror steamed up, and these letters appeared. I just saw them as you walked in. This could be serious."

"What do you mean by 'serious'?" Gabe questioned. He shut the bathroom door.

"These letters were written after your grandfather arrived," Lorenzo said.

"Anyone could have done that," Gabe countered. He ran his fingers through his hair as he tried to sort out what he'd just stumbled upon.

"No, Gabe. We clean the mirrors when we prepare the room for each new patron."

"It could have been missed by housekeeping," Gabe speculated.

"That's not possible," Lorenzo countered. "I cleaned this room myself."

Gabe felt a chill run down his spine for reasons he couldn't explain. Perhaps it had been the fear in Lorenzo's eyes. Gabe and Lorenzo stared at the ominous letters in front of them.

Suddenly, the spell was broken by Francesca. "Gabe, are you still here? Did Lorenzo tell you how to dial the call?" It was evident by the sound of her voice that she was speaking to him from the balcony.

"She wants me to call my grandfather's friend. He's stateside. She can't see this," Gabe told Lorenzo as he pointed to the mirror.

"Hurry then. My wife can help you connect the call." Lorenzo looked back at the mirror and added, "But there's someone who *does* need to see this."

"The police?" Gabe asked.

"No! Not the police! Not yet, anyway. Someone else, someone who might have an idea about what your grandfather meant," Lorenzo said, "if it even was your grandfather who wrote these letters."

Gabe cracked open the door. "I'm on my way," he called to his grandmother.

But it was too late. She was coming in from the balcony and headed toward the bathroom. "Is everything all right?" she asked, concerned.

"Fine, Gram."

Lorenzo panicked and reflexively reached for a towel to wipe the mirror.

"No!" Gabe exclaimed in a forced whisper. He grabbed Lorenzo's arm and flicked on the exhaust fan. "That'll take care of the mirror for now."

Lorenzo nodded. A look of relief washed over his face. He squeezed Gabe's shoulder firmly. "I'll sit with Francesca while you go to the office," Lorenzo said.

Lorenzo stepped out of the bathroom first, and Gabe followed, turned out the light, and closed the door. Thankfully, Francesca had stopped at John's bedside.

"Francesca, my dear," Lorenzo said. He extended his arms as he crossed the room toward her.

Gabe headed upstairs to the office. He felt shell-shocked and confused, and he focused on his breathing to calm himself. The adrenaline surge reminded him of what he'd felt during a climbing fall when he wondered, in that precarious instant, if his safety line would hold.

His mind raced. *What is the significance of those letters? And Lorenzo Bonelli's reaction to them? What does he mean by, "This could be serious?"* Gabe needed some answers. But first, he needed to call Zach Beckett. He decided not to mention what they'd seen on the mirror. Mr. Beckett might have been his grandfather's trusted confidant, but Gabe didn't know the man, nor did he know Gabe.

He took the last few stairs three at a time and steeled himself for the call. He entered the office, and Lorenzo's wife greeted him warmly.

"Mr. Roslo, I'm so sorry about your grandfather," she said with concern. "Can I get you anything to drink? You look a bit flushed."

"No, thank you. I'm fine, really."

She led him to a private phone and showed him how to dial the international call, then closed the door and left.

Gabe thought for a minute. He had one other call to make before dialing Beckett—to his mother. She would, no doubt, be asleep. The phone rang seven times and then rolled to the recorder. He hung up and tried her cell phone—the same result. He chose not to leave a message. He'd have to try again later.

Gabe looked at his grandfather's phone list. There was a notation by Zach Beckett's name that read *24-hour line* by the number. He looked at his watch: 6:40 a.m.—just before midnight in Washington, DC. *Late, but not too late, given the seriousness of my call*, Gabe thought.

A woman's voice answered, "Mr. Beckett's office."

Gabe was surprised to get a live voice that time of night. He identified himself as John Roslo's grandson and said he needed to speak to Mr. Beckett immediately. The call went through after a series of clicks and a short pause.

"Beckett here."

"Mr. Beckett, my name is Gabe Roslo, John Roslo's grandson."

"Yes, Gabe, I've heard much about you over the years. Please call me Zach. What can I do for you at this hour?"

Gabe hesitated momentarily. "I'm sorry for calling so late, but my grandfather died last night in Amalfi, Italy. My grandmother and I are here with him, and she asked me to call you."

"Died? I'm so sorry. Where is he now? Where are you—and what happened?" Beckett asked.

"He's still at the hotel," Gabe said. "My grandmother found him about an hour ago. The hotel owner has arranged to have his body moved to a funeral home here in Amalfi."

"This could take some time to sort out since he died overseas," Beckett said, "but I can certainly arrange to transport him back to the US. Your grandmother does want him buried in the States, I presume?"

"Yes, I'm sure she'll want him close to her."

"Good. I'll take care of everything. Where are you calling from?" Beckett asked.

"The Amalfi Hotel. It's a small hotel owned by a friend of my grandparents. The innkeeper has offered to let us stay here until the arrangements are made."

Beckett picked a piece of lint from his knee. "Has there been any discussion of an autopsy?"

Gabe looked surprised at his end of the line. "No, should there be?"

"It's standard operating procedure in a lot of places. If asked, tell the coroner you'd prefer to have the autopsy done stateside. Your grandfather had a career with the US government, and I'm sure they can make any arrangements necessary as a professional courtesy."

There was a short pause before Beckett continued. "Gabe, it might be best if I came to Amalfi. That way, I can provide the most assistance. In fact, tell your grandmother I'm on my way. I'll be there in twenty-four hours. Please give Francesca my condolences. I'm so very sorry about your grandfather. He was my mentor as well as my friend."

With that, Beckett hung up and looked at his watch. *I don't have much time*, he thought.

He immediately logged off his computer and stepped outside. He looked around to take in the hectic pace of the city. The Italian sun was shining brightly, and morning rush hour traffic had hit its peak on the streets of Rome.

2

Gabe returned to his grandmother's room and found Lorenzo still consoling her. Francesca's eyes brightened when she saw him. Lorenzo smiled and gave her a kiss on the forehead as he stood to leave.

"I'll wait upstairs for the arrival of your cousins," he said. As he left the room, he motioned for Gabe to step into the hallway.

"Gabriel," he said in a hushed tone.

Gabe leaned down to hear him. He noticed that Lorenzo's bushy eyebrows and hairy forearms amply compensated for his balding head. Signore Bonelli looked like the quintessential pizza chef.

"You need to meet Paolo Castriotti. He was your grandfather's closest associate here in Amalfi. Paolo is the man who needs to see the mirror. Perhaps he can explain things. Are you willing to meet with him?"

"Of course."

"Good. I'll call him right away." Lorenzo hesitated, "I also want to show him the book you found."

"Is there a problem with it?" Gabe asked.

"No problem, at least not for now," he backpedaled. "But the book and the mirror might be connected. I don't mean to alarm you, Gabe. Let's just show Castriotti what we found in the bathroom and hear what he has to say."

Lorenzo quickly changed the subject. "Why don't you sit with your grandmother for a while? Her cousins should be here soon. I think we should encourage her to go with them to Ravello. Then we can concentrate on what happened here without worrying about her well-being. It will give us a chance to talk about it at length."

"They'll take good care of her?" Gabe asked.

"The best," Lorenzo replied, "and she'll appreciate their support. My friend from the funeral home is due here," he said, checking his watch, "in about fifteen minutes. I'll wait upstairs for him."

With that, Lorenzo turned and disappeared up the staircase.

Gabe went back to his grandmother's room and picked up the book he'd found in the bathroom. *What's going on?* he thought. He examined it for a few moments and set it back down. Hopefully, Paolo Castriotti would be able to shed some light on things.

He moved across the room and looked at his grandmother sitting in a chair next to his grandfather's lifeless body. The long trip had been grueling enough for Gabe, but she was contending with the loss of her husband. He was worried about the toll it would take on a person her age. *And to make matters worse, there are now bizarre circumstances surrounding his death,* Gabe thought.

At that instant, Gabe's mind snapped back to something his grandfather had said to him when they first planned the trip: "Should anything happen to me, I need you to look after your grandmother." Gabe had taken it as a passing comment and reassured his grandfather that he certainly would, even though they both already knew that's exactly what he would do.

Suddenly, he was struck by another thought. Had he been invited to Italy for reasons other than climbing? Was it possible that his grandfather had known his death was imminent? The thought made Gabe shudder. He pushed it from his mind and resolved to take care of his grandmother, just as he'd promised.

The balcony door was still open, so Gabe pulled a thin blanket from the drawer and placed it around Francesca's shoulders to counter the sea breeze. "Gram, what can I do for you? I'm worried about you."

"You've always been so thoughtful, a blessing to us," she said. She rested her forehead in her hand. "Just sit with me for a while, won't you?"

He pulled a chair next to her and sat down. After an extended period of silence, Gabe said, "Tell me about you and Grandfather."

She smiled. "What would you like to know?"

"Well, for instance, how did the two of you meet?" He adjusted his chair to get more comfortable.

"How did we meet?" she repeated with a slight laugh.

Francesca tilted her head, and her expression took on a pleasing, faraway look, her eyes drifting off to another place and time. After a long pause, she began.

"It was shortly after the liberation of Rome in 1944. I'll never forget it. American and British forces had just arrived as conquering heroes. I'd been working as a clerk in the central personnel office of the Italian Army in Rome, a job I had for most of the war.

"It was an important place," she continued, "because we kept track of all Italian Army personnel—records of names, rank, division assignments, well, many things. The central personnel office was a real nerve center for the war effort.

"After the German occupation of Rome, German officers took over our office. The Italian high command had moved to a safe location outside the city, but we were left behind to fend for ourselves. It was a horrible few months, but when it became clear that the Allied advance into Italy was unstoppable, the German high command ordered a retreat from Roman soil. Rome was declared an open city, and since the Germans no longer intended to defend it, the city was spared the devastation that had crushed so much of Italy." Francesca shivered and began to stand.

"What can I get for you?" he asked, jumping up.

"I'm still a bit chilly," she replied. "Would you mind getting my sweater from the bureau? It's in the middle drawer on the right."

Gabe got up and got the sweater. "Here," he said. He breathed a sigh of relief that she hadn't moved toward the bathroom.

"Thank you, Gabe."

Pulling on the sweater, she continued. "I'll never forget that morning long ago. I arrived at work late. I was expecting a severe reprimand but learned that Colonel Kessler had left the city during the night. There was a strange, eerie silence in our office that first morning. It was surreal, in fact. We wanted to explode with joy, but we were fearful the whole thing was a cruel German hoax to identify traitors. What if they returned to crush our joy with an iron fist?

"As the day wore on, we gradually became more comfortable. We spoke about the possibility of liberation, and by the second day, we knew the occupation had ended."

Her eyes welled with tears. "Later in the week, British and American tanks secured the perimeter of Rome, and the celebration began in earnest. It was early June, and the weather was beautiful. We danced in the streets, and more than one American GI was captivated by our beautiful young women. Of course, the sentiment was returned, and we treated those brave young men like heroes.

"Within a few days, Allied brass began arriving, and officers of the American Army secured control of our office. That's when I met your grandfather. He was assigned to an intelligence detail that specialized in monitoring personnel strength and troop movements. They were very interested in our records."

Francesca fell silent with a pleasant look on her face. She lovingly smiled at John and stroked his arm through the blanket. Gabe watched her savor the memory from so many years before. He did not interrupt her. Finally, she turned her attention back to her grandson.

"We met about two weeks later. I know it sounds trite now, but when he walked through the door between those two other officers, I knew he was the man God had chosen for me. All I had to do was convince John of that," she added with a laugh.

"We spoke several times that day, each conversation related to the war effort. But when we made eye contact, I knew he was interested. The third time he came to my office, he invited me to dinner. My face became so flushed. I can still feel the heat in my cheeks when I think of it. My English was only a little better than his Italian, but it was clear that his offer had been accepted."

She looked affectionately at John's body on the bed. "As an intelligence officer, your grandfather had many special privileges within the army that others of similar rank did not. For us, that turned out to be a wonderful thing."

"How so?" Gabe asked.

"As the war progressed, John traveled extensively between London and Moscow."

"Moscow?" Gabe raised an eyebrow in surprise.

"Yes, Moscow. Remember, the Soviet Union was an American ally during the Second World War, and it was good for the two of us that they were."

Gabe realized that the history he had studied was the life they had lived.

"Rome became a stopover for his trips between London and Moscow," she continued. "Your grandfather was secretly passing classified information between the Russians and Americans about troop strength, division placements, and German resistance levels. Those were tumultuous days, but John's visits were a breath of fresh air. The two allies used this critical information in their effort to crush Germany in the middle."

Just then, Francesca's cousins burst into the room, followed by Lorenzo. The cousins spoke Italian in rapid-fire succession, and Gabe, who did not understand a word, stepped out of their way.

The three women were similar in age, size, and facial features, and they were obvious first cousins. Gabe knew their respective mothers had been sisters. As they huddled around Francesca in their house dresses, he noticed their calf muscles looked like they belonged to mountain bikers, not old women. *They must do a lot of walking over here,* he guessed.

Gabe rested his back against the wall and ran his hand through his hair. After many tears, words, and more tears, they were all suddenly quiet. When he looked up, everyone was staring at him.

Lorenzo explained in English, "Your grandmother's cousins have invited her to stay with them at their home in the mountains. She told them she was thankful for the invitation but was concerned for your welfare. She doesn't want to go unless it's okay with you."

Gabe turned to them and smiled. "I think it would be best," he said. He and Lorenzo exchanged a knowing look. He then added, "We can take care of matters here."

Lorenzo translated the answer, and the cousins were obviously pleased.

"But I won't leave until I know John's safe," Francesca protested.

The funeral home director and his assistant arrived as if on cue, knocking gently at the door. "Signore Bonelli, your wife told me I'd find you here."

A round of grieving sobs sprung up anew among the cousins. Lorenzo, familiar with the custom, ushered them gently from the room. He consoled them in Italian and suggested they let Francesca say her goodbye in private. He turned back toward Francesca as he exited and offered to put her luggage in the car. She accepted. Gabe then followed him into the hall.

"Gabriel, Paolo Castriotti will be here by 10:30. Let's meet on the terrace before coming back here."

Gabe nodded and quietly returned to the room. Meanwhile, Francesca packed her things. The funeral director momentarily distracted him with paperwork and signatures. Gabe looked up and realized that Francesca had slipped into the bathroom unnoticed. A wave of panic ran through him. There was nothing he could do but hope she wouldn't notice the mirror. He waited several agonizing moments until he heard the toilet flush and the water stop running. Finally, she opened the door.

He was reassured by her distracted, tearful countenance. She dabbed at her eyes with a tissue, closed the bathroom door behind her, and placed her toiletry case in the luggage.

After a touching goodbye, the mortician respectfully covered John's face and prepared him to be moved. Gabe took his grandmother by the arm and helped her to the parking lot, where Lorenzo appeared a few moments later with her bags.

Once the body was loaded, Francesca turned resolutely to the mortician. "Please be careful with my John." She then turned to Lorenzo, "And you take care of my Gabe."

Francesca gently reached for Gabe's face and kissed him on each cheek. She smiled. He saw in her eyes the strength of an Italian widow who would survive.

"Are you sure you want to stay at the hotel?" she asked again.

"Yes," Gabe reassured her. "I'll be fine. Get some rest, and I'll call you later."

She got into her cousin's car. Morning traffic was brisk, so Lorenzo stepped onto the road and raised his hand. Traffic came to a stop. The cousins backed out, and in a flash, the car disappeared around a curve. A few moments later, they were climbing the mountain switchbacks toward their home in Ravello.

Gabe had kept up a good front for his grandmother but was relieved to have a few hours alone. He felt as though he'd been driving through a dense fog at great speed. Lorenzo had already excused himself to tend to the needs of his hotel, so Gabe went down to the room to collect his grandfather's personal belongings.

He again picked up the book. This time, he examined it more closely. It was an antique. He flipped through it and spotted the date 1921 on one of the pages. Still, he had a hard time making sense of its cryptic contents. *What does all this mean?* He thought back to Lorenzo's reaction earlier and decided to separate the book from his grandfather's other belongings. He checked the hall and carried it to his room, where he locked it in the safe. He returned to his grandfather's room, gathered his other belongings, and took them to Lorenzo.

"It'll be a few hours until Paolo arrives," Lorenzo said. "Why don't you try to get some rest?"

Gabe thanked him for the suggestion, but he had another idea. Gabe decided to do what he always did when he needed solitude. He changed into his running clothes and was back outside a few minutes later, heading up the coastal road toward Amalfi. Running would give him a chance to clear his head.

Although hilly, Gabe found the sea level elevation quite to his liking. There was plenty of oxygen compared to the Canadian Rockies. He rounded a bend and spotted the small coastal village of Amalfi shooting straight up from the sea. It clung to the sides of sheer vertical cliffs.

He had read about Amalfi in preparation for his trip and marveled at how this small village had become frozen in time. As far back as the eighth century, its citizens had made their living on the sea by trading throughout the Mediterranean with the Byzantines to the east and the Arabs of North Africa to the south. It had long been a thriving maritime village, and in the twelfth century, its residents invented the compass and introduced the magnetic needle into their navigation methods. Around the same time, they brought the art of papermaking to Europe from Arabia. The quality of Amalfi's paper was so high that it immediately became the standard for all official Vatican documents of that era. Even today, the Vatican State still uses Amalfi paper for its correspondence.

Gabe peered over the guardrail as he ran. He saw a wooden staircase winding down the cliff to a black sand beach no larger than a football field. Two small fishing boats had pulled up on the sand, and the beach was flanked by a harbor to the west and jutting cliffs to the east.

He could also see local traffic snaking around a turnabout at the entrance to the harbor marina. He followed the coastal road until it reached the turnabout, where he veered right. He turned away from the sea into the village and passed through a stone archway. He found himself in a large piazza. His attention was immediately drawn to a magnificent stone staircase that ascended to an ornate cathedral. *Must be Saint Andrew's,* he thought. He recalled that Amalfi had grown up around the cathedral where the apostle's remains were entombed.

The piazza bustled with early morning activity. Sounds of the sea mingled with Italian voices and chirping birds that roosted on ledges. Amid the tourists and shopkeepers, he saw local women hanging laundry from balconies and men with fishing caps perched on their weathered, leathery heads drinking morning coffee.

He jogged through the piazza and noticed buildings that had once housed old trade shops, now converted into an array of hotels, restaurants, and bars. The storefronts were filled with objects found in any coastal town on the globe—postcards, sand art, seascapes, and T-shirts, as well as local fare like the lemon liqueurs and the famous decorative tiles Amalfi was known for. Even though Amalfi clung to its heritage, it was clear that it now depended on foreign tourists and their euros for survival.

He left the square behind and headed up the main village road toward the hills that rose up behind town. High above and to the left, he saw a medieval castle perched on a cliff, keeping a vigilant watch over the village from a distance. It had a menacing look, but Gabe decided that his opinion was probably colored by the events of the morning.

He ran another hundred meters and heard rushing water below his feet. He peered through the ancient, rough-hewn iron grates and saw the raging flow of a river that ran beneath the streets of Amalfi. For ages, its steady flow to the sea had cut a niche into the mountain. Now the village was built on top.

As he continued deeper into the village, the asphalt lane ascended to a steep incline. Gabe was up to the challenge. He was an impressive physical specimen, shaped by years of a rigid workout schedule. Six foot two, with sandy blonde hair and green eyes, he resembled his grandfather in his younger years. He never smoked and had taken grief in college when he refused to partake in drugs and excessive drinking. Even so, he was quick-witted, and everyone liked him.

He thought back to the vow he'd made when he was young to never turn out like his father, a man who had failed to recover from the habits he'd picked up in Vietnam. Instead, he chose to follow his grandfather's lead with a military-style self-discipline that had paid off for him.

His mind drifted to the life he'd had with his grandfather, who'd recently celebrated his eighty-fourth birthday. Gabe was in Italy at his request, and he held a deep affection for him. His grandfather had been there for all of Gabe's important events: football games, baseball games, school functions, and the like. Gabe was deeply grateful for all the support he'd received from him. Indeed, John Roslo had been like a father to him, filling the void left by his father, Alex.

Gabe and Alex were virtual strangers. They rarely saw each other, and whenever they did, his father was drunk. Alex Roslo had made a lot of promises over the years that he'd failed to keep, and Gabe loathed his lies and deceptions. His father didn't even make it to the Virginia state championship game when Gabe's high school baseball team played for the title.

He hadn't been there from the beginning, Gabe thought bitterly. His father was serving a second tour of duty in Vietnam when Gabe was born, and he returned to the States a shell of a man. His mother eventually gave up on him and found a new home that included their young son but not Alex.

Gabe swiped a hand at the sweat that blurred his vision. He checked his watch. It was after 9:00.

The watch was a gift from his grandfather and had great sentimental value. He received it in honor of his full-ride baseball scholarship to the Colorado School of Mines. It bore a truly unique design with an iridescent blue face and Roman numerals that glowed in the dark. The crystal now had a slight crack just above the eight, something that had occurred during a rock climb near Banff in the Canadian Rockies. Even so, Gabe loved it and wore it everywhere.

Given the time, he turned back toward the hotel. His mind focused on the events of the morning. It reeled with questions. *What do the cryptic letters mean? Why are they on the mirror, and why is Lorenzo Bonelli so concerned? Was my grandfather involved in something?* Gabe knew his grandfather had retired after a long and distinguished career with the NSA, but was he involved in something new, perhaps something dangerous? Maybe something dishonorable?

Surely not, Gabe thought, but suddenly, his mind jumped to the next step. *If he was involved in something shady, did it mean he wasn't the man I always admired? Had our relationship been a sham, too?*

Gabe increased his stride. *No,* he concluded. *My mind is playing tricks on me.* Gabe pushed aside his doubts. His grandfather had been a man of honor and integrity. His work for the NSA had been a direct result of his patriotism, and so were his duties during World War II. John Roslo had lived a life surrounded by faithful friends and a loving wife. And he'd always been there for Gabe.

Gabe reached full stride and resolved to get to the bottom of things. He needed to know what had happened to his grandfather and was determined to find out. A few minutes later, he turned into the gate of the Amalfi Hotel. He bent over to catch his breath.

3

Gabe still had an hour before the meeting with Paolo Castriotti, so he took a quick swim in the sea to cool down, showered, and arrived on the terrace just in time. He entered the terrace and found Lorenzo speaking to a man who had his back to Gabe. Lorenzo abruptly broke off his conversation and stepped toward Gabe. The anxious look in Lorenzo's eyes confirmed there was trouble.

"Gabe, this is Paolo Castriotti."

Lorenzo motioned to the man by his side. Castriotti extended a hand as Gabe sized him up. Castriotti was in his mid to late sixties, Gabe guessed, about five feet eight inches tall, with a classic Roman nose atop a black mustache. His hair was salt and pepper and well groomed. Though casually dressed in black, Gabe could tell by his stature that this was a man of some substance, perhaps a local businessman.

"Gabriel, I am deeply saddened by the loss of your grandfather. I feel as though I've lost a brother," said Castriotti as he shook Gabe's hand. "He spoke of you many times and was very proud of you."

"Thank you," Gabe said. "He mentioned your friendship often as we planned this trip to Italy."

Castriotti switched gears and launched right in. "Lorenzo and I have already spoken. He told me about the strange message on the mirror and said you showed him the old book you found after John's death. Do you know where it is now? It was missing when Lorenzo checked your grandfather's belongings."

"Why did Lorenzo go through his things?" Gabe asked. The apprehension he felt showed on his face and was evident in his tone. He was glad that he'd locked up the book.

Castriotti exchanged a furtive look with Lorenzo before he continued. "Gabe, you must trust that we have your best interests and those of your family at heart. John was a dear friend of mine for many years. Francesca can also attest to that and to his friendship with Lorenzo."

Castriotti looked again at Lorenzo and then back to Gabe. He hesitated for a moment to find the right words and began again. "Gabe, we're suspicious about your grandfather's death."

"Suspicious?" Gabe repeated. He began to wonder if his earlier imaginings had been true.

"Yes," Castriotti affirmed. "The book you showed Lorenzo was not just a book of personal reflections. It was, in fact, a diary that belonged to your great-grandfather, John's father. I've seen it before. I know there are people who might be interested in getting their hands on it—in conjunction with the message on the mirror."

Gabe froze. "Do you mean..." he stammered, unable to finish his question.

"I mean, the fact that he died last night with that book in his possession and the cryptic message on the mirror—well, it just leads to many questions. Did you notice anything suspicious about his appearance when you found him?"

"He didn't appear to be shot or stabbed. The only blood was from a cut on his head that I presume happened when he fell to the floor."

"People can die in many ways. Is it possible he was poisoned?" Castriotti asked, turning to Lorenzo.

"Possible," Lorenzo replied, "but as Gabe said, there were no outwardly obvious signs."

Gabe felt himself tremble. He composed himself and asked, "Murder? Why would anyone want to murder my grandfather?"

"I don't know, but if it was to steal the diary, apparently they failed," Castriotti replied.

"Maybe not," Gabe countered. "When I found the book—the diary, as you say—it was damp, and some pages were torn out."

The color drained from Castriotti's face. "Where's the diary now, Gabe? May we have a look at it?"

"It's in my room. I'll get it."

"I want a look at that mirror, too," Castriotti added.

"Let me grab the key for John's room, and we'll take care of both things at once," Lorenzo said as he ushered the two men from the terrace.

Gabe nodded and retrieved the book from his safe. When he reached his grandfather's room, the door was ajar, and he could hear the two men talking in the bathroom. Gabe crowded into the cramped space with them and shut the door.

Lorenzo turned on the hot water faucets in the tub and sink. In seconds, the steam revealed the letters on the mirror. Seeing them this time, Gabe had the distinct impression his grandfather had scrawled them in a desperate attempt to communicate with *him*. Gabe wondered what he had been trying to say.

The three men stood in puzzled silence as the steam increased. Gabe felt a chill run through him despite the hot, humid conditions in the bathroom. He stepped out of the bathroom and grabbed a notepad and pen from the bedside table. Returning, he wrote precisely what he saw, tore the paper from the pad, and stuck it in his pants pocket. He then made two other copies and handed one each to Lorenzo and Castriotti. When the steam condensed and ran down the mirror, Lorenzo switched on the exhaust fan and suggested they return to the terrace.

"I won't let anyone else in here for now," Lorenzo said. "This room will remain unoccupied until we have some answers. If we need to get the police involved, we don't want to disturb a crime scene."

They went back to the terrace. Gabe laid the diary and his copy of the message on the table. Castriotti picked up the diary and began to scan its pages. Lorenzo poured three cups of coffee and sat down with the other two men.

"Maybe you can make some sense of it," Gabe said to Castriotti. "It meant nothing to me."

Castriotti nodded, deep in thought. The other two men looked at the letters.

"What could he have meant by this jumble of letters?" Lorenzo asked no one in particular.

"He was obviously trying to tell us something," Gabe said. "Did you notice the way the last letter trailed off down the mirror? I think he was in a hurry and knew he didn't have time to write it all out."

"Hmm, that's possible," Castriotti said. He swirled the coffee in his cup as he thought.

"There was no spacing between the letters either, just the fact that they were written in three lines," Lorenzo interjected.

"Do you think they're initials for something or someone?" Castriotti speculated, setting his cup on the table.

"Perhaps, but for whom?" Lorenzo responded.

Castriotti rubbed his mustache and continued, "Or did he just leave out some of the letters?"

"Yeah, buy a vowel," Gabe said under his breath.

The other men looked at him, puzzled. "What do you mean?" Lorenzo asked as he watched Gabe rip a fresh sheet of paper from the pad and start to scribble.

"Probably nothing. It's from a game show in America that I used to watch with my grandfather when I was little," Gabe grew more excited as he explained, "Players guessed at letters represented by blank squares to put together a phrase. They could guess consonants but had to buy vowels out of their prize money.

"The game is neither here nor there," he continued. "My point is that perhaps my grandfather left out letters that he knew we could figure out. Now, we just need to solve the puzzle to understand what he's trying to tell us."

"But there are already two vowels in it," Castriotti countered.

"I know," Gabe said. "He must have felt they were essential to deciphering the rest."

The men spent several minutes trying different combinations but grew frustrated. Gabe suggested that maybe the diary held a clue.

Castriotti laid out the diary. "I counted remnants of five missing pages. It appears they were torn in the middle of this diary entry." He pointed first to the left side of the diary and then to the right, where they saw fragments of entries in each case. They hovered over the diary, guessing from context what might have been on the missing pages.

Gabe looked closely at the dates. "The entries are in chronological order, and all the missing pages are from 1979. But he didn't make an entry every day, only sporadically over the years."

The three men spent twenty more minutes looking at the diary and the message.

"This is useless," Castriotti finally said. "We're getting nowhere here. Whoever wanted the information from this diary has it. Gabe, I hope you will—how do you say it in America—keep this close to the vest for now."

"Don't you think we should notify the police of our suspicions?" Gabe asked.

"I don't think involving the authorities just yet will be helpful in finding out what happened to your grandfather. The Carabinieri in Italy are not known for their speedy investigations, especially in small towns like Amalfi. If it had been an obvious murder, that would be one thing. But for now, we are operating on our suspicions. If we want to find out what happened to John and these missing pages, we should try to get some answers on our own first. Have you considered an autopsy?" Castriotti asked Gabe.

"Same question Zach asked," Gabe mused.

Castriotti leaned forward. "Who's Zach?"

"Zachary Beckett, a former colleague of my grandfather's at the NSA. My grandmother had me call him this morning about my grandfather's death. Beckett suggested that we not approve an autopsy—that it would be done stateside. In fact, he's on his way here now. He was catching the next flight from DC to help get my grandfather's body back to the States. He told me that his government connections would cut through any red tape. I expect him here tomorrow."

"Is he trustworthy?" Castriotti asked.

"I assume so since my grandmother asked me to call him. I have no reason to distrust him, but I've never met the man either. He said my grandfather was his mentor, and they were close friends."

"Then why have you never met him?" Castriotti wondered aloud.

"I guess the opportunity never arose," Gabe answered.

Castriotti's question caused Gabe to think. *Perhaps Zach Beckett and my grandfather were caught up in something together, something that led to my grandfather's murder. But what?*

The three men sat thinking quietly for several minutes, once again trying to decipher the message. Finally, Gabe broke the silence.

"This is futile. We need some help. Surely there's somebody who can help us."

Lorenzo tapped his fingers on the table in contemplation. He then turned his gaze on Castriotti. "Rome?"

"Exactly! But it may be difficult to arrange on such short notice given his schedule," Castriotti replied.

"True, but I don't think we have any other options at this point, do we?" asked Lorenzo.

"What about Rome? What are you talking about?" Gabe demanded.

"A couple of years ago, I introduced your grandfather to a contact of mine in Rome," Castriotti answered. "John had questions related to this diary, and I arranged for him to meet with a high-ranking official at the Vatican, Cardinal Friedrich Bauer."

"A cardinal?" Gabe asked, incredulous.

"That's right—Cardinal Bauer. He's a personal acquaintance of mine and well-connected within the walls of the Vatican. I know for a fact that he maintained contact with John after their initial meeting. He will certainly want to know about his death, and if anybody can help us, he can. The real question is whether he can see you on short notice. He's a very busy man and travels frequently on Vatican business."

"Let's call him then," Gabe said.

"You realize he's not the type of man you just call up for a chat, especially when you consider the gravity of the situation. You will need to go to Rome."

"Go there? What will happen to my grandmother if I go to Rome now?" Gabe asked. "My grandfather specifically asked me to take care of her if something ever happened to him. I can't abandon her at a time like this, and if someone did kill my grandfather for this diary, how do I know she won't be next?"

"Don't worry about Francesca," Lorenzo jumped in, "Right now, she's completely safe at her cousins' house. Paolo and I will keep an eye on her; besides, nobody but us knows where she is. Perhaps you can tell her that you need to go to Rome to attend to some details to return John's body to the States. We'll cover for you and handle the rest."

Gabe hated the idea of deceiving his grandmother. Lying for any reason was completely foreign to him. It was bad enough that she didn't know what was going on, but now they were asking him to go to Rome under false pretenses. The entire idea ran contrary to Gabe's nature. All he wanted to do was protect her and keep her from getting hurt.

"I don't think going to Rome is a good idea," he said.

"Gabe, what choice do you have? Cardinal Bauer might be the only person who can help you," Castriotti protested. "And your grandmother might be in greater danger if you don't meet with him."

Gabe suspected Castriotti was right. He didn't like it, but he reluctantly nodded his assent.

"Okay. I'll go. I'll meet with him if it'll help me get to the bottom of this. If I must go to Rome, so be it."

Castriotti pulled out his cell phone. "With your permission, I'll call him immediately to arrange a meeting time. Hopefully, he's there today."

Gabe consented, and Castriotti stepped away from the table to place the call. Minutes later, he returned.

"We have a meeting for you, Gabe. But you'll have to leave for Rome immediately. Cardinal Bauer is traveling tomorrow but can meet with you this afternoon. He's working from his residence today. I'll drive you to Naples to catch the next train.

"I have a niece in Rome," Castriotti continued, "Her name is Anna. I can arrange for her to pick you up at the station in Rome and take you to the cardinal's residence."

"What about the diary?" Gabe asked.

"You should take it with you. Show it to Cardinal Bauer when you get there—along with the message. I'll get my car. We'll call Francesca from the road and tell her about your trip. Can you be ready in fifteen minutes?"

Gabe nodded and took a long, slow sip of coffee while contemplating the gravity of what he was about to do. He wondered where all this was headed. He set down his cup and rose from the table to pack his overnight bag. As he left the terrace, he saw Castriotti and Lorenzo exchange a look that filled him with trepidation.

4

ONE YEAR EARLIER: ISTANBUL

The mysterious Master of the Royal Secret had watched world events unfold and was contemplating his next move. He stood behind his intricately appointed Indonesian mahogany desk while leaning against the back of his lush Swedish leather chair. Preoccupied, he stared out the window of his penthouse office, lost in thought, until his phone broke the silence.

"Yes," was all he said when he picked it up.

Had anyone been in his office at the time, they would have been both enamored with and afraid of the man. He was strikingly handsome with dark hair and intense gray eyes. His suit was custom tailored with attention to every minute detail. This was a man accustomed to being in a position of control. He presented a confident and charismatic demeanor, but inside, he was ice cold. Behind his eyes was a chilling lack of conscience.

"I agree," was his only response after listening for a few moments.

He hung up and buzzed his assistant. "Gather the Istanbul Group," he said in a low tone when she entered the office. "Have them at the villa by 17:00 tomorrow. Everyone must be here, no excuses."

With that, he waved her off and returned to his chair. He looked back out the window with a measured smile creeping across his lips.

Within hours, prominent men from Eastern and Western Europe, Asia, South America, and the US began the journey to Istanbul.

JACK ALLBRITTON WAS IN A BOARD MEETING at Allbritton Enterprises when his chief operating officer, Robert Durand, was handed a note. He leaned toward Jack and whispered in his ear.

"The rest of the agenda will have to be postponed," Allbritton informed the board. "I have urgent business that needs my immediate attention. We'll pick up the unfinished items at our next meeting. Brenda, see that these gentlemen receive refreshments before leaving. Robert, come with me, please. Gentlemen, until next month…"

He gave a brief nod to the group and received warm, collegial smiles in return.

Jack Allbritton was a well-respected captain of industry, smooth and gracious, with a chameleon-like ability to be whatever a particular audience wanted to see in him. It was a talent he'd nurtured since childhood, and it had paid off well. He took pride in the fact that no one, absolutely no one, knew the real Jack Allbritton. Combined with his self-described ability to read everyone else's motives, he privately fostered an air of superiority that always made him the most confident man in the room.

He and Robert Durand picked up their luggage—pre-packed bags that remained at the office for just such contingencies. Allbritton's driver loaded the bags into the limo, and both men slid into the back seat. When the door closed, Allbritton asked Durand if he knew the reason for the meeting.

"None given," was the brief reply.

On the tarmac at Dulles Airport, Durand received a call. He listened momentarily then hung up. He turned to Allbritton and informed him that they would be stopping in Paris to pick up Claude Arneau before continuing to Istanbul.

"Great," Allbritton replied, "I haven't spoken with Claude in weeks. Maybe he can shed some light on the urgency."

They boarded the plane and taxied down the runway, Paris bound. Seven hours later, Claude Arneau came aboard at Charles De Gaulle airport. The atmosphere was relaxed and friendly as the men settled in for the rest of the trip. When Allbritton queried Arneau about the upcoming meeting in Istanbul, he was met with a wary glance.

"My dear friend," Arneau leaned forward and replied in a conspiratorial tone, "I know your people are surely trustworthy. However, it would be best to redirect our conversation until we arrive."

He revealed with his glance that he was referring to the crew member within earshot.

"Of course," Allbritton replied. "Janice, please bring us a bottle of champagne. I would welcome Mr. Arneau's opinion on our latest case."

The rest of the flight centered on discussions of crude oil prices and the prolonged war on terrorism. Arneau glibly commented on the gullibility of the American people, who are so easily manipulated in matters of consumerism and politics.

"That's what makes me so proud to be an American—a very successful American," Allbritton chuckled at his own humor. "If you know the nature of the people, you can figure out how best to play on it."

Robert Durand made no comment. He just shook his head and smiled.

5

Gabe carefully placed the diary in his jacket pocket, grabbed his overnight bag, and locked the hotel room. Castriotti was anxiously waiting when he reached the top of the stairs.

"Got everything?" he asked.

"Yes, sir," Gabe replied.

"Good. Let's go then."

Gabe threw his bag in the back seat of the black Alfa Romeo and got in. Castriotti dialed his cell phone, spoke briefly in Italian, and handed it to Gabe.

"Your grandmother is coming to the phone."

Castriotti stepped on the accelerator, and Gabe felt a knot tighten in his stomach. He was a terrible liar, yet he knew he needed to sound convincing. Hopefully, she would not become alarmed or suspicious about his need to go to Rome. Gabe watched the second hand on his watch tick as he waited for Francesca.

Finally, he heard the soothing sound of his grandmother's voice. True to her nature, she immediately concerned herself with Gabe's well-being rather than hers. When he asked how she was faring, she dismissed it as a secondary concern, consistent with that inner toughness Gabe had seen so many times in her life.

"Gram, there's something I need to do," he said. "Given our situation, documents must be filed at the US Embassy in Rome. I'm so sorry, but I need to go there immediately. If I leave now, I can be back tomorrow."

Francesca protested, not on her behalf, but for Gabe's sake. After some back-and-forth, she reluctantly agreed that Gabe should do whatever was necessary. She assured him that she would be well cared for at her cousins' and that he was not to worry.

Gabe flipped the phone closed and breathed a sigh of relief. "That went better than I thought it would," he said. "I think she's in good hands for now."

"Excellent!" Castriotti said. He made a sharp right turn off the main route. "We'll avoid the coastal road to save time. The tourist traffic will only slow us down."

The road to Naples was by no means a straight shot. An endless series of winding switchbacks climbed the nearly vertical ascent of the rugged coastal mountains.

"Please, buckle your seatbelt," Castriotti said.

Gabe needed no further warning. He watched sheer drop-offs zip by as they continued to pick up speed during their climb to the top. Castriotti was obviously comfortable with the driving conditions. He only slowed down when they encountered an obstacle, like a parked car or an oncoming bus.

They passed through small villages every five kilometers or so. *Italy is truly a stunning place,* Gabe thought as he looked out to sea. He scanned the mountainous terrain. He'd never seen such a mixture of cactus, evergreen, ferns, and flowers in one place. He could see why his grandfather had encouraged him to come there to climb, and the sheer limestone cliffs beckoned him.

The homes were quaint but well maintained. The houses on the upside of the mountain were visible, but he could only tell there were homes below the cliffs because of the iron gates that dotted the roadway. Driveways dropped off abruptly, and the gates appeared to open into empty space with only the Mediterranean Sea in view. Many entrances were bordered by trellises covered with bougainvillea, but they, too, seemed to disappear into the sea. It was mesmerizing. From an aesthetic standpoint, the Amalfi Coast was everything his grandparents had promised it would be.

Castriotti picked up his cell phone. His voice broke into Gabe's thoughts. "Anna, it's me, Uncle Paolo. Yes, we're on the way. I called, and I think Gabe can make the early afternoon train. You should be at Roma Termini to pick him up at 15:30, but the cardinal will not be expecting you until 18:00. Could you do me a favor? Would you please run Gabe by his grandfather's flat in the meantime?"

He now had Gabe's full attention. Gabe had no idea that his grandfather kept an apartment in Rome. *What else am I clueless about?* he wondered.

"Ciao, Anna." Castriotti finished and hung up the phone just in time to downshift.

"What flat?" Gabe asked, taken aback.

"Your grandfather has been coming to Italy for many years. After the unfortunate disaster in your country on September 11, the frequency of his visits increased decidedly. I do not fully know the nature of his work, but…"

"Nature of his work! What are you talking about? My grandfather was retired." Gabe was now incredulous.

"Perhaps I have misspoken," Castriotti said. "Whether John's time here was related to paid employment or not, I do not know. But I do know that he was intent on finding out certain information. As I told you earlier, I sent him to meet Cardinal Bauer. It was shortly after 9/11. I would trust Cardinal Bauer with my life as I would trust him with yours. Go meet with him, Gabriel, and perhaps we'll all have a better idea of what John was doing."

At that instant, the phone rang. Castriotti answered and listened without saying a word. "I understand," he said finally, then hung up.

Gabe saw the look of horror on Castriotti's face. Castriotti struggled to find words and pulled off the road.

"What's wrong?" Gabe demanded. "What the hell is going on?"

Castriotti began to slowly relay the message he'd been given. "That was Lorenzo. Francesca's cousins suggested a memorial service for John here in Amalfi. Francesca asked Lorenzo to make the arrangements, and when he called the owner of the Amalfi funeral home a few minutes ago, the funeral director was surprised. He asked Lorenzo when they wanted to hold the service because he'd already released the body for an autopsy."

"What?" Gabe shouted.

"He said that three official-looking men had come to the funeral home an hour earlier and had taken the body for an autopsy. They had the necessary paperwork, so he released John's remains. His body is gone."

Gabe felt an agonizing jolt rip through his gut. He slammed his fist on the dashboard. "How did this happen?" he roared. "How in the world could this have happened?"

Castriotti didn't say a word. Gabe clenched his fists and grimaced as he considered the implications. *What am I going to do now? What will I tell Gram?* He wasn't sure, but one thing was now perfectly clear. He no longer had any doubt that his grandfather had been murdered. But by whom and why?

"Get me back to Amalfi," he demanded, "I want to know who was responsible for this."

"So do I, Gabe, but we won't find that out in Amalfi. His body is gone, and those men weren't local. John could be anywhere by now. This development makes the meeting with Cardinal Bauer even more urgent. At the moment, you have nowhere else to turn."

They shared the same thought: to Rome—and fast.

Castriotti pulled his Alfa Romeo back on the road and had it back up to speed in an instant. They rode along in tortured silence as Castriotti navigated the descent into Naples. When they hit city traffic, there was not a second to talk as he dodged pedestrians, scooters, dogs, cars, and buses.

When they reached the train station, Castriotti looked directly into Gabe's eyes. "I don't know what this is all about, so be careful. The ticket counter is just inside, marked with a sign that says *Biglietto*. Buy a first-class ticket and get some rest on the way to Rome. I've described you to Anna. She'll be waiting when you arrive."

Castriotti put one hundred euros in Gabe's hand. "Please, take this. You won't have to worry about making exchanges. Consider it a gift from your grandfather, for he has taken care of me many times."

Gabe grabbed his bag from the back seat.

"Oh, and Gabriel," Castriotti continued, "the pickpockets on the trains and in the stations tend to be a problem. Keep the diary close. Don't let it out of your sight. Also, watch out for the well-dressed gypsies. They know the Americans, and they always beg for money. Just pass them by. They can be very persistent. God be with you, Gabriel."

Gabe nodded. He turned to enter the terminal, his mind spinning with questions.

6

Gabe was grateful for Castriotti's advice about getting a first-class seat. He'd never ridden on a European train and hadn't expected it to be so comfortable. The cars were like business class on a wide-body jet. Gabe found a seat and settled in. He took a moment to survey his surroundings. The nearest passenger was across the aisle and three rows up. A few moments later, the train rolled out of the station right on schedule.

He was still numb from the disappearance of his grandfather's body. The rapid succession of events left him feeling disoriented and confused, the way most Americans felt on the morning of 9/11. Who was responsible? How could this have happened? What would happen next?

The train gained speed and, within minutes, was out of Naples and into the Italian countryside. The scenery flew by in a blur. As Gabe stared out the window, two thoughts ran through his mind over and over. *Who tipped off the perpetrators? Who stole my grandfather's body?*

His confusion and anger gave way to a powerful sense of betrayal. Gabe went through a mental checklist of the people who knew his grandfather had been taken to the funeral home: Gram, her cousins, Lorenzo and his wife, Castriotti, Zach Beckett, the funeral home director, and his assistant.

Gabe immediately dismissed Gram and her cousins. But what about Lorenzo or Castriotti? Neither of them had wanted to call the authorities, and they seemed awfully interested in getting him out of Amalfi. Gabe considered the possibility that the mirror and the trip to Rome were all part of an elaborate coverup, but he quickly rejected the idea. He doubted that both men could have faked those looks of stunned shock—Lorenzo when he discovered the mirror and Castriotti when he was told that the body was missing. *No,* he concluded, *Lorenzo and Castriotti are trying to help me.*

What about the funeral home director or his assistant? Perhaps, but it seemed more likely that they innocently turned over the body to men who claimed it with the proper documentation. Plus, Gabe recalled that the funeral director was Lorenzo's friend, and he picked up the body as a courtesy.

That left Zach Beckett, but he was en route from America. Gabe had just contacted him in the States that morning. Besides, Beckett was an associate of his grandfather.

So, who was it? Gabe wondered, concluding that someone unknown must be involved. The feeling of betrayal began to dissipate. Nevertheless, Gabe and his family had been severely violated, and Gabe was incensed. He'd been disoriented that morning from the speed at which things had happened, but he was getting his bearings. From now on, he'd have his guard up and treat everyone with appropriate suspicion. He needed to protect his grandmother, but he also needed to bring those who were responsible to justice. It wasn't his nature to run from a challenge, and his growing sense of indignation made him more determined than ever.

Gabe began to nod his head as if agreeing with himself. *I will not be intimidated,* he thought. *No, I'll fight back!* He reached into his pocket and pulled out the message from the mirror. He stared at it and renewed his commitment; he'd find out who killed his grandfather and why.

But the letters still made no sense.

THBST
ISHR
SA

He tried a variety of combinations but came up empty every time. Frustrated, he thought about Castriotti's advice. With nowhere else to turn for answers, he'd meet with Cardinal Bauer to find out what he could learn. He'd also visit his grandfather's flat and search for clues.

Gabe made one other decision as he headed to Rome. Castriotti and Lorenzo had dissuaded him from calling the authorities, but it was now clear that his grandfather had been murdered. If he didn't have any answers by the time he got back to Amalfi, that was exactly what he intended to do: call the Carabinieri.

With his mind resolved, Gabe pulled out the diary and examined it closely. It was very cryptic and strange; some of it was written in a foreign language. The earliest entries were in Russian. He also noticed that someone had started to translate those entries into English. The handwriting in the margins looked like his grandfather's.

He continued to read, but the steady hum of the wheels on the rails had a sedating effect. Despite the tension, or perhaps because of it, his eyes felt heavy. He put the diary back in his coat pocket and drifted off to sleep.

Gabe didn't wake up until the train slowed to enter the Roma Termini. As it ground to a halt, he reached for his overnight bag and checked his breast pocket to make sure he still had the diary. He did. He looked out the window and scanned the platform. People were everywhere. Some were anxiously awaiting the arrival of loved ones, and others were looking for business associates.

One woman stood off to the side. She searched each face that disembarked. She was tall and fit, with olive skin, inquisitive brown eyes, and shoulder-length black hair pulled back in a sleek ponytail. Gabe took a moment to appreciate her beauty. *Perhaps that's her*, he thought as he headed for the stairs at the back of the car. When he stepped off the train, she stepped forward.

"Welcome to Roma, Mr. Roslo," she said kindly, extending her hand. "I'm Anna Castriotti, Paolo's niece."

"Please, call me Gabe. Thank you for meeting me here." He returned the handshake.

"Uncle Paolo has asked me to take you around," she began.

"I hope it's not too much trouble being away from work."

"No problem. I'm a property manager here in Rome. As long as I have this," she said, pointing to the cell phone in her other hand, "I'm always at work. I'm so very sorry to hear about your grandfather's death. Please accept my deepest condolences. He was a wonderful man."

Gabe nodded and thanked her as they turned toward the terminal. He looked around and was grateful she'd come to meet him. The terminal was bustling in controlled chaos, full of people in a hurry.

Anna had double parked near a side entrance. "In Roma, the painted lines are merely suggestions," she winked as she unlocked her car.

But Gabe's mind wasn't engaged in the small talk. He barely noticed as Anna darted into traffic. "I'd like to go to my grandfather's flat right away," Gabe said. He then checked himself, "if that's possible."

"No problem. I'm headed there now," she replied. "My uncle wanted me to take you there. The meeting with Cardinal Bauer isn't until 6:00."

"How will we get in? I don't have a key. And my grandmother wasn't available to ask for one."

"I strongly doubt she'd have one," Anna replied. "But it's no problem. Your grandfather's flat is in the property I manage. In fact, it's in the same complex where I live. I'll get a key from the office to let you in."

"How long has he kept this apartment in Rome?" Gabe inquired.

"Many years, I suppose. He had it before I took over management five years ago," she said. She turned off the main boulevard and drove uphill.

To Gabe's right was a huge stone wall. She saw him look at it and answered his unspoken question.

"Those are the walls of Vatican City. If we weren't so close, you'd be able to see the dome of Saint Peter's Basilica. It's a beautiful sight, visible from most places in Roma, except from the bottom of the wall, that is. Saint Peter's is an architectural wonder built to intimidate those who enter with the awesome magnificence of heavenly subjects. Did you know it was constructed over the bones of Saint Peter himself?"

"No, I didn't."

"It's true. After Peter was crucified, he was buried outside the walls of Nero's Circus. Centuries later, the basilica was built over that very spot. Today, Saint Peter's is the gateway to Vatican City, and no one escapes a feeling of awe when they enter, no matter what they believe."

Anna took a sudden left into a driveway and changed the subject. "Here we are, your grandfather's home in Roma," she announced as she pulled through the gated entrance.

She turned left a second time and entered an underground garage. The spaces were incredibly tight, but Anna easily slid into her reserved spot. She shut off the engine and led Gabe up a staircase to the ground level.

He looked around as they stepped back into daylight. There were several buildings of dark gray brick, three stories tall. Each was detailed in white marble with white iron balconies. The scalloped pattern of the stone-paved drive and walkways caught his attention. As with every place he'd seen in Italy so far, there were blooming flowers in white clay pots everywhere. Statues and fountains abounded, and Gabe could see the walls of Vatican City looming across the street.

Anna retrieved a key for Apartment 312A and led the way. They crossed a courtyard, and rounding a corner, she abruptly stopped. She threw an arm across Gabe's chest and pushed him back behind the bricks with a finger to her lips.

"Do you know that man—the one at the door of your grandfather's flat?" she asked.

He peeked around the corner and caught a glimpse of a stranger opening the door to the apartment. Gabe only saw him from the back, but he didn't know him. The man was tall and athletic. He appeared middle-aged and wore a black wool overcoat.

"No, I don't know him," Gabe whispered, "but I'm going to find out who he is." He strained against Anna as he started around the corner.

"Are you armed?" she asked.

"No, of course not," Gabe shot back.

"Well, maybe he is!" she exclaimed. She dropped her arm and stepped back. "Just hear me out. All visitors must ring the office to gain admittance. When I picked up your grandfather's key, no visitors were mentioned. This has to be a break-in."

"Yeah, and I bet he knows who killed my grandfather." Gabe pressed forward again.

"Are you crazy?" she said.

Gabe stopped and exhaled hard.

"Please, don't take a foolish chance by rushing in there alone," Anna pleaded. She pulled out her cell phone and dialed. "We have security here. Let's at least call them so you can go in together. It's safer that way."

"All right," Gabe reluctantly agreed, "but I'm staying right here. If he comes out before security gets here, he's mine."

INSIDE 312A, THE intruder locked the deadbolt, removed his coat, and got to work. He dropped his set of keys on the entry table, switched on the light, and took a moment to scan his surroundings.

The flat was rather small but had high ceilings and a marble inlaid floor. The entryway opened into a sitting room, and to the right of the entry was a hallway and galley-style kitchen. The hall led to a bedroom and bathroom.

He entered the kitchen and saw a telephone and some notes jotted on paper on the breakfast table. He read them, picked one up, and put it in his pocket. He then walked down the hall, peered into the bedroom and bathroom, and, finding nothing, returned to the sitting area.

Just past the TV cabinet, the intruder found what he was looking for—a desk in the corner piled high with books and papers, a telephone, and a flat-screen computer. It was adjacent to a French door that led to the patio. The automatic shutter, so popular in Italy, was closed to prevent daylight from entering the room.

The intruder crossed the room and switched on the floor lamp beside the desk. He scanned the titles on the bookshelf above it, mostly religious topics. He took a seat and fired up the computer. He could hear the whir of the hard drive, and as it ran through its boot-up routine, he pondered John's urgent request a few days prior for a clandestine meeting in Italy—a meeting of utmost importance.

John was usually not so cryptic in his communications, but when he'd asked John about the purpose of the meeting, he wasn't only evasive but downright obstinate in his refusal to divulge any information.

The login screen appeared, and Zach Beckett carefully entered the username and password. He hit enter, and the opening screen greeted him with "Welcome, Mr. Roslo."

It took a few moments to scan John Roslo's files for anything notable that might help Beckett decipher the purpose of the requested meeting. He looked at Roslo's calendar and noted with interest an entry from the prior week. It was a reminder to call the Red Cap and confirm arrangements.

"Hmmm," Beckett muttered to himself, "the same day I was supposed to meet with John in Amalfi."

Beckett pulled a zip drive from his pocket and plugged it into the computer. He clicked a few instructions and began a dump of the user files. A few moments into the process, the phone beside him rang. He reached for it as he pulled up John's contact log to review names.

"John Roslo here," he answered smoothly. The caller ID was blocked.

"Mr. Roslo, this is Italia Security. We received a report of a possible break-in at your location. Can you please provide us with the security code?"

"Excuse me, would you repeat that?" Beckett fumbled a little. He was buying time.

Damn, he thought, *I should have considered the code.*

"This is Italia Security. Please provide us with the security code, or we will notify the police. A break-in has been reported," the voice repeated.

Beckett didn't respond.

"The code, Mr. Roslo, the code!" demanded the voice at the other end of the line.

Beckett didn't have it. He placed the receiver on the desk and clicked the print icon to get a copy of John Roslo's contact records. He could hear the voice through the receiver that continued to threaten action. He hung up, made a final sweep of the flat, grabbed the zip drive, and headed for the kitchen.

Gabe heard sirens approaching as he waited and grew impatient. Finally, he decided to go in. As he neared the front door, security guards rounded the corner and motioned for him to stop as they flattened their backs against the walls on either side of the door. With their weapons drawn and ready to fire, one of the guards tried the handle. The door was locked. They kicked it in and stormed into the apartment with Gabe on their heels. But it was quiet—too quiet.

The guards worked their way methodically through the flat in search of the intruder.

"We won't find him today," one called from the kitchen.

Gabe rushed toward the voice. He entered the kitchen and saw that the window above the table was ajar, the curtain dancing, fanned by the breeze.

OUTSIDE THE FLAT, Beckett detoured through the garden and exited a pedestrian gate to the road. He jumped in his car. He could hear the Carabinieri sirens approaching and chuckled to himself. He saw security guards and police scrambling to surround the now vacant flat as he pulled out. A few blocks away, he pulled over and took a closer look at John Roslo's contact records. Some he recognized. Others, he didn't. One of the unfamiliar names caught his attention—Cardinal Bauer.

Cardinals wear red caps, don't they? he thought to himself.

"I guess I'd better pay the good padre a visit," he said aloud as he slammed the car into gear.

7

Gabe and Anna drove the short distance to the cardinal's residence in complete silence. He was still fuming about the intruder's escape. The security company had screwed up when they called and tipped off the intruder. And he was frustrated with himself. He'd taken the cautious route and allowed his first solid lead to slip through his fingers. Being timid was not in his nature, and he resolved that things would be different next time, regardless of the personal risks.

Gabe glanced at Anna as she confidently maneuvered her BMW through rush hour traffic. He knew she'd only been concerned for his safety when she held him back. He felt his anger soften and composed himself for the meeting with Cardinal Bauer.

She turned down a side street and parked just east of the colonnade outlining Saint Peter's Square. Via Rusticucci was a narrow lane, more of an alleyway, flanked by four-story flats on either side. To ease her anxiety about the intruder's escape, Gabe smiled and thanked Anna for escorting him around Rome as they got out of the car.

"This way," she smiled in return. "And you're welcome."

Anna located Cardinal Bauer's name on the building directory and buzzed his flat. When a voice answered, she addressed it in Italian.

"Gabriel Roslo è qui per incontrare il Cardinale Bauer."

"Ah, sì," the female voice responded. "The Cardinal is expecting Signore Roslo. I will buzz you in. Come up the stairs to the second floor. We're the first door on the right."

"Grazie," Anna replied.

Gabe reached for the door. "After you," he said.

Anna registered a pleasant look of surprise at the courtesy and stepped into the entry hall. It took a moment for their eyes to adjust to the dim light in the building. To their right was a wide, white marble staircase that inspired hushed, respectful tones. As they ascended the stairs, Gabe turned to Anna.

"I've never met a cardinal before. How should I address him?" he asked in a half-whisper.

"I believe you should call him 'Your Eminence,' take his hand if it's offered, and perhaps bow," she replied.

Anna knocked on the door. A cheerful, middle-aged nun in a full black habit answered. She invited them in and ushered them down the hall to a faintly lit parlor. She then asked them to wait while she told the cardinal of their arrival. Gabe perused his surroundings, which included two ceramic cats and an exceptional Steinway baby grand piano in the corner.

"They don't waste money on electricity in this building, do they?" he teased, relieving the tension while they waited. Anna smiled.

Five minutes later, Cardinal Bauer stepped into the room. "Please, forgive me. I've kept you waiting." He extended his hand first to Anna and then to Gabe.

Gabe noticed the skeletal structure of his hand and was surprised by the strength of his firm handshake. The cardinal had an impressive appearance. He was a towering, lanky, yet noble gentleman in his late seventies, dressed in a black cassock, with a pleasant face that belied his serious disposition. His eyes were warm yet intensely focused. Gabe surmised that the cardinal had the wisdom of years and a wealth of experience.

"Gabriel, I am honored to meet you. Please accept my condolences for the loss of your grandfather. He was an honorable man, and he is in my prayers."

"Thank you, Your Eminence," responded Gabe. He bowed his head slightly.

With a sweep of his hand, the cardinal motioned for them to be seated. He and Gabe sat facing each other in wingback chairs at opposite ends of the coffee table, and Anna sat on a small couch between them. The cardinal turned to the nun, who waited silently by the door. He asked that she bring tea for his guests.

"Right away," she replied. She bowed slightly and left the parlor.

With businesslike efficiency, Cardinal Bauer spoke first. "Paolo Castriotti sounded distraught this morning when he called me. He alluded to foul play. I encouraged him to notify the authorities, but he insisted that I meet with you first. The urgency in his voice was uncharacteristic. So, how can I help you?"

The cardinal patiently waited while Gabe collected his thoughts.

"Cardinal Bauer, many things have happened in the short time I've been in Italy. This morning, we found my grandfather's body on the bathroom floor of his hotel room. We assumed he'd died of natural causes. He was eighty-four years old. Then we discovered these."

Gabe pulled out the diary and the message. He laid them on the coffee table for the cardinal to see.

"This book was on the floor near my grandfather's body. It was damp, and some pages were missing. We suspect the perpetrator killed my grandfather to get those pages."

"And why do you think that?"

"Because we also found this," Gabe said. He pointed to the message. "It's some type of cryptic message from my grandfather. He wrote it on the mirror before he died. We think he knew he was dying and didn't have time to write a complete message."

Cardinal Bauer leaned forward and picked up the piece of paper. "What do you think it means, Gabriel?"

"I don't know. That's what I wanted to ask you. We're operating under two possible theories. One is that the letters are initials for someone or something. The other is that certain letters were purposely left out."

Cardinal Bauer looked at the jumble of letters again but offered nothing.

T H B S T
I S H R
S A

"I'm sorry," he said finally with a look of disappointment. "I'm at a loss."

Gabe was disappointed, too—another dead end.

The room was quiet. The grandfather clock ticked in the foyer. Gabe's gaze fixed on the cardinal, and at last, Cardinal Bauer broke the silence.

"Gabriel, I wish I could explain the message. The circumstances surrounding it are strange indeed, and I share Paolo's concern about it. Have you told me everything you know?"

Gabe took a breath and explained, "There's something else. On the way here, I learned that my grandfather's body is missing. Three men showed up at the funeral home and presented the necessary documents to claim his body. They said they were taking it for an autopsy, even though we didn't authorize one. Then, just in this last hour, Anna and I witnessed a stranger breaking into my grandfather's apartment. I wanted to confront him, but we thought he might be armed, so we called the security company instead. The guy had escaped out the back by the time they arrived. The Carabinieri are investigating it as a break-in, but so far, we don't know anything."

Cardinal Bauer took a deep breath and let it out slowly. "I see."

"It seems pretty clear that someone has killed my grandfather, and I think the message and this book hold the clues."

Gabe picked up the diary. "What do you know about this?" he asked. "Paolo Castriotti said it originally belonged to my great-grandfather, and he was immediately concerned when he saw it. In fact, that's when he suggested my grandfather's death might be the result of foul play."

Gabe paused. He expected a reaction from the cardinal. There was none, so he continued. "This morning, Castriotti said that my grandfather came to Italy frequently and even kept a flat in Rome. He said he was working on some type of project and that he'd discussed it with you."

While Gabe was speaking, Anna received a page from the security company. She excused herself and asked the cardinal if she could step into another room to return the call. At the same moment, the nun re-entered the room, balancing a tea tray. She set it on the coffee table and filled each cup as they watched.

Cardinal Bauer said to Anna, "Sister Maria Regina will show you to my library. You'll have privacy there."

Anna followed the nun, and the two women headed down the hallway. As they left, the cardinal leaned in toward Gabe.

"Gabriel, I am grateful for this moment to have a private word with you. Yes, I am familiar with the book. It is the same one your grandfather asked me about a few years ago."

"What is it?" Gabe asked. "I looked through it at the hotel and again on the train but couldn't make sense of it. It keeps referring to the Brotherhood but never mentions who they are. Then there's the question of the missing pages. Why is this diary so important?"

"Shortly after 9/11, John came to me," Cardinal Bauer replied. "He sought information about apparitions and locutions."

"Apparitions?" Gabe asked. "Do you mean those stories I see on the cover of the tabloid magazines?" Ridiculous headlines about Martians landing in the desert and giving birth to atomic babies flashed through Gabe's mind.

"No, Gabe, I'm referring to authentic apparitions and locutions. Within the walls of the Vatican, I'm considered one of the foremost authorities on the subject."

"I've heard of apparitions, but what are locutions?" Gabe asked.

"An apparition occurs when God Himself, or one of His representatives, appears to a human being. With an apparition, the person sees the supernatural visitor. With locutions, the person doesn't see the visitor but only hears them or experiences them mystically through an interior perception. These events are considered supernatural because they are caused by forces outside of nature. Sometimes, they are accompanied by physical signs as further proof of their occurrence. An example of a locution is when God spoke to Moses at the burning bush. He heard God's voice but didn't see Him. The most famous example of an apparition is the appearance of Jesus to Saint Paul. It was accompanied by a bright light, which threw Paul to the ground and temporarily struck him blind. Paul had an apparition of Jesus. He saw Him and heard Him."

Gabe recalled these stories from his youth.

Cardinal Bauer continued, "However, apparitions and locutions are not just the appearance or voice of God the Father or Jesus. They can be holy people sent by God as well. For instance, Moses and Elijah appeared when Jesus was transfigured to his glorified state. And they had been dead for centuries."

Gabe nodded as he listened.

"Those apparitions and locutions are not disputed among Christians," the cardinal said. "They are accepted by all of Christianity as authentic because they are contained in the Bible. However, subsequent apparitions and locutions are more controversial because they are not recorded in the Bible. Many Christians reject them solely on that basis. Nevertheless, it is well established that many such instances have occurred over the course of the centuries, even recently.

"Recently?" Gabe asked with surprise. "How recent?"

"Recent enough to catch your grandfather's attention."

Gabe raised an eyebrow at this disclosure.

"You see," Cardinal Bauer added, "God's supernatural interactions with man did not stop after the Bible was written. In fact, their frequency has increased in recent centuries. Your grandfather was investigating them as part of his work."

"But surely these claims are hoaxes," Gabe countered.

"Indeed, many are. The authenticity of every reported apparition is disputed, investigated, and researched. But I assure you, some of them are authentic."

"Are you saying that these things are investigated in some official capacity?" Gabe asked.

"That's correct—investigated and researched. Many apparition claims have been investigated, but only a few have been declared authentic."

"So, most of them are hoaxes, right?"

"I didn't say that," Cardinal Bauer replied. "I said only a few have been declared authentic. Some have been rejected as hoaxes, but quite a few fall into a gray area where there isn't enough evidence to rule one way or the other. That group is the most controversial of all."

"So, what happens then?" Gabe asked.

"The official ruling is 'not enough evidence.' In essence, the apparition might be authentic, but maybe not," the cardinal said. "Imagine this scenario: you apply for a job but only fill out part of the application. You give your name, address, phone number, and date of birth but leave the work experience section blank. Then you leave. What happens?"

"Well, I suppose the employer would throw out the application," replied Gabe.

"Perhaps, or maybe the employer would just set it aside and wait for more information."

"I hear what you're saying," said Gabe. "The lack of information doesn't automatically mean the person isn't qualified to do the job. Maybe he plans to provide more information."

"Exactly!" exclaimed Cardinal Bauer. "The same thing happens with apparition and locution investigations. Just because there's a lack of sufficient evidence to confirm authenticity does not automatically mean it's a hoax. It might, indeed, be the work of God."

"Hmmm, that makes sense," Gabe said. "I suppose, then, if a person believes in an all-powerful God, they ought to consider the possibility that these apparitions or locutions are real—at least some of them."

"Well said," Cardinal Bauer replied.

Gabe thought for a moment then said, "I'm still missing something. Why do they happen in the first place? In other words, what purpose do they serve if it's unclear whether they're real?"

"Good question. Authentic apparitions happen for a very specific reason. They assist people through difficult times in human history."

"Is that why my grandfather was looking into them?" Gabe asked.

"I believe so. I know for a fact he was beginning to see a strong correlation between certain apparitions and the current geopolitical situation."

Gabe wondered how this could relate to his grandfather's death. It was interesting, but it didn't sound like a murder motive.

The cardinal continued. "Apparitions never teach us anything new about our Christian faith. They assist people in living out their faith more fully, especially in times of difficulty. Apparitions often warn about the consequences of ignoring the principles of Christian teaching. I'll give you a recent example. Do you remember what happened in Rwanda in 1994?"

"Are you talking about the genocide—the massive slaughter?" Gabe asked.

"Exactly," replied Cardinal Bauer. "Kibeho, Rwanda, was home to a series of extensive apparitions during the 1980s. Both Jesus and the Virgin Mary appeared to seven people there for a period of several years. Among other things, they were encouraged to pray more and to live out the teachings of Christianity properly, but they were also warned."

"What do you mean by 'warned'?"

The cardinal reached for the teapot to refill his cup. "During the apparitions, they were warned of an oncoming slaughter. They were shown horrific visions of abandoned, decapitated bodies strewn everywhere and were warned that unless the people of Rwanda changed their ways by returning to God, the slaughter would occur. Those warnings were documented in books and films long before they occurred. In the summer of 1994, those visions were fulfilled in a spasm of violence."

"It was awful," Gabe said. "The news stories were horrid. People were chopped up with machetes and dumped into the river. Men, women, children—no one was spared. My grandfather and I talked about it. He told me that nearly a million people perished in just weeks—*one-seventh* of the country's population. It was just gruesome."

"Yes, it was monstrous, Gabe, and the tragic fulfillment of those warnings was evidence of their reality. Yet, the Rwandan apparitions were not declared authentic until 2001."

Gabe was confused. "If they weren't authenticated until after the slaughter, what use were they?"

"Authentication is not the issue," the cardinal replied. "It's how people respond that matters. No one is required to believe in apparitions, but everyone is encouraged to think about them and consider the gravity of their content. As I said, these mysterious happenings are intended to help us during difficult times, but sometimes we reject the help. The slaughter in Rwanda could have been averted. You can't have genocide without an absolute rebellion against the Fifth Commandment."

Gabe pondered the cardinal's words. "And my grandfather was investigating these things?"

"That's correct. He came here to learn about apparitions and locutions. Out of courtesy to Paolo Castriotti, I accepted the meeting. That first meeting led to others; in time, we became confidants. Eventually, John showed me the diary. He said he found it in an attic among his father's belongings. The diary was indeed your great-grandfather's."

"What significance did he see in it?" Gabe asked.

"As I told you, he came here asking about apparitions, so I gave him some reading material. That, in turn, led to questions about the diary. Your grandfather was trying to decipher a connection between the diary and certain apparitions. I don't know every aspect of his investigation, but I do know that he had a growing concern about its relationship to secret organizations and the global struggle against terrorism.

"Gabriel, I pray that your grandfather was not murdered. It's my sincere hope that this is not the case. But I must say, when Paolo told me of your suspicions, I was not totally surprised. Your grandfather was delving into a very complex maze of intrigue and deception."

Gabe felt a tremor run through his body as he placed his cup on the table. His hands began to shake ever so slightly. He suddenly had doubts about what he'd gotten himself into. He didn't know what to expect, but it certainly wasn't this.

He closed his eyes and took a deep breath to regain his composure. He then recalled the distinct impression that formed when he looked at the message in the mirror that morning. He was certain it had been directed toward him. *I need to find out where this is going,* he thought. He opened his eyes and locked his gaze on the cardinal.

"I'd like to read the material you gave my grandfather. Can you point me in the right direction?"

Cardinal Bauer nodded and stood up. "Most certainly. In fact, I'll give you a copy of the same book I gave him." The cardinal perused his bookshelf and took down a blue paperback volume. "Here it is in Italian. Do you speak Italian, Gabriel?"

"No, unfortunately not," he replied, "but if you give me the title, I'll get a copy at the bookstore."

"No, that won't be possible. This book is not distributed commercially. You can only obtain copies through the national offices of the organization in each country."

After thinking for a moment, the cardinal remembered where he might have an English version. He stepped out momentarily and returned with another copy that looked almost identical to the first.

"Here it is," Cardinal Bauer said as he handed it to Gabe.

Gabe looked at the title: *To the Priests, Our Lady's Beloved Sons.*

"This book is also a diary of sorts," Cardinal Bauer said. "I suggest you flip through the index and review the titles."

Gabe opened it to the index and scanned each year beginning with 1973. He gave no response, but the look on his face revealed that he was struck by the weighty topics, even if he didn't understand them.

"Gabriel, please be careful, especially if you return to John's flat. It's apparent that someone else is interested in what your grandfather was doing. Until we know who that is, please exercise extreme caution."

At that moment, the nun reappeared and handed a message to Cardinal Bauer. "Please excuse the interruption," she explained, "but this is important. Your Eminence, the caller is holding. He said it's an urgent matter of national security."

The cardinal unfolded the note and glanced at the caller's identity without changing his expression. "I'll take the call. Please ask him to wait a moment while I see my guests out. We were just finishing."

Gabe was astonished by the nature of the interruption. He realized that Cardinal Bauer was a man of considerable power. Evidently, the cardinal's duties stretched beyond the Vatican. He already knew the cardinal was a high-ranking clergyman, *but how could he put a call like that on hold?* Gabe wondered.

The cardinal was already on his feet. He led Gabe to the foyer and stepped toward an entryway table. He pulled a pen and sheet of paper from the drawer and scribbled something on it. He thought for a moment and continued writing. When he finished, he folded it and handed it to Gabe. "This should be of interest, too."

At that instant, Anna returned from the library.

"Gabriel and I were just finishing," Cardinal Bauer said. "I apologize for my abruptness, but I have an important call waiting."

He turned to Gabe and added, "I've included my direct cell phone number. It bypasses my secretary. Please keep me informed."

With that, Cardinal Bauer excused himself and disappeared from the room. Sister Maria Regina ushered Gabe and Anna from the apartment and bid them farewell.

Gabe opened the piece of paper as they descended the staircase. In addition to the cardinal's phone number, it contained a website address with no explanation.

Back in the apartment, Cardinal Bauer hesitated before picking up the call. He whispered a brief prayer for Gabe and wondered if he'd make it back.

8

Zach Beckett finished speaking and clicked his phone shut. He removed a breath mint from its wrapper and popped it in his mouth. He scanned John Roslo's contact records to locate the name and number of his property manager, Anna Castriotti. She was in flat 103A.

I'd better pay her a visit as well, he thought. Beckett didn't want the police involved in his business again. One persuasive meeting with Ms. Castriotti should throw any onlookers off the trail.

"No time like the present," he whispered. He swung his vehicle into the chaotic Roman traffic and headed back in her direction.

9

Anna maneuvered her car into evening traffic and said, "I spoke with the head of security. He told me the video cameras captured a good image of the intruder. The valuables appear intact—computer, television, DVD, etc. The Carabinieri just finished dusting for prints, but the analysis will take a little while. He also said there was no evidence of forced entry. The intruder had a key. Maybe he had your grandfather's permission to be there."

"Or perhaps he stole it from my grandfather," Gabe countered. "If he had permission, why did he run?"

"Good point. Hopefully, the fingerprint analysis will reveal something. So far, they have no leads," she added.

Gabe sighed in frustration. "Whoever he was, he's long gone now."

Anna dodged a group of motor scooters and changed the subject. "I see Cardinal Bauer gave you a book."

Gabe was a little embarrassed. He wondered how to broach the subject they had discussed. *Apparitions and locutions? She'll think I'm crazy,* he thought. He turned the book over.

"I'm familiar with it," she said.

"You've read this?" Gabe asked, surprised.

"Yes, quite a bit of it."

Relieved, Gabe launched in. "Look at this—it's huge. Cardinal Bauer called it a diary of sorts. The index shows hundreds of separate entries from 1973 to 1997. He told me he gave the same book to my grandfather."

"And now he wants you to read it, right?"

"Aren't you the observant one?" Gabe answered, grinning. "Cardinal Bauer said my grandfather came here asking about supernatural phenomena. He called them apparitions."

"I'm familiar with those, too," she said.

Gabe took a close look at Anna as she zipped through traffic. There was obviously more to this woman than met the eye. *She has intelligence and depth, as well as beauty,* Gabe thought.

Anna reached her apartment and triggered the security gate. She slid her BMW into its underground parking space.

"If you don't mind, I'd like to go check out my grandfather's flat right away," Gabe said.

"Certainly," she replied, "I still have the key."

They walked across the courtyard and reached the apartment. Gabe insisted on entering first. He swept the apartment but found nothing of significance. He invited Anna in, and they moved to the sitting room.

"I need to check out this website," Gabe said. He pulled the folded paper from his pocket. He sat down at the computer and hit the power button, but his login attempt failed. "No go. It's password protected."

"Don't worry about it," Anna reassured him. "We can use my computer. Are you hungry?"

"I'm famished." Gabe checked his watch. It was nearly 8:00. He realized he hadn't eaten since breakfast.

"Let's go to my apartment," Anna replied. "I'm sure I can scrounge up something for us to eat—perhaps a little wine. It'll give us a chance to talk about the book Cardinal Bauer gave you."

"That sounds great—if it's not too much trouble," Gabe said.

"No, none at all," she said.

As they left, Anna flipped off the lights and locked the door behind them. Gabe was curious to know more about this woman. She wore no wedding band, *but surely, she has a boyfriend,* he guessed. She exuded beauty and confidence, which is evident in many Italian women, but she also had an easy manner and amiability that made her quite approachable. They reached her apartment, and Anna unlocked the door.

"Make yourself at home. The bathroom is down the hall if you need it. I'll grab the wine and cheese," she called over her shoulder as she ducked into the kitchen.

Gabe entered the living room and took a moment to observe the surroundings. Anna's floor plan was similar to his grandfather's. It was simple yet warm and welcoming, with an eclectic, contemporary décor that reflected her personality.

"African masks, rain sticks, a Beleek china pitcher, llama skins—you get around, don't you? Or are you just an eBay junkie?" he teased.

"Wouldn't you like to know?" she countered with a grin as she returned with a tray of bruschetta and a bottle of Chianti.

They sat on opposite ends of the leather sofa. Anna removed her shoes and casually tucked her feet beneath her. She handed Gabe a glass of wine. He would have preferred a glass of water but was resigned to developing a taste for wine. *While in Rome,* he thought.

"Cardinal Bauer wants you to read the Gobbi messages," she said.

"Gobbi?" Gabe questioned, unfamiliar with the term.

"I'm sorry," Anna replied. "That blue book. It's commonly referred to by the name of the man who received the messages, an Italian priest named Stefano Gobbi. Father Gobbi received over six hundred locution messages between 1973 and 1997."

"From where?"

"From the mother of Jesus," she said. "The blue book's a compilation of all those messages."

"Cardinal Bauer referred to it as a diary," Gabe said.

"Well, I suppose it is. Each message is considered a diary entry. In fact, I think an index in the back lists them all."

"It does," Gabe said. "Cardinal Bauer mentioned it, too."

Gabe flipped to the index and scanned the list a second time. One of them mentioned revealing a secret. *What secret?* Gabe wondered.

Anna continued. "It's said that Mary delivered these messages to Father Gobbi during his prayer time and requested that he record them to share with his brother priests. Each message is considered a diary entry; over the years, they were compiled into this book. Most deal with issues of priestly piety, but some contain explicit information about the growing threat of evil in the world and the Book of Revelation."

"Really—the Book of Revelation? Do you think the messages are real?" Gabe asked.

"Well, actually, I do. History shows that this type of supernatural phenomenon has accompanied periods of difficulty. Humanity is struggling against itself. Global terrorism is proof enough of that. So, it makes sense to me that this type of thing could be happening," she said.

"Cardinal Bauer mentioned the War on Terror, too," Gabe said. "He told me that my grandfather was trying to decipher a connection between apparitions and terrorism and said that apparitions were intended to help people through difficult times, just like you said."

"And these are difficult times," Anna replied. "However, the messages have also given me hope. To me, they say this craziness will end someday, and I take great comfort in that."

"Hope—I hadn't thought of that." Gabe recalled a message title he'd seen earlier indicating the powers of hell would not prevail. "Have these messages been investigated for authenticity?" he asked.

"I'm not sure about that, but I know they haven't been officially confirmed. That would be a huge step, and I suspect it will take years, maybe even decades, before that type of statement occurs. Still, the Gobbi messages have been reviewed by no less than four cardinals and determined to be free of doctrinal error. That means they don't contradict any of the truths revealed by God through the scriptures and teachings. That, by itself, was a big step. They haven't been declared authentic officially, but you need to consider what it means when a clergyman of Cardinal Bauer's stature hands something like this to you. It certainly adds to their credibility."

Gabe was surprised by Anna's candor, and her knowledge and conviction were impressive. *Maybe there really is validity to these messages,* he considered, *but how do they relate to my grandfather's murder?*

"The Gobbi messages have been published in a multitude of languages," she added. "Hundreds of thousands of copies have been distributed worldwide. Even though the messages were originally directed to Catholic priests, they're available for anybody to read."

Gabe leaned forward and reached for a piece of bruschetta. He thought about how to phrase his next question.

"When I asked Cardinal Bauer for reading material, I wasn't expecting a thousand-page tome," Gabe said. He pointed to the blue book. "Is there any chance you could help me digest what these messages mean and how they might be related to my grandfather's murder?"

Anna nodded.

Just then, they were startled by a loud rap at the door.

10

ONE YEAR EARLIER: ISTANBUL MEETING, 5:00 P.M.

The assembled group of men casually mingled while servants supplied cocktails and hors d'oeuvres. When the Master of the Royal Secret entered, a hush fell over the room at the sight of his commanding presence.

"Gentlemen," he began, "I thank you for honoring me with your presence today. Please take a seat, and we'll begin."

He motioned toward the extravagant dining table surrounded by twelve upholstered chairs and took his seat at the head of the table. It was set for a sumptuous meal.

Jack Allbritton and Robert Durand sat next to each other at the far end, with Claude Arneau seated across from Allbritton.

After all the men had settled themselves, the Master methodically made direct eye contact with each of them, one after the other. Their loyalty was unquestioned.

"I call you here today with a heavy heart. We each know that the glory of true enlightenment belongs to us. Yet, we must ask ourselves, can the enigmatic tribesman from Saudi Arabia usurp the influence of the Brotherhood? Can Osama bin Laden reach the pinnacle of authority? No, I declare! We have come too far. Achieving global supremacy is our destiny—not Islam's. We have the power, and we have the authority!"

The room erupted in spontaneous applause. Waiting a few moments, he lifted a hand to silence the group and began again.

"Gentlemen, after 9/11, the initial war cry was to destroy Islamic terrorism. This unity of purpose among Americans reassured us. The world order was intact. But now, I tell you, things have changed. The balance of power has shifted, and we are slipping.

"On 9/11, we watched the radical branch of Islam attack an America that we had successfully weakened in faith and morals. The aftermath of the attack brought with it an initial resurgence of faith but, more importantly, a call to increased violence. Defending the homeland became the battle cry! But predictably, the resurgence in faith faded quickly.

"Their so-called faith should have led the American people to trust in the hereafter, but instead, it drove them to trust in their sensibilities—their power! This apparent contradiction between faith and power is exactly what we've thrived on for decades.

"The utter disgust and horror that filled the hearts of the American people after 9/11 galvanized their collective will. 'Do something,' they begged! And indeed, their government did. Homeland Security is now an American mantra."

The Master paused. He again stared each man in the eye, one after another.

"Yet, it made no difference in Spain. When the bombs exploded on those Spanish trains before their elections, reality set in. International terrorism is alive and well. America and its Western allies have attempted to manage the danger, but they still feel vulnerable. Why? Because they *are* vulnerable, and with every new explosion, there's a growing sense of helplessness against the 'invisible' enemy of terror.

"America invaded Afghanistan and Iraq to take the War on Terror to foreign lands. However, people now wonder if it'd be better for America to be out of these wars altogether. 'Is it worth the cost?' they ask. The disgust and indignation they felt on 9/11 have been replaced with doubts. America is no longer unified and galvanized in its quest to protect the homeland. America is no longer unified and galvanized in its quest to destroy the enemy. America is now divided against itself.

"Normally, the Brotherhood would feed off this polarization. We would play one side against the other, as we have done so many times in American politics. But this time, things are different. Polarization, our usual ally, has become our weakness. The current polarization of America is at cross-purposes with our plan for global ascendancy."

The Master studied his guests. The room was perfectly quiet.

"Gentlemen, we have a duty to ourselves. The time has come to raise the stakes. We need to galvanize the American people once again, but this time, absolutely!"

The room again erupted in applause. It lasted several minutes. The Master sneered, emboldened by their total and absolute support. When the ovation finally subsided, he continued.

"At first, I thought the invasion of Iraq would ensure our destiny. But now, as I observe the American people, I'm concerned the Iraqi situation is our greatest risk. One only needs to read Osama bin Laden's 1998 fatwa to know that his hatred is founded largely upon his view of American interference in Iraq, a document published five full years before the invasion."

The Master took a sip of water. He let the significance of his statement set in upon the men assembled.

"1998–*the mythical year*... We must now ask ourselves: Is this man capable of usurping our destiny? Is Osama bin Laden capable of uniting Islam and growing his improbable influence to global proportions? I put these questions before you, gentlemen. Will the Islamic world rise to his call? Will the one-billion-strong Islamic world unite under the banner of Allah and succeed where they have historically failed in destroying the 'Christian' West?

"My fears are not that they will overrun Christianity. The trunk of that tree is already ours. This we know. The church in Rome is rotting on the vine because of our work. No, Christianity is not my concern. That we have dealt with."

Nods of agreement and arrogant chuckles were exchanged among those assembled.

"My true concern is the maniacal behavior of Islamic zealots. There is no greater zeal than that which connects people to their eternal beliefs. That zeal once filled the hearts of the Christian martyrs. They died for their cause. They died willingly, bearing nothing more than the hope of a better future. Little good did it do them."

A new round of haughty laughter filled the room.

"That zeal is now present in Islam's youth, fueled by devotion to Allah. It is an all-powerful force, a zeal that could propel the Pan-Islamic cause to proportions never imagined.

"So, I ask: Can Islam achieve global domination? Can it reach the zenith of global supremacy? Painfully, the answer is yes. Through fear, terrorism, and radicalism, Islam is already on the path.

"But that, I tell you, is *not* our destiny! The summit of world transformation is within our reach, gentlemen, but we must capture the moment.

We must unify our rage against the unenlightened and propel humanity into the next age. If we fail and allow Islam to get the upper hand, we risk losing everything. Are you with me? I tell you: now's the time to act!"

The Master pounded his fist on the table for emphasis.

He took a deep breath and placed both hands on the table, palms down. In an even, measured tone, he explained his intentions.

"Gentlemen, we must orchestrate an event. We must orchestrate an event that makes it appear that the zealots have struck at the heart of the West again. However, this time, the result will be chaos. And from those ashes, we will arise as the sane, unifying force providing a final solution."

Not a single face at the table flinched.

"Gentlemen, here is my proposal…"

11

The knock had surprised them. Anna flashed a worried look at Gabe.

"Were you expecting someone?" he asked.

"No," she said.

She set her wine glass on the table and crossed the small room to the door. Gabe's gaze followed her. Anna crouched down to peer through the peephole. She stepped back immediately and shot a terrified glance in his direction.

"It's him," she whispered, "the intruder!"

Gabe bolted off the couch. He brushed past Anna to look. It was definitely him—the man who had entered his grandfather's flat.

Gabe moved close to Anna's ear and whispered, "You get the door. I'll be right here. It'll be okay. This time, we have the element of surprise."

He patted her on the back to reassure her then positioned himself behind the door to listen. He would not let this man slip through his fingers again.

Anna regained her composure. She looked at Gabe and mouthed, "Be careful." She clicked the deadbolt and hesitantly pulled the door ajar.

Gabe had a clear view of the man through the crack at the hinges. Gabe stood with his back plastered against the wall and remained perfectly still to avoid drawing attention to himself. The man didn't notice him.

"Hello," rumbled a deep voice. "Are you Anna Castriotti?"

"Yes, I'm Anna Castriotti," she replied. Her voice quivered slightly. "And who are you, may I ask?"

"Are you the property manager?"

"Yes, I'm the property manager. But you didn't answer my question—and how did you get past security?"

The man ignored her question a second time. "I'm looking for information on one of your tenants."

"Excuse me, sir, but you still haven't identified yourself."

Gabe watched the man's hand slide into the breast pocket of his coat. That was all Gabe needed to react. Gabe was hypersensitive and trained to respond instantly to danger because of his years of climbing experience. He grabbed the door, swung around it, and slammed into the unsuspecting stranger. The impact caused the two men to stumble over the threshold into the breezeway, but the stranger regained his balance almost immediately.

The two were well-matched. Gabe's physical condition was excellent, and he was years younger. However, it became immediately obvious that his adversary was well-trained in methods of self-defense. He was also a lot stronger than Gabe had expected.

Gabe drove his shoulder into the man's stomach and reached around his waist. He tried to push the man to the ground and felt hot breath on the back of his neck. The stranger strained to put Gabe in a choke hold, but the man's cumbersome overcoat tangled between them. Gabe had a momentary advantage, but suddenly, the man pulled back. The change in momentum swung Gabe around, slamming him into the breezeway wall. Gabe pushed off the wall for leverage and drove the man backward into Anna's apartment. They crashed into an entryway table, shattering a glass vase. Anna jumped out of the way as the two men struggled.

Somehow, the stranger freed himself from the sleeves of his coat. He grabbed Gabe by the arm and used a kung-fu hold to immobilize him. He slammed Gabe face down to the floor and pressed his cheek against the cold tile. Gabe felt the stranger's knee crush into his spine.

"What the hell are you doing?" the stranger demanded. He put his face close to Gabe's.

At that second, Gabe freed his arm and thrust it upward. He drove it squarely into the man's groin. His foe doubled over. Gabe rolled onto his back and grabbed the man by the throat. The man was still on top.

"I saw you break into my grandfather's apartment," Gabe said through clenched jaws. He felt the man's weight straining on top of him. Gabe tightened the throat hold and, with a quick thrust, forced the man off his chest. In an instant, Gabe rolled over and lunged on top. He had regained the advantage. Gabe leaned all his weight into his adversary.

"Wait a minute, wait a minute," the stranger gasped. He grabbed Gabe's wrist as it tightened around his windpipe. "Your grandfather? John Roslo is your grandfather?"

"Was my grandfather—but the question remains: who are you, and what were you doing in his flat?"

Gabe glanced up. He could see Anna's pale and terrified look. She had backed up against the bookcase during the confrontation.

"Ease up that grip, and I'll tell you, Gabe," the stranger said, struggling to speak.

Gabe was astonished. The man had used his name. Gabe eased his grip on the man's throat but maintained the pressure on his chest.

"I'm Zach Beckett," the man said hoarsely.

"Zach Beckett? Can you prove that?" he shot back. Gabe kept his guard up.

"I could if you get off me," Beckett groaned. "My identification's in the breast pocket of my coat."

"Anna," Gabe motioned with his head.

She retrieved the jumbled coat and searched the breast pocket. She found a wallet. It contained his NSA identification.

"It's here," she said, showing it to Gabe.

Gabe glanced at it. He released Beckett slowly but wouldn't let him stand up. Gabe wanted to maintain the advantage in case the man was lying. Gabe was still suspicious.

"When I called you from Amalfi, you said you'd be here in twenty-four hours. So, how was it possible that you were at my grandfather's apartment this afternoon if you were stateside when I called this morning?"

"Very observant, Gabe. But I never said I was stateside. I was already in Rome. In fact, I came to Italy at the request of your grandfather—for a meeting."

"A meeting—a meeting about what?" Gabe asked. He stood up.

"I don't know," Beckett replied. "He wouldn't elaborate. He only said it was urgent and he'd tell me when I arrived."

Beckett sat up and rubbed his throat.

"What were you doing in my grandfather's flat?" Gabe demanded. He felt his anger rising again. "And where the hell is my grandfather's body?"

Beckett paused momentarily. "It's standard NSA practice to comb field operations for loose ends in situations like this."

"NSA business?" Gabe exclaimed. "What would my grandfather still be doing for the NSA?"

Beckett flipped the conversation. "Gabe, the more immediate question is, what are you doing in Rome? Why are you here instead of Amalfi with your grandmother?"

Beckett's demeanor had become very authoritative.

Gabe considered his response. *Where is this going?* he wondered. He then said, "Two friends of my grandfather were suspicious of his death. One of them, Anna's uncle, sent me here."

"For what reason?" Beckett demanded.

Gabe did not immediately reply. He offered Beckett a hand and helped him to his feet. Anna motioned for the two men to have a seat in her living room and closed the door. She straightened Beckett's coat sleeves and placed it over a chair. Each man took a seat. After cursory introductions, she retreated to the kitchen for another wine glass.

Gabe looked at Beckett. *How much should I tell him?* he thought. Gabe was suspicious. He weighed his options. *Beckett had been his grandfather's colleague, but why did he withhold that he was already in Italy?* Gabe decided to proceed cautiously.

"I came to Rome to meet with a Cardinal Bauer," Gabe answered finally. "They thought he might shed some light on the subject—whatever that means."

Gabe noticed Beckett raise an eyebrow for an instant.

"Do you know something about this?" Gabe demanded. "Do you know Cardinal Bauer?"

Beckett glanced in the direction of the kitchen. His face became stealth-like, cool, and without emotion.

"No, I don't," Beckett replied. "I've never met the man."

Gabe was unconvinced. "What do you know about the disappearance of my grandfather's body from the funeral home?"

"What do you mean disappearance?"

"The director said three men with official papers took him for an autopsy. You'd asked me about an autopsy. Given my grandfather's age, it seemed like a strange question at the time. Now, his body is gone."

"Hold on a minute," Beckett protested.

Gabe's voice began to rise. "Sounds like the stuff the NSA might do. I think you know about this. What's going on?" Beckett didn't answer.

Gabe scrutinized him carefully. Beckett looked like standard-issue Secret Service, tall, about six-three, with a Marine-like posture that attested to his former military service. His hair was brown and close-cropped. His face was clean shaven with a square, set jaw. Beckett appeared to be in his mid-fifties and physically fit. *This man doesn't have much fun,* Gabe thought. Beckett's intense expression magnified his apprehension.

Anna returned from the kitchen. She lifted the wine bottle to pour a glass for Beckett. He raised his hand to cover the glass.

"I never drink. It only clouds the mind," Beckett said.

At least we have one thing in common, Gabe thought. He refused when Anna tried to refill his glass.

Gabe found Beckett's mannerisms highly suspicious. His demeanor was cold and calculating. *What did his grandfather see in this man that had constituted their long and close association?* Gabe wondered. It didn't add up. Beckett was hiding something.

"Well, what do you know about this?" Gabe demanded. He went on the offensive to regain control of the conversation.

Beckett avoided Gabe's question a second time. Instead, he changed the subject. "I'm concerned about Francesca. Where is she?" he asked.

"I left her in Amalfi," Gabe replied. He did not reveal her specific whereabouts. "Friends are looking after her until I return from Rome."

Gabe was irritated by Beckett's attempt to redirect the conversation. Nevertheless, Gabe maintained his composure and acted as if he hadn't noticed.

"Who else knows where she is?" Beckett questioned.

"Just me," Gabe replied, lying deliberately.

"I want to see her as soon as I get there," Beckett said. "How's she holding up, by the way?"

"Fairly well," Gabe answered, "but she doesn't know about his disappearance. She'll be frantic when she finds out, and she certainly has no suspicions he was murdered."

"In that case, don't you think it would be prudent for you to return to Amalfi?" Beckett asked.

Gabe felt he was being manipulated. He looked Beckett straight in the eye. "You still haven't told me what you know about the disappearance of my grandfather's body!"

"And you still haven't told me about your meeting with Cardinal Bauer," Beckett countered. "Listen, Gabe, we're on the same side here. John and I were colleagues for many years. He was my mentor, and I was his protégé during my early years with the agency. Why don't we work together, and we'll both get our questions answered?"

Beckett's tone and expression had changed. Now, he was acting like a concerned ally. Gabe sensed a masquerade. *Two can play this game,* he thought.

"I think you're right," Gabe replied. "We're on the same side. We both want to find out what happened to my grandfather." Gabe paused momentarily for effect. He then pretended to confide in Beckett. "This afternoon, Anna and I visited Cardinal Bauer. He extended genuine condolences, but unfortunately, he couldn't answer any of my questions."

Gabe was testing Beckett. He chose not to reveal anything about his conversation with the cardinal. He didn't mention the diary, the message, the blue book, or the fact that Cardinal Bauer was unfazed by a possible murder.

"Then perhaps it would be better for you to return to Amalfi," Beckett suggested again.

Beckett failed the test, Gabe thought. "Perhaps you're right," he said.

Gabe pretended to agree. He saw Beckett's face relax. His suspicions were heightened. Beckett wanted him out of the way. *But why?* Gabe wondered.

"In Amalfi, you could comfort Francesca," Beckett added. "I'm sure she'd like your support."

Gabe was annoyed, but he decided to make one more attempt. "So, what about my grandfather's remains? What do you know about their disappearance?"

Beckett exhaled. He looked at the glass on the table. "I would prefer a glass of water if you don't mind."

Anna nodded and headed for the kitchen. Beckett leaned in and spoke in a hushed tone.

"I don't know your grandfather's whereabouts, but I can use my contacts to locate where the autopsy is being done. There must be a paper trail."

A moment of silence ensued. Gabe pondered his options. He was out of leads. *Who was this man, Zach Beckett? He obviously had powerful connections,* Gabe thought. He decided to acquiesce, at least until they located his grandfather's body.

"Perhaps you're right," Gabe said. "I should go back to Amalfi and support my grandmother. It would be best for now."

Beckett nodded. He seemed pleased with Gabe's decision.

Anna returned with a glass of water. She'd overheard their conversation.

"I can take you to Amalfi," she said. "We could leave in the morning. Uncle Paolo asked me to assist you in any way possible. I'd be happy to help."

She hesitated for a moment and looked at Beckett. She then looked down at her hands. When she raised her eyes, she met Gabe's gaze.

"Thanks, Anna," Gabe said. "That'd be great if you can spare the time."

She blushed slightly. "It's no problem at all." She quickly regained her composure. The interchange between Gabe and Anna had not escaped Beckett.

"It's settled then," Beckett added. "I'll remain in Rome to make some calls about the autopsy. Our people will run down the leads to see where your grandfather has been taken and by whom. We can apply official pressure and get some fast answers. We'll find him, Gabe."

Beckett rose from the sofa. His business was finished. He picked up his coat from the chair and extended his hand toward Gabe. "I hope our next meeting begins with a more pleasant greeting," he said with a firm handshake. He stared Gabe straight in the eye. "If your grandfather was murdered, the people who did it could be very dangerous. You need to be extremely careful."

Beckett started toward the door then stopped. He pulled a business card from his pocket and handed it to Gabe. "You can reach me via cell or through my office anytime, day or night. I'll be in touch with you."

Beckett nodded toward Anna then walked out the door. She watched him disappear down the hall and then shut the door. She turned around and faced Gabe. "Do you trust that guy?"

"I honestly don't know who to trust," he sighed with a frown, "but he leaves me no choice at this point."

Gabe noticed that Beckett had not asked for his number. Yet, he doubted Beckett would have any trouble finding him if needed. He then recalled the note from Cardinal Bauer. He checked his pocket. It was still intact.

Gabe looked at Anna. "I really appreciate your offer. If it's still good, could we leave for Amalfi first thing in the morning?"

"Of course," she replied.

Gabe looked at the slip of paper Cardinal Bauer had given him. It contained a web address. He handed it to Anna. "Would you mind if I checked out this website?" he asked.

"Not at all," she replied. "This way."

She went to her computer and sat down to log on. Gabe watched over her shoulder as she keyed in the address. A website appeared on the screen. It was titled *Humanum Genus, Encyclical of Pope Leo XIII on Freemasonry.*

"*Humanum Genus*? What does that mean?" Gabe asked.

"It's Latin for the human race," she answered. "I'm familiar with this document. It's an encyclical letter written by Pope Leo in the late 1800s. It warned humanity about the spread of evil throughout the world. Evil was definitely on the rise at the time. Tragically, the horrors of the twentieth century proved his point."

"Why would Cardinal Bauer direct me here?" Gabe wondered aloud.

"It deals with Freemasonry." Anna hesitated, "Was your grandfather a Mason?"

"I don't think so, but I couldn't rule it out either. I'm not aware of any Masonic connections."

"Perhaps he was investigating the Masons," Anna suggested.

Gabe shrugged his shoulders. Then it hit him.

"Wait a minute—the diary!" he exclaimed. "My great-grandfather's diary kept mentioning the Brotherhood. I asked Cardinal Bauer what the Brotherhood meant. He never answered directly but gave me this website as we left his apartment. He must have known about a connection to the Masons."

Gabe turned back to the monitor and scrolled to the end of Pope Leo's document. "I'd better print this. Do you mind?" he asked.

"Be my guest," Anna replied. She checked the paper tray.

Gabe reached past her to click the print icon. He moved within a few inches of her and, for an instant, caught the pleasant scent of her hair. She stood to move out of his way.

"Would you like an espresso?" she asked.

Gabe looked at his watch. It was nearly 10:00 p.m. He felt the fatigue of the day, and his muscles ached from the altercation with Beckett. He'd been awake since a little after five in the morning. Gabe rubbed his shoulder.

"It's been a long day," he replied, "but I'll take some if it's not too much trouble."

"None at all."

Anna went to the kitchen. All was silent except the sound of the printer and the rustle of the brew passing through the machine. Gabe watched the pages print.

Just then, Anna popped her head around the corner. "I have a furnished, unoccupied apartment across the complex," she said. "I'd be happy to get the key and let you in—free of charge,of course. It would be more convenient than getting a hotel this time of night."

"I don't want to be any trouble," he replied. He respected the fact that she hadn't offered her couch. *I could just stay at my grandfather's apartment,* he thought, but he decided to accept her hospitality. "The apartment would be great if the offer's open."

"No trouble at all," she said. "I'll run to the office and get a key."

She returned from the kitchen and handed him a cup. "Enjoy your espresso. I'll be back in a few minutes," she said. She opened the door.

"Are you sure you don't want an escort?" Gabe asked warily.

"Not necessary. Who else could visit us tonight? I'll be back in a flash," she quipped bravely and closed the door behind her.

12

A silver Audi A8 slid into a parking space along Via Fontanini in Naples. It was just around the corner from the Palazzo Medici Hotel, where the driver planned to check in for the night. Sitting behind the wheel was a man in his early thirties, single, and dark complected. He was dressed completely in black, including his gloves.

He'd been driving rather aimlessly for the past several hours, but the time for making contact approached. He placed his €65,000 luxury automobile into park and flipped open his cell phone. The voice on the other end said one simple word.

"Report…"

"It's done," replied the Audi driver. "I stuck him in the neck with a direct hit. It will look like a heart attack, as you requested—natural causes. Rest assured, you won't be hearing from Mr. Roslo again."

"Very good," was the reply. "I like clean work. We've confirmed the result. Drive to the marina. You'll be met by an agent at Pier 19 in one hour. He'll have the balance of your payment."

"Grazie. It's always a pleasure doing business with you."

The sentiment was not returned. Instead, there was a momentary pause followed by a proposal. "Something's come up. I have another job, and this one might be more important than the first."

The assassin was the consummate professional, methodical and deliberate in his manner. He was unflappable. Experience had taught him to move in efficient silence and quietly execute his duties without asking questions. All he needed were the essential details—and he was well paid. By that point in his career, specific contract terms had become perfunctory. He pulled a pencil from his pocket and asked one question. "Location?"

"An apartment complex just outside the walls of the Vatican. Here's the address…"

13

Anna returned from the office with a key and showed Gabe to the vacant apartment. He brought the printout of the encyclical and the blue book with him. She unlocked the door and handed Gabe the key. "I'll call you in the morning when I'm ready to go," she said with a smile. "It should be around 9:00."

"Great," Gabe said. "I'll be ready. I appreciate all your help."

"Can I get you anything else before bed?" she asked.

"No, thanks. I'm all set." He lifted the printed pages. "I've got my bedtime reading material."

Anna wrote her phone number on a piece of paper and handed it to him. "In case you need to reach me." She then turned and headed to her flat. When she arrived, she found the shattered vase and flowers still strewn across the floor. She picked up the flowers and placed them in a glass of water to revive them. She then swept up the shards of glass.

Anna couldn't take her mind off the puzzling jumble of letters. *What could they mean?* she thought as she cleared away the dishes from the evening. She walked into the bathroom and prepared for bed. She brushed her teeth and hair, but she found sleep impossible once tucked in. Her thoughts kept drifting toward Gabe, all he'd been through, and the hurdles he faced trying to find out what happened to his grandfather. She tossed and turned for an hour and finally picked up a book to distract herself. It didn't work.

Meanwhile, Gabe was pouring over Pope Leo's letter on Freemasonry. He highlighted various sections as he read. He found the statements both peculiar and illuminating. He'd been reading for over an hour and began tapping his fingers on the table. He reached for the phone and then hesitated. Just then, the phone rang.

"Gabe, did I wake you?" It was Anna.

"No, I'm still reading. Is something wrong?" he asked.

"Not really," she replied, "but I can't get to sleep. I keep thinking about the message. Have you made any progress solving it?" she asked.

"No, I haven't," Gabe answered. "I've been reading this document about Freemasonry, but I don't know what to think. It's given me more questions than answers. I haven't been able to solve the puzzle, but I might've found a connection between Freemasonry and my grandfather's murder. At best, it's a loose connection, but it's all I have. Do you want to see it?"

"I'll be right there," she replied and hung up.

Gabe heard the handset click and then a dial tone. He stretched to get himself awake. He was exhausted, and it showed when he looked in the mirror. He splashed water on his face, combed his hair, and brushed his teeth. He finished just in time to answer the knock at the door.

"Come in," he said. "I'm glad you're here." He took her coat and hung it over a chair.

Anna started toward the dining table where his papers were laid out.

"Why don't you get comfortable on the couch? I'll bring these over. Would you like something to drink?" he asked.

"No, thanks," she replied with a pleasant smile. She took a seat on the couch, kicked off her shoes, and tucked her feet beneath herself. "What did you find?"

Gabe gathered the pages. He carried them to the coffee table and laid them in front of her. He then sat next to her on the couch.

"I've been thinking about Cardinal Bauer. Why wasn't he surprised by suspicions of foul play? And why did he point me to this website? There must be a reason."

"I would think so," she replied.

"I have a working thesis," Gabe said. "Let's suppose my grandfather's murder was somehow—in some way—connected to the Masons. It's only conjecture at this point, but it's a plausible scenario given Cardinal Bauer's input." He flipped through the packet of papers and found a highlighted section. "It doesn't provide any concrete evidence, but check this out," he said, reading it aloud.

The partisans of evil seem to be combining together and struggling with united vehemence, led on or assisted by that strongly organized

and widespread association called the Freemasons. No longer making any secret of their purposes, they are now boldly rising up against God Himself.

Gabe looked at her when he finished. "That's a pretty bold accusation, don't you think?"

She nodded in agreement, not in support of Gabe's statement but of the pope's. "The Masonic organization *is* revolting against Almighty God in every possible way," she said, "just as Pope Leo wrote. The evidence is everywhere—confusion, division, political polarization. These things are not accidents. They're deliberate, and they occur through crafty messaging. The Masonic organization makes masterful use of the media to amplify its nefarious ideas. The pope wrote it with keen insight. He was also prophetic. The technology explosion of the twentieth century brought it all to fruition in our media-driven society. Tragically, these actions are shrouded in secrecy, so the public is unaware."

"Secrecy?" Gabe protested. "According to the pope, their purposes are no longer secret."

"Well, yes and no," Anna replied. "The Masonic seat of power has become more emboldened, but their actions are still hidden—hidden in plain sight. Secrecy is the very essence of Masonry's existence. It's how the Masonic organization hides its unsavory actions. A favorite expression of Masons goes something like this: 'Perhaps the most misunderstood aspect of Freemasonry is its secrecy. Freemasonry is not a secret society, but rather *a society with secrets.*'"

"What kind of crazy double-speak is that?" Gabe asked.

"It explains how the Masonic organization has come out of the shadows without revealing any of its methods and secret agenda. Rest assured, that which occurs behind the curtain of the lodge is still a strictly guarded secret, especially the rituals."

"So, the public will never know?" Gabe asked.

"Precisely, and not just the public. Some of Freemasonry's own members don't know."

Anna spoke slowly for emphasis. "Freemasonry presents an illusion of goodness to the initiates at the bottom of the organization. It's characterized as a fraternal organization, a brotherhood, but Masonic literature deliberately weaves layers of deception into the fabric of its teachings and rituals to hide its real purpose, even from low-ranking members. The deception protects their ultimate aims—those things promoted at the highest levels of the organization."

"And what exactly is that?" Gabe asked.

"That's the great mystery. But you've been given a glimpse in Pope Leo's letter," she replied.

"That's insane!" he said.

"Or perhaps very clever," she countered. "It allows Masonry to present itself in a good light while secretly conducting all sorts of nefarious activities. Have you ever wondered why you've heard of Freemasonry but don't know anything about it?" she asked.

"No, not really," Gabe replied, "but you're right."

"You're not alone, and that's *by design*," she said.

"By design?"

"Absolutely," she said. "It's no accident the public knows *of Freemasonry* but doesn't know *about Freemasonry*. Take a poll. You'll see what I mean. Nearly everyone will give the same answer. Sure, they've heard of Masonry, but they can't tell you much about it."

Gabe found that latest revelation striking. *Perhaps it explained how he could've been unaware of a connection between his grandfather and the Masons,* he thought. Then he had another thought.

"How do you know all this?" Gabe asked. "How do you know so much about Freemasonry?"

"From my Uncle Paolo," she answered.

"Is *he* a Mason?" Gabe asked.

"Absolutely not!" she exclaimed. She was obviously offended by the question.

"Please, forgive me, but you said the only people who really know about the Masonic organization are its high-ranking members."

"That's not exactly what I said. Do you remember the murder of Roberto Calvi, the infamous Italian banker?"

"No, I've never heard of him," Gabe answered.

"Not surprising, but here in Italy, he was front-page news," she said. "In the early eighties, his body was found hanging from a bridge in London after the bank he ran fell into financial trouble. Officially, it was ruled a suicide, but everyone suspected murder. There were allegations connecting Calvi to the Masons, the Mafia, and even the Catholic Church. Fingers were pointed in every direction, but nothing was ever proven. Uncle Paolo was intrigued by all the theories. He even had his own. He tried to prove it for years but, ultimately, gave up in frustration. Uncle Paolo learned a lot about Freemasonry through his investigations. He discovered their organizational structure, their rituals, and their history. He has stacks of books and pamphlets and has done tons of research. And we talked about it—*extensively*. I was intrigued by every discovery, and each one led to more investigations and revelations."

"I apologize," Gabe said. "My comment sounded like an accusation."

"No harm done," she replied with a smile.

Gabe leaned back and thought for a moment. *My grandfather never mentioned a Masonic affiliation. He wasn't a religious man either, but he was an intelligence officer.*

He looked at Anna. "When we left Cardinal Bauer's residence, he had a call holding," Gabe said. "His housekeeper said it was a matter of urgent national security. I was astonished by the nature of the call but didn't think it was noteworthy at the time." Gabe shuffled through the papers. "Then I found this, and it got me thinking. Listen to this statement from Pope Leo's document."

> **Their ultimate purpose forces itself into view—namely, the utter overthrow of that whole religious and political order of the world, which the Christian teaching has produced, and the substitution of a new state of things in accordance with their ideas, of which the foundations and laws shall be drawn from mere naturalism.**

Gabe turned toward Anna and said, "Maybe Cardinal Bauer knew more about this than he let on—*the overthrow of the religious and political order of the world*—serious matters."

He leaned back against the couch. *There must be a political angle,* he thought.

Anna broke the silence. "Pope Leo knew what he was talking about. That's been the Masonic aim for centuries. The Masonic goal is to undermine Christianity and change the political order of the world. It continues to this very day."

He looked at her quizzically. *What have I gotten myself into?* he wondered. He then said, "My grandfather wasn't a religious man, which is strange because Cardinal Bauer told me he was investigating supernatural phenomena. But he spent his entire career battling men who were trying to overthrow the political order of the world—first Hitler, then the Soviets." Gabe paused. He searched for the right words. "If my working thesis is correct and my grandfather was killed by the Masons, I need to understand what I'm up against. I need to understand this."

Anna brushed the hair back from her face. She hesitated.

"What's wrong?" he asked.

"Well, no… it's just that—I'm not sure where to begin. I mean, be careful what you ask for. You might not like the answer."

"What are you talking about? I want to know about this. Hell, I *need* to know."

Gabe reached for Anna's arm instinctively. He then drew it back. He felt a bit awkward, but she smiled. He realized at that moment that she was having an effect on him. Anna bit her lip.

"Okay, I'll tell you what I know, but you must promise you won't share it with anybody. It can't be traced back to me. I need your absolute silence about anything I tell you."

Gabe found her request peculiar, but under the circumstances, he agreed. "You have my word on it."

She nodded and began. "The Masonic organization has both a political side and a religious side. The political side embraces global politics at the highest levels. Roosevelt, Truman, and Churchill were all Masons. They defeated Hitler to preserve the freedoms and ideals of Western society. However, Masonry has also been the catalyst behind numerous revolutions with mixed results. Take the American Revolution, for example. George Washington and his Masonic brothers gave birth to a great nation. Then look at France. French Masons were the driving force behind the French Revolution—and look what happened there: thirty thousand people had their heads chopped off. So much for liberty and justice."

"What about today? Who's in charge of Masonry now?" Gabe asked.

A sardonic grin formed on Anna's face. It was followed by a heavy sigh.

"Is something funny?" he asked.

"That's a little like asking where a circle begins. You can't find it. Masonry claims to have no single spokesman or representative, but outsiders don't know for sure. Whether someone's supremely in charge is another carefully shrouded mystery."

"But someone has to be in charge," Gabe retorted.

"Perhaps, perhaps not. Masonry's organizational structure was a closely guarded secret for centuries, just like its rituals. There's been a public effort to be more transparent in recent times, but Uncle Paolo thinks that's just another layer of deception to cover up the real agenda."

Gabe thought about Anna's stern warning. He felt a sense of unease. *How would he make progress against an invisible and secretive adversary?* he wondered. His thoughts then flashed to his grandparents, especially his grandfather, lying on the bathroom floor. The image made his blood boil. *No!* he thought. He would not give up. Gabe was resolute. He determined to find out who was responsible—no matter where it led. *This is unfamiliar territory,* he thought. He needed to know more about his rival.

Gabe looked at Anna and said, "If I'm going to make any progress, I need to understand more. Can you tell me what else you know? Will you help me?"

"Yes," she replied. She then repeated her warning, "But none of this can be traced back to me."

"Agreed," Gabe said. "Let's start with the organizational structure."

Anna nodded and launched in. "Masonry is organized into lodges. Each lodge is governed by a Worshipful Master who presides over its meetings, initiations, and secret rituals."

"Worshipful Master?"

"Bizarre, isn't it? Makes you wonder what they're worshipping," she said.

"You can say that again," Gabe replied.

"Local lodges are grouped into regions," she continued. "These regions are sometimes called valleys or orients, and each region is governed by a grand lodge. The grand lodges are the key to the Masonic organization. That's where the power lies."

"Where are they located?" he asked.

"In America, you have at least one in every state. Each grand lodge is governed by a Grand Master, who holds absolute authority in his region. In official Masonry, they're considered Sovereign Masters. They're the men in charge."

"Sovereign Masters?" *Masters of what?* he wondered. "How many Sovereign Masters are there?" he asked.

"Worldwide, perhaps hundreds," she replied.

"Hundreds?" Gabe sighed. "This is going to be a lot harder than I thought. If my working thesis is correct and my grandfather was killed by the Masons, the order could have come from anywhere."

Gabe rose to his feet and began to pace. Now, he *knew* he was in over his head. Still, he was filled with indignation. The image of his grandfather lying on the floor was fresh in his mind; he had been murdered in cold blood. He stopped and faced Anna.

"Are the Sovereign Masters accountable to anyone?"

"That's hard to say, but here's something to consider. The Ancient and Accepted Scottish Rite of Freemasonry is the largest type of Freemasonry in the world. Scottish Rite Freemasonry has divided the world into specific jurisdictions. Every grand lodge falls into one of those jurisdictions and is governed by a Supreme Council. In America, there are two Supreme Councils. One of them is considered the *Mother Council of the World*. Guess where that's located?"

"Where?" Gabe asked.

"None other than Washington, DC, home of the most powerful government on Earth. The capital of America is the global power base of modern Masonry. If I remember correctly, Uncle Paolo said there are forty supreme councils around the globe, but the one in Washington wields the most power and influence. If you want real answers, that's where you must look."

"Do you think the location is merely coincidental?" he asked.

"Highly doubtful. You'll find Masonic influence wherever there's power. These people think of themselves as gods among men. These men believe they are worthy of wielding power. So, if someone wants to wield global power, no place offers greater opportunity than Washington, DC."

Gabe stopped pacing and sat back down. "Just think about America's military capability," he said, pausing for effect.

"And its economic power," she added. "The scale of the American government is so outsized it's mind-numbing. Do you realize that America's federal budget alone is larger than the economies of every nation on Earth except Japan and Germany? Every cent of that money is controlled in Washington—more than $2 trillion a year. With a war chest like that, you could accomplish nearly anything."

No wonder Washington was a target on 9/11, Gabe thought. *New York and Washington are the heart of America's political, military, and economic power.*

Gabe ran his hand through his hair. Washington, DC, was also home to the NSA, where Zach Beckett now operated and his grandfather had served for years. He looked at Anna and said, "DC is the perfect choice for Masonic power, isn't it?"

"Indeed," she replied. "Before that, it was London when the British Empire dominated the world. London has a powerful supreme council, too."

The British capital—another coincidence? *Doubtful,* Gabe thought.

"And here's something else," Anna added. "The British Grand Master is none other than the Duke of Kent, Queen Elizabeth's cousin!"

Gabe was blown away—absolutely astonished that Masonry's influence had penetrated such high echelons of society. *If British royalty is caught up in this, who else might be involved?* he wondered.

He stood and began to pace again. He then walked to the window and pulled open the curtain. He could see the majestic dome of Saint Peter's towering above the Vatican. The cross on top was silhouetted by the nighttime sky. *Here I am in Rome,* he thought, *the very place where the pope's scathing condemnation of Freemasonry had been written more than a century earlier.* The circumstances were beyond surreal.

Two days earlier, he'd left the pristine serenity of the Canadian Rockies bound for Italy. He'd planned to get away, see his grandparents, and do some rock climbing. Instead, he found himself in the middle of a perplexing web of intrigue. *How did it come to this?* he wondered.

Anna was still seated on the couch. Gabe could see her out of the corner of his eye.

"How did Freemasonry become so prominent?" he asked. "This couldn't have happened overnight."

"You're right," she replied. "Masonic influence has grown for centuries. It's not new. Some people trace its roots back to the Middle Ages, others to the formation of the first grand lodge in London in 1717. Others will tell you it dates to the Egyptians because it incorporates large swaths of ancient pagan rituals and beliefs. Frankly, no one really knows. However, one thing is certain. Its influence is everywhere."

"And you think this will continue?"

"Without a doubt!" she exclaimed. She then raised her hand for emphasis. "Rest assured, the darkest Masonic plans are shrouded in complete secrecy, but someday, they'll unfold before our very eyes."

Gabe turned around to face her. "Maybe my grandfather discovered those plans."

"Maybe he did."

14

Beckett placed a call from his cell phone, which was picked up after the first ring.

"Zach Beckett here. I need pass clearance to get in the gate. Can you contact the guard post?"

"Certainly, sir," a man's voice replied.

Beckett made small talk and asked the man about his wife and kids but didn't listen to the answer. He was distracted. He was focused on the disk he'd downloaded from John Roslo's computer. Beckett veered off the main thoroughfare, turned onto a side street, and approached the heavily guarded iron gate. He produced his NSA identification for inspection and handed it to the armed soldier.

"Good evening, Mr. Beckett. Working late, I see," the Marine commented cheerfully. He handed back Beckett's ID.

"Work never ceases for those of us protecting the homeland, does it?" he said in return. "Keep up the good work."

The Marine let him pass. He pulled into a space reserved for the Regional Security Office. He grabbed the disk, locked the car, and proceeded to the US Embassy. The corridors were brightly lit and well-watched. Three checkpoints later, he was in an office. He took a seat at a computer.

Beckett put the zip disk into the drive and began transmission. In the process, the data passed through the most sophisticated encryption technology known to man. When the transmission was complete, he sent an encoded communiqué to his agents in Washington. He instructed them to scan all the files for proper names, aliases, code names, and pseudonyms.

Most importantly, he asked them to look for possible connections to current watch list subjects.

He received a reply two minutes later. It read:

Request received. Will take some time due to volume of coded priorities. Your location tomorrow?

Beckett thought about his response. He then wrote:

Run it through the main office with the message Signal Fire. I'll respond to you then.

He received confirmation, logged off, and headed to his hotel to sleep.

15

Gabe stared out the window as he contemplated the possibilities. *What if my grandfather stumbled upon something accidentally,* he thought, *or became privy to a plot because of his former association with the NSA? That still doesn't explain his association with Cardinal Bauer or his investigation of apparitions. Still, Cardinal Bauer was the one who brought Freemasonry into the equation.* Gabe wanted to know more. He turned and looked at Anna.

"So, the organization has ranks?" he asked.

"Precisely. Masonry is structured like a pyramid. Members advance through ranks, called degrees, to ascend the pyramid. Scottish Rite Freemasonry has thirty-three degrees, but many of its members never make it past the third degree. Third-degree Masons hold the title of Master Mason, but they're still neophytes. Authentic Masonic ideology is deliberately hidden from them."

"To shroud Masonry's ultimate aim, right?" he asked.

"Exactly," she replied. "The members of the first three degrees see Masonry as a fraternal organization. They use it to develop business contacts, promote civic duty, and develop a personal code of morality, as taught by Masonry. This group tends to vehemently defend the Masonic organization on the basis that it does good things and promotes goodwill. However, Masonry has many more levels. That's where the esoteric knowledge lies."

"Esoteric?" Gabe asked. He was unfamiliar with the term.

"Esoteric knowledge can only be comprehended by a person with sufficient knowledge to understand its meaning. In Masonic circles, only a select few are considered worthy of this privilege. They're the innermost circle—the ones who successfully ascend through the Masonic degrees."

"How is that accomplished?" he asked.

"Through study and ritual," she replied. "Masonic teaching uses a system of symbols and allegories to instruct its members. These symbols have a secret double meaning that conveys one thing to Masonry's highest-ranking members, the so-called 'enlightened,' and something completely different to everyone else, the so-called 'profane.' Both low-ranking Masons and the general public are considered profane."

"That's revolting!" Gabe exclaimed.

"It is," she continued. "Sadly, most Masons never learn this, nor do they uncover the true meaning behind the Masonic symbols. Only the few who are willing and able to ascend to Freemasonry's highest ranks are considered worthy of true Masonic light. Those who advance through the higher speculative degrees are granted this privilege."

"Speculative degrees?" Gabe queried.

"The fourth through the thirty-third degrees of Masonry are known as speculative degrees, and each has a title," she said

"Like what?" he asked.

"Prince of the Tabernacle, Prince of Mercy, and Scottish Knight of Saint Andrew."

"Those are Christian titles," Gabe said.

"Yes, they are," she replied, "but rest assured, these titles have a hidden meaning that's anything but Christian. In fact, just the opposite. Remember, Freemasonry aims to overthrow the entire religious and political order of the world produced by Christian teaching. As a man passes through the speculative degrees of Freemasonry, he's systematically indoctrinated with Masonic ideology consistent with this aim. He also makes further pledges of secrecy to hide and protect the secret symbols and beliefs. Then, as he approaches the pinnacle of the Masonic pyramid, his instruction becomes entirely oral. Nothing is written for fear of exposure. This methodology is exactly the reverse of Christianity, which has always used public preaching and the written word to convey its teachings to the world. Masonic instruction, on the other hand, is passed along in secret by the great Adepts, those men who are the real masters of Freemasonry."

How did my grandfather become involved in such a tangled mess? Gabe wondered. It was bizarre, to say the least. *Still, my grandfather's entire career had been rooted in a world of secrecy.*

Anna interrupted his thoughts. "At the top of the pyramid is the Brotherhood's highest honor: the thirty-third degree. It's where the final Masonic secrets are conveyed. The thirty-third degree is so secretive that it's debated whether it exists at all, but it does. Those who ascend to the top of the pyramid find the demonic realm, where the darkest symbols, beliefs, and rituals are jealously guarded. It's the seat of power—the place where the world's most enlightened Masons promote Masonic ideology around the world."

Gabe turned and looked out the window a second time. *Perhaps she's right*, he thought. *She warned me to be careful about what I asked for.*

At that instant, he snapped the curtain closed. He stepped back and quickly turned off the floor lamp. The room was thrown into total darkness. He returned to the window and cautiously pulled back the curtain's edge to peer out. He waited for his eyes to adjust to the darkness. He then rushed to the front door and clicked the deadbolt.

"What's wrong?" she asked.

"I saw someone in the courtyard. He's going door to door," Gabe replied.

At that instant, the doorknob rattled. Someone was trying to open it.

Anna gasped. She sprang from the couch and bumped into Gabe in the darkness. They untangled themselves, and she leaned forward to look through the peephole. As her eye drew level, there was a rapid knock on the door. It startled her, and she was thrown back into Gabe a second time.

"What do we do?" she whispered.

Before he could respond, they heard a deep, baritone voice from outside the door.

"Night security."

Anna flipped around and looked through the peephole a second time. She then switched on the light, unlocked the deadbolt, and opened the door.

"Good evening, Ms. Castriotti," the security guard said. "A prowler has been reported in the vicinity. I'm checking all doors to make sure they're locked. I saw the lights on, but I knew this flat was supposed to be unoccupied. My apologies if I startled you, but I wanted to check it out after what happened here this afternoon. Is everything all right?"

"Si, si," Anna replied. "Thank you for your concern. We're fine. I've loaned the apartment to an out-of-town guest for the night. I appreciate your diligence. Please keep up the good work."

"Yes, ma'am."

Anna closed the door. They both took a deep breath and exhaled in relief. Gabe grinned as the two of them retreated to the couch. He reached over and turned the floor lamp back on.

"I'm a little edgy," he said.

"Perfectly understandable," she replied.

Gabe draped an arm over the back of the sofa. He glanced at his watch: 12:30 a.m. It was getting late. He needed sleep, but one question still rolled through his mind. "Cardinal Bauer said my grandfather was investigating apparitions. Even if my working thesis is correct and the Masons were involved in his murder, what do they have to do with apparitions?" he asked.

"That's where the Gobbi messages come in," she replied. She pointed to the blue book. "Read it, and you'll understand."

He eyed the massive, blue volume. It was nearly a thousand pages thick. He felt exasperated.

"You look tired," she said. "It's late, and I've given you plenty to consider—enough for tonight, anyway." She rose from the couch.

Gabe got up as well. He picked up the blue book. "I'll never get through all this tonight. Where do I begin?" he asked.

Anna thought for a moment. "I'd start by reading the messages from 1989. Actually, start a bit earlier. There was a message given on September 11, 1988. Start there and read forward to the end of 1989."

"9/11?" he queried.

"Ironic, isn't it? But that's where I'd start," she replied.

"Will do," Gabe said. He retrieved her coat and helped her into it. "Thanks for coming. I couldn't have gotten this far without your help."

Anna placed a reassuring hand on his arm. Gabe considered kissing her but held back, given the circumstances.

"Goodnight, Gabe," she said. "I'm very happy we met, and I'll continue to help in any way I can. Arrivederci."

She kissed him on the cheek, turned, and left before he had a chance to respond. Gabe watched her disappear through the dimly lit courtyard and closed the door.

He returned to the couch and sat down. He then made notes of the things she'd told him. He felt the stress of the day and needed to get some sleep, but more than that, he wanted to read the Gobbi messages.

He picked up the blue book and wondered about apparitions and locutions. Were they real? He'd heard about them over the years but had not taken them seriously, much less studied them. The blue book supposedly contained over six hundred messages from the mother of Jesus. It seemed like an awfully big stretch. Yet, the book had been given to him by a cardinal of the Catholic Church. If that weren't enough, his grandfather had been researching them, too. *There must be something to this,* Gabe surmised, *but what?*

He decided to lie down on the couch to read. The floor lamp at the end of the couch had a three-way bulb. He turned it to the brightest setting, propped a pillow under his head, and opened the book to the index. He searched for the entry dated September 11, 1988. He turned to that message and read the words supposedly given by the mother of Jesus. Gabe hadn't given Jesus much thought in recent years, but he found it incredibly poignant given what happened on that date exactly thirteen years later.

He flipped back to the index and scanned the other titles from 1988 and 1989. One caught his attention. It was dated October 13, 1988. It mentioned opening the sealed book. He turned to the message and found an intriguing statement. The mother of Jesus said she was opening the sealed book so the secrets it contained could be revealed. Gabe continued reading, and one thing became painfully clear: He was going to need his strength for what lay ahead. These were no ordinary secrets.

16

ONE YEAR EARLIER: ISTANBUL MEETING, 5:30 P.M.

The Master leaned on the table for emphasis and again made eye contact with each man around it. Tension filled the room as the men awaited his proposal.

"Gentlemen, there is only one thing that would galvanize America absolutely: the cleansing of an American city."

With those words, eyes darted around the room as the men at the table looked to see the others' reactions. A certain degree of discomfort was evident as they shifted in their seats, but no one spoke a word.

"The key to our success depends on two factors. First, we must achieve absolute surprise, just as al-Qaeda did on 9/11. The event must shock the country beyond anything that has ever happened. Second, it must look like it was orchestrated by Osama bin Laden and his al-Qaeda network. We must make it appear to be entirely the work of radical Islam. In this way, we will bring about the unity of purpose that we seek."

He paused to allow his words to resonate with each man. He studied them carefully to observe their reactions before continuing.

"The United States now has ground forces in Afghanistan and Iraq and looks at Iran and Syria with suspicion. America fights its War on Terror in each of these places to promote the cause of freedom and, more importantly, to assure the free flow of oil by its expanding presence in the Middle East.

"Gentlemen, you know what Osama bin Laden thinks about Arabian oil. He sees it as Allah's gift to the Islamic people. You also know what he thinks about America's presence in the region. He wrote about these at length in his fatwas against the United States. America depends on Arabian oil, and Bin Laden intends to defend the sacred ground in which it lies. The battleground has been set!"

"When Osama bin Laden fired the first shots of this war on 9/11, he enraged a nation. The terror strikes on 9/11 made his earlier attacks look like child's play, but the lack of a follow-up event has lulled the American nation back to sleep. The country is now completely divided over Iraq.

"The initial anger has faded, and the resurgence in faith experienced in America after 9/11 has diminished. The American people have gone back to their everyday lives—*marrying and being given in marriage.*"

The derisive use of the Biblical reference brought laughter from those gathered. It momentarily broke the tension in the room.

"Gentlemen, I'm confident we can achieve total surprise. Our event will be so shocking that it will first crush the hearts of the American people in paralyzing anguish. However, from that pain, a raging fury will arise like nothing we've seen in the history of the world. America will seek its revenge."

The room erupted with spontaneous applause.

When the noise died down, he began again. "Remember, the final ingredient is to make it look like the work of Osama bin Laden. That, my friends, will be the easy part."

17

"Don't move a muscle."

Gabe opened his eyes. He squinted to see past the automatic weapon pressed against his forehead. The man hovering over him was dressed completely in black, including his gloves. Gabe couldn't see his face behind the black ski mask.

"We already have what we want, Gabriel Roslo. Don't be a hero," the man said. He motioned with his head.

Gabe glanced at the coffee table and saw the diary lying open to the missing pages. He struggled but felt the gun press heavier against his forehead. He was pinned against the couch.

"What did you do with my grandfather's body?"

"Never mind that—you ought to be more concerned about your grandmother. I would hate to see the same thing happen to her."

Then, unexpectedly, Gabe saw his grandfather come through the doorway. The intruder stood up. He charged his grandfather and stabbed him over and over in the stomach. Gabe wanted to shout but was paralyzed. His legs felt strangely heavy. He tried to get up but couldn't lift his head. Then, suddenly, his body jolted, ripping him from sleep. He shuddered from the gruesome nightmare.

It took Gabe a moment to get oriented. As he gained consciousness, he realized the lamplight was still on. He shook himself awake and recalled where he was. He sat up trembling. The sequence of images was appalling. His shirt was soaked with sweat. He got up, went into the bathroom, and splashed water on his face. Now fully awake, he checked his watch. It was 5:30 a.m., twenty-four hours since he'd learned about his grandfather's death.

Gabe returned to the living room, sat down, and reopened the blue book. He scanned the pages to find his place. He'd made it halfway through the 1989 messages before falling asleep. He read the next four messages with great interest. When he turned the page, his eyes locked on the title.

"My God," he said, aghast. "That's it!"

He grabbed his grandfather's diary and pulled out the sheet of paper with the message from the mirror. He carefully smoothed it out on the table before him. He then set the Gobbi messages beside it.

"Buy a vowel," he said in a half-whisper. *That was the key,* he reasoned. He shook his head in disbelief. He turned the paper over and hurriedly wrote his version of the message. As he filled in the final letter, he was horrified by what the message contained, stunned by its simplicity but certain it was accurate. He'd just unraveled a huge piece of the puzzle.

Gabe felt a strange queasiness because of it. His grandfather's cryptic message bore a surreal quality. It reached deeper into the mystery of evil than he cared to imagine. *But who should I tell?* he wondered. He ran through the list of people he'd met the past day and settled on Paolo Castriotti. His grandfather had obviously trusted him with his search for information, and Castriotti had sent him to meet Cardinal Bauer. Gabe resolved to contact him as soon as he returned to Amalfi. Yes, he'd be the one to tell.

Gabe turned his attention back to the blue book. He waited impatiently for Anna's call as he pored over its contents. Finally, the phone rang at 8:30. Anna asked if she had disturbed him. His alert response reassured her. He was fully awake.

"I'm already up," he said. "I've been reading since 5:30, and I could use a distraction. Are you ready for the drive?"

Anna said she'd be ready to leave in thirty minutes. She suggested they grab coffee and breakfast on the road.

"That would be great," he replied.

Gabe continued thinking about the diary, the message's meaning, and his need to see Paolo Castriotti. Several scenarios played out in his mind as he got himself ready. He also found himself whistling in the shower as he anticipated spending the day with Anna. He knew the train was faster, but Anna's company would be well worth the delay. Besides, they still had things to talk about, and her assistance was much appreciated.

Gabe finished getting ready, grabbed his things, and met Anna as she exited her flat. The morning was overcast but had the promise of clearing skies.

"Buon giorno," he said.

"Buon giorno," she replied. Her pleasant greeting included another kiss on the cheek. She then led them to the parking garage, where she fired up her BMW. Anna shifted gears and merged into the early morning traffic.

They left the ancient walls of Rome and sped along the Via Appia Antica, the Appian Way, a route used by the ancient Romans to get to their main naval seaport. Anna followed it to the GRA, better known as the Great Ring Road, which encircles Rome. She took the GRA southeast to reach the A1 and merged into traffic.

"The Italian Autostrade is similar to the interstate system in the United States," she told Gabe. She steered into the leftmost lane, where they drove for a few minutes. Suddenly, her BMW careened right. Gabe was surprised by the jolt and turned his head to see why they moved into the right lane. Just then, a Mercedes scorched past in the left lane.

"He nearly ran us over," Gabe said, a note of irritation in his voice. "That guy didn't even try to slow down. He must've been going two hundred kilometers per hour."

Anna laughed.

"Speed limits out here are considered mere suggestions," she said. "Italians ignore them, and cars in the left lane expect you to move out of the way. It's just the way it works. My apologies. I only had a second to react."

She moved back into the left lane and slammed down the accelerator. She went 160 km/h as they headed south on the A1 toward Naples. Anna navigated the crazy traffic with confident ease, and Gabe began to wonder about this woman.

What was it like for her living in the Roman metropolis? he wondered. His whole life had been focused on avoiding places like Rome. He grew up in a quiet little Virginia town seventy-five miles from the nation's capital. He spent every summer as a child with his grandparents in Alexandria. His grandfather made those summers very special. Still, Gabe never really liked the hectic pulse of the city.

She seemed totally at peace in her environment. She was an attractive, energetic, intelligent woman and exuded a sense of contentment that Gabe found engaging. Here he was, deeply immersed in the mystery of his grandfather's murder but with a growing sense of curiosity about this woman, Anna Castriotti.

She broke into his musings. "Why'd you come to Amalfi?" she asked.

"My grandparents invited me," Gabe replied. He hoped she hadn't noticed him staring at her. "I love climbing mountains. My grandfather told me the mountains in Amalfi are fabulous and that there's great climbing all over Italy."

"Do you climb often?" she asked.

"It's my life, really. I moved to Canada after graduating from college and became a climbing guide in Banff. I take experienced and not-so-experienced climbers into the Rockies so they can encounter nature in a real, tangible way. It's beautiful there," he said with a faraway look. "It never gets old."

Gabe did not mention the other reason for his visit. It was time to get over his breakup with Sarah. His grandparents had invited him because he needed a change of venue. Gabe was finally exiting the celebrated blue period that follows the demise of every long-term, once-promising love. Gabe accepted their invitation and anticipated new adventures and a fresh start.

"My original plan was to go climbing in Amalfi then head to the Alps. I planned to be in Europe for a total of six weeks, but that's all up in the air now," he said with a sigh. "What about you?" he asked.

Anna brushed her hair back off her face. "Me?" she stammered slightly. "Well, I've lived in Rome my entire life. I grew up in a nice little neighborhood near Trevi Fountain. I'm the youngest of four, the only girl, and I was spoiled my whole life as a result, especially by my Uncle Paolo. I love the Amalfi Coast. I spent every summer there when I was growing up. He and my aunt treated me like a daughter. I still spend as much time there as I can."

She paused a moment, thinking. "Anyway, after university, I found my degree to be of little use, so I became a property manager. That's served me well, but my interests still lie in the study of politics."

"Is that what you studied in college?" Gabe asked.

"It is," Anna replied. "I've always been interested in politics. My undergraduate degree is in political science. In school, I was particularly interested in the contrast between the American system of liberty and the Soviet system of tyranny. I was fortunate to spend a year in America at Georgetown University. It was quite an eye-opening experience for me. I was able to work on my English and see firsthand how your system of government works."

"An intellectual," Gabe teased with a laugh.

Anna blushed. "Where'd you go to college?" she asked, deflecting attention from herself.

"The Colorado School of Mines. That's where I developed my interest in climbing and outdoor sports. I went there on a baseball scholarship. I had some success with baseball and was even recruited professionally, but my real love was the mountains. After college, I took a job as a climbing guide with a company in Calgary. I later moved to Banff and started my own expedition business. I get a lot of Americans who want to get away from it all and commune with nature."

"Do you live there alone?"

"I do."

Gabe carefully avoided the subject of Sarah and their breakup. He'd been in love with Sarah since their college days and wanted to marry her. She refused. *In the end, it was about money,* he thought bitterly. Sarah wanted "the good life." She made it clear what she really wanted: the privileged life and financial fortune of a professional athlete. When Gabe turned away from the limelight, Sarah's feelings faded. They didn't correlate with living a rugged existence in the Canadian Rockies, and she moved back to the US. A year had passed, and Gabe was ready to move on with his life. As his mind wandered, he suddenly remembered his mom.

"Anna, I need to call my mother. I tried her yesterday but couldn't reach her. Could we stop and find a phone?"

"No problem," she replied. She reached into her purse. "Use mine."

"Thanks," he said.

"Just dial zero, one, one, then the number," she added. "It works internationally."

Gabe felt his heart race as he punched the last number. She answered on the fourth ring. There was a distinct grogginess in her voice. He'd obviously awakened her.

"Mom? It's me, Gabe."

"My dear, I was asleep. How's Italy? Did you make it safely? What time is it? How are you? Is everything all right?"

"I'm fine, Mom. Umm, well, I'm fine—but everything's not okay. I have some very bad news. Grandfather passed away."

He heard a loud gasp. She had been quite fond of her father-in-law.

"When? Where?" she asked.

"During the night," he replied. "Evidently, he fell. Gram found him on the bathroom floor yesterday morning."

"Oh, my God! How is she? She must be devastated."

"She's taking it pretty well," he answered. "She was more concerned about me. She's at her cousins' house. She stayed there last night. I'm headed there now."

Gabe could hear his mother's voice break. "I know how much he meant to you. How are you holding up?"

"I'm doing okay," he said. "My main concern is Gram."

"What about the arrangements?" she asked. "You're going to need help. I'll come right away."

"No, Mom. Stay in Virginia. As much as I'd love to have you here, it would be better to have a familiar face at the airport when we get back. I can handle the arrangements. Mom, I love you."

Gabe could hear her crying.

"I love you, too, son. Please tell your grandmother I'm so sorry."

"I will."

With that, he hung up and handed the phone back to Anna. Neither spoke. Gabe laid his head against the headrest and turned his thoughts to the day before. It had been a day like no other. First, he was awakened by the news of his grandfather's death. Then he discovered it was probably murder. Lastly, it was somehow connected to the peculiar secret society of Freemasonry.

Until the prior evening, Gabe had never even thought about Freemasonry, much less studied it. Now, he was tracking the elusive and secretive brotherhood to figure out why his grandfather had been murdered. However, based on what he'd read that morning in the blue book, a dreadful new twist connected it all to the deepest mysteries of evil.

He looked at Anna and felt an affinity toward her. He was truly thankful for her assistance. He then said, "I thought about what you told me last night as I read the Gobbi messages. I think you were right when you cautioned me about Masonry."

Anna glanced in his direction but said nothing.

"I know Pope Leo's letter made reference to the overthrow of both the political *and* religious order, but I wasn't prepared for what I found in the Gobbi messages."

Anna shot a second glance at Gabe. It looked like she was going to speak, but she stopped. She turned her eyes back toward the road and twirled her hair nervously.

"You know something, don't you?" Gabe pressed forward.

"Nothing specific," she replied. "I mean... nothing specific about your grandfather."

"Do you mind telling me what you do know?" he asked.

Anna stopped twirling her hair. She pushed a CD into the changer and adjusted the volume. "Like I said last night," she started. "I will tell you what I know, but you must promise that you won't reveal your source—no matter what."

"Agreed," he replied.

"This condition is absolute. You can't imagine how deep and widespread the Masonic organization is," she continued.

"I promise. I won't say a word to anyone."

She eyed him cautiously. "I didn't want to tell you this last night," she said, "but Masonry has plans to replace Christianity with something altogether different. Most people have no idea about this, but the agenda is a completely unsavory web of political and religious complicity. If you look closely at what Pope Leo wrote, he talked about the *kingdom of Satan* and pointed his finger straight at the Masonic organization."

"After reading the Gobbi messages, I'm beginning to see why," he said.

Anna nodded.

They drove silently for a while. Gabe felt uneasy and wondered whether to press the topic further. Still, he was intrigued about what he'd read that morning and the night before. His mind was filled with questions. In particular, he was curious about something from *Humanum Genus*. Pope Leo wrote that Masonry's ultimate purpose was to substitute a new state of things, where foundations and laws would be drawn from mere naturalism. *What exactly does that mean?* he wondered.

He turned to Anna and asked, "Pope Leo talked about the overthrow of the religious and political order of the world produced by Christian teaching. What did he mean when he said Masonry's aim was to substitute a new order of things based solely on naturalism? What did he mean by *naturalism?*"

"Naturalism is the idea that God is the cosmos," she replied. "This is not a new idea, of course, but it directly conflicts with Christianity, as well as Judaism and Islam. They all start with the idea that God is the creator, separate and distinct from the creation."

"And naturalism merges the two?" he asked.

"Exactly," she said. "For an upper-level Mason, there's no distinction between God and creation. They are merged into one thing—nature. Do you see where this is going?"

"I do," he answered.

"Think about it," she continued. "Naturalism strips God of his power and hands it to the cosmos. It tears down belief in the Almighty and exalts the creation instead. Naturalism draws our adoration away from God and places it upon things of this world. In subtle and cunning ways, Masonry uses this philosophy to undermine every aspect of Christian teaching and to attack the divinity of Christ. There was a reason Pope Leo connected the Masons to the kingdom of Satan."

Gabe was floored.

Anna continued without prompting. "I don't know if you're a Christian believer or not, but here's something you need to understand. According to naturalism, humanity possesses within itself all the creative powers necessary to generate more human life. In simple terms, man is god. Therefore, Masonry glorifies mankind because humanity sits at the pinnacle of nature. In other words, man reigns supreme, and any belief in a supreme deity is tolerated publicly but ridiculed privately. It also lays the foundation for all the modern-day attacks on Christian beliefs."

Gabe began to grasp the deeper significance of Pope Leo's letter. He didn't consider himself a Christian believer, but he wasn't an unbeliever either. He certainly believed in God. He just didn't think about it very much.

Anna continued, "Naturalism has another ramification, and this one's huge. Because the Masonic philosophy of naturalism focuses on earthly life, where the power of man reigns supreme, it directly conflicts with the Christian belief in eternal life, something that was purchased at a high price: the blood sacrifice of Jesus. The media now promotes a new wrinkle, the idea that Jesus had a purely human bloodline that has been passed on from generation to generation in secret, adding insult to this mockery. Such utter nonsense is a perfect example of how naturalism and the Masonic deception take Christian belief and pervert it by denying the divinity of Jesus. On top of that, they've had the audacity to suggest the Catholic Church has hidden this fact for centuries in an elaborate coverup."

Gabe had recently finished a book claiming exactly that. It was the premise put forth in Dan Brown's *The DaVinci Code*. He wondered, *Was it possible that Masonic influence had penetrated even there?*

"Let me see if I understand this," he said. "By focusing solely on the historical, human nature of Jesus, people are coached to forget his divinity. In essence, he's reduced to just another good man."

"You've got it!" she exclaimed. "And that lays the foundation for all the modern-day attacks on Christ himself."

"But how do they do it?" he asked. "How does it happen without people knowing?"

"It all goes back to Masonry's many deceptions," she answered. "For starters, Masonry claims it is *not* a religion—an absolute lie. All religions are systems of belief, and Masonry has a very well-developed system of beliefs. It also conducts specific rituals in the secrecy of the lodge. It's anyone's guess what those truly entail, but the real Masonic method is best explained through a metaphor."

"Which is?" he asked.

"Darkness and light," she replied. "Darkness is the absence of light, right? Darkness is also used to describe evil. Take your popular American movie series, *Star Wars*, for instance. All things evil are referred to as the dark side, but light represents goodness and truth. Masonry puts a new twist on that. To cover the darkness of its reality, Masonry creates artificial light."

"The appearance of goodness!" Gabe interjected.

"Exactly," Anna replied.

She reached up and hit the pause button on her CD changer. All became quiet except for the muffled hum of road noise.

"By masking the darkness with artificial light," she continued. "Masonry can systematically extinguish true light without most people ever knowing. That's why Pope Leo warned us so strongly. Masonry has waged this war of deception against Christianity for centuries."

"Unbelievable," Gabe said. He ran his hand through his hair. "Artificial light to cover the darkness," he repeated several times. "Masterfully clever."

"Just about everything Masonry touches manufactures artificial light," she continued, "but when you peel back the curtain of secrecy, you find layer after layer of duplicity, deception, and blasphemy against God Himself."

Gabe digested her words, unable to conceal a frown.

"We need fuel," she said. Anna pointed to the gauges of her BMW.

She steered into the right lane and exited the freeway. She eased into a spot at the pump, shut off the engine, and turned toward Gabe.

"If the Masonic organization stood up and announced its true nature to the world," she said, "there would be an outrage like none seen in history. But it can't do that. Everyone would understand that it stood in darkness. Instead, Masonry creates artificial light to shine brightly in the eyes of free society and cleverly deceive it. By doing that, Masonry unfolds its great plan without detection."

She finished speaking and jumped out of the car to fill the tank. A few minutes later, she popped her head in the window. "Are you hungry?" she asked. "I'm famished. This would be a good place to eat."

"Sure, I guess," Gabe replied. He was lost in thought.

He opened the door to get out just as she hopped back into the driver's seat. "I'll find a parking place and be right with you," she said.

Anna started the car and pulled around to the Autostop entrance. Gabe met her inside.

MEANWHILE, CARDINAL BAUER was finishing a phone call in his office.

"Yes, that's correct—Gabriel Roslo, John Roslo's grandson. He's here in Italy. He visited me yesterday after learning of his grandfather's death. He came here to ask about his grandfather's research."

The cardinal listened carefully to the instructions.

"I understand perfectly and agree with your assessment. I'll see to it immediately." With that, he hung up and redialed.

18

The Autostop hovered over the freeway. It spanned the width of the Autostrade and served traffic from both directions. It reminded Gabe of the oasis stops he'd seen years earlier in Illinois along Chicago's Tri-state Tollway.

They worked their way through the crowd toward the restaurant. Gabe studied the faces of those they passed. The building was abuzz with travelers, including two busloads of adolescent students. He noticed that certain men seemed to stare at him, holding their glances a bit too long. *Am I being watched,* Gabe wondered, *or just being paranoid?*

They entered the nearly full restaurant and were greeted by a pleasant-faced, middle-aged hostess, who led them to an empty booth in the far corner. Once seated, a waitress appeared and took their drink orders. Anna asked for orange juice and hot tea. Gabe ordered coffee and a bottle of water.

"I'll be right back to take your order," she said in English.

"Grazie," replied Anna.

The waitress returned a few minutes later with their drinks and took their breakfast order—eggs, toast, and a plate of fresh fruit to split.

After she left, Gabe leaned in and said in a low whisper, "With everything you've told me, it's still not clear if my grandfather was murdered for political reasons or religious reasons. He spent his entire career in the intelligence services but had more recently been investigating religious phenomena."

"Perhaps it was both," Anna suggested. "It wouldn't be the first time that religion and politics were tangled together."

"That would explain why both Cardinal Bauer and Zach Beckett are involved in this," Gabe said.

"From what I know about Cardinal Bauer," she continued, "I don't think he would've pointed you toward the Masons unless he thought there was a political and religious connection. At his level, he sees these connections all too clearly."

She's probably right, Gabe thought. The overlap of the political and religious implications was becoming clearer. He contemplated those implications and then asked, "What did you mean when you said Masonry creates artificial light to shine brightly into the eyes of free society?"

"For Masonry's deception to work," she said, "society must first be completely indoctrinated with the idea that freedom is an inalienable right, the overriding ideal of society."

"That's a good thing," he said, "The foundation on which America was built."

"Si, si," she answered. "Many good men have given their lives to defend this ideal. The preservation of freedom and liberty are hallmarks of American society. They reflect the positive side of Masonry. Freedom and liberty are good things—absolutely. No one takes exception with that."

"So, where's the deception?" Gabe asked.

She answered. "Once liberty and freedom have been established as the supreme ideals, Masonry goes to work in the shadows to convince people they possess within themselves the right to choose anything permissible under civil law, ignoring spiritual repercussions for those choices. That's the artificial light—the colossal lie. Freemasonry makes phenomenal use of the media to advance that lie. People have steadily accepted Masonic thinking without even realizing it."

"It sounds like brainwashing," Gabe said.

"The media are powerful instruments," she replied. "They feed us a steady diet of propaganda. The messaging reinforces the notion that we're in total control of our lives. This creates a tremendous conflict between freedom and choice. Freedom is an inalienable right, but choice has consequences. Masonry works to blur the line, which makes Masonic ideology so difficult to understand and so spiritually dangerous."

Gabe raised an eyebrow.

The waitress returned with breakfast and set it before them. Anna took a bite of toast. She then continued.

"It might sound like brainwashing, but here's the rub. We all make choices freely, so it's no wonder people confuse freedom and choice. It's part of the Masonic agenda."

"How so?" he asked.

"Freemasonry has a plan to systematically neutralize Christian teaching in Western society. This plan has been evolving for a long time. The Soviets tried to destroy Christianity altogether when they proclaimed atheism, but that didn't work. When put to the test, people chose death over tyranny. The Masonic agenda is far more cunning. Don't get rid of Christianity—neutralize it. Let everyone practice it freely and work in secret to slowly suffocate its message. The real prize is the disintegration of baptized Christians, especially Catholics."

"That's a lot to take in," Gabe said. "And it seems far-fetched."

"Gabe, I assure you this is real, just hidden. Not every revolution is fought with guns. This one's being waged with ideas, especially inside the American legal system. It has been for decades. It's all part of an ongoing Masonic effort to overthrow the religious and political systems produced by Christian teaching. I'm not making this up."

"So how does this neutralization happen?" Gabe asked.

"Do you remember last night when I said that Masonic revolutionaries helped birth a great nation?"

"Yes," he answered.

"Because of their success," she continued, "America was born—and without the French Reign of Terror, I might add. Nevertheless, the dark side of Masonry's influences developed along other lines in your country. Take the case of Roosevelt and Truman—political giants at the seat of Masonic power. Roosevelt was a thirty-second-degree Mason, and Truman held a thirty-third degree. Their Masonic influence has left an indelible mark on American culture."

"How?" Gabe protested. "Roosevelt and Truman were great American patriots," he continued. "They defeated Hitler and guided the nation through its greatest trial."

"While that's undoubtedly true," she countered, "there's more to the story. While they were saving the West, they laid the foundation for some of today's most divisive cultural clashes."

"What do you mean?" Gabe asked.

"Why do you think the phrase 'separation of church and state' is so ingrained in American culture?" she asked.

"It's in the First Amendment, of course," Gabe answered.

"That's what most people think, but you're wrong," she replied.

"But surely the Constitution guarantees the separation of church and state," he protested.

"That's how the Constitution's been interpreted," she countered. "However, the phrase itself is not in the Constitution."

Gabe was incredulous. "So, where does it come from?" he asked.

"The Danbury Letter," she replied.

"Never heard of it."

"It was written by Thomas Jefferson to the Danbury Baptist Association in the early 1800s. Check it out yourself," she said. "Jefferson referenced the First Amendment. It stipulates, 'Congress shall make no law respecting an establishment of religion or prohibiting the free exercise thereof.' Jefferson then added, 'thus building a wall of separation between church and state.'

"Jefferson believed strongly that no one should be coerced into joining a particular church, especially one forced on them by the government, as had been the case in England. He made that abundantly clear in the Danbury Letter when he reassured the Danbury Baptists that the wall of separation between church and state safeguarded these things. The First Amendment was designed to protect society from government-mandated religion while ensuring everyone's freedom to worship as they choose."

"The Danbury Letter. So that's where the phrase comes from—a letter written by Thomas Jefferson," Gabe confirmed.

"Precisely, but most Americans believe it's written into the Constitution because of what happened in 1947," she said.

"What happened in 1947?" he asked.

"That's where the Masonic agenda really takes flight. A century and a half after Jefferson wrote the Danbury Letter, the Supreme Court turned the phrase into a constitutional principle. In a landmark case, Justices on both sides of the ruling cited the 'wall of separation' phrase to support their opinions, effectively enshrining it into constitutional law.

"Their actions allowed the legal system to flip the meaning of Thomas Jefferson's words. Rather than protecting the rights of its citizens to worship freely, the 'separation of church and state' became the legal basis for challenging Christian influence in public places, including schools. Suddenly, cases sprang up everywhere seeking to eliminate Christian presence in the public sphere. The results profoundly changed society and laid the foundation for today's deep cultural divides.

"After that, the media linked the phrases 'first amendment' and 'separation of church and state' with such frequency that most Americans now accept them as one and the same thing."

"But how do the Freemasons figure into this?" Gabe asked.

"That's the clincher," Anna replied. "In 1947, the Supreme Court was stacked with Masons, and every one of them was appointed by Roosevelt or Truman. Seven of its nine members were confirmed Masons—a perfect setup. It was far more cunning than atheism."

Gabe thought about the sheet of paper in his pocket. His grandfather had left a puzzling riddle, indeed, but Gabe was convinced he had the correct translation—and the implications were staggering. *Even giants of the American political scene were in league with the Masons,* he thought. If the Masonic organization aimed to replace the influence of Christianity with a system based on naturalism—and Gabe had every reason to believe it did—what else was it involved in? And what might his grandfather have known about those plans that got him murdered? The range of possibilities was endless. No wonder Anna was being so cautious.

19

Anna picked up her fork. Gabe couldn't help but notice her attractive figure. She wore a light blue sweater that accentuated her trim but curvaceous shape. Her shoulder-length hair partly covered her face. It highlighted her near-perfect features. They ate quietly for several minutes when suddenly Gabe pulled the diary from his coat pocket.

"There's something I wanted to ask you about," he said. "I found this written in my great-grandfather's diary." He flipped through several pages and then passed the book to Anna. She looked at the page. "See here," he said. "There's something written in the margin."

Anna examined the page. A look of disdain crossed her face.

"Any idea what it means?" he asked.

She nodded her head in the affirmative. "It's Latin," she said. "Do you remember last night when we talked about how Masonry assigns a secret double meaning to its symbols and allegories to create an esoteric body of knowledge known only by the higher-ups?"

Gabe nodded.

"One of the tactics is to take common Christian symbols and twist their meaning. What's the best-known Christian symbol?" she asked.

"The cross, I suppose," he said.

"Right, the cross. Have you ever seen the letters INRI at the top of a crucifix?"

"Sure, my grandmother's house was full of them," he said.

She turned the page around and read the words aloud. "*Igne Natura Renovatur Integra*—INRI. That's the occultic interpretation of the letters

INRI. It's derived from ancient paganism and secretly incorporated into Freemasonry. The true meaning of the letters, of course, comes from the statement Pontius Pilate hung above the cross of Jesus. It read, 'Jesus of Nazareth, King of the Jews.' Latin has no J, so the first and last words are expressed with the letter I. The N stands for Nazareth, and the R stands for *Rex*, which means king. To Christian believers, those letters point to Jesus' blood sacrifice. They also signify resurrection, triumph over death, and eternal life. The Masonic derivation makes a mockery of this sacrifice. It glorifies human sexuality instead."

Anna pointed to the words written in the margin. She continued, "The Latin phrase, *Igne Natura Renovatur Integra*, translates to 'All of nature is renovated by fire.' This Masonic fire refers to the fire of man's passion. It is the fiery drive behind human sexuality. It's also the driving force behind human reproduction—the power to renovate nature. As such, sexual passion exalts man and his human nature to godlike status. All under the banner of sexual freedom, of course. If you extend this to its furthest conclusion, every form of sexual passion is to be fueled, adored, and fed without limit. Look at our society—we're there."

Man ruled by his passions, Gabe thought. He contemplated what she said. Undoubtedly, society was fed a steady diet of desirable eye candy. Still, he'd chosen a life ruled by self-discipline for himself—not that he wasn't drawn to the beauty of the female form. He most certainly was. Women found Gabe's good looks and athleticism hard to resist, and Gabe held women in high esteem. He appreciated their personalities, hopes, dreams, and thoughts. For Gabe, women were subjects of interest rather than objects of pleasure.

He looked up and made eye contact with Anna. "How do you know all this?" he asked.

"I told you—from my Uncle Paolo," she replied. "The Masonic organization keeps these alternate meanings hidden to accomplish their purpose. Only those who move through the higher degrees are told. Low-ranking members are allowed to believe the Masonic interpretation of the cross holds the same meaning as its Christian significance. If not, Masonry might not be able to attract new initiates."

Gabe took a bite of toast. He contemplated what he'd read in the Gobbi messages the night before and thought about what she'd just said. He was making connections.

Anna grabbed a napkin and started drawing. When she finished, she turned the napkin around for Gabe to see.

"The same ideas are embodied here. Do you recognize this?" she asked as she pointed to a drawing of an interlocking compass and square with the familiar G in the middle.

"Sure," Gabe replied. "It's a Masonic insignia, right?"

"Exactly, and it contains layers of meaning—things like God and man, body and spirit, truth and lies, male domination and female inferiority."

"No way!" he exclaimed. "And I suppose the G stands for God?"

"That's a common misinterpretation," she answered, "but it secretly means generative, signifying copulation."

"You're joking," Gabe interrupted.

"I wish I were, and it's totally bizarre," she said.

Anna pointed to the insignia again. "Officially, the G means geometry—literally, earth measurement. Masons display this symbol publicly because it honors the original stonemasons, the great builders of Europe. The top of the symbol is a compass, which is used for drawing circles. The bottom is a carpenter's square, which is used for making right angles. These basic geometric shapes are used in building.

"However, the secret meaning is altogether different," she continued. "In the esoteric, hidden meaning, the square signifies the female, what the ancient pagans referred to as the divine feminine. Look at the diagram again."

Anna used her pencil to trace the carpenter's square.

"See, she lies flat on her back, legs wide open. It's her symbolic duty to passively await the male, which is symbolized by…"

"The compass point," Gabe guessed.

"Exactly. The compass point is a Masonic phallic symbol, what the ancient pagans referred to as the divine masculine. See how the symbols interlock—the dominant, superior male presses down upon the passive, inferior female."

"That's pathetic," Gabe said with a look of disgust on his face. "Why doesn't the women's movement scream about this? It's insulting."

"Hell, Gabe, I'm insulted by it, and I'm not even an activist. Any woman would be. It's truly wretched."

"So much for equality between the sexes," he said. He lifted his coffee cup to his mouth.

"This absurd, chauvinistic attitude," Anna continued, "helps explain why women were prevented from voting in the United States for over a century. The Founding Fathers did not assign equal dignity to women, despite America's claim of equality among its citizens. Women were simply considered inferior. So were slaves."

"But all that's in the past," Gabe countered.

"True, but pagan principles are still incorporated into Masonic teaching and ritual. In Egyptian paganism, Osiris was the sun god. Isis was the moon goddess, and their sexual union brought forth Horus, their divine offspring. In Freemasonry, it's called the Generative Principle of Life. That's the hidden Masonic meaning behind the letter G appearing inside the compass and square."

"That's pretty weird," Gabe said.

"It is, but the symbolism explains a lot. Osiris is the male sun god because sunlight dominates the sky. Hence, in the Masonic adaptation, men are deemed dominant and superior because they choose when and where to sow their seed. They possess godlike qualities in their reproductive capability—the power to create life."

Gabe took a deep breath and raised an eyebrow.

"Stay with me, Gabe. You haven't heard the worst part. Isis is the female moon goddess. Her light is inferior. Therefore, women are considered passive and inferior. They're the receivers of the seed, and their duty is illustrated by the carpenter's square," she said. "Just lay back and await the male."

Gabe shook his head in disbelief. Anna took a few bites of melon, and Gabe finished his eggs. They ate quietly for a few minutes. He thought about what she'd said earlier. If the devil had a language, the words would say one thing but mean another. These deceptions were darker than people realized.

Anna interrupted his thoughts. "There's one more thing you should know."

Gabe looked up at her.

"Hidden Masonic ideology proffers one more idea that starkly contrasts Christian teaching. Masonry teaches that the human soul is completely incorruptible—never capable of being damaged by human action. Our physical nature, on the other hand, is considered animalistic and hopelessly corrupted by the desires of the flesh. These beliefs have far-reaching consequences. First, this idea makes a complete mockery of the crucifixion. There is no need for a Savior if the human soul is incorruptible. If you watch *The Passion of the Christ*, the film exposes the depth of this mockery because it captures the reality of what Jesus endured. Second, this belief unleashes the physical passions to satiate every human desire, regardless of spiritual consequence. Give in to your passions—it's simply nature."

Anna finished her eggs and took a few bites of toast and jelly. Gabe pondered her statements. These were heavy thoughts, yet they raised his curiosity. He glanced at her and wondered, *Who is this woman?* Anna Castriotti was a walking encyclopedia—both brilliant and beautiful.

He thought for a moment then asked her the obvious question. "So, what happens to this incorruptible Masonic soul when we die?"

"That's the worst part, Gabe. At the end of life, the Masonic soul loses its identity. It becomes either nothing at all or is reincarnated. In either case, there's no heaven. There's no hell. There's no entrapment of souls and no spiritual consequences to our actions. And that, my friend, is one powerful lie. In Freemasonry, the focus is on our intellect. Enlighten the human mind with knowledge. Knowledge is the food that propels us toward glory—a path that can be achieved through our efforts. In effect, our ability to reason makes us divine."

Anna pointed to the Masonic symbol once again. "Because the sexual union between men and women has the power to bring about newly created life, the Masonic symbol is put forth as evidence that human beings are gods with both the physical power to create life and the intellectual power to choose which ones live and which ones die. And that, Gabe, is the most divisive issue of all."

Gabe was flabbergasted. He'd never felt strongly one way or the other about human reproductive issues. Yet, Anna had put the debate into an entirely new context. Evidently, the present-day battle between the right to life and the right to choose was buried inside a much deeper conflict. Based on what he'd read that morning, he was beginning to understand why. Gabe wondered if there was any place where Masonic influence had failed to penetrate. Suddenly, he felt overwhelmed by the task at hand.

He glanced at his watch. It was nearly noon. He took a deep breath. "We'd better get going," he said. "We still have a long drive."

Gabe threw twenty euros on the table to cover the check, and they got up to leave. When they reached the car, they were approached by two men begging for money. Anna waived them off. One of them persisted in Italian, even to the point of leaning into her door as she got in. Anna didn't flinch, but Gabe was unnerved. She pulled the door closed, started the car, and dropped it into gear.

"Gypsies," she said with a grin. "He washed my windshield while we were eating and demanded payment."

Gabe laughed as they hit the highway ramp. Paolo had warned him about the gypsies.

They zoomed south on the A1. The morning clouds were breaking up, and patches of clear, blue sky emerged. The rolling scenery offered one treat after another. Gabe noticed an impressive stone structure built atop a huge, craggy mountain to the left of the freeway.

"What's that?" Gabe asked.

"Montecassino," she answered. "The famous abbey founded by Saint Benedict. It's been there for fifteen hundred years. Talk about history. The place has been destroyed and rebuilt no fewer than four times over the centuries. The most recent destruction was during World War II when the Allies tried to recapture it from the Germans. They reduced it to a heap of rubble in less than three hours. Sadly, hundreds of defenseless civilians had taken refuge there and were crushed to death under the debris."

"What a tragedy," Gabe said.

Anna made no response. She seemed completely content to drive in silence, and no further conversation followed. Gabe thought about how easy she was to be with—how she respected his space but was always willing to engage his questions. Some people needed to fill the void with chatter, but not Anna.

He looked out the windshield and watched the colorful oleander whisk by in the median. The concrete median formed a continuous ribbon from Rome to Naples, except for periodic crossover points. It blurred by on the left side of the car. After twenty minutes or so, the hypnotic effect began to take its toll. Gabe's eyelids grew heavy.

"If you don't mind, I'd like to catch some sleep. I only slept four hours last night."

"Be my guest," she replied. She moved back into the fast lane and stepped on the accelerator. "I usually make good time from here."

Gabe dozed into a deep sleep. He propped his head against the side window. Fatigue had finally caught up with him.

20

ONE YEAR EARLIER: ISTANBUL MEETING, 6:00 P.M.

The Master of the Royal Secret was energized by the adulation of the powerful men seated around the table.

"It's an ingenious plan," the Master said. "We will galvanize the American people in their resolve to fight fire with fire. Raging indignation will reunite the American people in their willingness to strike back with nuclear weapons. 'Forget Homeland Security. Nuke 'Em!' will be their motto.

"Through this orchestrated event, we will ensure the most powerful military force on Earth will be unleashed against the militant zeal of Islam—or anyone else who dares to stand in its way. And it will appear that radical Islam has brought this doom upon itself."

The room again erupted in applause. He glowed in their praise. When it finally died down, he began again.

"In doing so, we will most assuredly neutralize the rising Pan-Islamic movement and its extremists. Now, gentlemen, what city should serve as our sacrificial lamb? It must be far enough from the country's power base on the East Coast to preserve New York and Washington but large enough to matter. In my opinion, the perfect target would be America's heartland. Remember the shock that spread across the country when a terrorist struck in Oklahoma City? I have prepared a list for you to consider."

The room fell into subdued silence as a flat panel screen dropped from the ceiling, illuminating potential targets. A quiet eeriness hung over the room. The Master read their minds as each man contemplated the consequences.

He continued, "Some of you have holdings in these cities—in certain cases, substantial holdings. However, I will not allow you to liquidate them in advance. It's true that they will be worthless afterward, but the bigger prize awaits us. Therefore, it's imperative that you avoid any activity that could cast suspicion either before or after our mission is accomplished."

The room was again quiet.

Jack Allbritton had major holdings in each potential city and didn't like any of the choices. He understood the need, but he wondered if the same could be accomplished by striking against a target outside of America. After a period of contemplation, he raised the question.

"Did you consider other targets—the Vatican, perhaps?"

The inquiry produced snickers and derisive comments among the participants.

"Of course, we considered the Vatican. My staff even speculated on the pleasure of killing two birds with one stone, but I see things differently. An attack against the Vatican would produce outrage, especially in Europe, but it would not achieve the galvanizing impact of a nuclear strike against an American city. Our goal is to guarantee the ironclad unity of the American people in the support of their government to use nuclear weapons in retaliation."

He then straightened to his full and imposing height. A sinister look flickered in his eye as he added, "We need the Catholic Church to serve as our mouthpiece. We have many well-placed associates within their ranks to stir dissent against the pope. If we cut out its heart, people might sympathize with his message and fail to hear ours. We cannot have this. Dissidents within his ranks are already making spectacular headway in neutralizing what the pope teaches. Belief in the ridiculous superstitions of Christianity is waning and has practically disappeared in Europe. In time, America will follow suit. The Catholic Church has over one billion members—more than all the other varieties of Christianity combined. It must continue to function if it's to serve our plans. Adolf Hitler recognized that to succeed in the destruction of an inferior race of people, you must first strip them of their core beliefs and then strike with absolute force. Today, we stand inspired by his words in our quest to accomplish the same. However, this time, we have one crucial difference to ensure we succeed where he failed. Through our efforts, a vast multitude of people will discard their core beliefs by their free choice."

Heads nodded in agreement. They contemplated the significance of his words. After a moment of quiet reflection, one of the men present asked the question on many minds.

"Where would we get the weapon? Obviously, America, China, and India are out of the question. Security over their nuclear arsenals is ironclad."

The Master of the Royal Secret grinned slyly, obviously pleased with the question.

"Never underestimate the White Lodge. The fall of the Soviet Union has produced many cracks in the security of its aging nuclear arsenal, and Pakistan is an obvious consideration. However, before we continue, I suggest we eat."

With a wave of his hand, female servants entered the room, weighed down by trays loaded with sumptuous food.

21

When Gabe awoke, they were descending a series of switchbacks and were no longer on the A1. He wasn't sure of their location, but the view of the sea was fabulous. The sky was completely clear now, and its deep, cerulean blue reflected off the Mediterranean.

"Well, aren't you the sleepyhead?" Anna teased.

"How long have I been out?"

"A little more than two hours," she replied.

Gabe looked at his watch. It was just before 2:30 p.m. *Hopefully, I didn't drool,* he thought, wiping his mouth just in case. He was slightly embarrassed but grateful for the nap.

"Where are we?"

"Just a few minutes from Amalfi," she replied.

Gabe stretched to get himself fully awake. He thought about his game plan as they sped toward Amalfi. He wanted to speak with Paolo Castriotti first. Anna mentioned that her uncle was very familiar with the blue book. Gabe felt a growing sense of trust toward Anna and her uncle. Based on what he'd read that morning, he was sure that Castriotti held the key to unlocking the next clue. He also wanted to find out what Castriotti knew about Zach Beckett.

It was now perfectly clear that his grandfather's murder was more than a local incident. Gabe concluded that it was pointless to involve the local authorities. At best, they'd get in the way, or worse, they might lead the people involved directly to the trail of evidence—or worse still, to his grandmother. The fewer people who knew what was going on, the better.

"Anna, I'd like to go straight to the hotel. I want to see your uncle right away."

She glanced at the clock on her dashboard. "Perfect, just in time for wine time. He should be there when we arrive."

"Wine time?" Gabe asked, puzzled.

"Every afternoon at 3:00, my uncle and his friends gather on the terrace of the hotel to drink wine and solve the world's problems." Anna winked at him. "Your grandfather always joined in when he was here. Uncle Paolo never misses it unless he's away on business."

He started to ask Anna who else might be there when she suddenly took a sharp right turn. They pulled into the parking lot of the Amalfi Hotel. She shut off the engine and yanked up the parking brake.

"We're here," she said.

Gabe reached for the door handle but was startled by Lorenzo Bonelli's contorted face at the window.

"Gabriel, I am so glad you're here. There's a man who wants to meet you," he said as Gabe opened the door. "He's downstairs."

Lorenzo was completely flustered and out of breath. His forehead was beaded with sweat, and worry engulfed his face. He'd obviously been waiting for them. He then remembered his manners and hastily kissed Anna on both cheeks when she got out of the car.

"It's good to see you, Anna."

He allowed no time for a response and turned to Gabe. "I didn't know what to do. Paolo's not here yet. I've been up here waiting for you. I'm so sorry; I just didn't know what to do," he repeated. He began to pace anxiously with his hands on his head.

Gabe's mind raced. Who was this person, and how did he know where to find him?

"Who's here?" Anna asked. She was bewildered by Lorenzo's behavior. "Who wants to meet with Gabe?"

"Andre Gotto," Lorenzo informed them.

Anna's face softened. A broad smile formed across her lips. "He's part of the wine time group," she said. She took Gabe by the arm to reassure him. "He's another close friend of Uncle Paolo's. Your grandfather knew him, too. He's a local fisherman—very likable."

However, the dreadful look on Lorenzo's face hadn't changed. "He brought Gino Caruso," Lorenzo said.

Anna's face went slack. Her pleasant smile transformed into a look of stunned apprehension.

"I'm so sorry," Lorenzo continued. "These last two days have been so unsettling for an old man like me. Andre was away on a fishing trip, and I forgot to cancel wine time in all the commotion. They arrived just a few minutes ago."

"What's going on?" Gabe demanded. "Who's Gino Caruso?"

"He's a local politician," Anna replied. "Well-connected up and down the Amalfi Coast. He's nosy too—into everyone's business and always looking for an angle, a way to get ahead. He periodically stops in for wine time to see what kind of local gossip he might pick up. His arrival here today couldn't have come at a worse time."

Gabe turned back to Lorenzo. "Do they know about my grandfather's disappearance?"

Lorenzo twisted his wedding band nervously and stumbled over his words. "Well, um, well… let me explain…"

"Do they know he's been murdered?" Gabe demanded.

Lorenzo winced, "Well, they do now…"

"How?"

"I told them."

"Why on Earth did you do that?" Gabe asked sharply.

Lorenzo's face collapsed. "It's not what you think. They want to help you," he said.

Gabe could not begin to imagine how.

"They caught me off guard," Lorenzo continued. "I didn't know what to do. Caruso's always snooping around. We have a crime scene here. At least, I think we do, so I felt he should know since we haven't called the police yet. I didn't want to compromise his political standing. I mean, how would it look to the public?"

"Lorenzo, I understand your reasoning, but you might've placed this Caruso in an even worse position," Gabe said. "If he denies knowing anything now, it'll be a lie."

Lorenzo winced again, realizing his error in judgment. He scratched his balding head and looked out from under his dark gray eyebrows. "I guess you're right. But I can't undo what's been done. What should we do now?"

Gabe was extremely apprehensive. The circle of confidants was growing. Lorenzo had a good heart, but he totally lacked discretion. Gabe looked at Anna. The worried look on her face had not changed. He decided to wait. It would be better if Lorenzo were out of the way before he asked her what she was thinking.

"Where's Paolo?" Gabe asked Lorenzo, restraining his agitation.

Lorenzo checked his watch. "He should be here any minute," he replied.

"Perfect. Then here's what we're going to do," Gabe said. "Anna and I will wait here until he arrives. I want you to go back down to the terrace and keep them entertained for the time being. Don't mention we've arrived."

Anna followed Gabe's cue and took Lorenzo by the elbow. She gently nudged him toward the staircase. "We'll bring Gabe down when Uncle Paolo gets here," she said.

"Perhaps that would be best," he agreed.

They reached the top of the stairs, and she turned toward him. "Just be yourself and try to act like nothing unusual has happened," she coached him.

Lorenzo started down the steps but stopped suddenly. He turned back toward them and said, "I nearly forgot. I have a message for you, Gabe. It's from Zach Beckett. He called just before you arrived. You can reach him at this number."

Lorenzo pulled a note from his pocket. Gabe glanced at Anna and stepped past her to take it.

"I guess he had no trouble finding me," Gabe said. "I hope it was as easy finding my grandfather."

"He found your grandfather?" Lorenzo interrupted, hopefully.

"I don't know—possibly," Gabe answered. He wished he'd kept his mouth shut. "We ran into Mr. Beckett in Rome."

"I thought he was in the United States," Lorenzo said.

Gabe and Anna exchanged another look. "I thought so too, but evidently not. He was already in Italy. Let's just say our initial meeting wasn't on the best terms. In any case, he offered to help me. He thought he could use his NSA connections to locate my grandfather's body quickly. He said he'd get back to me when he did."

A look of relief erased the worry lines in Lorenzo's face. He was obviously delighted with this promising development. Lorenzo felt deeply responsible for the disappearance of John Roslo's remains. He was buoyed by the news and asked Gabe to notify him of any developments.

"I will," Gabe assured him, "Just don't mention that we're here when you get downstairs."

"I most certainly won't," he replied.

"By the way, have you heard from my grandmother?" Gabe asked. "I need to check on her."

"Yes. As a matter of fact, I spoke to her this morning," Lorenzo said. "She's fine but anxious to see you. She wants to take you out for a nice Italian meal tonight."

"Did she mention where?"

"No, but I have a suggestion," Lorenzo replied confidently. He was back in his element of hospitality. "A friend of mine owns a very secluded restaurant up the mountain. It would be the perfect place for a quiet, private dinner for you and your grandmother. I would be pleased to call Alessandro and arrange everything if you allow me."

The thought of a quiet evening with his grandmother sounded like a terrific idea. Plus, it would give him an opportunity to gain insight into his grandfather's recent activities. Gabe lifted his hand to massage the headache forming at the base of his neck.

"Thanks, Lorenzo," he said. "I would appreciate that. The privacy of a secluded location would be much better than taking her to a restaurant overrun with tourists," *or anyone else, for that matter,* he thought.

"It is my pleasure." Lorenzo bowed slightly, turned, and headed down the staircase.

The instant he was out of earshot, Anna grabbed Gabe by the arm and dragged him back up the stairs. The terrified look was back on her face. This was not the confident woman he'd come to know in the past twenty-four hours. She checked in all directions, making sure no one was around. She then took hold of his forearms and looked him square in the eye. "Caruso's a Mason. I don't know his rank, but Uncle Paolo never liked him. He's one of the most self-serving people I've ever met."

"Could it be a coincidence that he showed up here today?" he asked.

"You tell me." She shrugged. "I smell a trap. It's good you followed your instincts. If only Uncle Paolo were here."

Gabe's head was spinning. "I want to check on my grandmother right now."

Anna pulled out her cell phone. Gabe reached for it but reconsidered. "Maybe you should call," he said. "That way, if one of her cousins answers, I won't have to deal with the language barrier."

Anna nodded and dialed the call. It rang several times, then the message machine picked up. She said something in Italian and hung up.

The look on Gabe's face gave away his apprehension.

"I'm sure they're just outside," she said calmly. "Those ladies spend most nice days in the garden. I've asked her to call the hotel when she returns."

The words were still coming out of Anna's mouth when the sound of churning gravel announced the arrival of Paolo Castriotti. His black Alfa Romeo whipped into the parking area and slid into a narrow space.

"Sorry I'm late; I got stuck behind one of those infernal tourist buses ten kilometers back," he said, sniffing at his sleeve. "I smell like diesel exhaust. Thanks for waiting for me. I wasn't sure you'd be here yet."

Paolo embraced Anna with a kiss on each cheek then shook hands with Gabe.

"We're so glad to see you," Anna said. She checked in both directions to make sure they were still alone. "We've only been here a few minutes, but there's been an unexpected development. We've been hiding out up here waiting for you."

"What's going on?" Paolo questioned. His eyes darted between Anna and Gabe.

"Andre arrived shortly before we did, but he brought Gino Caruso with him. Evidently, Lorenzo told them about the murder. Now, they want to meet Gabe. Lorenzo said they've offered to help, but we thought it would be better to speak to you first."

Paolo clenched his fists. "I didn't see this coming, but you did the right thing." He turned toward Gabe. "Do they know about the missing body or the message on the mirror?" he asked.

"As far as I know, they're aware of the murder possibility and the disappearance of his body. They don't know about the message. At least, I don't think so," Gabe answered warily.

"But it gets worse," Anna jumped in. "We met with Cardinal Bauer yesterday. He directed Gabe to *Humanum Genus* and the Gobbi messages. We don't know this for sure, but we suspect the murder has something to do with the Masons."

Paolo's eyes took on the appearance of saucers. He stroked his mustache with one hand and began to pace. "And Gino Caruso's definitely a Mason," he said, thinking aloud. "However, if Caruso's involved, I can't imagine he'd be stupid enough to come here today. No, he must be here for other reasons."

"The man makes it his business to know everyone else's business," Anna suggested.

"You're right," he replied.

Paolo stopped pacing and turned toward Gabe. "We need to approach this with extreme caution. Let's be sure we don't give him anything he can use. Who knows where this is headed? However, one thing's for certain: your grandfather's death goes beyond the local authorities. I suspect the motives have far broader implications than we first imagined."

"My thoughts exactly," Gabe replied.

Paolo tapped his fingers on the roof of his car. "What about the diary, Gabe? Does he know about that?"

"I don't know. Lorenzo didn't say, but I still have it safely in my possession where it'll stay." Gabe confidently patted his coat pocket.

"You made a wise choice to wait for me," Paolo said. "Lorenzo is well-meaning, but we need to diffuse the situation downstairs."

"What do you have in mind?" Gabe asked.

"I'll go down first and downplay our concerns. I want you to join us on the terrace in fifteen minutes. Act like you've just arrived. I know this will put you in a compromising position, but you can't ignore them completely. It'll look suspicious. I'll make a short introduction. Just smile and exchange appropriate greetings, but don't sit down. And bring your overnight bag. It'll give you a perfect excuse to go to your room. It might seem rude, but it's much better than the alternative."

Gabe and Anna exchanged a wary glance.

"Okay," Gabe replied, "but I still need to talk to you—about the message we found on the mirror."

"I'll meet you in your room after wine time," Paolo said.

With that, Paolo turned and disappeared down the staircase.

Anna took Gabe by the arm. "I don't feel good about this," she said. "I trust Uncle Paolo, but I wish you didn't have to go down there."

"I'll be fine," he reassured her.

Yet Gabe was anything but fine. Fifteen minutes seemed like an eternity. His headache was worsening, and he was bursting with nervous energy. He wanted to take off running and began to pace without even realizing it. *Who is this character, Caruso, and what does he want?* Gabe wondered. Images of *The Godfather* flashed through his mind. *And what about the other guy, Andre Gotto? Lorenzo said they'd arrived together. Why would a local fisherman be hanging out with a politician? What's the connection?* he thought. Gabe couldn't push aside the mafioso images. Suddenly, he stopped and faced Anna, grimacing.

"I don't speak a word of Italian."

Anna laughed. It eased the tension. "Gabe, that's the least of your concerns. They'll speak English just like they did when your grandfather was around. Just be yourself and try to relax."

He nodded and realized he wasn't hiding his anxiety very well. He grinned and said, "You're right. I just need to calm down."

He checked his watch. It was time.

Anna led the way. "Remember, Gabe, this is a simple meet and greet. Exchange pleasantries and move on."

"Got it."

When they arrived on the terrace, four men were seated at a slate table. The table was one of several arrayed along the seaside edge of the terrace. A stone retaining wall was built around the perimeter of the terrace to protect them from the hundred-foot drop to the sea. It was lined with large ceramic pots of red geraniums and multicolored impatiens. The view of the Mediterranean formed a spectacular panoramic backdrop under a perfectly blue, cloudless sky.

The afternoon sun was warm, so the men had the umbrella raised above the table. Gabe could see Paolo and Lorenzo easily, but the umbrella cast a shadow across the two other men. He could not distinguish their faces. *At least there's no one else on the terrace,* Gabe thought—a temporary relief from the knots in his stomach.

"Gabriel and Anna are here," Castriotti said. He stood to announce their arrival. His tone was pleasant and animated. "Please allow me to introduce you. Gentlemen, you know my niece, Anna," Paolo said. She smiled and leaned in to get a kiss on each cheek from her uncle. "And this is Gabriel Roslo."

The other three men followed Paolo's lead and stood to greet their guests.

Paolo noticed that Gabe was looking at Caruso, so he introduced him first. "Gabriel, this is Gino Caruso, one of our local politicians. He was born in southern Italy but has been a fixture along the Amalfi Coast for years."

Caruso was polished, in his mid-sixties, with perfectly greased silver hair, and had an easy, confident manner about him.

"It's a pleasure to make your acquaintance, Gabriel," Caruso said. He extended his perfectly manicured hand. "I only wish it had been under better circumstances. I am very sorry about your grandfather."

Gabe solemnly nodded as they shook hands. "Nice to meet you," he said. His polite manner concealed his true thoughts. *This guy's name could easily be Don Corleone.*

Gabe looked at the other man. He was the antithesis of Gino Caruso. He was the quintessential Mediterranean fisherman with rolled-up jeans, a handwoven woolen sweater, and a blue knit cap. His sweater was clean but permanently stained from days on the water. His hands were callused, and he had blackened fingernails from years of hard work. Still, his salt-and-pepper sideburns outlined a pleasant demeanor. His blue eyes sparkled with an intelligence that belied his appearance. He didn't wait for Paolo's introduction.

"Andre Gotto, I'm a true native, son. I've never lived anywhere but Amalfi." Andre stretched out his arms and placed his hands on Gabe's shoulders. He looked him straight in the eye. "I am so very sorry about your grandfather. He was a good man and our friend. Please accept my deepest condolences." He gave Gabe a strapping bear hug, much to Gabe's surprise.

He moved Gabe back to arm's length. He paused for emphasis then added, "If we can be of any help to you or your grandmother, we are at your service."

Lorenzo motioned for everyone to sit as he reached for a second bottle of Chianti.

"I would love to," Gabe responded, "but my grandmother is expecting my call. I told her I'd call as soon as I arrived. Do you mind if I take a rain check?"

"Not at all," Paolo boomed before anyone else could speak. "We understand completely. What about you, Anna?"

"I would be pleased to join you," she said. She pulled back the chair next to her uncle.

Gabe seized the opening. He thanked them for the offer, picked up his overnight bag, and turned to leave. His abrupt departure was a cultural faux pas but nothing more. The plan had worked. He was in the clear and headed for the staircase. He was halfway across the terrace when suddenly he heard Lorenzo's voice.

"Gabriel! Please tell Francesca I'm making dinner arrangements for you. I'll call Alessandro and take care of everything."

Gabe's heart sank. His easy exit had failed. He took a deep breath, steadied himself, and turned around.

"You're having dinner at Alessandro's?" Caruso asked. "Excellent choice. It's very private, and the view is superb. The tourists don't know about it either. In fact, I doubt they'd be able to find it."

"Thank you, Lorenzo. I'll tell her," Gabe said. He nodded as if nothing had happened.

Gabe turned and headed toward his hotel room. He couldn't believe it. *Why did Lorenzo announce my plans in front of Caruso and Gotto?* It seemed as if the man had no sense of discretion at all. Now, he really needed some ibuprofen and a few minutes of peace and quiet.

THE FIVE OF THEM sat down after Gabe departed. Lorenzo and Anna sat on either side of Paolo. The other two sat across the table.

Lorenzo turned over a fifth wine glass. He filled it along with the others. He lifted his glass and proposed a toast to the memory of John Roslo. "May the memory of John's life be cherished always by those of us who had the good fortune to know him."

Everyone lifted their glass and took a drink.

Paolo directed the conversation. "Anna, it's always a pleasure having you here. I was just telling these fine gentlemen about Lorenzo's overactive imagination. He seems to think foul play was a factor in John's death, but there's no evidence to suggest such a thing."

"What about the missing body?" Caruso interrupted. His tone expressed notable irritation at Paolo's assertion. "I think we should call the Carabinieri. If Lorenzo suspects foul play, let's get the police involved. Let them sort out the details."

"Gino," Paolo replied, "you know how it is around here. John's body isn't missing; it's just misplaced—an oversight. I'm sure his remains will be returned as soon as the autopsy is complete. Lorenzo was understandably upset by what happened. After all, the funeral home recommendation was his, but I'm sure everything will work out fine. There's no need to sound the alarm, at least not yet. Just give it a couple of days."

"I think Paolo's right," Andre Gotto said as he set down his wine glass. "I may be a simple fisherman, but John was eighty-four years old. Certainly, he died of natural causes. Why are we making an issue? Calling the Carabinieri would accomplish only one thing—upset Francesca unnecessarily."

"Uncle Paolo and Andre are right," Anna chimed in. "The poor woman just lost her husband—in a foreign country, no less."

"What if this so-called mix-up doesn't get straightened out by Saturday?" countered Caruso. "What will you tell her at the memorial service—that John's body disappeared into thin air?"

"Don't be ridiculous," Lorenzo protested. "The people performing the autopsy had the proper papers. Paolo's right. Let's not panic. Let's just wait and see if the guy from the NSA can find him before Saturday."

"The NSA?" Caruso asked. He raised an eyebrow. "What on Earth does this have to do with NSA?"

"Nothing," Paolo replied. He felt a lump form in his throat. *Damn it*, he thought. *Why can't Lorenzo keep his mouth shut?*

Paolo calmly squeezed Lorenzo's knee under the table—hard.

"I think Lorenzo was referring to one of John's former colleagues from the NSA," he continued. "Gabriel called him yesterday to request his assistance with the arrangements. He wanted help getting John's remains back to the States since he died overseas. John had a distinguished career with the NSA, and Gabriel was looking for a professional courtesy."

"That's right," Lorenzo jumped in. "When Gabriel told him what happened, he said he'd use his connections to track down the paper trail. I suppose if anybody could find out where an autopsy was taking place, it would be someone from the NSA."

Caruso leaned back in his chair and stared out to sea. He was not buying the story; at least, that's the way it looked to Paolo.

"Perhaps you're right," Caruso said after a long pause. "I'm going to put out a few feelers of my own. I'm not comfortable knowing there's a missing body in my district."

He made no further comment. From that point forward, he listened intently but offered little to the conversation.

Paolo directed the conversation to lighter topics. Anna followed suit. Lorenzo heeded Paolo's silent warning and held his tongue. They carried on for another hour. Caruso looked at his watch: 16:30.

"I better get going," he said, pushing his chair back.

"Then I guess I'm leaving, too," Gotto added. "You're my ride." He checked his watch.

They exchanged farewells, and the gathering slowly broke up.

Gotto left with Caruso. The two of them climbed the stairs to the parking area and got into Caruso's car. Caruso backed out and turned his Jaguar toward Amalfi.

Paolo and Anna remained behind with Lorenzo. Paolo had words of caution for him. "Lorenzo, my friend, be careful what you say in front of people. Things are much worse than we thought, and we both know that the walls of Amalfi have ears."

Lorenzo nodded. He was ashamed of his absent-minded lapses. "I'll be more careful."

Paolo and Anna walked with him to the hotel lobby, where they found Lorenzo's wife working behind the desk.

"I need to make dinner arrangements with Alessandro," Lorenzo said. He excused himself and picked up the phone to dial.

22

Gabe entered his room and dropped his suitcase on the bed. He nervously looked at the phone message from Zach Beckett. *I better call him first,* Gabe thought. *I need answers before speaking to my grandmother.*

He picked up the phone and dialed. Beckett answered on the second ring.

"Zach, it's Gabe Roslo."

"Gabe, thanks for calling back," Beckett paused. "I'm sorry to report that we still haven't located your grandfather's body. I've been assured we'll have something by tomorrow or the next day at the latest."

"What's the holdup?" Gabe demanded.

"I can guarantee you that we are on top of this," Beckett replied. "My people are chasing down leads up and down the Amalfi Coast as well as in Rome. I'll call you as soon as I know something."

"What should I say to my grandmother? She still thinks we're having a memorial service on Saturday."

"For now, nothing," Beckett said sharply. He hesitated momentarily and added, "Maybe you should get her out of Amalfi for a while."

Gabe wondered if the suggestion was meant for his grandmother's safety or Beckett's convenience. He decided to play along and find out. "I'm taking her to dinner tonight at a place in the mountains. Lorenzo Bonelli has assured me it's very quiet and secluded."

"What's it called?" Beckett asked.

"Not sure, but it's run by Lorenzo's acquaintance. He's making the arrangements for us."

"Sounds good," Beckett said, "but I was referring to something a little longer, a day or two. Do you have any other ideas?"

"She loves Capri. She goes there every time she's in Amalfi," Gabe said. "It's an easy trip. I could suggest it to her. We could leave in the morning, maybe even spend the night."

"Perfect," Beckett replied. "It'll help take her mind off things for a while. I'll join you in Amalfi as soon as I can. I still have some things to take care of."

"When will…"

Dial tone. Beckett had hung up.

Rude bastard, Gabe thought. Once again, he wondered whose side Zach Beckett was on. He pulled out his great-grandfather's diary, gave the exterior a cursory glance, and started flipping through the pages. A name caught his eye. The entry was dated October 27, 1933:

> Hitler's blatant hatred for the Jews worries me. In Mein Kampf, he called for effective propaganda and the use of absolute force against the Jews. He now is striking fear into the hearts of Jews by enflaming national sentiment against them. The propaganda machine is in full swing. Will absolute force be next?

Another message was dated February 16, 1934. Gabe read:

> The German government has begun collecting information on people it views as enemies of the state, including Jews, Marxists, and Freemasons.

Hitler opposed Freemasons. Gabe found that peculiar at first but reasoned that the Nazis opposed every form of power. He turned a few more pages and found an entry from March 14, 1934:

> I think the time has come to escape the growing risk to liberty. With Stalin to the east and Hitler to the west, Poland will inevitably be crushed yet again. As both an academic and a Freemason, I have dual reasons to leave Poland for the liberties of America. Although the US economy remains mired in depression, I would rather stake my family fortune on liberty than lose it to either the Germans or the Soviets.

Gabe was still staring at the message when the phone rang. He answered in English, but the voice on the other end spoke Italian. He heard a flurry of words followed by a pause. He then heard the rustle of the receiver being passed.

"My dear, it was so good to get your message. How are you?" his grandmother asked.

"I'm fine, Gram. The more important question is how are you?"

"Well, Gabe, I feel as well as can be expected under the circumstances. What did you learn in Rome? Were you able to make the necessary arrangements?"

Gabe paused. He did not want to answer. "This process is taking longer than we thought. I went to the embassy to file the paperwork, but there was a lot of red tape. I'm not sure when it'll be resolved."

He heard his grandmother's disappointed sigh. It lingered in his ear.

"Gram, are you all right?"

"Oh, to be honest, I need some rest. I love my cousins dearly, but they love to talk. I'm feeling a bit fatigued."

"I have an idea," Gabe said. "What if the two of us go to dinner? Lorenzo told me about a secluded place in the mountains above Amalfi, a little family-owned restaurant. It overlooks a canyon and the sea, and it's private. We'd probably be the only two people there. I promise to have you back in time for a good night's sleep."

"Oh, sweetheart, that sounds wonderful. I think a quiet evening together would be perfect. How about seven?"

"Seven it is," he replied. "Goodbye, Gram."

He hung up, pulled clean clothes from his suitcase, took a shower, and shaved. As he got dressed, he thought about suggesting a trip to Capri. It would be a nice diversion, and the anonymity of folding into a flood of tourists was appealing. Plus, he might have a chance to do more reading in the diary and blue book. Gabe was eager to revisit those 1989 messages. *But will Gram agree to the trip?* he wondered.

MEANWHILE, ZACH BECKETT placed a call of his own. The duty officer at the military hospital answered on the first ring.

"MH Block 5, your PIN, please."

"67YQ49—Zachary Beckett."

"Thank you, sir. I'll put you through."

A tech answered after two rings. Beckett identified himself. "How much longer on the autopsy?"

"The screens are still in process, sir. We'll notify you the minute we have something."

"Stay on top of it," Beckett demanded. The frustration in his tone was evident. "People are asking too many questions."

He hung up without waiting for a response.

23

The car was silent as Gino Caruso and Andre Gotto drove to the marina in Amalfi. Neither spoke—each preoccupied with his concerns.

Gotto got out of the car when they reached the docks. He tipped his head slightly and then walked to the slip where his boat was docked. He tried to maintain his normal routine as much as possible.

Caruso pulled out of the marina and turned toward home. His mind wandered as he negotiated the twisting coastal road. He thought for a moment and pulled out his cell phone. He hit speed dial. The call was to a long-time associate in Salerno, approximately twenty-five kilometers to the east of Amalfi.

Salerno formed one of the bookends to the famous Amalfi Coast. All along the coast, mountains rose majestically straight from the sea, but it flattened to sea level in Salerno. Consequently, it had a major port. Under the command of General Mark Clark, the port served as the landing site of the American Fifth Army during World War II. The Allied invasion in September 1943 led to the liberation of Rome the following June.

Salerno was now an industrial hub and an important cargo shipping center. Its streets were lined with row after row of five- and six-story housing complexes like the ones found in the old Soviet bloc. Salerno was a working man's town. It made up in function for what it lacked in beauty.

Caruso waited for his call to be answered. He kept one eye on the road as he wound his way up the mountain.

"Marco here…"

"Marco, this is Gino. I have a report for you. John Roslo, the American, died early yesterday morning in Amalfi."

"Died, really? He was pretty old, wasn't he?" Marco asked with feigned compassion. He shifted the receiver to his left shoulder and grabbed his pen. "Are there funeral arrangements?"

"Not yet. The funeral will be in the States; however, they're planning a memorial service on Saturday in Amalfi. But here's the strange part—Roslo's body is missing."

"What do you mean by 'missing'?"

"Evidently, a couple of suits with official papers picked it up. They said they were taking it for an autopsy."

"That's strange. Keep your ear to the ground," Marco ordered.

"I will," he replied.

"What's the status of Roslo's wife?" Marco asked.

"She wasn't at the hotel. She doesn't know about the missing corpse either. There's something else. Roslo has a grandson. He's here in Amalfi. Name's Gabriel."

"I see," said Marco. He was taking notes.

"He came here with his grandparents," Caruso continued. "He's assisting with the arrangements. I just met him after he returned from Rome."

"Rome? He went to Rome?"

"Yes. He went there overnight."

"For what purpose?" Marco asked. He strained to keep the edge out of his voice.

"Bonelli said he visited a friend of his grandfather's. He wanted to notify him in person of his grandfather's passing."

"Did he give a name?" Marco asked.

"As a matter of fact, he did. It was a cardinal—Cardinal Bauer, no less," Caruso replied.

Marco quickly scribbled the name on his notepad.

Caruso thought for a moment then added, "He also ran into an American, a government official sent to assist with Roslo's arrangements."

"What was his name?"

"Bonelli didn't say, but he works for the NSA. I got the impression he was a former colleague of Roslo's."

Marco made another note on his pad.

"I think you should know something else," said Caruso. "They suspect he was murdered."

"On what evidence?" Marco's voice was devoid of emotion.

"Not much, really—just the fact that his body was picked up from the funeral home for an autopsy without his family ordering one."

"Have the authorities been notified?" Marco asked.

"Not yet," Caruso answered. "They didn't want to alarm his wife unnecessarily. But they'll have to soon if they don't find the body."

Good, Marco thought. "Where's this NSA official now?" he asked.

"I'm not sure. Bonelli didn't say, but evidently, his agency is also trying to locate the body."

"I appreciate the information. Keep me informed of any developments."

"I will. Do you have any other orders?" Caruso asked.

"No. Just keep me posted."

With that, Marco hung up.

Caruso closed his phone and placed it back in his pocket.

As he continued his drive home, Gino Caruso reflected on his longtime relationship with Marco Sorrentino. Over the years, he'd assisted Marco many times. In return, Marco was a constant source of political support. It was a mutually agreeable arrangement that kept the wheels of progress turning. Still, it was clear who was in charge.

They'd met in 1978 when Caruso joined Salerno's Masonic lodge as an Entered Apprentice. Marco was a sixteenth-degree Mason at the time. He held the title *Prince of Jerusalem*. Marco had ascended to the coveted thirty-third degree in the years since. In the privacy of the lodge, he was known as the Worshipful Master. In public, he preferred to be called Marco. It was part of his carefully crafted persona. He exhibited a humble, relaxed manner that put others at ease and him in charge.

Marco was a major real estate developer and a true builder at heart. He also ran a successful shipping enterprise in Salerno. He'd taken a liking to Caruso from the beginning and always inquired about his family and friends. For his part, Caruso made it his business to know what was going on along the Amalfi Coast. He kept Marco informed of pertinent developments, and Marco took advantage of this knowledge from time to time when it proved helpful to his businesses. Even though Gino Caruso was still a low-level Mason, his lodge connections had aided his lengthy political career over the years.

Caruso's thoughts returned to John Roslo. He'd known him for many years. They'd been introduced by Lorenzo Bonelli at wine time. His earliest recollections of Roslo were nothing special, just an American who'd married a local woman after the war. However, when Marco learned of their acquaintance, he encouraged Caruso to nurture the relationship. Caruso knew not to ask why. It was a matter of strict obedience.

Caruso was still daydreaming when his cell phone rang.

"Gino, this is Marco. We need to meet, just the two of us—tonight."

"Tonight?" Caruso asked. "I'm on my way home." *Can't this wait until tomorrow?* he thought.

"It's urgent. I'll meet you at Wally's at 21:00."

Marco hung up without waiting for a reply.

24

Gabe waited on his balcony for Paolo and Anna to arrive. He stood in the same spot he'd been two nights earlier when he'd watched the party below. Suddenly, he remembered the fishing boat. That night, he'd thought the three flashes of light were for the revelers below. However, he now gazed out to sea and wondered if there was any connection to what had happened. Then another thought hit him: *Andre Gotto is a fisherman.*

The afternoon sun was warm. Gabe sat down and contemplated the link between his great-grandfather's diary, the Gobbi messages, and the pope's letter on Freemasonry. There was definitely a connection—*but what was it?*

The previous night, Anna had directed him to a message dated September 11, 1988. She suggested he read from there until the end of 1989. In one of the messages, the mother of Jesus said she was opening the sealed book so the secrets in it could be revealed.

That left a strong impression on him, but at first, he didn't grasp what she meant. As he worked his way through the 1989 messages, it became clear. The mother of Jesus was unlocking the Book of Revelation and the mysterious secrets contained within its cryptic text.

The 1989 Gobbi messages explained in phenomenal detail the meaning of Revelation's most mysterious symbols, secrets that had been hidden from the beginning. To Gabe's alarm, several messages referred to the Masonic societies specifically. He'd found it hard enough to contemplate his grandfather's murder from the standpoint of a global, secret society. Now, he was being forced to put it into the context of supernatural evil on a Biblical scale.

Gabe shook his head. It was strangely surreal—crazy, actually. He would have discounted it completely were it not for three inescapable facts: his grandfather was dead, someone had stolen the body, and a prominent cardinal of the Catholic Church had pointed him toward the clandestine abyss of Freemasonry.

Gabe picked up Pope Leo's scathing condemnation of Freemasonry and reviewed the sections he'd highlighted. He'd been incredulous the night before. Some of the statements sounded heavy-handed, outrageous, and even fanatical. The pope had accused secret Masonic societies of leading the kingdom of Satan. He declared that they were spearheading the ongoing battle between the forces of good and evil—statements written in 1884. Gabe pondered this. He realized that, in the context of the Gobbi messages, the world had become exactly what Pope Leo warned about over a century earlier.

Gabe now saw the Masonic organization as a formidable force, and its influence was everywhere. Yet he drew courage from a Gobbi message that indicated the forces of hell would not prevail. He needed that encouragement, especially after reading one of the pope's more ominous statements about Freemasonry:

> **Moreover, to be enrolled, it is necessary that the candidates promise and undertake to be thenceforward strictly obedient to their leaders and masters, with the utmost submission and fidelity, and to be in readiness to do their bidding upon the slightest expression of their will—or, if disobedient, to submit to the direst penalties, even death itself. As a fact, if any are judged to have betrayed the doings of the sect or to have resisted commands given, punishment is inflicted on them with such frequency, audacity, and dexterity that the assassin very often escapes detection and the penalty of his crime.**

Gabe swallowed hard. He'd been operating under the premise that his grandfather was an outsider, murdered as someone unaffiliated with the organization. But what if his grandfather was an insider? Skilled assassins, crimes escaping detection, murky chaos…

Gabe leaned back in his chair. Clearly, his great-grandfather had been a Mason. That was evident from the diary. *But was my grandfather one too?* he wondered. He wasn't aware of any Masonic affiliations, but maybe his grandfather had kept it secret. Gabe's mind raced. Then it hit him. He could ask Gram. Surely, she would know.

A knock at the door broke into his thoughts. He got up and checked his watch—4:50 p.m. He opened the door and was greeted by the dead-serious countenance of Paolo Castriotti.

"Where's Anna?" Gabe asked.

"She had to make a few calls. She'll join us momentarily."

Gabe led him to the balcony, where they both took a seat. Paolo's face was all business.

"Caruso's not convinced," Paolo began. "I tried to downplay the murder, but he wasn't buying it. He became very quiet and barely said a word. That's completely out of character for him. He said he'd try to locate John, but it's my guess he's trying to figure out a way to take advantage of the situation. That said, I can't think of anyone else who's more in touch with what's going on along the Amalfi Coast."

"What should we do?" Gabe asked.

"Nothing, for now. There's nothing we can do. We'll just need to see how this plays out. Thankfully, he agreed not to call the local police out of respect for Francesca—at least for now. That's the last thing we need," Castriotti said with a sigh. "Tell me about Rome."

Gabe nodded and quickly recounted everything that happened in the past twenty-four hours.

"When's Beckett supposed to get back to you?" Paolo asked.

"I don't know, as soon as he has some information. Personally, I don't think he'll be any help. His demeanor is very calculated. I think he's hiding something," Gabe said.

"Perhaps," Castriotti replied, "but he's with the NSA, right? And he was the first person stateside that Francesca had you call yesterday morning."

"That's true, but he went out of his way to dodge questions about my grandfather's body. And it sure looked like he was trying to get me out of the way. He wanted me to go back to Amalfi."

"I hate to admit it, Gabe. You're in the same boat with Beckett as you are with Gino Caruso—and it's not a great position. You have two people looking for your grandfather, and neither one is trustworthy. One might have a competing agenda, and the other surely does. For now, all we can do is wait and see."

"I guess you're right," Gabe said with a sense of resignation. "Hopefully, one of them will locate my grandfather before Saturday."

"We can only hope," Castriotti said. He paused and added, "But if we're still in the dark on Friday, we'll need to think about calling the local authorities and perhaps the American embassy in Rome. We don't want it to come to that because I suspect whatever's going on runs a lot deeper than the Italian police or the Americans are ready to handle."

Gabe exhaled a long, frustrated sigh. He didn't like it, but he accepted Castriotti's assessment. "You're right, Paolo. This is something completely different—and very strange. Cardinal Bauer wasn't the least bit surprised by our suspicions of foul play. That fact has me more concerned than anything else that's happened, and I think I know why."

Castriotti's face tightened. "What do you mean?" he asked.

"I've read the Gobbi messages," Gabe replied.

Castriotti raised his hand to stroke his mustache.

"They're like a code book," Gabe continued. "They systematically explain the symbolism in Chapters 12 and 13 of Revelation."

Gabe thought back to the description of the bizarre, seven-headed monster he'd read about that morning. The creature's image was seared into his memory. However, the vivid explanation of the creature left the strongest impression.

"Paolo, I was stunned by the Gobbi messages. They identified the seven-headed monster as Freemasonry—specifically. Do you know what that means?"

Castriotti nodded his head almost imperceptibly. "It means the Book of Revelation foretold the rise of the Masonic secret societies," Castriotti said. "It also means Pope Leo knew what he was talking about when he referred to them as the kingdom of Satan."

Gabe swallowed hard. He'd already made the connection. "Those ramifications have been rolling through my mind all morning," he said. "However, there's something I can't figure out. The Gobbi messages also identify the seven-headed monster as atheistic communism. How can it be both?"

"It's not. The Book of Revelation has *two* seven-headed monsters," Castriotti explained, "but they're not the same thing. The monsters look similar, but they're two distinct symbols. The first is found in Chapter 12. The other is in Chapter 13."

"How can you tell them apart?" Gabe asked.

"The explanation is quite straightforward," Castriotti explained. "Both monsters have seven heads and ten horns, and both are wearing crowns, referred to as diadems in some Bibles. However, the primary distinction between the two is how they wear their crowns. That's the key to understanding.

"The other thing to remember," he continued, "is the monsters are metaphors. They are not to be interpreted literally. People have been frightened by these monsters for generations. They imagine horrible creatures roaming the earth, and they're repulsed, which is understandable. They should be. The monsters are ugly. But they're ugly because of what they symbolize. The seven-headed creatures described in Revelation are not grotesque organisms but rather ungodly organizations—organizations bent on tearing down truth and bringing humanity to spiritual ruin."

Gabe leaned back in his seat. He stared at the blue waters of the Mediterranean and let those words sink in.

"The rise of these powerful organizations was foretold from the beginning of Christianity," Castriotti continued. "Atheistic communism was last century's menace, but with the collapse of the Soviet Union, Freemasonry is now coming out of the shadows to take center stage."

Out of the shadows, Gabe thought. How ironic.

"Do you have *Humanum Genus?*" Castriotti asked.

"Right here," Gabe said.

Castriotti scanned through it. "You might not have understood the significance when you read it, but Pope Leo's foresight was brilliant. He linked these two organizations and the unified threat they presented to nations and governments. See, look here."

Gabe started reading.

(With) fear of God and reverence for divine laws taken away, the authority of rulers despised, sedition permitted and approved, and the popular passions urged on to lawlessness with no restraint save that of (civil) punishment, a change and overthrow of all things will necessarily follow. Yes, this change and overthrow are deliberately planned and put forward by many associations of communists and socialists, and to their undertakings, the sect of Freemasons is not hostile but greatly favors their designs and holds in common with them their chief opinions.

"Pope Leo recognized a common bond between the communists and Masons," Castriotti continued. "He saw this more than a century before they were identified as the two seven-headed monsters of Revelation in the Gobbi messages. He saw similarities in their philosophy, opinions, and objectives and wrote about it before the Bolshevik revolution. Everyone knows what happened in Russia after the revolution. It was the story of the twentieth century. Communist aggression destroyed freedom, devoured Christians, and pursued a reckless path toward global domination. One can only imagine what's in store for humanity in the twenty-first century at the hands of Freemasonry."

Castriotti leaned in for emphasis. "But here's something you need to remember—no matter what the future holds. Not every war is fought with guns. The great battles of the twenty-first century will be waged over ideas."

"That's the same thing Anna said last night," Gabe said. He leaned back in his chair and again looked out to sea. "You said that the distinction between the two seven-headed monsters is found in how they wear their crowns. What does that mean?"

Castriotti pulled up his chair and spoke with passion. "At first blush, the two monsters appear identical. They both have seven heads and ten horns and wear crowns. However, the first monster wears *seven* crowns on its seven *heads*, while the second monster wears *ten* crowns on its ten *horns*. The crowns define how they claim their authority.

"Soviet communism claimed *divine* authority—the state itself was god, supreme in all matters. The Masons rely on *civil* authority—purely human. In other words, the rule of law and the Constitution are supreme in all things—man's law.

"What do you know about the symbolic meaning of numbers seven and ten from a Biblical standpoint?" Castriotti asked.

"Nothing, really," Gabe answered.

"I'll explain. In Christianity, seven is the sacred number for completeness. The number three represents God: Father, Son, and Holy Spirit. The number four represents the world: His creation, referred to as the earth's four corners. Three plus four equals seven: the sacred number for completeness. Many ancient cultures found spiritual meaning in the number seven. The ancient Egyptians had it, but so did the Native Americans a continent away."

"Like the creation story," Gabe said.

"Exactly," Castriotti replied. "God and creation, the completeness of existence.

"What about the number ten?" Gabe asked.

"In ancient Hebrew tradition, the number ten also signifies completeness, but it's a worldly number for completeness. It is man's number for completeness."

"Like our base-ten numerical system," Gabe surmised.

"Precisely," Castriotti replied. He held up his hands, fingers apart. "Ten—designed by God and given to man, just like the Ten Commandments. Our ten digits are perfect for counting. The Ten Commandments became the foundation of Jewish law. Christianity, of course, adopted this understanding as well. It's easy to see why ten became humanity's symbolic number for completeness."

"Interesting," Gabe said.

"It is interesting, and it's not surprising the two symbols are interconnected. They reflect the relationship between God and man."

"How so?" Gabe asked.

"The Ten Commandments are divided into two parts. The first three delineate our duties to God—our highest duties. Jesus called one the greatest commandment: 'Love God above all else.'

"The next seven delineate our duties to ourselves and to humanity. Jesus summarized them with the Golden Rule: 'Love one another as you would have them love you.'"

"And the two parts form the whole," Gabe concluded.

"You've got it. The Ten Commandments define our duties to God and man. Notably, our duty toward our parents is at the top of the second list—father, mother, child, the foundation of human existence."

"That is noteworthy," Gabe repeated. He felt a sudden twinge of remorse. It had been a long time since he'd honored his father in any way at all. His father's pathetic pattern of lying and empty promises left Gabe deeply bitter. Yet he was moved by these symbolic interrelationships. They were cause for reflection.

Castriotti broke into his musing. "The communist monster wore seven crowns on its seven heads. The crowns signify royal dominion, rulers over their subjects, but the language is symbolic. The crowns do not signify kings literally but figuratively—supreme rulers. In this sense, a string of Soviet dictators rose up to fulfill this Revelation prophecy. They ruled over their empire with crushing force, especially Stalin."

"But how does that work? Seven is a sacred number for completeness."

Castriotti was touched by his budding inquisitiveness. He held his hand up to postpone an answer to the question. "Stay with me, Gabe. The atheistic ideology of the Soviet Union attempted to usurp God by crushing all religion and putting forth the idea that the Soviet government itself was god—the beginning and end of all things. The Soviet government made a claim of godlike authority. It established itself as the absolute and supreme ruler of humanity."

"And they spent the better part of the twentieth century forcing that idea on the whole world," Gabe said, finishing Castriotti's thought.

"Exactly. The rise of the Soviet Union in the twentieth century was Biblical fulfillment—the completeness of evil. Even President Ronald Reagan called it the Evil Empire. The media had a field day with that one, but he was right. The Soviets suppressed freedoms of every kind. Not only did the Soviet

Union establish an iron-fisted dictatorship over its people, but it also ruthlessly crushed Christianity. Under Stalin, this misappropriation of power was the absolute embodiment of evil. He was the king of evil. The Soviet Union represented the rise and fall of an atheistic superpower and good riddance."

Gabe worked through the logic in his head. "If the seven crowns foretold the Soviet claim of divine authority, the ten crowns must foretell the Masonic claim of civil authority—man's law as supreme."

"Precisely!" Castriotti exclaimed. "Freemasonry is rooted in the laws of civil society. In the United States, the Constitution guarantees its right to exist. Under the freedom of assembly, Masonry is allowed to operate in virtual secrecy, protected from scrutiny, and accountable to no one. It makes no claim of divine authority because its existence depends entirely on civil authority. This sets up the ultimate Revelation showdown—man against God."

Gabe shifted uncomfortably in his seat.

"Masonry pretends to place all belief systems on an equal footing," Castriotti continued. "Christianity, Islam, Buddhism, and the eastern religions, even Judaism—they're all treated the same."

"Meaning it defends the freedom of religion?" Gabe asked.

"It does, but behind that freedom lies a deception. Freemasonry treats Christianity and all major religions with disdain. They're considered equally inferior to what Masonry calls 'pure religion.' But Masonic pure religion is a system devoid of truth and clear principles. No matter how ridiculous, all points of view are considered equally valid. The Masons in your country have misused the Bill of Rights to build their empire of influence and sow confusion among the people. We see the same issues over here. The framers of the European constitution are trying to define human rights while rejecting the Christian foundation on which they're built. The freedom of religion, the freedom of assembly, the freedom of speech, and the freedom of the press are all used to advance the Masonic version of liberty. Look again at the symbol of the monster. Where does it find its royal power? Where does the Masonic monster wear its crowns?"

"On its ten horns," Gabe answered.

"Correct—on its ten horns. The horn is an instrument of amplification to make one's message known. In ancient Biblical times, the ram's horn, called a shofar, was used to announce important proclamations. The Masonic monster has ten horns."

"The world's number for completeness," Gabe said, finishing Castriotti's statement. "The global influence of media and modern social communication—I read about it in the Gobbi messages."

"That's right, Gabe. Think about the technological advances of the twentieth century. The global dissemination of the Masonic message could not have reached its current proportions without television, satellite communication, and the internet—innovations with incredible amplification powers. Never in the history of the world has it been easier to blast images, ideas, and information around the globe, regardless of content. The media are used to formulate public opinion, inculcate the youth, and fill our minds with thoughts of every kind."

Gabe sat back in his chair. He contemplated the George Orwellian scope of Castriotti's words. He thought about his clients who complained about the constant bombardment of the media. They came to Banff to escape it all, but after three days in the wilderness, they'd go crazy, craving to know what was happening in the world. The media is a drug that tells us what to think, what to care about, and what to believe.

"But it's not hopeless," Castriotti said. "People lament the mass media because of its content, but the media are not alive. The word media is plural for medium, which means channel. These channels can be used for good or evil purposes. The media are inanimate objects. It's the content that matters. Pope John Paul II recognized this and made masterful use of the media to deliver his message of hope and peace in Jesus Christ. He once said, 'If it doesn't happen on television, it doesn't happen.' He understood perfectly the vast influence of television."

There was a knock at the door.

25

Gabe answered the door. It was Anna.

"My apologies for being late," she said.

"I'm glad you're here. Paulo and I were waiting for you."

She walked out onto the balcony and took a seat next to Paolo.

"Can I get either of you something to drink?" Gabe asked.

"I'd like a bottle of water," Paolo answered.

"So would I," Anna replied. "Grazie."

Gabe pulled three bottles of water from the mini bar and brought them to the table. He sat down to collect his thoughts. He'd been waiting to speak to the two of them together all day. He'd made a discovery earlier that morning and wanted to tell Paolo and Anna at the same time.

"I had a nightmare this morning," Gabe said. "I dreamt an intruder was in the apartment. He put a gun to my forehead, threatened me, and warned me to stop the investigation. Then my grandfather walked into the room. As I watched, the shadowy character charged him and murdered him in cold blood. The image ripped me from my sleep."

He paused, took a deep breath, and then turned to Anna. "Have you ever seen a leopard in the wild?"

She looked puzzled. "In the wild? No. Was there one in your dream?"

He shook his head no. "What do you know about leopards?" he asked.

"Well, not that much, I guess. Why do you want to know?" she asked.

The sea breeze kicked up and was blowing hair in her face. She pulled it back into a ponytail.

"I'll get there," he said, "but what do you know about a leopard's characteristics?"

Anna was mildly amused by Gabe's mysterious line of questioning. Still, it was outside her realm of expertise. "I'm sorry," she shrugged. "I don't really know anything about leopards."

"Well, I do," Gabe said. "And I've been thinking about them a lot today. I've always had a keen interest in wildlife. Growing up, I read a lot of *National Geographic* and watched a lot of *Discovery Channel*. Somewhere along the way, I learned about leopards."

Paolo listened intently. He said nothing.

"Leopards have massive skulls," Gabe continued, "and powerful jaw muscles. It makes them formidable killers. They're sleek animals with relatively small bodies. They can take down prey over twice their size. They also have soft, padded paws with retractable claws. This allows them to prowl around unnoticed. And they're active mostly at night. They stalk and kill most of their prey under the cover of darkness—*darkness*."

"Interesting," Anna replied. She pursed her lips.

"Leopards stalk their prey in the shadows," Gabe added. "Then, in a final unsuspecting rush, they pounce upon their victims and devour them completely."

"Nice image," she said with a hint of sarcasm. "And the point is?"

"I read something this morning," Gabe said. "It described in detail the spiritual significance of Freemasonry—things you mentioned these past two days. I was struck by the irony of the simile. Like a leopard, the beast is a perfect description of Masonry."

Paolo stroked his moustache. "The comparison is straight out of Revelation," he said.

"I know," Gabe replied. "I have a working theory. What if Zach Beckett's telling the truth?" Gabe continued. "He said he was in Italy at my grandfather's request."

"Did he say what that was?" Paolo asked.

"He said he didn't know, only that my grandfather wanted him here for a meeting. He would learn the details when he arrived. According to Cardinal Bauer, my grandfather was investigating supernatural phenomena. As you probably know, he wasn't a religious man. He worked in intelligence. He spent his entire career with the NSA protecting America—until he retired, of course."

"Go on," Paolo said.

"He was a trained intelligence officer. He made a career out of keeping and investigating secrets. Perhaps he didn't tell Beckett the purpose of the meeting because he knew he was being watched. Maybe he was being extraordinarily careful because he knew someone or something was after him—something like the leopard."

Paolo and his niece exchanged worried glances.

Gabe picked up his great-grandfather's diary. He turned to the missing pages and laid it on the table. He then pulled out a piece of notepaper tucked in the crease.

"I believe I've solved the riddle from the mirror—at least the first part, anyway," Gabe said.

Paolo stopped stroking his mustache. Anna leaned forward in anticipation, focused on the jumble of letters again.

THBST
ISHR
SA

"I tried countless combinations yesterday on the train," Gabe said. "I tried rearranging the letters, reversing them, adding letters, deleting letters, but came up with nothing. However, it clicked after reading Revelation and the Gobbi messages this morning."

Gabe flipped over the sheet of paper. "By adding the right vowels, I came up with this:

TH<u>e</u> B<u>ea</u>ST
ISHR
SA

He'd underlined the additional letters for emphasis.

"The beast!" Anna gasped. "The beast I, S, H, R. The beast is H, R. The beast is—what? What does HR stand for?"

"The only thing I could come up with was human race," Gabe replied. "*Humanum genus* is Latin for the human race."

"The beast is the human race? That can't be right," she countered. "The beast is not the human race. The beast is Freemasonry. Besides, it doesn't fit the pattern."

Gabe looked at the letters again and realized she was right. He rearranged the letters yet again. All three leaned in to study the pattern.

<pre>
    T H e
    B e a S T
    I S
    H R
</pre>

"If it's not the human race, what else fits?" Gabe asked. "What if we add an E?"

"The beast is her? Her who?" Paolo said. "I don't think so."

"How about two?" Anna suggested. "Add another E."

<pre>
    T H e
    B e a S T
    I S
    H e R e
</pre>

"The beast is here," Gabe said, reading it aloud before she finished.

Paolo gasped at the full weight of its implications. "The beast is here," he repeated in a barely audible whisper. "Your grandfather was telling us his death was the work of Freemasonry—the beast of Revelation."

Paolo's chin dropped. His head fell forward, eyes closed. Gabe saw a change in his expression—a look of bitter disappointment and tremendous grief. He tried to speak, but his lips quivered as he held back tears. Gabe and Anna watched him sympathetically. After a long pause, Paolo collected himself and regained his composure.

He lifted his head and looked Gabe square in the eye. "I tried to warn him," he said. "I told John he was treading on exceedingly dangerous turf. I told him that his very life was at risk because of the things he was uncovering. I warned him that if he continued to probe the dark secrets of Freemasonry, it would eventually catch up to him."

Paolo reached for his water. He took a slow drink. "John was a fearless warrior," he continued. "He fought the Germans in World War II. He battled the Soviets during the Cold War. He defended liberty in America at every turn."

He paused and took another drink.

"Last week, after Lorenzo told me that he and Francesca had arrived, I spoke to him by phone. I asked John what his plans were in Amalfi. He simply stated, 'I have a duty to do,' then quickly changed the subject to your impending arrival. I just had no idea, Gabe. I'm so sorry."

Paolo's voice trailed off, and the sadness in his eyes renewed Gabe's sense of grief. His grandfather had been a good, principled man. He spent his life fighting for the greater good. Gabe felt his own lifestyle reflected that strength and resilience, traits that had skipped a generation because of his father's drug and alcohol addictions.

Gabe leaned back in his chair. He scanned the horizon of the Mediterranean. Fishing boats and pleasure craft moved in random directions. The water glowed orange in the late afternoon sun. It was blissful. However, Gabe's eyes were now opened to the dangers lurking in the shadows. The contrast between his grave discovery and the tranquil surroundings was penetrating. Still, he drew inspiration from Paolo Castriotti's words. Gabe let the powerful force of those words filter through his mind. He felt a renewed indignation and a new sense of purpose. Now, *he* had a duty to do.

Everyone at the table believed their suspicions had been confirmed. John Roslo had done his duty; for that, he'd been hunted and killed by the Masons—the beast of Revelation, the beast like a leopard.

There was a long silence. Anna finally broke it.

"What do you suppose the letters S and A mean?" she asked.

Gabe was wrestling with the same question. Did they represent a person or possibly a place? Were they initials? He had no leads, and two letters weren't much to go on.

"This is just a theory," Anna said, "but if the first part of the message was a reference to Revelation, perhaps the second part is, too."

"I'm not so sure," Gabe said in response. "If he used the first part to tell us who murdered him, maybe he used the second part to tell us why."

Paolo nodded his agreement. "That would make sense, but I think Anna's on to something, too. Perhaps the letters refer to some further aspect of Revelation symbolism, something that explains why he was killed."

"Maybe the S stands for seven, as in seven-headed monster," Anna speculated.

"Maybe it stands for Satan-Antichrist," Gabe countered. "The Book of Revelation is all about the Antichrist, right?"

Paolo's eyebrows furrowed. He tilted his head slightly. Anna's face also displayed a perplexed look. Paolo turned to Gabe.

"The Antichrist doesn't come from Revelation," he said.

Now, it was Gabe's turn to look confused.

"He's right, Gabe," Anna added. "The word Antichrist doesn't appear anywhere in the Book of Revelation. A lot of people think it does, but that's not the case. It's a common misconception."

Gabe wasn't sure how to respond. He was a touch embarrassed and still skeptical. "So where does the word come from?" he asked.

Anna's response was immediate and authoritative. "There are four references to the term 'Antichrist' in the Bible. All four are in letters written by John the Apostle. They're part of the New Testament, but they're not in Revelation."

She sounded quite certain of her facts. Gabe was impressed. Still, she maintained a modesty and humility that belied her intellectual status.

Gabe looked at them. "For some reason, I thought the Antichrist and the beast of Revelation were the same thing," he said.

"The beast of Revelation is not the Antichrist," Paolo interjected. "They're not the same thing."

"Are they related?" Gabe asked.

"They are related, closely related," Paolo replied. "However, they're not the same. Freemasonry, the beast of Revelation, is a preparation for the Antichrist. The beast lays the foundation by building up the kingdom of Satan."

"The same term used by Pope Leo."

"Exactly, Gabe. Masonry precedes the rise of Antichrist," Paolo continued. "And it's far more diabolical than atheistic communism because it works through deception. It convinces the world to accept its lies with free will and consent. And when the moment's right, the person of Antichrist assumes the helm."

Gabe looked at Anna, who was nodding her head in agreement.

"You see, Gabe," she said. "The two monsters of Revelation are frequently interpreted as the Antichrist and his prophet, a sort of evil parallel to Jesus and John the Baptist."

"That's the way I've heard it explained," he said.

"But that's not right," she continued. "I know a lot of people expect the emergence of these two evil men, but it can't be that obvious. I mean, what would the so-called false prophet do? Get up on a podium and announce the King of Evil? Doubtful. People would see it and reject it. It doesn't make any sense, does it?"

"I suppose not," Gabe replied.

"The powers of evil are far too crafty for such an obvious disclosure. That's why the Masonic deception has been so stealthy. It hides behind the artificial light it creates. As you said about the leopard, Masonry operates in the shadows, stalking its prey before devouring it in a final unsuspecting rush."

Gabe was intrigued and repulsed at the same time.

"The symbolism in Revelation is deep and complicated," Anna continued. "However, the basic theology has been understood from the earliest days of Christianity. It's about the battle between good and evil—the struggle of believers against those opposed to the message of Christ. But in the end, the victory goes to those who persevere and resist the deception."

Anna leaned in for emphasis.

"When the Antichrist finally shows himself and walks upon the earth, that event will bring about the final ruin of evil. And like every good epic, the forces of evil will be defeated through the heroic efforts of the underdog. Jesus—the invisible God, seemingly far away and irrelevant—will manifest Himself in absolute glory and power to crush the legions of evil forever."

"But not before a multitude fall victim to the deception," Paolo said. His tone was somber.

Gabe did a long exhale. He focused on the sheet of paper once again.

"We still don't know what the letters S and A mean," he lamented. "They mean something, but what?"

Both Paolo and Anna shook their heads.

"I don't know, Gabe," Paolo said in reply.

"Maybe it has something to do with the Catholic Church," Gabe theorized. "Why else would Cardinal Bauer have reacted like he did? He immediately pointed me in the direction of the Masons. Are the Masons connected to the Catholic Church?"

"They're totally incompatible," Paolo answered. "Masonry and Christianity are diametrically opposed. Pope Leo pointed out in *Humanum Genus* that Masonry seeks to destroy the Catholic Church and end the papacy. He also declared that it would never happen because the foundation of the Catholic Church is too strong to be overturned by the efforts of men. Its resilience is girded by supernatural power. Whenever the church is on the ropes, almighty God has a way of bringing forth powerful leaders to defend the faith, people like Pope John Paul II."

"Then why do you think my grandfather was looking into this?"

"Because the Masons haven't failed to rip apart the flock," Paolo continued. "Every possible means has been used to entice people away from Christianity and to repudiate their belief in Jesus. The Masons couldn't make the Catholic Church go away, so they made the people go away. They also developed a sinister tactic—infiltration. Even though Pope Leo reaffirmed the express prohibition against Catholics from joining the Masonic societies, the Masons have continued to find Catholic initiates, even among the clergy in some cases."

"The clergy—are you serious?" Gabe asked.

"Absolutely, even in Rome."

"Is this prohibition still in effect?"

"Most certainly," Paolo replied. "However, the Masonic infiltration has continued anyway in secret, and Cardinal Bauer knows it. The full extent is unclear, but it's happening. The beast of Revelation has found its way into the Catholic Church."

"Does any of this relate to the infamous number 666?" Gabe asked.

Just then, there were three loud thumps at the door.

"Gabriel, it's me, Lorenzo."

Gabe stood to answer the door. Paolo grabbed him by the elbow. "No more conversations in front of Lorenzo," Paolo said flatly. "He means well, but he has trouble with discretion." Gabe nodded. He would heed the warning.

Gabe opened the door and found Lorenzo Bonelli's beaming face.

"Gabriel, I've made your dinner arrangements. Everything's set. Alessandro and I even planned the menu. You need not worry about a thing. Dinner is at seven. It should be very nice and private, just you and Francesca." He handed Gabe a sheet of paper with directions to the restaurant.

"How long will it take to get there?" Gabe asked.

"Perhaps thirty minutes," Lorenzo said.

Gabe checked his watch. It was already past 6:00.

"You'll need to leave right away if you plan to be on time," he added.

"Thanks, Lorenzo. It was kind of you to arrange this. We will very much appreciate a quiet dinner. Thank you for your hospitality."

Paolo and Anna overheard the conversation. They came in from the balcony.

"We were just leaving," Paolo said. He checked his watch. "Anna is anxious to see her aunt." He turned to Gabe and added, "We'll pick this up tomorrow."

"Actually, I'm thinking about taking my grandmother to Capri tomorrow. The diversion should do us both well," he said. Gabe extended his hand to shake Paolo's. "We might spend the night there."

He then turned toward Anna. She put one hand behind his head and pulled it toward her. She leaned in and whispered in his ear, "Be careful." She then slipped a note into his hand and kissed him on the cheek.

26

Meanwhile, approximately twenty-five kilometers down the coast, the cargo freighter, *Ruse of the Sea*, sailed into Salerno's harbor under the watchful eye of Marco Sorrentino. Marco's penthouse suite overlooked the docks and gave him a view of the entire port. The elegance of his office portrayed a man of success, polished and refined in every regard. Awards and placards recognizing his accomplishments hung throughout.

Marco controlled nearly 80 percent of the shipping container business that passed through the Port of Salerno. He built an empire that generated tremendous wealth over the years. His cut-throat tactics and hardnosed business dealings were legendary. He bought most of his enterprises at distressed prices when others panicked. The shipping business and the global economy fell into a deep recession in the late 1970s due to high fuel costs. As businesses slid into bankruptcy, Marco was a buyer. He paid only a fraction of the true worth of the enterprises he acquired.

He also carefully cultivated a demeanor that tricked people into thinking he was helping them in their time of need. It was nothing more than opportunistic positioning. His business strategy succeeded, and he rose to prominence.

Marco also served as an advisor to SOLAS, the International Convention for the Safety of Life at Sea. SOLAS established regulations for the shipping of hazardous materials on the high seas. Those regulations were eventually incorporated into the International Maritime Dangerous Goods Code, the international standard.

His experience offered invaluable assistance to the commission that developed the regulations. He received useful insights and information in return. Always opportunistic, he became intimately familiar with the regulatory schemes of both maritime safety and the international policing of cargo shipments that were potentially dangerous to national security. Marco never did anything unless there was a payback.

Marco, the one-time Masonic Prince of Jerusalem, watched as the *Ruse of the Sea* was guided into its docking berth.

"Careful, boys," he said. A thin smile formed on his face.

27

Gabe closed the door after the Castriottis left and looked at the note from Anna. It had one instruction: *Read Gobbi Message #407.* He checked his watch—not enough time. He slipped it into his pocket. It would have to wait until after dinner.

He picked up the diary, placed it in his coat pocket, and grabbed his keys. He locked the door. A few minutes later, he was on the road to Ravello to pick up his grandmother.

The mountain road to Ravello was a challenge. It was even tighter than the twisting coastal road. At one point, it narrowed to a single lane, and stop lights controlled the flow of traffic. Gabe had seen this system used in construction zones but with work crews on-site to ensure traffic moved in just one direction at a time. These lights were permanent.

The sun was low on the horizon, and it was getting dark in the canyons. The peaks were still lit, but Gabe was driving in the shadows. He approached the red light and stopped. The single lane made a sharp, ninety-degree righthand turn and disappeared around a rocky outcropping. To his left was a sheer drop into the gorge below. A rounded mirror was installed at the turn, allowing drivers to see oncoming traffic. Soon, the road ahead was clear.

Gabe waited for the light to change and mulled over possible meanings of the letters S and A. *SA, Satan-Antichrist, SA, Satan-Antichrist,* he kept repeating in his head. It was a convenient solution, but he doubted it was right. His grandfather might've been killed by the Masons, but he wasn't killed by the Antichrist. There had to be another meaning. *But what?* he wondered.

A black sedan approached from behind and stopped three feet off his bumper. The driver tapped his fingers on the steering wheel. He looked impatient. *You gotta love 'em,* Gabe thought. *The Italians sure have style. Only here would someone wear black leather driving gloves.*

The car behind had crept even closer. *What's with this guy?* he thought. Perhaps he was getting ready to blow through the red light and go around him. It would've been no surprise. Italian drivers took regulations as mere suggestions.

Gabe looked in the mirror again. The driver had stopped tapping. He was leaning into the passenger seat like he was fishing for something in the glove box.

Suddenly, Gabe was struck by a thought. *This is a perfect place for an ambush. There are no escape routes, no witnesses, and no sound—a perfect trap.* His adrenaline surged.

The driver was now sitting upright and staring straight ahead. Gabe couldn't see his hands. He wondered if he should blow through the light. Not a single car had come from the other direction. The man with the black gloves was still staring at the back of his head.

"It's now or never," Gabe said aloud. He slammed the car into gear, let out the clutch, and shot around the ninety-degree turn. He blazed through several more turns, the black car close on his heels. Still a single lane, the road stretched into an S-curve. Gabe accelerated. So did the other car. They rounded a curve. A warning sign appeared—another ninety-degree turn. The light was already red. Gabe downshifted but didn't stop. He cranked his wheel into the blind turn.

Suddenly, a set of headlights appeared. Gabe found himself face-to-face with a silver Audi. Everyone screeched to a halt, Gabe sandwiched in the middle.

He checked his rearview—nowhere to go. He looked forward—no room to pass. He considered ramming the Audi but didn't want to go over the edge. *Don't panic,* Gabe thought. He stared into the driver's eyes. No one moved.

A few seconds later, the Audi driver threw his car in reverse. He backed up fifty meters to a place where the road widened slightly. He instinctively pulled to the side and pressed as close to the mountain as possible.

Gabe crept forward to pass. The sedan followed. Their side mirrors missed the silver Audi by inches. After they passed, the Audi pushed onward.

Gabe again accelerated. He snaked up the mountain, the sedan tailgating and pulling within a few feet of him several times. Gabe kept his focus on the single-lane road. They swerved around curve after curve. *How much further is the next traffic signal?* he wondered. After ten harrowing minutes, the road widened again and became two lanes. The instant it did, the sedan barreled around him and quickly disappeared around another curve.

"These people are crazy," Gabe said to himself, laughing out loud. He was relieved and shook his head in admiration. *No wonder Formula One is so popular in Europe,* he thought.

Lorenzo's directions proved accurate. Gabe arrived in Ravello shortly before 7:00. Within minutes, he found the house. His grandmother was ready. She translated an obligatory round of small talk with the cousins. A few moments later, they were off to the restaurant. Francesca navigated. She was already familiar with the mountain passes.

Gabe remembered Lorenzo's words: "My friend, Alessandro, will have everything ready when you arrive. We've planned the entire meal for you. It should be completely secluded. Just go and enjoy." Gabe began to relax.

Lorenzo was right about the seclusion. The final leg of the drive was also a one-lane road but without any traffic control devices. They slowly wound their way along the edge of the mountain. Gabe saw no signs of civilization anywhere. They passed through an arched tunnel, and the road turned to gravel. A few old, rundown buildings appeared on the other side. They were nothing like the attractive, well-kept places he'd seen along the coast.

"Where's Lorenzo sending us?" Gabe asked.

"Not to fear. We're almost there."

At last, they rounded one more curve and came to a dead end in a parking lot—if you could call it that. In truth, it was just a couple of empty parking spaces with a donkey path trailing off behind the lot. Gabe didn't see any cars or people, only an antiquated, three-wheeled truck about the size of an American four-wheeler.

"Pull in here," Francesca said, pointing to one of the empty spaces.

Gabe complied. He looked up and saw a tiny village perched on top of a rock staircase. The sun was setting, and the mountains were cast in shadows. He could see houses and lights at various places all the way to the top of the mountain. He surmised the donkey path was their only access.

Gabe took Francesca by the arm and helped her up the stairs. They slowly climbed the sixty-three uneven stone steps. As they walked, he thought about his game plan. He needed to know what involvement, if any, his grandfather had with the Masons. He also needed to find out if she had any insight about the letters S and A. *This isn't going to be easy,* he thought. His grandmother was intelligent and perceptive, and he didn't want to alarm her. And he certainly couldn't tell her, "The beast is here."

The top of the staircase opened into a small piazza. Gabe saw two old men sitting on park benches in the center, hunched over a board game that looked like checkers.

"They're playing Quarto," Francesca said. She patted Gabe's arm.

Gabe was astonished to see any life at all. *Do people actually live up here?* he thought.

Several young boys ran along the top of a stone retaining wall on the far side of the piazza. They were seven or eight years old and were playing a game. Their fun abruptly stopped at the sound of their mother's voice scolding them from the third-story window of a stone house at the edge of the square.

Gabe and Francesca crossed the piazza and turned right. They found themselves in a narrow, brick alleyway and discovered a pizzeria. Gabe peered into the glass entry and saw ten or twelve neatly arranged tables. It was a pleasant atmosphere but not the seclusion he'd hoped for.

"Gabriel Roslo, welcome!"

Gabe spun around. A man rushed toward them. He'd burst into the alley from an unmarked doorway on the other side.

"Welcome, signore," he said again. "I'm Alessandro." He shook Gabe's hand. He then turned toward Francesca. "Signora Roslo, welcome. My sincere condolences for the loss of your husband." *Alessandro speaks more truth than he knows,* Gabe thought. Francesca accepted the proprietor's kind words. Gabe was reassured that she still knew nothing about her husband's missing body.

Alessandro gestured toward the door on the opposite side. "Our terrace is this way," he said. He took Francesca by the arm and escorted her to the entrance.

The opening to the terrace was a nondescript, arched gate encased in plaster. What they found on the other side was nothing short of spectacular. They stood on a private veranda built into the side of a V-shaped gorge. It was covered by a lattice canopy of bougainvillea, and the far side was open air. Alessandro guided them to the best of four empty tables along the exterior rail. He explained that the veranda was often used for private dinner parties, but he expected no one else that evening.

Gabe walked to the rail and took in the view. To the right, he saw the stunning Mediterranean more than two thousand feet below. To the left, he saw the interior of the gorge, terraced and lushly vegetated. He looked up and saw a majestic villa built along the rim on the far side. It was surrounded by umbrella pines.

He and Gram took their seats. Gabe sat facing the sea, where the sun touched the horizon. The craggy walls were bathed in orange light, highlighting the terraces. Gabe also noticed a gibbous moon rising from behind the mountains as the sun disappeared.

Once they were seated, Allesandro busied himself at the serving cart. The views were extraordinary, but more importantly, they were alone.

Francesca had also been surveying the surrounding beauty. She had a look of contentment on her face.

"I love Amalfi," she said. "This is my true home. I miss it. It's where I grew up and spent my youth." She reached over and squeezed Gabe's hand lovingly.

"I love America too, of course," she continued. "However, it was really your grandfather's love for America that I so cherished. He was always grateful for the life he had there, and his enthusiasm was infectious. He poured himself into everything he did, you know."

"Yes, he did," Gabe replied.

Alessandro brought water in a blue bottle. He poured a glass for each of them and placed the remainder on the table. He then left for the kitchen and returned with a Caprese salad of vine-ripened tomatoes topped with soft mozzarella, olive oil, and cracked black pepper. He placed a basket of fresh, steamy bread on the table along with the pitcher of red table wine that accompanied every evening meal in Italy. He bowed slightly and excused himself.

Gabe anxiously waited for Alessandro to move out of earshot. He then steered the conversation toward the pressing questions on his mind. Just as he was about to speak, he heard voices coming from the entrance. He pretended not to notice, but the voices grew louder, and before he knew it, Alessandro led two men to the adjacent table.

They were dressed in flawlessly tailored Armani suits, replete with Bruno Magli shoes. They could not have looked more out of place. *What happened to privacy and seclusion?* Gabe wondered with grave suspicion. He made eye contact with Alessandro, who shrugged and looked bewildered.

The two men spoke in Italian. Gabe tried to eavesdrop but couldn't understand a word. He could see them over his grandmother's shoulder. She paid little attention to them, but images of *The Godfather* flashed through Gabe's mind for the second time that day. *Just business associates out for dinner,* he tried to reassure himself. He would need to take his conversation in another direction for the time being.

"Gram, yesterday morning, you were telling me how you and Grandfather met. When your cousins arrived, we got interrupted. Would you tell me the rest of the story?"

"I'd love to," she replied. "Where'd we leave off?"

"Grandfather was covertly moving information between London and Moscow during the war."

"Ah, yes, I remember," she said. "It was mid-1944, right after the D-Day invasion of France. The Allies had just launched their final assault on the German war machine. Western Europe was still heavily defended by the Nazis." A distressed look came over her face. "Did you see the movie *Saving Private Ryan?*" she asked.

"I did," Gabe answered. "On the big screen. I don't think I exhaled for the film's first twenty minutes. It was horrible. No wonder the memories are so intense for those who survived."

"Those brave American boys—they were just slaughtered at Normandy," she said. She paused for a moment. "It was different for us. The Germans declared Rome to be an open city rather than defending it to the end. We were so thankful. Countless human lives were spared, and the city's priceless art treasures and architectural wonders were preserved."

"I saw Montecassino this morning on the drive from Rome," Gabe interjected. "Anna Castriotti told me how it had been leveled by American bombers during the war."

"That was tragic," she said. "Montecassino was a German stronghold. It was being used to slow the Allied advance toward Rome, so the Allies had little choice. It became a casualty of war like so much of my country. Still, the Italians of my generation feel deep gratitude toward the American people for their sacrifices here in Europe. That type of courage fueled John's patriotism and pride in America."

"It's why Tom Brokaw called it the greatest generation," he added.

"It was heroic," Francesca said with a look of pride. "And my personal hero carried out his dangerous mission traveling back and forth between the British and Soviet capitals. To avoid the German Army, John had to travel either a northerly route across the North Sea and Scandinavia or a southerly route across Spain, the Mediterranean Sea, Italy, and the Baltics. Guess which one he preferred?"

"North?" Gabe replied with a playful grin.

"Given John's long-held affinity for the Amalfi Coast, I hardly think so. Plus, the journey required a stop in both directions," she quipped, winking at Gabe.

"I take it these dual stops brought him to Rome often," he said.

"They certainly did, and John never failed to visit my office," she answered.

Gabe studied her expression. He imagined the youthful beauty his grandfather must have seen so many years earlier. Francesca was a very beautiful young woman.

"How old were you?" he asked.

"Twenty-four," she said. "I was born in 1919, right after World War I. I guess you could say I was a product of the first baby boom. My father had been a sergeant in the Italian Army and fought in the trenches against the hated Germans."

"How did Germany and Italy end up as allies in the Second World War if there was so much bitterness between them after World War I?" he asked.

"Times of war make for strange bedfellows," she replied. She stared at the lemon in her water glass. "Italy became Fascist when Benito Mussolini rose to power. I think it was around 1922. He was Europe's first fascist dictator, a full decade before Hitler. It was only natural for him to forge an alliance with Hitler that later ended up bringing Italy into World War II on the wrong side."

"What a tragedy," Gabe said.

"Most Italians hated the idea of being aligned with Germany," she continued, "but you must remember, with a dictator, the will of the people is rarely considered."

She paused to replenish the olive oil and pepper. She dipped a piece of bread and offered one to Gabe.

"Politically, Italy and Germany were allies during World War II, but in truth, the Germans were more of an occupation force than anything else," she continued. "You might say our marriage of convenience kept us from shooting at them. In fact, after Mussolini was ousted late in the war, the Italian royal family escaped into exile and declared war on Germany."

"I didn't know that," Gabe said. He peered over her shoulder again. The two men were still engaged in conversation. It looked like they'd just ordered their meal.

"It's a little-known fact of the war," she said. "It lifted our hopes for freedom, but it's also when the Germans decided to occupy Rome. The alliance with Germany and Japan was never the will of the Italian people. Hitler called it the Axis on which the world turned, but in the end, it brought nothing but death and destruction to our country." Francesca's face was forlorn.

"Wasn't Mussolini executed?" Gabe asked.

"Indeed, he was," she said. Francesca provided a surprisingly graphic answer. "Toward the end of the war, he and his mistress were arrested by the Italian Resistance. They were executed, and their corpses were hanged in the streets of Milan for public viewing. It was gruesome, but like my father, members of the resistance battled valiantly in the trenches during World War I. They witnessed firsthand the slaughter of countless thousands of their countrymen at the hands of the Germans and held a deep hatred for the German war machine. Mussolini forgot that, and for his arrogance, he paid with his life."

As she finished speaking, Alessandro approached with a heaping platter of pasta.

"Tonight, we have linguine with lemon. Amalfi has some of the best lemons in the world," he explained to Gabe as he set the linguine on the table. "Very big and juicy with a lovely scent. Perhaps you've noticed them hanging from the pergolas along the coast. Enjoy. I'll return with your entree in twenty minutes." Alessandro smiled graciously.

He turned to leave, and one of the two gentlemen at the next table asked him a question. He replied in Italian, and a brief dialogue ensued. Gabe again tried to listen, but eavesdropping was pointless. His grandmother didn't appear concerned by the conversation. *Perhaps I can ask my questions after all,* he thought.

Gabe offered his grandmother a serving of linguine and then helped himself to a healthy portion. He kept an eye on the next table. Alessandro nodded firmly, turned, and left. The conversation between the two men resumed, but before Gabe could speak, Francesca continued.

"The First World War opened a wound in my father that never really healed. He was only too happy to return home to the comforting arms of his young bride. The peace and serenity of these mountains were the perfect antidote for the horrors he'd witnessed," she said. She gestured with a wide sweep of her arm.

Gabe refilled his grandmother's water glass.

"Thank you," she added with an affectionate smile.

"You were close to your parents, I take it," Gabe said.

"Oh yes, very close, which made it particularly hard for them when John and I decided to marry."

"Why was that?" Gabe asked. He looked up from his plate, surprised.

"Because John planned to take me to America. I would've followed him to the moon, but my parents were living here on the Amalfi Coast. I think my mom suspected she'd never see me again. In those days, intercontinental travel was a rare and expensive proposition. It just didn't happen for people of our means."

Gabe reflected on how much bigger the world would have seemed in those days. And yet, in a single lifetime, his grandmother's generation had witnessed the greatest changes in the history of the world. He watched her twirl her linguine without stopping to take a bite.

"My father tried to discourage me at first. He really did," she continued. "He warned me that our relationship was nothing more than John's attempt to separate a young woman from her virtue." She chuckled as she remembered the scene. "But it was no use. We were completely in love. Like so many young women, I'd fallen head over heels in love with an Allied soldier. Sadly, many of those other relationships were as fleeting as the passing summer season, but ours was different."

Gabe saw her eyes sparkle with the joy of youth.

"Almost immediately, we began discussing our plans for the war's end. John was so confident. He wanted to return to the US and continue his career in the intelligence services. I, on the other hand, had only one goal in mind—get as close to this man as I could and hold on to him for the rest of my life."

Alessandro returned to the table and noticed Gabe's empty plate. He asked if they were ready for their entrees.

"Yes, please," Francesca replied.

Francesca sat back in her chair. She neatly folded her linen napkin and placed it on the table. Gabe helped himself to the rest of the linguine.

She continued to reminisce. "I'll never forget the first time John met my father. My father was a rotund man, only five-foot-four. He always stood ramrod straight and was strong as an ox. John, as you know, stretched to six-foot-four. Despite their enormous difference in size, it was clear who held the upper hand. My father was a bull of a man with a broad mustache. He was also deeply religious with a heart of gold—kind, compassionate, and generous. But don't let that fool you. He had a way of controlling situations despite his unimposing size."

Gabe laughed. He'd been on the short end of that same stick himself one time when he'd met Sarah's father over Christmas break his senior year in college.

"When John entered our family home," she said, "he reached for my father's hand and introduced himself as Captain John Roslovsky. My father eyed him carefully before shaking his hand. I could tell Papa was not impressed—if not outright hostile toward him. We all just stood there, waiting for my father to respond. It was so quiet I could hear the Swiss clock ticking in the foyer."

"Finally, my father said, 'Roslovsky, you say. Your name is Roslovsky?' He spoke in Italian, of course, so I had to translate.

'That's correct, sir. Captain John Roslovsky, US Army.'
'What, if I may ask, do you do for the Army?'
'I'm in special services,' John replied.
'Special services?'
'He's an intelligence officer, Father,' I interrupted.
'An intelligence officer!' my father exclaimed. 'That's worse. How do we know he's not a communist spy?'"

Francesca shuddered as she recalled the moment. "I felt my throat go dry. I wanted to swallow my words, but then I saw my father's face transform into one of his classic smiles. I'd seen that smile a hundred times before. Then I knew. He liked John. It had been a bluff. My father wanted to be sure John knew who was boss." She smiled and shook her head fondly at the memory.

Alessandro appeared with the main course, a delicious local fish grilled and served whole. He began removing the bones while Gabe and Francesca waited patiently. When he finished, he served the fish and asked if they needed anything else.

"Grazie, no," Francesca replied. "Thank you so kindly for your hospitality, Alessandro. This is a lovely meal." He nodded graciously. With that, he refilled their wine glasses and left the table.

She ate sparingly, but Gabe had plenty of appetite. It had been an incredible two days, and a good meal was just what he needed. Still, he slowed the pace of the meal, hoping the two men would finish first and leave. He looked over Francesca's shoulder. They hadn't received their entrees yet. He wanted to ask his questions but decided to continue with a safe conversation.

"Were you married here or in the United States?" he asked.

"We were married in Italy. My father insisted. It was his final condition before granting his blessing."

"Blessing? Wow! Your father's blessing—you don't hear that much anymore."

Francesca frowned at Gabe. "In those days, young man, it was entirely proper for a man to gain his future father-in-law's blessing. I know things are different today, but in those days, it would've been a huge scandal to run off and get married without my father's blessing. John was the perfect gentleman. He always did the right thing," she sighed. "We were married here at the end of the war. John and my father developed a great mutual respect that lasted throughout their lives."

They made small talk about a variety of subjects unrelated to Italy or his grandfather. Eventually, Francesca stopped eating altogether. His plate was empty.

Alessandro returned to the veranda and cleared their plates. "For dessert tonight, I made the house special," he said. "May I suggest coffee to accompany your dessert?"

They both accepted. Moments later, Alessandro returned with coffee and tiramisu. Gabe could see the meal was winding down, and he still needed to get his questions answered. The two men were now completely engrossed in their meal. He decided to launch in.

"Gram, I spent some time looking through the book I found in the bathroom."

"What about it?"

"Well," he began. He lowered his voice and leaned in. "I noticed it contained some strange symbols—Masonic symbols." He said the last two words in a whisper, virtually mouthing them.

Francesca froze mid-bite. She glanced over her shoulder and set her fork down. It was the first time she'd paid any attention to the men behind her.

28

She picked up her napkin and wiped her mouth, clearly caught off guard by Gabe's comment.

"What do you mean?" Francesca asked in an equally low tone.

"Was Grandfather ever involved with the Masons?" he asked.

The conversation at the next table stopped cold. Gabe felt his heart race. *I'm such an idiot,* he thought to himself. The silence was scorching.

He kept his head down to avoid making eye contact. He couldn't tell whether the two men were looking in his direction or not.

They hadn't resumed their conversation when Alessandro's voice broke the silence. "Gentlemen, could I interest you in dessert?" He'd been watching the men from across the terrace, but he was now standing at their table. When he departed, their conversation resumed.

Francesca eavesdropped momentarily. She quietly whispered to Gabe, "They're talking about the shipping business in Salerno."

Gabe decided it was time for them to leave. The place was incredibly secluded, and it was now dark outside, which presented security issues.

"Gram, I don't have much left in me," he said, feigning a yawn.

"Oh, me neither," she replied. He noticed a discernable sigh of relief.

Alessandro returned as if on cue. Gabe reached for his wallet, but Alessandro threw a hand up. "No, signore. We have already taken care of your meal. It was my pleasure serving you both. Please, enjoy the rest of your evening."

Gabe was pleasantly surprised by Alessandro's refusal to accept payment. He made a mental note to thank Lorenzo when he returned to the hotel. They exchanged pleasantries and rose to leave.

Gabe carefully monitored their surroundings. He saw no one as they passed through the piazza, but it was impossible to tell if someone lurked in the shadows. Gram took his arm when they reached the staircase, and they started the slow descent down the steps. At last, they reached the car. He opened her door and helped her in.

Gabe made one last visual sweep of the perimeter—nothing but shadows. He quickly slipped into the driver's seat and fired up the engine.

ALESSANDRO RE-ENTERED THE TERRACE with cannoli and steaming cappuccinos for the two gentlemen. *That's odd,* he thought as he approached the table. *Where did they go?*

Ample payment laid on the table to cover the bill. He shrugged, pocketed the money, and turned back for the kitchen.

A HEAVY SILENCE HUNG in the car as they started down the mountain. Dinner had called for discretion. Gabe was disconcerted by what happened, but he still needed answers to his questions. He had to ask again.

"Gram, please forgive me. I shouldn't have asked about Grandfather's book in public, but I need to know. Was he ever a Mason?"

"As a matter of fact," she began slowly, "he was involved with the Masons for a time after the war. It was the early 1950s. His father encouraged him to join."

"So, he left?" he asked.

"That's right," she said.

"But I thought Masonry was a lifetime deal."

"Well, usually it is," she said, "but he quit—and for good reason."

"Which was?"

"He left because he rejected their rampant racism. He was a member of a segregated lodge, which was the norm back then. In fact, I don't think black men were even allowed to join the Masons in those days. Publicly, his lodge brothers spoke of equality among men, but privately, they ridiculed people of color.

"Your grandfather told me that most of them believed African Americans were an inferior race. He was truly sickened by it. He couldn't stand the contradiction it represented. He'd fought against the tyranny of Nazi racism and hated it with a passion. Racism was still a huge problem in America at the time, and the Masons weren't immune."

She paused a moment then added, "Quite frankly, I was glad when he got out. Masonic membership is strictly forbidden by our church. I was never comfortable with it. That was his last involvement, as far as I know."

"What about his father?" Gabe asked. "I think the book belonged to him. What was his involvement with the Masons?"

"John's father was a lifelong member as far as I know—high ranking, as well. He was very influential. It was a point of contention between them. They simply agreed to disagree."

"I see," he said. He paused momentarily then continued, "I have one more question for you. This one's more generic, but I need to pick your brain. Do the letters SA mean anything to you?"

"SA—are they initials?" she asked.

"I don't know. I was hoping you could tell me."

She thought for several minutes. "I have no idea. Why do you ask?"

"I found the letters SA written in the margin on one of the pages. I was just wondering if you had any idea what they meant or what they might've meant to Grandfather?"

Gabe regretted his lie, but it was better than explaining the truth. An accumulating lie was unfamiliar territory for him, but so was investigating his grandfather's murder. He decided to change the subject.

"Hey, I have an idea. Why don't we go to Capri tomorrow if you feel up to it? We could make it a day trip or even spend the night and come back Friday. We'd have plenty of time before the memorial service. There's nothing we need to do beforehand. The distraction might be nice for both of us."

"Oh, Gabe, I'd love that! The drive along the coast is one of my favorites, and I'd certainly enjoy spending more time with you. This evening was a gift," she said, patting his hand. "It would be great if we could spend the night on Capri."

"It's settled then," he said. "I'll pick you up in the morning."

They drove quietly for a few minutes.

"Turn here," she said. Gabe turned into the driveway of her cousin's house. He helped her out of the car and walked her to the door. When they reached the doorstep, she turned to him.

"Gabe, could you do a favor for me? I'd like to go to Mass at the cathedral in the morning. It would be so nice if you could accompany me. Mass is at 8:00, and I'm a little slow these days. We'd need to leave here by 7:15 if that isn't too early for you."

"Sure, Gram, I'd be happy to take you to Mass. I wanted to see the cathedral anyway. I'll be here promptly at 7:15."

"Oh, thank you, Gabriel," she said with a beaming smile.

"Get some sleep now," Gabe said. "We'll talk more tomorrow. I love you."

He kissed her on the cheek and helped her into the house under the yellow glow of lamplight. She closed the door. For the first time, he realized she

THE AMALFI SECRET

was now an old woman. He got in his car and wondered if he could fake his way through Mass—in Italian, no less. He hadn't been near a church in years.

He retraced the route back to the Amalfi Hotel, where he found Lorenzo Bonelli seated behind the desk in the lobby.

"How was dinner?" he asked.

"It was delicious," Gabe said. "My grandmother was so thrilled." He thanked Lorenzo for graciously making the arrangements.

Lorenzo nodded with delight. He then became serious. He rose and came out from behind the desk. "Did you speak to Zach Beckett? Has he found your grandfather's body?"

Gabe shook his head. "I spoke to him—no leads," Gabe said.

"I'm so sorry. Is there anything else I can do for you tonight?" Lorenzo asked, his face drawn.

"No, thank you. I appreciate everything you've done. The meal was wonderful. Alessandro told me that you…"

"Say no more," Lorenzo interrupted. He raised his hand. "It was my pleasure."

Gabe was eager to get back to his room to read message #407. The conversation with Paolo Castriotti and Anna had been abruptly cut off, and he wanted to find out what the message contained, so he said good night to Lorenzo.

He turned to leave but stopped short. "Lorenzo, there's one thing you could do for me. I'm leaving early tomorrow to take my grandmother to Mass. Then we're going to Capri to spend the night. Could you make hotel reservations for us?"

"I would be pleased to assist," he said. A wide smile covered his face.

"If possible, I'd like adjoining rooms," Gabe said. "Just let me know the arrangements in the morning. I'm leaving around 6:45."

Lorenzo nodded politely.

Gabe headed downstairs to his room and changed into a pair of shorts and a T-shirt. He brushed his teeth, pulled a bottle of water from the mini bar, lay on the bed, and picked up the blue book of Gobbi messages.

He flipped it open to message #407.

What Gabe found was completely shocking as it explained the number 666. He broke into a sweat. A myriad of images flashed through his mind as he considered the consequences of the message. Filled with trepidation, he jumped up and began to pace across the room. He felt an ominous but powerful sense of dread gnawing at his soul.

Suddenly, he stopped. His mind locked onto a single image—the face of Cardinal Bauer.

29

While Gabe and Francesca were at dinner, Gino Caruso left his home high in the hills above Amalfi. He snaked his way down to the coastal road and turned right toward the village. He passed the turnabout at Amalfi's main intersection and drove up the winding hill toward Wally's Pub, an English brew house run by a big, burly Brit aptly named Wally. The place catered mainly to English-speaking patrons. On most nights, it was filled with Americans, Brits, and Aussies. Several small tables lined the darkened walls, which virtually guaranteed Italian-speaking patrons would go unnoticed.

Caruso exited a tunnel and curved to the right. The pub came into view. Finding a parking space on the narrow road during high season would have been impossible, but the tourist season was slowing. Caruso had no trouble squeezing his Jaguar into a spot behind a bank of scooters.

The pub itself was built into the side of the mountain. Its back wall was the recess of a hollowed-out cavern. The façade was not much more than a wooden door and a window set into the bedrock.

There were only four patrons in Wally's Pub when Caruso entered: a twenty-something Australian couple and a redheaded American woman were seated at the bar. The Australian couple was discussing their round-the-world trip. They'd just spent a week in Rome viewing masterpieces at the Vatican. The Australian woman was explaining her reaction to the depiction of Saint Bartholomew the Apostle, who'd been flayed—literally skinned alive—for preaching along the shores of the Caspian Sea. The image left her stunned, to say the least.

She told the redhead that she'd been raised a complete atheist by her father and knew nothing of the apostles or their various martyrdoms. The American woman provided a catechism lesson while the jovial bartender added his take on Christian history. All carried on famously as the cheery barkeep provided a continuous flow of drinks, oblivious to the soccer match blaring from a television in the corner.

Caruso found the fourth patron sitting below the television. Marco Sorrentino was snacking on honey-roasted peanuts and nursing a Carlsberg 47 Danish pale lager. There was a second bottle for Caruso on the table.

He greeted Caruso with a nod but no handshake. Marco motioned for him to have a seat. As expected, the other patrons were unaware of their presence. He wasted no time on pleasantries. His questions were direct and pointed.

"Why was Gabriel Roslo in Rome?"

"I already told you that—to personally notify Cardinal Bauer of his grandfather's death," Caruso replied.

"Don't you find that strange?" Marco asked. "Why didn't he just call or send a telegram?"

Caruso did find it strange, but he didn't answer.

"Did he see anyone else?" Marco asked.

"Not sure, but he returned to Amalfi with Anna Castriotti."

"Castriotti's niece? She's involved in this?"

"Involved in what?" Caruso asked.

"Roslo's death."

"I have no idea what her involvement is," Caruso replied, "but she's here in Amalfi."

"I'm more interested in the NSA man—the one who's been assisting with the arrangements. Where is he now?" Marco asked.

"I have no idea."

"You don't know, or you haven't told me? Which is it?" Marco demanded sharply.

Caruso was surprised by his directness.

"And what about Andre Gotto? Where's he now?" Marco pressed.

"I dropped him at the docks this afternoon when we left wine time. He was headed out to sea."

"Did he say anything?"

"No, he seemed uncharacteristically quiet today," Caruso said.

"What does he know about John Roslo's death?"

"I'm not sure. He didn't say anything but wanted to keep the authorities out of it."

"Really? Now we're getting somewhere," Marco said, slamming his beer on the table. His normally relaxed manner was suddenly forceful. "Do you know if the NSA man is coming to Amalfi?"

"No, I don't," Caruso replied.

Caruso smelled blood. Marco was searching for something and that spelled opportunity. "Why are you so interested in John Roslo anyway?" he asked. "What do you have on him?"

Marco's face was ice cold. He provided no answer.

"Well?" Caruso demanded. "What do you know?" Caruso maneuvered to see where the opportunity might lead. Marco did not answer. "Come on, bring me up to date," Caruso said.

Still nothing from Marco.

Caruso looked at his watch. He decided to employ an old political tactic. He declared the meeting over and abruptly stood up. "Then I guess we've got nothing else to discuss," Caruso said. He tossed drink money on the table and headed for the door.

"Short stay, mate?" he heard Wally ask. Caruso waived his right hand and hurried out the door without turning or speaking. He jumped into the driver's seat and started his car.

He pumped the clutch and squealed the tires. The car jerked forward then backward in a series of motions. Once pointed in the right direction, he sped back down the coast to the center of Amalfi. He reached the turnabout and pulled into the marina instead of continuing home. He slipped into a parking space, the motor still running. He stared at the harbor. He could see the lights of a passenger ferry entering the Amalfi marina and a variety of fishing boats and pleasure craft moored at the docks.

Something big is going on, he thought. Why else would Marco be so demanding with his questions and so tight-lipped with any answers? Caruso had been a politician for a long time and had learned years earlier to be shrewd in his tactics and dealings, even with people he knew well.

He pondered the obvious. Marco wanted information, and he was in the information business—a natural component of his political life. Marco's tone was completely out of character—*no doubt a clue as to how important the information is,* he thought to himself. A smile formed at the corners of his mouth. Caruso ran the conversation through his mind. He realized the name of the NSA man and his whereabouts had great value, information that would be worth a lot of money.

He thought about his options. Marco was a longtime lodge brother and always willing to pay for the right information. The payment was usually in the form of political contributions. In other cases, payment garnered intangible benefits. However, this information was worth straight-up cash. *How much would Marco pay?* he wondered.

Caruso thought about John Roslo. *Was he murdered? Maybe, maybe not. But what difference does it make? An old man is dead, end of story.* Marco wanted information, valuable information. He'd paid for it in the past. Why should this be any different? After all, this was business, a simple information exchange. He just needed to put the right deal on the table. Even John Roslo was fond of the expression, "All the important decisions are made by people with the most money, the biggest guns, and the best information."

Caruso felt his resolve strengthen. This was an opportunity. He needed to make the most of it. Even honest politicians found ways to earn extra euros for services rendered. He flipped open his phone and hit speed dial.

"Marco here." He was still finishing his beer.

"I think I can help you," Caruso said. "I want to propose a deal."

"I'm listening..."

"I never make it my business to ask why," Caruso said. "Frankly, I don't care, and in my opinion, this should be no different. What do you want to find out?"

"I want to know the name of the NSA man," Marco replied. "I want to know where he is, why he's here, his activities—everything. I also want to know the connection between Roslo and Cardinal Bauer. Most importantly, why did Roslo's grandson go to Rome?"

"Got it. Anything else?"

"Si. Roslo owned a diary. I want to know what happened to it. Learn its whereabouts. That by itself could be worth a handsome reward. Do you understand?"

"Perfectly," Caruso replied. He paused momentarily.

Caruso knew Marco was a dealmaker and worth tens of millions. He would pay for important information. If John Roslo had indeed been murdered, this information could be worth a tremendous sum of money. He felt emboldened.

"Here are my terms," Caruso said. "I want 200,000 euros for the name of the NSA man, his location, and the reason he's in Italy."

"100,000," Marco countered.

One hundred thousand euros was more than Caruso's annual salary—a lot of money for information he could gather easily. Still, incriminating evidence had a high price, and hiding it was worth even more. Plus, he had a political career to deal with. He'd been involved in plenty of sleazy deals but never murder. He thought a deal like this would have to be worth the risk, and he knew Marco was willing to pay.

"200,000 firm," Caruso said. "I want another 200,000 to find out how Roslo was connected to the cardinal."

Now, it was Marco's turn to pause. "You're proposing a lot of money. What about the diary?" Marco asked.

"If you agree to my terms, I'll throw it in for free."

"We've known each other a long time. This can't go beyond us. I need your sworn pledge," Marco said.

"My lips are sealed."

"Good," replied Marco, "but I have one condition. I want you to arrange a meeting with Gabriel Roslo. Tell him you have information about his grandfather's disappearance. Can you do that?"

"Of course," said Caruso.

"Set up lunch at the Seaside Café in Salerno," Marco said. "You know the place."

"I know it well," Caruso replied. The Seaside was an open-air garden café across from Salerno's marina.

"Invite the wine time group to avoid suspicion, and make sure they bring the Castriotti girl."

Caruso furrowed his eyebrows. Why did he want Anna Castriotti there? He didn't like it, but he was in no position to protest now. Reluctantly, he agreed. He then added a condition of his own.

"I want 10,000 euros wired into my Swiss account as a down payment."

The line was silent as Marco paused to consider it—cheap, by his thinking. "I'll have it sent as soon as you arrange the meeting. Call me when it's done."

Caruso looked at the clock on his dashboard. It was nearly 22:00. "Give me twelve hours."

"Perfect," Marco replied. He closed his phone and called for another Carlsberg.

The barkeep brought it over but remained fully engaged in the lively conversation at the bar. He looked at Marco briefly. "Four euros fifty."

Marco handed him a five and motioned for him to keep it. Wally nodded his appreciation and returned to the bar without missing a beat. Marco was once again anonymous. He took a long drink of his beer. He then flipped open his phone and hit speed dial.

"Caruso wants to make a deal. He thinks he can get what we need, but he's asking for 400,000 euros."

Marco studied the people at the bar as he impatiently listened to the voice on the other end. "That's correct," he said when the voice finished. "Lunch at the Seaside, and the Castriotti girl will be there. Thank you."

Marco showed no further emotion as the voice on the other end gave final instructions. With that, he closed the phone and headed out the door. The beer on the table was three-quarters full.

GINO CARUSO LEFT THE MARINA and drove up the mountain ascent. He turned into his driveway, switched off the engine, and sat motionless for a few minutes. His eyes were heavy. He could hear the *tink, tink* of the engine as it cooled. He thought about his life. This was no time for remorse or regret. He convinced himself that he was simply doing what anyone would do in his position—taking care of number one.

He got out of the car and, once inside, found his wife asleep. He kissed her on the cheek and crawled into bed next to her. He drifted off, pleased with himself. He'd wanted to exit politics for a quieter life for some time. The days until retirement had just been shortened considerably.

30

Gabe awoke to the sound of crashing waves. An overnight storm stirred up the sea, and waves were pounding against the rocks beneath his window. It had been a fitful night of tossing and turning. He looked at the clock on the side table. It was 6:15 a.m. He had thirty minutes to get ready and still have enough time to retrace his steps up the mountain to Ravello and drive back down to Amalfi for Mass at the cathedral.

He jumped in the shower, dressed, and hastily packed his overnight bag. He made sure the diary was secure in his coat pocket. He locked the hotel room door and headed up the stairs. When he reached the top of the staircase, Lorenzo was waiting to assist him.

Lorenzo led him to the parking area and handed Gabe a note. "Here's the name of the hotel," he said. "Just give it to the taxi driver when you arrive on Capri. He'll know where it is."

"Thank you, Lorenzo. I very much appreciate your help," Gabe said.

"Enjoy this time with your grandmother. I'll contact you at the hotel if I hear anything."

"I'll do the same," Gabe replied. "Otherwise, I'll be back tomorrow."

Gabe hopped into his rental car and prepared to back up. Lorenzo stepped behind the car and held up his hands to stop traffic in both directions. *Now that's service,* Gabe thought. He backed out, slammed the car into gear, and was gone in a flash.

He wound his way up the mountain to Ravello. The trip was much easier the second time. Francesca was ready and waiting when he arrived. They said farewell to the cousins, he loaded her bag, and they headed out.

Francesca had him turn onto a narrow street when they arrived in Amalfi. It led to a small parking lot behind a municipal building, home to Amalfi's civic administration. It was early—just past 7:45—so several parking places were still available. Gabe slid into one outlined in blue.

"Sorry, Gabe, we need to move over there," Francesca protested. "This is a handicapped spot."

"How would a tourist ever know that?" Gabe laughed. He backed up and moved the car one space to the right.

"They don't," she grinned. "Parking tickets are a steady source of local revenue."

They got out of the car, and Francesca took Gabe by the arm. She led him along a back route to Saint Andrew's Cathedral. They followed a maze of tunnels, staircases, and hidden alleyways until they reached a nondescript, green double door in the side of a wall. She pushed it open, and they stepped inside. They were standing on the landing of a wide marble staircase.

"Where does that go?" Gabe asked, pointing upward.

"To the main sanctuary. It'll be open after Mass, but we're going this way," she said. She led him downstairs to the crypt.

They maneuvered into one of the four old wooden pews. It was a tight squeeze for Gabe. His feet hit the wall behind them as he knelt beside his grandmother. She said her prayers and sat back on the pew. Gabe followed her lead. After they were seated, he surveyed the room.

"This crypt was built eight hundred years ago at the request of Cardinal Pietro Capuano," she leaned over and whispered. "In 1208, he had Saint Andrew's remains brought here from Constantinople on his return from the Fourth Crusade."

Gabe was intrigued. The ceiling of the crypt was cross-vaulted and covered in frescoes from the seventeenth century. It looked like some of them had been recently restored to reveal the beautiful artistry, while others were dark and discolored. He spent a few minutes trying to determine the subjects of the paintings but to no avail. Time and burning lamp oil had covered them in black veils.

The crypt had a marble communion rail. It bordered an ornate marble altar that was built into the wall. There were more blackened frescoes behind the altar. Gabe couldn't make out what they depicted either. Dim sconces and a small amount of natural light filtering through thick-paned, grilled windows at the east end of the crypt provided light.

The most prominent artifact was an impressive, majestic bronze statue of Saint Andrew. It loomed above the altar, flanked by two smaller statues set in arches. Francesca later explained that Saint Stephen and Saint Lawrence were the first deacons of the Eastern and Western Christian churches. Gabe could see a golden grill below the altar encasing thick glass.

"Those are the bones of Saint Andrew the Apostle," Francesca whispered.

To Gabe's left were eight gray-haired women of faith, clearly all Italians. One turned to him and asked, "Communion?"

Gabe was confused by her question, so he opted for "no." He thought it was the safest answer to almost any question when he couldn't understand what was being said. He noticed a look of momentary disappointment on his grandmother's face.

An elderly priest emerged from a hidden door promptly at 8:00. The door was camouflaged in the wall behind them. He crossed in front of those gathered and entered through the communion rail. He made the sign of the cross and began the opening prayer in Italian. Strangely, the priest faced the altar with his back toward the people. The altar was built into the wall, and its direction had not been reversed after the Second Vatican Council.

Gabe couldn't follow the Italian, and his mind began to wander. He thought about his grandfather, his father, and the mysteries connecting the past and present. He wondered about his Italian ancestors and imagined what life must have been like in Amalfi a thousand years earlier.

Midway through the service, Francesca reached for his hand. "Time for the Lord's prayer," she whispered. She gave his hand a loving squeeze.

Gabe's mind snapped back to the present. He knew Holy Communion would follow shortly. A few moments later, those present lined up to receive the body and blood of Jesus. Gabe had not been to Mass since he was sixteen years old. He was not religious, but strangely, at that moment, he was struck by the thought of Andrew the Apostle being present at the very first Holy Communion at the Last Supper. Now, thousands of years later, people were still gathering to commemorate that event—at 8:00 in the morning on a weekday, no less.

The Italian ladies broke into a spontaneous acapella hymn immediately after communion. Gabe couldn't understand a single word, but as their voices reverberated off the marble walls, he experienced the strongest sense of serenity. He felt a powerful connection to the faith of the ages. He would've been hard-pressed to explain it, but a true sense of peace welled up in his heart. He savored the moment quietly after Mass ended.

The elderly ladies started shuffling up the stairs. Francesca turned to him. "Have a look at the main sanctuary upstairs. It's impressive. I promised John that I'd remember him to Saint Andrew. I'll be along in a minute to meet you there." With that, she bowed her head in prayer.

Gabe moved toward the staircase and saw a man sitting in the shadows. The man was sitting in the domed cove attached to the back of the crypt. Gabe hadn't noticed him during Mass. He was dressed entirely in black. Unbeknownst to Gabe, the man had been watching him since they arrived.

Gabe's immediate instinct was to return to his grandmother, but the man was now moving toward him. *Stay calm, stay calm,* he thought as he climbed the marble staircase. The man followed at an uncomfortably close distance. Gabe reached the sanctuary and heard the man's footsteps directly behind him. His heart was pounding, but at least he'd led the man away from his grandmother.

The dimly lit cathedral was cavernous. The main lights were turned off, and the only source of light came through the stained-glass windows. Gabe looked in both directions. He saw no one. *It's now or never,* he thought. He stopped, whipped around, and confronted the man. What he saw caused him to freeze in place. Standing before him was one of the men from dinner the night before!

The man stopped and looked Gabe square in the eye. Gabe's adrenalin surged. After what seemed like an eternity, the man nodded and continued walking. He never said a word and disappeared out the cathedral's front door. Gabe immediately headed for the crypt to check on his grandmother.

She was coming up the steps as he rounded the corner of the staircase. She took him by the arm and led him back into the impressive structure.

"Let me show you around," she said proudly. "This is the church I grew up in."

Gabe's heart was racing. He employed a controlled breathing technique to decrease his pulse rate. He kept a wary eye on the entrances as they slowly walked to the front of the cathedral.

Behind the main altar was a huge painting of a crucifixion. It depicted a man hanging on an X-shaped cross. Gabe found this curious because it was so different than any image of the crucifixion he'd ever seen.

"That's Saint Andrew," she said, patting his arm.

"Saint Andrew?" he asked.

"Oh yes, he was crucified too," she said, "a martyr for the faith."

They spent a few quiet moments looking at the scene. She then gave him a tour of the other paintings, statues, and relics displayed throughout the cathedral before leaving. The crypt was now locked, so they left through the front door, the same one used by the man Gabe had seen at dinner.

The exit led to the main portico built along the front edge of the cathedral. They were perched high above the street. Gabe scanned his surroundings.

Thankfully, the man was nowhere to be seen. Francesca again took his arm, and they began the fifty-seven-step descent to street level.

"Gram, do you remember the men seated near us at dinner last night?" he asked.

"Vaguely, why?"

"Have you ever seen them before—at the church, maybe?" Gabe pressed.

"Not that I recall. Why do you ask?"

"Just curious. Thought they might be locals," he said. He changed the subject and pointed to a rough spot on the staircase. "Watch your step."

Amalfi's main piazza was at the foot of the steps. Gabe had run past that very spot two days earlier. To their right was the main route into the village of Amalfi. To their left was a short, one-block walk to the coastal road and the marina.

The sun shone brightly and felt warm on Gabe's face. He looked up and could see the ancient castle high in the mountains. It stood sentry over Amalfi, as it had for centuries. It was the same castle he'd seen the morning his grandfather was murdered.

Francesca caught Gabe by the arm and turned him back toward the cathedral. "I think you'll find this interesting," she said. She pointed to the façade. He looked up and saw a huge mosaic just under the roof line of the cathedral.

"That image was a favorite of my father's," Francesca said wistfully. "*Cristo in trono ossequiato dai potenti della Terra.*"

Gabe looked puzzled.

"Christ enthroned, worshipped by the powerful on Earth," she quickly clarified in English. "It's a picture of the apocalypse from the Book of Revelation. Many people think of the return of Christ as a scary time, but my father always told me it was the time to long for—a time of great hope. He said that during his most frightening moments in the trenches during the First World War, he would think of this image and be comforted.

"Notice the roofline," she continued, "above the mosaic. The pitch on one side of the roof is different than the other. We Italians are more concerned with beauty than perfection," she smiled.

She again took him by the arm. They strolled through the piazza and passed a public water fountain. In the center of the fountain was a large marble statue of Saint Andrew. The statue was on a platform supported by angelic cherubs.

The statue of Saint Andrew was impressive, but the statue below the platform frequently caught the tourists' attention. It was a woman with drinking water pouring from her breasts. Gabe chuckled when his grandmother suggested it might be time to turn off the tap.

31

Gabe and his grandmother continued to stroll. They eventually left the piazza and circled the municipal building back to the car. Another car was now in the handicapped space; sure enough, it had a parking ticket on the window.

"I'm glad you warned me," he laughed. He opened his grandmother's door and helped her in. Gabe jumped into the driver's seat, and in a flash, they were headed to Sorrento.

Gabe found the drive was much like a video game or a bad driver's education film. He dodged an endless stream of pedestrians, buses, scooters, and parked vehicles. It required his constant vigilance, but he found it to be a fun challenge—all part of the Amalfi Coast experience.

The city of Sorrento formed the other bookend to the Amalfi Coast. On the way, they passed famous landmarks like the Arch Bridge, the Emerald Grotto, and the picturesque town of Praiano. Gabe could see that the passing scenery lifted his grandmother's spirits. The exquisite beauty of the terraced landscapes was stunning indeed.

The narrow, twisting road was slow going, and by the time they reached Positano, Gabe was hungry. He suggested they stop for breakfast. Francesca said it was a smashing idea and offered to pay.

Positano was built into a horseshoe-shaped curve in the mountain. It was terraced from sea level all the way to the top. Hotels, restaurants, and cafés lined the narrow streets that wound through town. The mountains on both sides of Positano curved forward, forming a natural bay in the sea below.

Gabe found a breakfast café in the middle of the horseshoe with a spectacular panoramic view. Once they were seated, he ordered two Sicilian cannoli and a mixture of fresh fruit to share. Francesca requested a pot of tea, and Gabe ordered coffee. He felt relaxed as they blended in with the tourists.

"Gram, I truly enjoyed our conversation last night. I was fascinated to hear about your life here and how you two met. It left me wanting to know more about Grandfather's family."

"Well," she replied, raising her eyebrows, "the Roslovsky story is most interesting—but also very tragic. Before World War I, the Roslovskys were a prominent, wealthy Russian family. It would be fair to say they were nobility."

"What? I didn't know that!" Gabe exclaimed.

"It's true. However, when the war broke out, everything changed. John's father was commissioned to the Russian Army and served as an officer. He commanded a unit sent to the western stretches of the Russian Empire. That territory is now Poland."

"What do you mean? Poland didn't exist?" he asked.

"That's right," she replied. "Many people don't know this, but the nation of Poland was erased from the map for more than a century. In the late 1700s, it was divided among Austria, Germany, and Russia. Poland had long been a territorial hot spot and wasn't restored as a nation until after World War I."

Francesca took a long sip of her tea. "In any case," she continued, "John's father, Ivan, was battling the Germans there at the same time my father was fighting them in the Italian Alps. Ivan Roslovsky witnessed even more bloodshed than my father. In 1915, the second year of the war, a massive German offensive captured the cities of Warsaw and Vilna, resulting in a million Russian casualties. It was unlike anything the world had ever seen.

"The Russian Army tried to mount a counter-offensive the next year but was completely unsuccessful. Your great-grandfather did his best to lead his unit, but morale was low, and despair had set in among the troops. Defections were rampant. John's father tried to rally his troops, but the men on the front lines knew their families were starving to death at home. This was especially true for Russia's peasants who'd been conscripted into the army by the millions."

Gabe cringed at the gruesome magnitude of the suffering.

"The suffering of the Russian people stoked revolutionary sentiment," she continued, "and in 1917, the Bolsheviks rose to power. They promised a better life for the working class, but that was a total lie. In the decades that followed, Russian life became a living hell as the true nature of Soviet communism became known."

My God! Gabe thought, *the birth of Revelation's first seven-headed monster. My great-grandfather, Ivan Roslovsky, lived through the birth of atheistic communism. Humanity had committed a gruesome atrocity against itself, a carnage foretold at the very foundation of Christianity, and my great-grandfather had been there.* Gabe wondered if his grandmother knew the meaning of the seven-headed monster.

"For the Roslovskys, it was clear from the beginning that the new regime would be disastrous for people of means," Francesca continued. "The Bolsheviks immediately seized their family business and all its assets, just like they stole every other piece of property in Russia. Collectivization for the benefit of the working class proved to be a complete lie, too. The only thing the working class got was fear, misery, and tyranny. Under Stalin, quotas were developed for every town, village, and city."

"Production quotas?" Gabe asked.

"They had those too, but I'm talking about human quotas," she said. "After Stalin rose to power, he was so paranoid that he set quotas for the number of people to be rounded up and executed in every Soviet city. Local party leaders generated lists of names, and everyone lived in terror. You never knew when that fateful knock might come in the middle of the night. Entire families disappeared. Millions, perhaps tens of millions, were murdered as enemies of the state. The entire Roslovsky clan perished at the hands of Stalin, everyone except Ivan."

"My God!" Gabe exclaimed.

He couldn't believe it. Not only did it look like his grandfather was murdered by the Masons, but his ancestors before him had been executed by communists. Gabe didn't like the sick feeling in his stomach, but he wanted to know more. He was fascinated by his family history.

"How did my great-grandfather manage to escape the same fate?" he asked.

"During the last year of the war, the Bolsheviks forged a separate peace agreement with Germany, which took Russia out of World War I. Part of the agreement reestablished Poland. It became an independent nation for the first time in more than a century. The agreement put Russia at peace with Germany, but the Russians were immediately plunged into civil war. It brought more death and brutality. Russian landowners, the so-called White Army, battled the Soviet Red Army and tried to stop the Bolsheviks. John's father found himself fighting his own countrymen, but of course, the Soviets prevailed. Ivan was without a home. I think that was around 1921."

"Is that when he went to Poland?" Gabe asked.

"Actually, he was already there. During the Russian Civil War, the Polish army reclaimed much of the eastern borderlands previously controlled by the Polish Lithuanian Commonwealth—essentially Lithuania, Belarus, and Ukraine. However, Lenin had other ideas. He saw Poland as a land bridge into Europe. He wanted that territory to be used as a corridor for spreading communism westward.

"War swept into Poland, and that's when your great-grandfather met Marianne Golec. Like many Polish women, Marianne was beautiful and had a strong Catholic identity. She and Ivan fell in love and married in 1919. Their oldest, my darling John, was born the next year."

Gabe absorbed the disquieting struggle of his family and was struck by a profound thought. He wouldn't be alive if Ivan Roslovsky hadn't survived the rise of Soviet communism—Revelation's first seven-headed monster. He would not have been born. Gabe let that sink in for a moment.

He looked up. "What happened after that?"

"Poland successfully repelled the Soviets the year John was born. The new Polish nation was preserved, but sadly, the Russian White Army wasn't as fortunate. The Bolsheviks tightened their grip on power, and the Soviet Reds emerged victorious. It was clear to John's father that returning to Russia would be impossible. He stayed in Poland and waited for the Bolsheviks to collapse, but of course, that day never came."

How could it have happened? Gabe thought. *Why did it happen? Could it happen again,* he wondered? It wasn't beyond the realm of imagination. Russia was still struggling to recover from its communist past. *And who was Vladimir Putin? Would the newly elected president of Russia advance the cause of freedom, or would he backslide into oppression, possibly reigniting a new Cold War?*

Gabe looked at his grandmother. "What did he do there? I mean, how did they afford to live?" he asked.

"He took a teaching position at the Warsaw School of Economics. It had a different name then, but it's Poland's oldest and most prestigious economics school. He and Marianne lived in Warsaw and had four more children—all daughters. They were quite happy there."

"So why did they move to America?" he asked.

"John's father was savvy about European politics. With Germany on Poland's western border and Russia on its eastern border, he correctly predicted that Poland would once again be crushed in the middle, this time by two ruthless, opposing egomaniacs. He watched Hitler rise to power in Germany while Stalin terrorized his people in Russia, so he was convinced it was time to disappear. He looked around Europe and didn't like what he saw. That's when he moved his family to America. He believed that American liberty and personal freedom were more important for his future than any hope of reclaiming the Roslovsky family wealth in Russia."

"So they became poor European immigrants?" Gabe asked.

"Well, not exactly," she replied. "Prior to World War I, the Roslovskys used their international business dealings to stash money in various European banks. It was still there when the war ended. It was nothing like the wealth they'd lost, but it was substantial. That money became the lifeline by which Ivan and his family survived the Great Depression."

Francesca ate several fresh peach slices and took another drink of tea before continuing. "So, in 1934, he took Marianne and their children and sailed to the United States. John was just shy of his fourteenth birthday. They arrived at Ellis Island but chose not to stay in New York. Ivan spoke English and landed a position teaching economics at Georgetown University. They settled in Alexandria, Virginia. He immediately started the process to obtain full US citizenship. That fall, John was enrolled at Georgetown Preparatory High School.

"John felt a great sense of pride when he moved to America. He was inspired by his father's patriotic encouragement to embrace the ideals of the new country. Ivan insisted that John study English from the time he was eight years old. It wasn't easy, but John managed. By the time he entered high school, he was fluent. Like his father, John was intelligent, and he made up for whatever he lacked in natural ability with tenacity and hard work."

"How did he end up in the army?" Gabe asked.

"John went to Georgetown in the fall of 1938 to study mathematics and logic."

"Hmm, that's interesting," he said. "Anna went there, too."

"Really?" she said. "I didn't know that. Things started out great for John, but Germany invaded Poland the next year. He tried to cut his studies short and enlist, but his lack of citizenship kept him out of the US Army until 1941. That's when full citizenship was granted to the entire Roslovsky family. John joined the Army in December, right after graduation. He graduated on Saturday and was commissioned the very next Monday."

"Wasn't that when Pearl Harbor was bombed?" he asked.

"It was, and when America entered World War II, John was ready. Even though the Japanese had attacked the US, John's skills were more useful in Europe. He spoke fluent Russian, Polish, and English and was assigned to the intelligence branch after receiving his commission. Second Lieutenant John Roslovsky became a rising star in the US Army."

"Lucky for you," Gabe said.

"It was lucky for me—and you too," she said with a relaxed grin.

"How did he end up in Italy?" he asked.

"He spent the first part of 1942 training in the art of intelligence gathering. In June, he was sent to London, where his training was put into action. His first assignment was advance preparation for the Allied landings in North Africa later that year. That took him to places like Tunisia and Morocco, where he gathered intelligence on German troop strength and underground resistance levels.

"The following year, he was sent to Moscow for secret briefings for the first time. He was a natural for that assignment because of his language skills. Those missions continued for the remainder of the war, resulting in the fortuitous stopovers in Rome."

Just then, a young waiter brought the check. Gabe reached for it, but Francesca intercepted it. "This one's on me," she said with a warm, grandmotherly smile. "Let's pay and get going. Capri will be exquisite on a day like today."

"Sounds good to me," Gabe said with a wink. "I've been told it's incredible."

They returned to the car and meandered through the narrow streets of Positano until they reached the main coastal road. Gabe turned left and headed for Sorrento. He veered toward the mountain pass at the Saint Agata fork at his grandmother's urging. She said it was the better route.

The road began to climb from the coast. When they reached the summit, the sea reappeared on the other side. The illusion surprised Gabe. He didn't know it, but the Sorrento end of the Amalfi Coast was a peninsula. They'd just crossed from one side to the other. His grandmother was right—the views were amazing as they descended from the top.

He could see Sorrento below them and the glistening city of Naples across the bay. It certainly looked better from a distance than it had up close. Sorrento, on the other hand, was fabulously beautiful. It stood in stark contrast to Salerno. It catered to tourists and served as Capri Island's main port of call.

Sorrento was abuzz with midmorning activity when they arrived, and like everywhere else in Italy, people drove like maniacs. Gabe darted around busses, scooters, and pedestrians as they made their way to the dock. The port was in the city center at the base of two-hundred-foot cliffs.

They followed a narrow road to the water's edge built of ancient paving stones. It was bordered by steep, brick walls blackened by soot from years of exhaust from buses climbing and descending the twisted switchbacks. Their tires generated a rhythmic clacking sound as they rolled across the stones. It reminded Gabe of when he clipped a playing card to his bicycle spokes as a child.

At the bottom of the road, a parking garage materialized on the left. It was carved into the wall of the cliff and had a small, single-door opening. They pulled inside and parked. Gabe locked the car, and they walked the short distance from the garage to the ticket counter, purchased tickets, and prepared to board.

Sorrento's harbor was picturesque. Colorful sailing vessels of all types were moored at the docks. Gabe saw a schooner anchored in deeper water that was perhaps a hundred feet in length. Fancy hotels lined the cliffs. *You could not travel here on a tight budget,* he thought.

The boats to Capri were more like an extension of the bus system rather than cruise ships. They operated every hour. Each boat held several hundred passengers for the thirty-minute ride to Capri. They made their way onto the vessel and found comfortable seats inside. An exterior deck was available, but it was standing room only. A busload of Japanese tourists arrived just before departure and descended upon the hydrofoil, and they filled most of the remaining seats.

Gabe checked his surroundings—no sign of anything strange. They were safely nestled among the tourists. The morning sun streamed into their eyes as the boat backed out of its berth and turned toward Capri. Gabe adjusted the plaid, rainbow-colored curtains.

"I'm going to get some fresh air," Gabe said.

"I'll be here," she said and smiled.

He headed outside to have a look at the upper deck and walked the length of the boat—no suspicious faces and, more importantly, no familiar ones. The ride was smooth, and ten minutes into the trip, they began to hydrofoil. The vessel settled into a rhythmic motion. Gabe positioned himself in the sun and felt its healing warmth on his cheeks as the boat glided across the sea. That and the wind blowing in his face made him feel alive again.

They sped past the end of the peninsula into open water. The coastline was gorgeous. Large cliffs rose from the sea in front of them. It was the magnificent Capri Island. He checked his watch, and despite Italy's general transportation chaos, the boat was on time to the minute. He headed back inside to sit with his grandmother until their arrival.

Capri was an island of limestone-exposed cliffs covered with deciduous vegetation. Homes and hotels were strewn about the hillsides. The port was charming, full of small skiffs and sailboats, and brightly painted. There was also one large ferry from Napoli. The hydrofoil reduced its speed and pulled into the harbor. Gabe and his grandmother gathered their belongings and disembarked. They shuffled along with the crowd toward a bustling piazza at the end of the dock.

The piazza reminded Gabe of a Moroccan bazaar with colorful tents and street vendors everywhere. With the harbor behind them and the cliffs in front, the place was truly enchanting. He saw couples waiting in a long line in the middle of the bazaar to make arrangements for open-air taxis. The scene exuded romance, and for a moment, he imagined bringing Anna there.

You weren't allowed to bring your own vehicles to the island, so transportation was by bus or taxi. The buses were small and crowded, so taxis were a much better choice. Gabe stood at the end of the queue and found himself negotiating with a man whose job it was to make such deals.

"Signore, would you like a tour of the island?" the man asked with a pleasant but businesslike demeanor. "One hundred twenty-five euros for four hours."

Gabe turned to his grandmother, and she nodded enthusiastically.

"It's truly worth it, Gabe. The sights are stunning. My treat," she said.

The man put their bags in the trunk of the first available taxi. The driver helped Francesca into the back seat, and Gabe got in on the other side. They felt like celebrities touring Capri in the back of an open-air limo.

Gabe suggested they drop their bags at the hotel and check-in before taking the tour. The driver nodded and immediately climbed a steep incline to Hotel Caesar Augustus. When they pulled up in front, Francesca leaned over and smiled. "This is my treat, too."

She and John had stayed there before. It was a fabulous five-star hotel high above the sea with a spectacular view. Gabe arranged for adjoining rooms. The bellhop took their bags to their rooms, and they set out to tour the island.

One of the first stops was atop Mount Tiberio, where they walked among the ruins of Villa Jovis, the largest of the twelve Roman villas on Capri. From there, Tiberius Caesar ruled the Roman Empire from 27 to 37 AD. The massive structure covered an area of almost two acres. It was on a terraced landscape built into the rocky, rugged countryside. The site was rediscovered in 1938, and they were still working on its archeological restoration.

From there, they went to Piazza della Vittoria, located at the base of a chairlift that climbed to the highest point on Capri. The lift featured hundreds of single-seat chairs that rose to the summit, almost two thousand feet above the surrounding sea. Francesca insisted they ride it to the top "for old times' sake."

Amazed at her spunk, Gabe put his grandmother on the lift ahead of him. He couldn't help but laugh as she took off in the rickety chair, bound for the top. She looked completely content with her purse in her lap and her legs dangling in the air. She'd been to the top before and knew what a delight was in store for Gabe.

The trip took twelve breathtaking minutes. Gabe stepped off the lift and was not disappointed. The scenery was staggering. The blue water reflected a perfectly cloudless sky. He could see the mainland clearly, and now he understood why the water appeared to change sides as they crossed over the top of the peninsula.

Down the right side of the peninsula was the Amalfi Coast. It stretched into the distance. On the left side of the peninsula was the Bay of Naples. He could see Sorrento on the near side and Naples in the distance. Sailing vessels of all kinds moved in the bay and around the island. Cargo ships, passenger ships, commuter boats, and individual pleasure craft dotted the seascape. The sight was truly awe-inspiring.

He turned a slow, 360-degree revolution. As he did, he thought about how men had traveled these seas for centuries. That expanse of time produced a feeling of awe and made him feel incredibly small. He imagined men sailing the Mediterranean Sea before radios and modern navigation. He imagined the Roman naval fleet dominating the region and sailing past these very same mountain cliffs.

Then he was struck by another thought that gave him the same sense of wonder he'd experienced at Mass that morning. Saint Peter had sailed past that very place on his way to Rome to establish Christianity in the heart of the Roman Empire. It was one thing to read about in history books. It was quite another to see it firsthand. Gabe was seeing the same sights Saint Peter had seen two thousand years earlier.

Francesca was looking at him, and she had a huge smile on her lips. "You look just like John did when he saw this place for the first time," she said.

Gabe embraced his grandmother.

She took his arm. "Let's see what kind of trouble we can get into now, shall we?" she said with delight as she steered him back toward the chairlift.

32

Zach Beckett had just finished lunch when his phone rang. "Beckett here."

"Sir, we've finished the toxicology screen. Your hunch was correct. Mr. Roslo was poisoned. We found tetrodotoxin."

"Tetrodotoxin—what the hell is tetrodotoxin?" he asked.

"TTX for short. It's an extremely potent neurotoxin found primarily in pufferfish."

"Pufferfish? You think he died from eating poisonous fish?" Beckett asked.

"No," his contact replied. "Japan's the only place crazy enough to serve pufferfish. You won't find it anywhere in Italy. Even the Japanese require training and a special license to reduce toxicity levels. Still, several hundred people a year get sick from the strange delicacy. Half of those cases are fatal. Only an insane person would put it on the menu. This was no accident. Mr. Roslo was deliberately poisoned."

"You're certain?" Beckett asked.

"Absolutely. TTX is one hundred times more lethal than black widow venom and ten thousand times deadlier than cyanide. One to two milligrams of purified TTX can be lethal. We calculated fifty milligrams in Roslo's bloodstream, yet nothing in his digestive tract, so he didn't eat it. We also found a puncture mark on his neck. He didn't have a chance."

"How does it work?" Beckett asked.

"It blocks the voltage-gated sodium channels on the surface of nerve membranes."

"In English!" Beckett demanded.

"Sorry," his contact replied. "The brain sends messages to the body using electrical impulses. They instruct our muscles how to behave—for example, the heart. Sodium and potassium ions stimulate nerve cells to produce the right responses. Nerve cells need both to function properly, but TTX attaches to the sodium ions. It prevents them from reaching their destination. Simply put, the entire message-sending process shuts down, paralysis sets in, and death is assured when the vital organs stop functioning."

"Did he suffer?" Beckett asked.

"It's hard to say. Symptoms appear almost immediately. Death can occur in as little as twenty minutes. But consider this: even though the victim becomes totally paralyzed, he's frequently conscious and lucid to the very end. Some victims survive up to eight hours, but Mr. Roslo wouldn't have lasted nearly that long due to these concentrations."

"Damn!" Beckett exclaimed. "Frozen stiff, unable to move or speak, yet completely in touch with his faculties. He would've known he was dying, yet unable to do a thing about it." Beckett paused for a moment then asked, "Does TTX have any commercial use?"

"None that I'm aware of."

"Terrorism or weaponry?" Beckett probed.

"No terrorist use, but Japan tried to weaponize it during World War II. They tested it on Chinese prisoners at Unit 731 but never deployed it on the battlefield."

"What about now?" Beckett asked.

"It isn't produced in large enough quantities to use in modern weapons—at least as far as we know. But someone coming up with a dose of fifty milligrams is a stunning development. With enough volume, it would make a terrifying weapon. Almost nothing is known about its inhalation toxicity, and TTX has no known antidote."

"Anything else?" Beckett asked as if he hadn't heard enough already.

"Well, yes, actually. It turns out that tetrodotoxin is used in the practice of voodoo, both in Haiti and Western Africa. TTX is an ingredient in zombie powder. I guess you could say it turns people into zombies." The technician chuckled at his own weak humor.

"Not funny," Beckett snapped. "John Roslo was a personal friend of mine."

"Sorry, sir. Please accept my apology. I didn't mean to be insensitive. But the whole thing is pretty weird. Of all the things a person could use to poison someone, TTX would fall way down the list. It's potent but extremely rare. This might sound strange, but do you think someone was trying to send a message—a really twisted message?"

Beckett exhaled. "Perhaps that's not as strange as you think. Make sure the autopsy is properly concealed, and hold onto the body until you hear back from me."

"Will do, sir."

Beckett hung up and pondered the possibilities. If the use of TTX had indeed been a statement, it suggested they were dealing with sophisticated people. It also meant that the national security threat took on a new characterization. It was already at the highest possible level but was now expanding into strange and unfamiliar territory.

His work in Rome was not yet complete. Beckett picked up his cell phone and dialed NSA headquarters. When the voice answered, he asked for his head of special ops, code name Signal Fire.

"One moment, please, Mr. Beckett," the voice said. He was placed on hold.

33

As Gabe and Francesca descended from Monte Solaro, he thought about the Caesars and their empire, which had been dead for a long time. The mighty had fallen, but little old ladies were still praying and worshipping at Saint Andrew's Cathedral, the final resting place of a poor fisherman crucified by the empire. He contemplated the irony.

Gabe helped his grandmother to a bench at the edge of the piazza when they reached the bottom. Their driver greeted them a few moments later.

Francesca turned toward Gabe. "Are you ready to continue, my dear?" she asked with a smile.

They stepped back into the taxi and completed their four-hour tour of the island. Afterward, they were hungry and decided to have a late lunch. The driver dropped them off at the hotel around 3:00 in the afternoon.

The dining room was traditionally appointed with heavy floral fabric chairs and tablecloths. The drapes had been drawn back to let in streams of sunlight. Gabe noticed floating dust motes reflecting in the rays. The hostess showed them to their table.

A waiter appeared with water and suggested the house wine. They ordered a light lunch of mixed salad and panini. Once their salads were served, Gabe reopened the family history conversation. He hoped to learn more about his grandfather's work.

"So what did Grandfather do after the war—you know, when he brought his new bride to America?"

Francesca smiled at the recollection of being a young bride.

"Well, John was still in the Army, so we didn't come to America right away. He was sent to Berlin after the war to monitor Soviet radio traffic. Relations between the Soviet Union and America were souring, and Stalin was reneging on his wartime promises. Everyone was concerned the war would flare up again, this time against the Soviets. John's new work grew in importance as the Cold War became icier. He ended up battling the red menace the rest of his career."

"What about you?" Gabe asked.

"I joined him in Berlin six months later, the longest six months of my life. I was so happy when my travel visa was finally approved. We met at the train station, and I was never so proud as at that moment. John was there in full dress uniform, a dozen red roses hidden behind his back. It was wonderful," she said. Her eyes grew misty.

"Life in Berlin was difficult after the war," she said, "but not impossible. We were buoyed by the prospects of peace the first couple of years. However, life took a decided turn for the worse in 1948 when the Soviets blocked access to the city. West Berlin was an island completely surrounded by Soviet-controlled East Germany. The Soviets had closed all road and rail traffic into the city. That was the beginning of the Cold War as we came to understand it.

"How did you survive?" Gabe asked.

"The entire city relied on airlifts. American, British, and French military units operated flights around the clock for nearly a year. They brought in food, medicine, everything. It was strangely surreal. There we were, defending Germany, our enemy in both world wars, against Russia, our ally during both world wars. It was a very tense time and very dangerous. Thankfully, they released the chokehold in 1949. John was finally sent back to the States a few months later, and our new life in America began."

The waiter quietly placed the panini in front of them and left.

"Is that when you settled in Alexandria?" Gabe asked.

"It was. We moved there and rented an apartment near his parents. John was assigned to an Army intelligence unit in Washington, a forerunner to the NSA. He was a fierce anti-communist. As the Cold War grew more serious, he shortened our surname from Roslovsky to Roslo. His Russian name belied his patriotic love for America. It was the era of McCarthyism, and he saw no reason to bring added suspicion upon himself. He was an American and wanted to be thought of as an American."

"How did his father feel about that?"

"He was okay with it. Ivan realized that any hope of ever returning to Russia was gone."

"So, when did Grandfather join the NSA?" Gabe asked.

"In the mid-1950s. The agency had been formed a few years earlier to coordinate all US communications security and cryptology activities, both military and non-military. He resigned his Army commission and joined as a cryptologist. The NSA was a perfect fit for John. He was an information junkie. He loved to solve riddles and puzzles. He searched for the hidden meaning in things. He was a master at spotting the connections between seemingly unrelated facts, and he found them in the most unexpected places. Those skills served him well at the NSA," she said with a smile.

"Your grandfather was also pragmatic about how things worked. I told him he should have more faith, but in his world, 'the ultimate questions were decided by the people with the most money, the biggest guns, and the best information.' That expression defined his worldview. He used it all the time. He said it was even reflected in the NSA insignia."

"How so?" Gabe asked. He was intrigued.

"The official NSA emblem is an eagle, which symbolizes courage, authority, and supreme power. Those attributes reflect the economic and military strength of the United States," she said.

Gabe thought back to his conversation with Anna. Washington, the capital of the most powerful nation on Earth, was also the seat of global Masonic influence. It was an apt description indeed.

"The eagle is clutching a silver key," she continued. "That's also symbolic. The NSA holds the key to national security, protecting America by gaining access to secrets. Your grandfather spent his entire career gaining access to Soviet secrets. The emblem designer borrowed the symbolism from Saint Peter, possessor of the keys to the kingdom. Your grandfather liked to tease me about that one."

Gabe felt a strange shiver run down his spine. The world of secrets was a twisted web indeed. *How many Americans knew the NSA had patterned its insignia after such an overtly Christian theme?* he wondered.

Secrecy, power, authority—all vested in the hands of men. Would humanity use them wisely, or would they be used for destruction again? History offered little consolation. And the Revelation prophecies foretold an impending evil worse than Hitler, worse than Stalin, worse than anything in the history of the world.

Francesca interrupted his thoughts. "John's monitoring efforts expanded in the 1960s to include Eastern Europe, China, North Korea, Cuba, and Vietnam—all victims of the spread of communism. Vietnam was the most galling. Johnson and Nixon knew the war was unwinnable, but they presented

Vietnam as a line in the sand in defense of Western freedom. In the end, it cost John his son."

Conversations about Alex Roslo were rare between Gabe and his grandmother. In recent years, they'd spoken about his father only a handful of times. Francesca looked out the window, a distant expression on her face.

"Your father was never the same after he left home. He went to Vietnam as a patriot and returned a bitter, angry young man. Like so many others, he filled his life with drugs and alcohol. The effects were already evident when he returned after his first tour of duty. After his second tour, he joined the antiwar protests and openly despised your grandfather for his work at the NSA. He even accused John of murdering innocent women and children."

Gabe lowered his head. Francesca extended her hand to take hold of his.

"Your grandfather stood his ground," she continued. "He'd seen the atrocities committed by the Soviets and knew it was necessary to stop their aggression. But your father saw something else. He'd witnessed firsthand the endless American bombing of Vietnamese and Cambodian civilians. That and the loss of so many American soldiers were bitter pills to swallow, especially when it was later revealed that US Defense Secretary Robert McNamara knew as early as 1965 that the war was unwinnable. A lot of good men were lost in Vietnam, even the ones who lived through it and came home. Your father fell deeper and deeper into drug and alcohol abuse. In the end, your mother moved on without him. I wish things had been different, Gabe. I truly wish they'd been different."

He felt a lump form in his throat and didn't respond. Francesca knew his feelings. Tears welled up in her eyes. She felt the same void in her heart—a pain that was unbearable at times. Few pains are more acute than the suffering experienced by a mother who loses her son.

"Your grandfather wrestled with his feelings," she said. "He hated losing Alex. They had a good relationship before Vietnam. John was proud when your father shipped out to defend freedom, but he couldn't accept his son turning against America, the nation that helped rescue Europe from the Nazis."

For the first time, Gabe understood the great divide between his father and grandfather. Gabe felt bitter toward his father, but perhaps there was more to the story. His father was yet another Roslo victimized by Revelation's seven-headed monsters.

Francesca smiled tenderly. "Gabriel, somewhere deep down inside, I know your father loves you. If only he could escape the demons that have hold of him."

Gabe looked up and smiled back. There was a long pause. He kept his emotions in check.

"Perhaps we should go," she said finally. "I wouldn't mind a little rest."

He nodded, paid the tab, and escorted his grandmother to her third-floor room. It was plush, spacious, and beautifully decorated. As with most places on the Amalfi Coast, the room was bright and cheerful. It had whitewashed walls with yellow and blue upholstered furniture and drapes. The windows were full length with tall, narrow, French-style doors that opened onto a balcony overlooking the sea. Gabe and Francesca stepped outside. The balcony was tiny, with a table and chairs for two, and was just large enough for them to stand against the wrought-iron railing and take in the sea air.

"It's beautiful, isn't it, Gabe?" she sighed.

"It is," he said. He checked his watch. "If you don't mind, I'd like to get in a workout and do some reading. Why don't you get some rest, and we'll meet later for dinner?"

"That would be perfect," she replied.

He left and went to his adjoining room. It was excellent. The corner room gave him a view of the sea in two directions. He opened the balcony door and stepped outside. The balcony was around the corner from his grandmother's. He took in the sights. Birds flew about, and he heard the sea crashing on the rocks far below. The sun was now well into the western sky.

He moved back inside and changed into his workout gear. After locking his great-grandfather's diary into the room safe, he checked the common doorway between their rooms. It was also locked.

He headed out and found the spa and exercise facilities outside in a secluded and tranquil corner of the hotel's clifftop garden. He was alone but surrounded by sweetly scented lavender and rosemary bushes. He attacked the StairMaster, and an hour later, he returned to his room drenched in sweat.

He threw his key on the table, wiped the sweat from his face, and pulled a bottle of water from the minibar. He downed it and headed for the shower. That's when he saw it—a knife. A butcher knife had been stabbed through his bed pillow.

He walked closer and lifted the pillow. The knife's serrated nine-inch blade had pierced a sheet of paper, pinning a handwritten note to the pillow.

34

The avenue outside the Vatican was suffocating with late afternoon pedestrian traffic. Crowds had gathered throughout the day as word leaked out. The pontiff's health had taken a turn for the worse. The sound of traffic and sirens blaring punctuated the atmosphere. Vehicles vied for space on the narrow thoroughfare, and the smell of diesel fumes and warm, rushing bodies filled the air. Beckett dove into an opening between a baby stroller and a man's briefcase when his phone rang.

"Beckett here," he said. He strained to hear the voice at the other end of the line. "Wait a minute. Let me get out of the noise." He ducked into a pizzeria. The sounds on the street became muffled as the door closed behind him. "Beckett here," he repeated.

"Agent Beckett, Signal Fire. Please confirm," the voice said.

"Three smoke rings signify a talented smoker," Beckett replied.

"Confirmed. We have information that one of Allbritton's ships has entered the port of Salerno and has docked at the shipyard."

"Salerno?" Beckett questioned. He was alarmed by the coincidence.

"That's right. Satellite recon has confirmed."

"Name?" Beckett asked.

"*Ruse of the Sea*, flying under a Danish flag. It arrived last evening. No on-loading or offloading so far, but it fits the profile. Should we send local agents to investigate?"

"Not yet," Beckett cautioned him. "Things are getting stirred up here at the Vatican, so keep it quiet for now. I want to check this one out myself. I'll call you when I have something. Just keep me posted with any developments. And Signal Fire," he added, "thanks for the heads-up."

Beckett hung up and walked to the counter. He ordered a slice of pizza and a soda. *One thing that always tastes the same worldwide is Coke*, he mused. He scarfed down the pizza, dropped several euros on the counter, and walked out the door. He folded into the crush of the crowd and headed straight for his car. *Next stop, Salerno,* he thought. Too much was at stake to allow any interference now.

35

Gabe ripped the note from the pillow and read the message. It had been scrawled in red lipstick:

> Gabriel Roslo, stop your search. Go back to America.
> There's nothing here for you but agony and heartache.
> You're being watched!
> WSB

Gabe's legs felt weak, and he immediately thought of his grandmother. He ran to the adjoining door—still locked. His heart raced. Unsure what he'd find on the other side, he composed himself. He took a deep breath and knocked. A moment later, he heard his grandmother's voice.

"Gabe, is that you?"

"It is," he replied.

"Finished with your workout already?" she asked as she opened the door between their rooms.

Gabe made a quick visual sweep of the room. Everything appeared to be in order.

"What's the matter, dear? You look pale. Are you all right?" she asked.

"Ah—oh, I'm fine. I just wanted to check on you." He forced a smile to mask his apprehension and walked into her room. "Has anyone stopped by?" he asked.

She shook her head. "Were you expecting someone?"

"No, but I noticed your deadbolt and safety chain were unlocked," he replied. He walked across the room and locked them. "Always a good idea."

"If you insist, but it's perfectly safe here," she said.

"Did anyone call?" he asked.

"No. Gabe, are you sure you're all right?"

"Yes, of course. I just need a shower," he replied. "I'm a little tired from my workout." He changed the subject. "When do you want to have dinner?"

"Around 7:30, perhaps?"

"Perfect," he said in reply. He headed back to the adjoining doorway. "Do you mind if we keep this door closed until dinner? I'd like to do some reading."

"That would be fine," she said, smiling.

Gabe closed the adjoining door and exhaled a huge sigh of relief. *Thank God she's all right,* he thought to himself. Then he remembered the diary and was at the safe in seconds. He entered the code and turned the handle, and the door swung open with a pop. The diary was right where he'd left it. He quickly thumbed through the pages. It was still intact. He put it back in the safe, closed the door, and reset the lock.

He looked around the room. *How could an intruder have entered?* he wondered. There were only two possibilities—the front door or the balcony. He'd left the balcony door open. The curtains danced in the breeze.

He stepped onto the balcony and looked in every direction. There were no easy footholds to climb up from below. That would've been a challenge, even for him. It was a straight drop to the rocks hundreds of feet below. The distance from one floor to the next was considerable, so the intruder most likely dropped in from above. It would've been daring but certainly possible. Gabe could've performed the feat easily. He was on the third floor from the top. There were two rooms above. *Whoever it was might still be around,* he thought.

He stepped back into the room, locked the balcony door, and grabbed his room key. He then did a quick search of the room before leaving. He looked in the closets, in the bathroom, under the bed, and in the drawers of his armoire. Nothing was out of place. The note was written in red lipstick, which suggested a woman was involved. He read it one more time and shoved it into his pocket.

Gabe cracked the door and checked up and down the hall—not a soul in sight. He went to the stairwell and climbed one flight. An elderly couple waited at the elevator. After they entered, the fourth floor was deserted, too. With no one in sight, Gabe pressed his ear to the door of room #426. He could hear a voice, a woman. It sounded like she was on the phone. She spoke, and then there was silence followed by more speaking—all in Italian.

Gabe exhaled, braced himself, and gave the door three firm knocks. The voice sped up and then stopped. Silence. He could hear someone moving about inside the room. Finally, the door opened—but just a crack. The door chain was still engaged.

"Excuse me. Do you speak English?" Gabe asked.

"A little," she replied. She held her hand up and gestured with her thumb and forefinger. She was wearing a hotel bathrobe and had a towel wrapped around her head. Apparently, she was just out of the shower. She was in her early thirties, curvaceous, and incredibly gorgeous.

"May I help you?" she asked. Her expression was polite, but she was obviously inconvenienced.

"I was…"

Just as Gabe started to speak, a toddler appeared at her feet, perhaps two years old. The little girl yanked on her robe and asked for something in Italian. The woman smiled, answered the child, and did her best to maintain her modesty, all the while remaining polite toward the strange man at her door.

"I'm sorry. I have the wrong room," Gabe said.

She tipped her head, grinned, and pushed the door shut. Gabe proceeded to the fifth floor. The entire floor was a gigantic master suite, but the door was propped open when he arrived. He stepped into the room and saw a maid cleaning the bathroom.

"Excuse me," he began. Evidently, he startled her.

She turned around and shook her head. "No English, no English," she repeated several times.

Gabe motioned to the balcony door, which stood open. The maid nodded and went back to her work. He walked to the balcony. He determined that a person could've rappelled from that room, but there was no evidence—no rope, nothing amiss.

He went back inside and motioned to the housekeeper to inquire about the guest who'd checked out. No luck. She gave him a blank shrug, but one thing was certain: at 250 pounds, it was clear it hadn't been her. Gabe smiled and backed out of the room.

He went down to the front desk. *Certainly, they'll have the name,* he thought, and he asked who'd occupied the fifth floor.

"I'm sorry, Mr. Roslo. We're not allowed to give out that type of information."

"Can you tell me when he or she checked out?" Gabe asked.

"One moment." He checked the computer. "It looks like she checked out thirty minutes ago."

"So it *was* a woman," Gabe mumbled to himself.

The desk attendant made no comment, but the disapproving look on his face confirmed that he'd said too much.

"I need to know that guest's name," Gabe demanded.

"I'm sorry, sir. I simply cannot. Our policies do not allow us to share that type of information."

"You don't understand. It's important," Gabe pleaded.

"I'm sorry. There's nothing I can do."

Gabe huffed in disgust and headed for the elevator. How hard could it be to learn the name of that guest? Surely, someone could find out. Maybe Lorenzo—*a courtesy extended to a fellow innkeeper?* he thought. He returned to his room and immediately called the Amalfi Hotel. After seven long rings, Lorenzo finally answered.

"Amalfi Hotel, how may I help you?"

Gabe could tell Lorenzo was out of breath. "This is Gabe."

"I'm so glad you finally called me back. I left that message for you this morning."

"What message?" Gabe asked, "I didn't have any messages."

"I left one at the hotel," Lorenzo said. "You should've received it when you checked in. I told them it was urgent."

"No one gave me anything," Gabe replied. A suspicious look crossed his face. "What was it?"

"I received an urgent call this morning from Gino Caruso. He wants to meet you for lunch tomorrow in Salerno. He said he has important information about your grandfather's death. He thinks he knows the people responsible but wants to tell you in person. Can you make it?"

Gabe felt a chill run down his spine.

"Of course."

"He wants us all there," Lorenzo continued.

"All who?" Gabe asked.

"You, me, the Castriottis—the whole wine time group except Andre Gotto. His fishing boat's been chartered for the day."

"What time does he want to meet?" Gabe asked.

"That depends on you. What time can you be back?"

"If we sail back in the morning, I can be in Amalfi by noon," Gabe said. "I'll take my grandmother to her cousins' house and meet you at the hotel."

"Good, we'll leave from here," Lorenzo replied. "We can drive together." He paused a moment then asked. "Have you heard from Zach Beckett?"

"No," Gabe replied. "Have you?"

"Nothing at all. But if I do, I'll give him the number for the Caesar and have him contact you at the hotel."

"Please do," he said. Gabe paused. "I have a favor to ask. Could you possibly find out a name for me? I need to know the name of the guest who checked out of the rooftop master suite earlier today."

Lorenzo exhaled hard. "I'll see what I can do," he said. "It would've been easy in the old days, but it's harder now. I still know people, though. I'll see what I can do."

"Thank you, Lorenzo. I'll see you tomorrow."

Gabe had no intention of mentioning this new message to Lorenzo. He hung up. Why did Caruso invite the whole group? He thought it could be a trap, but it wasn't his style to run and hide. The meeting was a crucial development. At present, it was his only lead to finding out whether the Masons killed his grandfather.

Gabe opened the adjoining door to keep a closer watch on his grandmother. She'd been napping. The sound of the door awakened her.

"Sorry for waking you, Gram. I was thinking that I'd like to take an early morning boat back to the mainland tomorrow."

"Why?" she asked.

Gabe looked away, not sure what to say. A long, uncomfortable silence ensued. Finally, a ferry whistle blew in the distance. He looked at her.

"Things have been strange since Grandfather passed away," he said. "I'm not sure what's going on, but it would be best if you were back at your cousins' house. I'd like you to stay there until I get it sorted out."

Francesca's eyes widened at his words. She walked to the window and stared out at the sea.

"Gram, what is it?" he asked.

She turned and faced him. "I know what you mean. Your grandfather acted strange when we arrived in Amalfi. For one thing, he went to Mass with me—twice. He never went to Mass, so that was unusual. He was also agitated before we made the trip. I wasn't sure what to make of it, but I learned long ago not to ask. So, I didn't. But something was definitely amiss."

Francesca had been a constant source of support for her husband throughout their lives. She'd long given up on senseless worry, even though she knew his work was dangerous. She was a strong woman, and Gabe knew she possessed an interesting character trait. She almost always knew more than she let on.

"Enough. If you need to get back early, then that's what we'll do," she said.

Gabe reached over and hugged her. "Thanks for everything."

"Now, tell me about Anna," she said with a wink.

"Let's order room service, and I'll fill you in," he suggested.

36

Dinner was delivered to Francesca's room around 7:45 p.m. Gabe pulled out a chair for his grandmother, and they both took a seat. The room service attendant removed the covers from their plates and asked if everything was to their liking. It was.

Gabe placed his napkin on his lap and began to explain his relationship with Anna Castriotti.

"After I learned that I needed to go to Rome, Paolo called Anna and asked her to meet me at the train station. He said she'd take me wherever I needed to go, which she did. She let me stay in a vacant apartment in the complex she manages. Then she drove us back to Amalfi. It sure beat the train," he said with a laugh.

Francesca's eyes sparkled.

"She's a fascinating woman," he continued. "She's smart and confident, and it goes without saying that she is beautiful. It's kind of strange, really. We come from totally different backgrounds, but there's a connection. I told her I originally planned to be here for six weeks, but it's all up in the air now. We'll see what happens. But don't be surprised if I come back here to finish my trip."

"That wouldn't surprise me in the least," she teased.

Gabe had said enough about Anna to satisfy her curiosity. He had a more pressing need to learn about his grandfather's recent activities. So, he asked her point blank what she knew about his latest project.

A look of apprehension washed over her face. "As you know, it was never my place to ask John about his work," she began, "but this project was different. It dealt with the spiritual realm. It went way beyond the usual scope of his work and involved things that were uncomfortably strange to him. So, on a few occasions, we violated our 'don't ask, don't tell' policy."

"What was he doing?" he asked.

"He was working on a project for Zach Beckett—official business. You know as well as I that he never really wanted to retire. They said it was budget cuts, but I think he was pushed out because of his age. Anyway, after he left, he maintained regular contact with Zach. It was an outlet for him. John's body might have aged, but his mind was still at the top of its game. They had lunch every couple of weeks. It kept his mind sharp, and Zach benefitted from your grandfather's keen insights."

She paused and took a sip of tea. "One day, he came home from lunch with Zach and asked me what I knew about Marian apparitions. Now, that was a topic I knew something about! I dug out a videotape, *Marian Apparitions of the 20th Century*, a film narrated by Ricardo Montalban. John teased me about it at first. I remember him walking down the hall saying, 'De plane, de plane,' but after he watched the film, he was intrigued—if not powerfully moved. The film chronicled some of the places where the Virgin Mary appeared during the century and warned people of the consequences of turning away from God—places like Yugoslavia, which subsequently collapsed into civil war, or Rwanda, which saw a seventh of its population wiped out by genocide a few years later.

"The film also connected with the same Cold War issues he'd tackled during his career. The connections between religion and politics had him stymied. The warnings were simple but direct. God loved humanity. God had not abandoned humanity. However, if humanity didn't turn away from its present wickedness, human suffering would only grow, and chastisement would inevitably follow as a consequence. Just look at the world. It's all coming true."

Gabe knew she was right and wondered how much she knew about the Masons and their role. He also saw a pattern emerging. His grandfather was investigating Marian apparitions for Zach Beckett. His investigations led him to the Vatican. Along the way, he discovered something that led to his murder, something that perhaps stretched into the bowels of hell itself.

Francesca continued. "As with everything else in his life, John poured his heart into this project. It occupied a great deal of his time, and it struck a chord with him. For most of his life, your grandfather struggled mightily with the big questions: Where do we come from? Where are we going? Why do people suffer so much? That last one especially bothered him. He always questioned why there was so much suffering in the world. I think his doubts were related to his sister."

"Which one?" he asked.

Francesca bit her lip. "His twin," she replied.

"His twin? What do you mean his twin?" Gabe was dumbfounded.

"John had a twin sister, Maria. He never ever spoke about her. None of the Roslovskys did—not for decades. We never even told Alex, but it's true nonetheless."

Gabe was stunned. "Does my mother know about her?"

Francesca shook her head.

"Why?"

"It was John's way of trying to forget a painful, awful memory," she said.

"What memory? What happened?" Gabe asked.

She pursed her lips and paused to think. "It feels strange to betray a decades-old family secret, but I guess it's okay to tell you now. John's sister was devoutly faithful and heavily influenced by their mother's Catholic faith. When Maria turned thirteen, she declared her desire to enter the convent. John's mother was delighted."

"At thirteen?" Gabe was incredulous.

"It wasn't at all unusual for a young girl to enter the convent at that age in the 1930s. Besides, it took years to declare final vows, and her devotion was real. It's what she wanted to do with her life. After a brief search, she found an order of nuns in Krakow who would accept her. She poured herself into the life of a religious.

"John's family emigrated to America a year later. Marianne Roslovsky pleaded with her daughter to leave the order and go with them, but she refused. Ivan could have forced her to go, but he said Maria was old enough to make her own choices, so he left the decision to her. She chose to remain in Poland."

Gabe saw his grandmother's mouth quiver. "The family maintained regular correspondence with Maria until Hitler invaded Poland—then silence. Nothing for three years. Finally, in 1942, a letter arrived that had been smuggled out of Poland by the underground resistance. Marianne learned that her daughter was still alive, but the harsh German occupation was taking its toll on everyone, especially the Jews. They were disappearing. Maria said they were being rounded up and deported, but nobody knew where. None had returned. She'd taken her final vows by that time and expressed hope of being able to write freely after the war. She closed with the words, 'Jesus, I trust in You.'"

Francesca took a deep breath. She continued slowly. "That was the last time they ever heard from her."

Gabe couldn't believe his ears. How could a family tragedy of that magnitude be hidden for so many years? "What happened to her?" he asked. "Did anyone ever find out?"

"After the war, the family heard absolutely nothing. John's mother repeatedly wrote to her daughter, the religious order, and her relatives back in Poland but never received a reply. The Germans were gone, but the Soviet occupation had begun. The flow of information was practically nonexistent. Then, one day, a letter arrived. It was from one of Marianne's cousins. It contained the bitter news they'd long expected but never wanted. John's sister had indeed perished during the war. She and several other members of her order were secretly hiding Jews. One day, they fell into a trap set by the Nazis. Nine nuns from her convent were loaded onto a train and sent to Auschwitz. Six others were shot in the back of the head, including Maria."

Gabe's head dropped. "I'm in shock. I don't know what to say."

She reached across the table and took his hand.

"How could something like that have remained a secret all these years?" he asked bitterly.

"Gabriel," she said with serious eyes, "the scars of war were painful for everybody. Virtually everyone had been touched by the tragedy of the war in one way or another. You never knew whose suffering and loss were greater than your own. We all kept the pain to ourselves. Your grandfather, especially, would not speak about it. He was a master at keeping secrets—even the dark ones."

Secrets, Gabe thought. He couldn't bring himself to tell his grandmother that one of those secrets had cost him his life.

"I know John suffered greatly from losing his sister," she continued, "and it caused him to question his Christian beliefs. In arguments, he would always come back to the same question. How could a loving God allow so much misery?" Francesca let a heavy sigh escape. She used her fork to rearrange the food on her plate.

"I tried to explain the redemptive value of suffering," she continued, "but he wouldn't accept that explanation. He understood duty, valor, and personal sacrifice for the greater cause. However, the suffering of the innocents left him perplexed and angry, and at the top of that list was his sister. I pointed out that God himself set the example. He suffered the supreme payment for the benefit of man, but John simply couldn't grasp it—at least not until recently. Over the past few months, I saw changes in him. It seemed as if he was putting some of the pieces together."

Gabe picked up a piece of bread and dipped it in olive oil and pepper. He offered some to Francesca, but she politely refused. They sat quietly for a while eating—she lost in memories and he in revelation. He refilled his water glass and then broke the silence.

"Was life difficult as an immigrant woman in a foreign land?" he asked, changing the trajectory of the conversation.

"Well, yes and no, thanks to John's mother. She was a great help to me. Marianne and I became very close over the years. She made me feel welcome. We shared a common faith. Our Catholic identity gave us a common bond as we learned to love and embrace our new country. That made life easier. However, learning English and the customs of a new country was challenging, and I greatly missed my family. I was so thankful in later years that we were able to travel here to see them."

"That must've been quite a joy for you," Gabe said.

"Indeed," she said.

"What about the Roslovskys?" he asked.

"Marianne also missed her home. She loved Poland the way I loved Italy. She told me stories of how her people maintained their cultural identity as Polish Catholics, even when their country ceased to exist for over a century. She had a favorite quote and repeated it often. She'd say, 'Poland has a destiny.' Evidently, that idea had become woven into the culture of the Polish people, a sort of rallying cry during their years of misery. I had no idea what to make of it, but it became perfectly clear one day. Poland's most famous son was also the world's most recognizable person."

"The pope?" he asked.

"Indeed, John Paul II not only revived the Catholic Church, but he was also the spiritual catalyst behind the collapse of communism in Eastern Europe."

Francesca leaned in for emphasis. "Some people even think his papacy was prophesied in the Book of Revelation. They're just beginning to figure that out, but it will become increasingly clear to everyone as time passes. Poland did indeed have a destiny."

Pope John Paul II had been famous, Gabe thought. Virtually everyone recognized him. The media were in love with him, and television and newspapers constantly reported on his travels. No person on the planet had been covered as widely as John Paul II—not even the President of the United States. Still, it seemed a stretch to think that his papacy was prophesied in the Book of Revelation.

"Was it surprising that everywhere he went, everything he did, and everything he said was reported on by the media?" he asked.

"Not at all," she replied. "John Paul II reached out to the entire world during his many years as pope. He wanted people to know there's still hope despite all the misery in the world. His book, *Crossing the Threshold of Hope,* was a bestseller. He made it clear that the mission of the apostles was still being carried out today. He wanted people to know that they're loved by their Creator, and he wanted them to enter the universal gathering of the people of God. That message went out to everyone—not just to Christians. He was truly preparing the world for an encounter with Christ, and I think he felt driven by a high level of urgency to get that message across."

Gabe thought about the message he'd read the night before that explained the meaning of the number 666. He felt a cold chill run down his spine.

37

Francesca was tired when dinner ended. Gabe suggested they leave the adjoining door open, and she agreed. She prepared for bed, and he carefully checked the deadbolts on his grandmother's hall and balcony doors. He then kissed her on the cheek and returned to his room for the night.

He settled into a chair in the corner of his room. He drew the curtain and left it open just enough to maintain a view of the balcony. He resolved to remain awake and watch over his grandmother while she slept. Whoever had entered his room that afternoon would not get in again that night.

Sometime later, his body lurched in the chair. He'd dozed off. Gabe jumped to his feet and checked on his grandmother. She was sleeping peacefully. Gabe checked the time. His watch face cast a blue glow in the darkened room. It was a few minutes past 1:00 a.m.

He desperately needed some sleep, but his mind refused to cooperate. Who or what was WSB? He got up, splashed cold water on his face, and did some push-ups to drive his body back into action. He pulled the diary out of the safe, poured a glass of water, and returned to his post at the window.

His working copy of the message from the mirror was tucked into the diary. He looked at the cryptic message and his partial translation: *the beast is here*. That meaning was clear enough, but what did the SA stand for? He combed his mental catalog for possible answers, trying to connect the conversations he'd had with his grandmother to the things he'd learned from Anna and Paolo.

He replayed their discussions in his mind but kept returning to the news about his grandfather's twin sister. His grandfather's suffering had been too terrible to share; it was a suffering Gabe would never experience because he had no siblings of his own.

He remembered his childhood and recalled how his grandmother insisted he attend church with her on Sundays, but she never pressed his grandfather to go. He remembered how unfair it seemed at the time. He had to brush his teeth, wear uncomfortable clothes, and head off to church early in the morning while his grandfather stayed behind, drank a cup of coffee, and read the paper. Now he understood why she never pressured him the same way. It wasn't that his grandfather was indifferent toward faith. Rather, he struggled with it. He was trying to make sense of it. He was trying to come to grips with why there was so much suffering in the world.

Gabe thought about his visit to Saint Andrew's Cathedral that morning. The visit had been both comforting and disturbing. He felt at peace during Mass in the crypt but experienced sharp trepidation when he was followed upstairs to the main sanctuary. It was a place of contrasts—the cold and clamminess of the crypt and the warmth and tenderness of the old women singing. He thought about the church's façade and meticulously crafted tile mosaic, the image of Christ sitting on his throne.

"That's it!" he said suddenly. He grabbed the translation of the message and filled in his working copy to read:

THe BeaST
IS HeRe
Saint Andrew's

Is it really that easy? he wondered. *Could Saint Andrew's be the missing piece?* If so, what was his grandfather trying to tell him, and how was the beast connected to Saint Andrew's? Was it someone in the church? Surely that wasn't it, or was it? Maybe Paolo or Anna would know. Gabe was now more eager than ever to get back to Amalfi.

The old clock on the bedside table ticked at a laboriously slow pace, and he drifted in and out of sleep the rest of the night.

The next morning, they were packed and ready to depart by 8:30. The taxi ride to the dock was uneventful. Gabe couldn't enjoy the magnificent scenery as he had the day before. They hadn't been followed, but he eyed every passerby with suspicion. They caught the 9:00 a.m. boat for Sorrento. The trip was short, and they disembarked twenty minutes later.

Gabe stayed vigilant as they walked to the car. Nothing appeared out of the ordinary. It was just another beautiful, sunny day in Italy.

When they reached the garage, Gabe placed their bags in the trunk. He helped Francesca get in and pushed the door closed. Just then, a set of parking lights flashed at the opposite end of the garage. It was a black Audi A8. A man in the driver's seat was talking on his cell phone. Gabe glanced at him, but the man appeared to pay no attention. *I'm just being paranoid,* he thought.

Gabe pulled toward the exit, but the gate was closed. He fished for his wallet to pay the waiting attendant, and when he rolled down the window, he noticed his side mirror was still pushed in. It was a common practice along the Amalfi Coast to keep parked cars from losing their mirrors in tight squeezes.

He paid the attendant, pushed the driver's side mirror back into place, and rolled up his window. He asked Francesca to do the same with the other mirror. The instant it snapped into place, Gabe saw the Audi directly behind them.

In the rearview mirror, he could see a man in his mid-thirties staring back. He was dressed in black, had a dark complexion, and was no longer on his phone. *Stay calm,* Gabe thought.

He swung to the right and punched it. They glided back and forth through high-walled switchbacks rising from the docks below to the city above, the Audi close behind. When they surfaced, they were in the heart of the city.

Sorrento's streets formed a twisted maze. Gabe wasn't sure which way to go, but Francesca told him to turn left, even though he was certain the coastal route was the other way. The Audi followed.

He drove seven blocks and saw a sign for Amalfi that pointed to the right. He whipped around the corner and hit the accelerator. So did the Audi. Gabe quickly scanned the horizon. A traffic light at the next corner was about to change from yellow to red. He slowed down and pretended to stop. Cross-traffic had already geared up to move, but he gunned the accelerator and ran the red light at precisely the right instant. He bolted through the intersection and nearly broadsided a bus. Cross-traffic screeched to a halt. The intersection was jammed, and the Audi was forced to stop.

Francesca laughed. "You need to be more careful," she said. "You're only a quarter Italian, young man. There's no need to drive like the full-blooded locals."

"Sorry," he replied with a sly grin. "I'll be more careful."

The Audi disappeared in his rearview mirror, and Gabe sighed with relief. He'd outrun it but kept a watchful eye as they headed up the mountain. Francesca offered light conversation as they drove and shared recollections of her young life.

When they crossed over the top of the mountain and descended to the other side, Gabe saw the blue waters of the Mediterranean and hit the coastal road toward Amalfi. After several kilometers, a fruit stand came into view, and Francesca asked him to pull over. She wanted to get some fresh peaches and grapes. He tried to dissuade her, but she was insistent. Gabe checked his mirror again and reluctantly pulled off the road. He positioned the car to the far side of the fruit stand and parked as close to the retaining wall as possible. The car was mostly out of sight.

They stepped out of the car, and Gabe gently ushered her to the rear of the stand, keeping a wary eye on the road as she picked over the stock. They'd been there about ten minutes when he saw the Audi rounding the bend. It slowed but did not stop. Gabe took a deep breath and slowly let it out.

Francesca finished her selections and paid in cash. They got back in the car and continued toward Amalfi. After approximately eight kilometers to the west, they passed a grove of pine trees. The site was a popular destination for picture takers because of the quaint inlet bay and mountainous backdrop. Traffic was congested and moved slowly. Gabe could see the Audi as they crept forward. It had pulled over and was parked among the other vehicles. The driver stood outside and leaned against the door, cell phone to his ear. He stared straight at them as they passed.

Gabe made eye contact and got a good look at his face. He didn't recognize him but felt his penetrating gaze. The driver made no attempt to follow, but Gabe was now certain he was being watched.

MOMENTS LATER, MARCO'S cell phone rang. He was in Salerno. He flipped it open, and the voice on the other end said without emotion, "They're headed your way."

GINO CARUSO AWOKE early that morning. He was nervous and walked down his narrow street to the fruit vendor at the corner. He bought some lemons and two peaches and picked up a bottle of water and a newspaper.

"Morning, Sal," he said.

"Morning, Gino. Looks like another beautiful day." Sal motioned to the skies with his thick, bushy eyebrows.

Caruso smirked. "Yes, it does. Today will be a stunning day." He checked his belt to confirm his cell phone was on. It was. He then glanced at his watch—7:15 a.m.

He went home and read his paper to pass the time. Finally, around 10:15, his phone rang. The caller ID showed it was Marco.

"They're on the way," Marco warned.

"Excellent. I'll pass it along," Caruso said. He hung up and immediately called Lorenzo Bonelli at the Amalfi Hotel. "We'll meet you at the Seaside at 14:30."

"Thank you," Lorenzo replied. "I'll pass it along to Gabriel and the Castriottis. Ciao."

He hung up and called Paolo Castriotti. "We'll meet at the Seaside at 14:30. Everything is set," Lorenzo said.

Castriotti thought about his response. He paused briefly then replied, "I'll see you there."

A FEW MINUTES LATER, Marco relayed the information to Istanbul. He was greeted with a single word when the phone was answered.

"Yes?"

"Lunch is served," Marco replied.

"Perfect."

GABE REMAINED VIGILANT, but the Audi never reappeared. He reached the turn to Ravello and waited for three cars to pass from the other direction. When all was clear, he turned left and headed up the narrow mountain road to Francesca's cousins'. They arrived safely, and Gabe helped Francesca to the door, carrying her bags. He hugged her tightly.

"It was a lovely trip," she said.

"Capri was truly spectacular," he replied. "I'm so glad we went, but I need to go. I'll call you later."

"Yes, please do," she said. "Perhaps we could visit the funeral home this evening."

Gabe froze. "Yes, perhaps we could," he said. He turned and beat a hasty retreat to the car. Francesca waved from the doorway.

He pulled into the last remaining parking space when he reached the Amalfi Hotel. On his left was a retaining wall; on his right was a familiar BMW. It was Anna's car. Paolo Castriotti was in the driver's seat with Anna beside him. Gabe got out of his car, grabbed his suitcase, and walked to the driver's side window.

"Where's Lorenzo?" he asked. He bent down to look in.

"He left already," Paolo answered.

Anna leaned across. "Don't ask questions, just get in." The look on her face was disturbing.

Gabe immediately straightened up. He quickly swept the perimeter—no sign of the Audi. Anna popped open her door. He jumped in the back seat and put his suitcase on the seat beside him.

38

Zach Beckett stood at the window of Salerno's Morretti Hotel. He looked down at the shipyards below. He was polishing off the orange juice that room service had just delivered. His phone rang.

"Beckett here."

"Zach, Signal Fire."

Signal Fire, aka Jason Hollingsworth, was head of special ops and Beckett's most experienced subordinate at the NSA. They'd worked together for fifteen years. Hollingsworth now served as Beckett's second in command.

"I just received the report on the contact list you sent from Roslo's computer," Hollingsworth said. "We searched for coded names and aliases. We also cross-referenced dates, times, and places against our database. Unfortunately, nothing of significance turned up."

"What about the files?" Beckett asked.

"We found one filled with names, but those people are already dead—names like Hitler, Stalin, Reagan, and the like. The document appeared to be a treatise, but it didn't contain any of the things we're looking for."

"When was that file last saved?"

"Let me check. Based on the file date, the last time it was saved was Sunday—five days ago," Hollingsworth said.

"The file name?" Beckett asked.

"He called it *Cold Darkness*."

"Good work," Beckett replied. He pulled a pen from his breast pocket. "Anything else significant?"

"We found one more thing—residue from a deleted file. The file was deleted shortly after *Cold Darkness* was last saved."

"Can you retrieve it?" Beckett asked.

"Not without the hard disk. The residue evidence transferred, but we need the actual disk to retrieve the contents."

"Right," Beckett said.

Beckett knew that John Roslo's computer was protected with a copy of the agency's encryption/decryption software. It prevented deleted files from being recovered with commercial disk utilities. Even sophisticated hackers were hopelessly locked out. When Beckett dumped the data from Roslo's hard drive, the NSA transferred and deciphered the encrypted content. The deleted file, however, had not been transferred because it no longer existed. Nevertheless, NSA's encryption software created a small, coded residual file when the original was deleted. The residual file contained the identification data, file name, creation date, and deletion date. However, the extraction routine could not function without the hard drive.

"Zach, if you want to find out what's on that deleted file, you'll need to get the physical drive itself. It's the only way we can retrieve it."

Beckett knew he couldn't get it until he returned to Rome—that evening at the earliest. "It'll take a few hours, but I'll transmit as soon as I get it," Beckett said.

"Check. We'll be waiting," replied Hollingsworth. "One last thing: we've seen an increased level of chatter in Turkey again—both internet and cell. I'll keep you posted. Our analysts are working on it."

"Good," Beckett said. "I want a follow-up report when I deliver the hard drive." He hung up and shifted his focus back to the shipyard below.

39

Paolo Castriotti backed out of the hotel parking lot and turned toward Salerno. Gabe scanned the coastal road again. There was no sign of the Audi, only local traffic, tourists, and pedestrians.

Gabe then looked at Anna. "What's wrong?" he asked.

"I don't think this meeting is a good idea," Paolo answered forcefully.

"Why not?" Gabe asked.

"It's too dangerous," Paolo replied.

"But we need to find out what Gino Caruso knows about my grandfather's disappearance," Gabe said.

"True, but why risk going there? It only puts you in danger. It puts all of us in danger. Why didn't he just tell you by phone?" Paolo said.

"How dangerous can it be?" Gabe said. "We're meeting in a public venue in broad daylight."

"I still don't like it," Paolo replied.

"Do you know something about this meeting?" Gabe asked.

"I have my suspicions," Paolo said.

"What kind of suspicions?" Gabe said. He saw Paolo's fingers tapping the wheel nervously.

"I'm starting to wonder about Lorenzo," Paolo began. "I know he's an old friend, but we've seen too many inconsistencies. First, there was the missing body, which he let slip to Caruso and Gotto. Then he announced where you were headed to dinner the other night. Now, he's arranged this meeting in Salerno. It just doesn't add up."

Paolo's allegations floored Gabe, but he was right. It didn't add up. *There have been too many blunders,* he thought. Lorenzo was the only person who knew where they'd stayed on Capri.

"And here's something else," Paolo continued. "We think your grandfather's murder was connected to the Masons, right? And Gino Caruso belongs to the lodge in Salerno, right?"

"Okay, so what exactly are you saying, Paolo?" Gabe asked.

"Do you remember the final letters in your grandfather's message? I think the letters SA were a warning to you about *Salerno*. Even Cardinal Bauer called to advise me about the dangers of going there."

"He did?" Gabe asked, stunned.

"That's right, he did the morning you came back from Rome."

Gabe's head dropped back against the seat.

SA—Salerno. *Of course,* he thought. That made a lot more sense than Saint Andrew's. He'd overlooked the obvious in his zeal to find answers about his grandfather's disappearance. But he'd been distracted. There was the threat from WSB, the chase by the Audi, and his concern for his grandmother's safety.

They rode in somber silence for the next few minutes. Gabe wondered whether to tell them about the threat from WSB. *It might complicate things further.* However, he risked throwing them completely into the fire if he hid it. This wasn't just lunch; Salerno was very possibly a trap.

Suddenly, he exclaimed, "Turn back—back to the hotel. I won't put you two in harm's way. I'm going to this meeting alone."

Paolo pulled over, idling the BMW alongside the road. He looked at Anna.

"I don't want to turn back," she said flatly. "We've come this far together. I want to help. Sure, it's dangerous, but like Gabe said, it's daytime, and there's strength in numbers."

Gabe raised his hand to stop her protest. "There's something I need to tell you. While I was in Capri, I received a threat, a note."

"Good God be with us!" Paolo exploded, crossing himself. "What did it say?"

Gabe reached into his pocket and pulled out the note. "It says, 'Gabriel Roslo, stop your search. Go back to America. There's nothing here for you but agony and heartache. You're being watched.' It was signed 'WSB.'"

Paolo immediately slammed the car in gear and shot back into traffic. He hit the accelerator. They passed two cars and a delivery truck. An oncoming scooter veered out of their way, narrowly missing the limestone cliff.

"We're going with you," Paolo declared. He left no room for discussion. "Anna's right. There's strength in numbers. We might not like the risk, but let's face it: we're already deeply involved. Besides, I know how these people are. If they really want to find us, they can—anytime, anywhere."

Anna turned toward Gabe. "He's right. We're not letting you go alone. Let's find out what Caruso has to say."

Gabe was unsettled by her insistence. There was simply no reason for them to go. *What if Lorenzo has, indeed, orchestrated a trap?* he thought. "We should call the meeting off," he said.

"We're going," Anna replied. She and Paolo exchanged a wary glance.

"But what if it's a trap?" Gabe demanded.

"So, what if it is?" she answered. "Whoever's pulling the strings had no trouble finding you on Capri. They won't have any trouble finding us either. We might as well push on, or else you'll never get your questions answered."

Gabe nodded his head cautiously. He didn't like it, but her logic was sound. "To Salerno then."

Gabe patted the diary inside his breast pocket. "They're just trying to scare me away," he said. "Besides, they might already have what they want." He was referring to the missing pages from the diary.

Paolo zigzagged through traffic and nodded in agreement. The BMW twisted along the coast and passed through quaint seaside villages. Gabe barely noticed the passing scenery. He had his eyes on the road. Thankfully, there was no sign of the Audi.

The drive to Salerno took nearly an hour due to the congestion, hairpin turns, and obstacles along the route. They entered the city and passed a large shipyard. Gabe saw a cargo ship sailing out to sea. Its top deck was loaded eight-high with shipping containers in varied shades of orange, brown, and gray.

"That's a lot of wine," he said, joking.

Paolo and Anna laughed, and it broke the tension in the car. The road dropped to sea level past the shipyard. They continued along the coast, which had flattened out. The mountains were further inland now. For the first time in fifty kilometers, the coastline wasn't a sheer drop into the sea.

Traffic began to build as they entered the city center. Five- and six-story tenement buildings lined the left side of the road. The coastal side was dotted with an alternating pattern of parks and beaches. The architecture was fair. Salerno was nothing compared to the Cinderella quality of Sorrento.

There were no parking spaces in front of the Seaside Café, so Paolo turned into the parking lot of a private marina. Gabe saw sailboats and pleasure craft moored in the slips. He checked his watch—2:20 p.m. They were ten minutes early.

They pulled up to the valet. The attendant handed Paolo a claim check, and they crossed the street to the café. Gino Caruso and Lorenzo Bonelli had already arrived and were seated in the outside garden. The garden was L-shaped and wrapped around the east side of the building. It was slightly elevated and provided a view of the marina across the street.

Caruso and Bonelli sat at a table in the far corner, away from the other patrons, and were also hidden from the road by a hedgerow. A stone retaining wall was at their backs. They exchanged formal pleasantries with the new arrivals, and Caruso thanked them for coming. He invited everyone to sit.

He seems calm, Gabe thought. But then again, Caruso was a politician. He was a master at playing the game.

A white delivery van was parked eight hundred meters away. The recording technician calmly smiled as he adjusted the levels on his console. He'd planted four microphones in the garden the previous night. "I'm getting excellent signal strength," he said.

"Perfect!" replied his colleague. He was perched above the café on a private balcony of the neighboring building. "My line of sight is clear and unobstructed. This will be easy," he whispered. He adjusted his earpiece. "I can hear her breathing."

The sniper slowly leveled his scope to examine the target area. He looked at each person at the table, one after the other. He then fixed his sight on Anna Castriotti. "I didn't know she was such a babe. What a shame."

"Let me take a look," the recording tech said.

"Not a chance," said the sniper, focusing.

The rifle scope was connected to a digital transmitter, but the sniper switched it off. The recording tech grinned. He manipulated a few switches and engaged the transmitter remotely. The screen flickered. A second later, her image was in full view.

"Wow, she's hot," the tech mumbled to himself.

The sniper surveyed the café. No rush. They hadn't even ordered yet. *I might as well enjoy the view while it lasts,* he thought. He watched the waiter pour water, first for Anna and then for the others. "Gas or no gas," the sniper said aloud.

"You never hear that question where I come from," the technician quipped.

"Only in Europe, my friend," the sniper replied. "Never in America."

At the table, Gino Caruso opened the conversation. "Gabriel, what have you learned about the disappearance of your grandfather's body?"

"Nothing, I'm sorry to say—no new developments," he answered. He avoided any details.

Caruso's lips straightened into a thin, hard line. "I was afraid of that. I have reason to believe the delay is intentional—meant to keep you here longer," he said calmly. He unfolded his napkin and laid it in his lap.

"What do you mean?" Gabe asked.

"That man, the one from America. Are you sure he's trustworthy?" Caruso asked. "What's he doing here?"

"He's helping arrange my grandfather's transport back to the States." Gabe realized he was being interrogated.

"Hmm," Caruso said. He clicked his tongue against his teeth. "I'm not so sure. I think he's looking for something—something you have."

"Like what?" Gabe asked. He felt the muscles at the back of his neck tighten.

"Didn't you say he was from the NSA? Well, think about it. What might he be looking for?" Caruso said.

"I have no idea," Gabe answered with a stone-cold gaze. Lying was becoming easier.

"I have reason to believe he's after your grandfather's diary," Caruso said flatly.

A stunned silence ensued. How did Caruso know about the diary? Gabe scanned the faces at the table. Lorenzo was expressionless. Paolo and Anna were silent. Gabe started to respond but was interrupted by the waiter.

"Today's specials are…"

The sniper continued to watch from his perch as each person placed their order—first Anna, then the rest.

When the waiter left, Caruso said, "I believe the diary contains information implicating the NSA man in your grandfather's death."

"What? How do you know this?" Gabe asked.

"I have my sources."

"What sources?" Gabe demanded.

"Think about it," Caruso replied. He ignored his question. "The NSA man was already in Rome when you called him about your grandfather. You saw him enter your grandfather's apartment. Then he came looking for you at Anna's flat. What other evidence do you need?"

Gabe felt his blood run cold. He ran his hand through his hair as he thought about his next move. Perhaps Caruso was right. Maybe Zach Beckett was after the diary. Gabe looked at Anna. He noticed her eyes dart back and forth between her uncle's and his.

"But how do you know this?" Gabe pressed again.

"I don't for a fact, but it's a strong suspicion. I mean, why haven't we met him? Do you know where he is? Do you even know his name?" Caruso asked.

"Of course, I know his name, and he's in Rome trying to locate my grandfather's body," Gabe said.

"How do you know he isn't the one who took it?" Caruso countered.

Lorenzo leaned forward as if to speak. He immediately felt a kick in the shin. Paolo flashed a glare in his direction. He sat back silently.

"At this point, I have no idea who took my grandfather's body," Gabe said. "That's why I came here today, hoping to find out. He and my grandfather were friends. I must trust their relationship was genuine."

"Of course," Caruso said calmly. "Nevertheless, I think it's extremely important the diary be kept safe. Where is it now?" he asked collegially. He leaned forward and placed a hand on Gabe's forearm.

Just then, the waiter reappeared in the sniper's sights. He carried a tray with their lunch order. The sniper followed the waiter as he served each person. After all were served, the sniper once again squared Anna in his sights. The waiter disappeared, and Caruso repeated his question.

All eyes were on Gabe. "It's at the hotel, locked in my room safe."

"I've got it," the technician whispered. "It's at the hotel, in his room safe."

"Superb," the sniper replied. "Now it's my turn."

"Wait, we still need to find out the name," the recording tech said.

The sniper paused, easing his finger off the trigger. "Very well. A few more minutes to admire the scenery."

Caruso looked around the table. He now had a key piece of information. He turned back to Gabe and continued to dig. "Does the NSA man know where you're staying?"

"He does."

"Then how do you know the diary is safe from—what did you say his name was?" Caruso asked.

"I didn't," Gabe replied, clearly suspicious. He didn't take the bait.

"Gabriel," Caruso said, "there are suspicions that your grandfather was murdered. Your friends think he died of natural causes, but how does that explain the missing body? The most obvious suspect is the NSA man unless someone at this table is responsible."

"Now, wait a minute!" Lorenzo Bonelli protested. "None of us had anything to do with this, and Zach Beckett was a personal friend of John Roslo."

"Zach Beckett?" Caruso asked, confirming the name.

Lorenzo had blurted out the words before anyone could react. Gabe was floored by yet another lapse.

"Did you catch that?" the technician asked. "His name is Zach Beckett."

"I heard it," the sniper replied, "loud and clear. It's time." He took one last look at the beautiful Anna Castriotti.

40

Just past 3:00 p.m., a loud crack echoed off the walls of the surrounding apartment buildings. Chaos erupted in the café. There was blood everywhere. Paolo shouted in Italian as Anna fell to the ground. Gabe instinctively lunged to his left, away from the direction of the sound. He dove under the table and could see Anna lying with her face to the ground.

"You arrogant son of a bitch," the tech groaned into his headset. "No silencer?"

"What fun's the shot without the bang?" the sniper laughed in reply.

Patrons were screaming and running in panic. Some dove under tables. Others hid behind large concrete landscaping planters. The waitstaff barked orders as glasses and dishes crashed to the ground.

Gabe tried to crawl through the table legs toward Anna, but he was grabbed from behind amidst the chaos. He jerked his head around to see who had a hold of him. To his shocked horror, he was staring straight into the barrel of Zach Beckett's Glock 18 semiautomatic weapon.

An instant later, Beckett pulled him to his feet. "Let's move." He shoved Gabe toward the door from the garden to the interior of the café. Gabe tried to resist, but Beckett jammed the gun into his side. "Now!"

Gabe's first instinct was to help Anna, but he was forced at gunpoint to abandon her. Gabe staggered into the café and out the front door. Beckett shadowed him with the gun still firmly planted in Gabe's side. "Get in the car!" Beckett demanded.

Gabe hesitated. His eyes made a quick sweep of the surroundings. Beckett was in no mood for delays. He pointed his weapon at Gabe's head, pulled the passenger door open, and shoved him inside. Beckett ran to the driver's side and jumped in behind the wheel. Within seconds, they sped away from the café. Beckett still pointed his gun in Gabe's direction.

They bolted down the coastal road, then turned right. Suddenly, Beckett pulled over and screeched to a halt. He jammed the car into park, got out, hurried around to the passenger side, and opened the door.

"Get out," he said.

They were parked in front of the train station. *Surely, he's not going to kill me here,* Gabe thought. He looked at Beckett and then toward the train station.

"Don't try to run. I'm an expert marksman," Beckett said. He opened the back door and demanded Gabe get in the back seat. Gabe complied.

"Slide over!" Beckett snapped. He slipped his semiautomatic back in its holster and got in next to Gabe. He flipped open his cell phone and hit speed dial. "We're here."

Gabe watched. He thought about making a break for it. The closest cover was at least twenty meters away, much too far. Beckett kept a close eye on him. A moment later, a man approached the car. To Gabe's horror, it was the same man he'd seen the prior morning at Saint Andrew's after Mass. The same man who interrupted the private dinner with his grandmother. Gabe reached for the door.

"Freeze!" Beckett ordered. "You're not going anywhere."

The man wore an ordinary gray suit. His face was emotionless. He moved methodically toward the driver's door. He hesitated to look around, opened the door, and got behind the wheel. The man put the car in drive and eased back into traffic.

"Where are we going?" Gabe demanded.

Neither man spoke.

"I thought you were my grandfather's colleague," Gabe said to Beckett.

They continued in silence. The driver turned into a deserted alley and maneuvered around a garbage dumpster. He stopped out of sight of the busy street and shut off the engine. He turned around and extended his hand.

"Gabe Roslo, I'm Agent Jenkins. I work for Mr. Beckett. Please don't be alarmed. You're safe now." Gabe was stunned.

The man smiled. "Sorry for all the cloak and dagger, but we needed to ensure your safety," he said. "You're in grave danger."

Gabe was not amused. He turned toward Beckett. "What the hell are you thinking?" he demanded sharply. "We need to help Anna. We need to go back *now*!"

"You've got to trust me," Beckett replied. "I can't let you go back in there. It would be suicide. These people will stop at nothing to get what they want."

"Mr. Beckett is right," Agent Jenkins said, his expression dire. "We can't let you back in there. It's my job to keep an eye on you. We got you out just in time."

"What?" Gabe exclaimed. "You've been watching me this whole time?"

Beckett leaned forward. "Do you remember Jenkins from dinner the other night?" he asked.

"Yeah, what about it?" Gabe replied.

"He and the other man are both agents. I sent them to protect the two of you after your grandfather was murdered. Agent Mallon has your grandmother under surveillance as we speak. He won't let anything happen to her."

Gabe shot a look at Beckett. "So, you're certain my grandfather was murdered."

Beckett's lips furrowed, but he didn't speak. Gabe saw an emotion shadow his face for the first time.

Beckett let out a long sigh. "There's no easy way to tell you this." He paused again. He looked down and pressed a wrinkle from his pant leg with his right thumb. "I never meant to hurt you or deceive you, but I had a job to do. Too much is at stake."

"You bastard!" Gabe shouted. He lunged at Beckett and grabbed him by the throat. "How could you?"

"Not us, you idiot. We didn't kill him," Beckett wheezed.

"Stop, Gabe! We're trying to help you," Jenkins roared. He reached over the seat to pull him back while Beckett fought to push Gabe away. Gabe slowly released his grip on Beckett and sat back in his seat.

"We didn't kill your grandfather, but we have proof he was murdered," Beckett said. He reached under his coat and calmly pulled out his Glock. He pointed it at Gabe's kneecap. "Son, if you do that again, you're going to walk with a permanent limp. Now sit still and listen. We know your grandfather was poisoned. It was confirmed by the autopsy."

"So, you lied to me," Gabe said.

"Under the circumstances, I had no choice. I couldn't risk telling you about the autopsy until we were certain. When you called me the morning John died, I immediately suspected foul play. I didn't want to alarm you or your grandmother. In international cases, an autopsy is often required. We were concerned that one might be ordered by the local authorities. We couldn't let that happen."

"Why not?" Gabe asked.

"Given the timing and nature of his death, poisoning was a natural possibility. We needed to know for certain. Standard autopsy procedures often miss sophisticated poisons, especially the rare and exotic varieties. So, we had our people do it. We ran all the necessary screens. I doubt the local pathologist would've even heard of TTX, much less found it. We had to be certain John was murdered, and we had to know how."

Gabe felt like he'd been punched in the stomach. "Why did you lie to me? My grandmother will be devastated when she finds out."

"I'm really sorry, but there was no other way. I know Francesca will be shocked by his murder, but I doubt she'll be angry over the autopsy. She knows full well that we were authorized to perform one without her permission."

"What are you talking about?" Gabe was incredulous.

Beckett and Jenkins exchanged glances. "Your grandfather was working on a project for me," Beckett said. "He was under contract with the agency. He was being paid a stipend for his work. Under the terms of his contract, the NSA has the right to authorize an autopsy without the approval of the family. I assure you Francesca understands this."

Gabe looked out his side window to digest what he'd just heard. His grandfather was under contract with the NSA. He'd been murdered because of it, and now there was even more bloodshed. The image of Anna flashed through his mind.

"We need to go back to the café!" Gabe demanded again.

"We have no authorization. Our job is to protect you," Jenkins said. "Returning to the café is an unnecessary risk."

"Then you're going to have to shoot me," Gabe retorted. "I'm going back." He reached for the door. It began to open.

Click.

Gabe froze.

"I'm not bluffing," Beckett said. "I'll shoot you if I have to. Close the door before you get yourself killed. You're of no use to us dead."

"Then shoot me."

Beckett pounded his fist on the back of the seat. "Damn it, you've got a hard head! Are you trying to get yourself killed? Close the door."

Gabe reluctantly complied.

Beckett exhaled hard, paused, and said, "Jenkins, get this thing moving—back to the café."

"Yes, sir," Jenkins replied, his lips set in a hard line. He fired up the engine and put it in drive.

Gabe eyed Beckett suspiciously. *Does he know about the possible Masonic implications?* he wondered. *What does he mean by rare and exotic poisons, and what was TTX? Above all, what does he know about Anna Castriotti?*

It took only a few minutes to retrace their path to the Seaside Café, which was now swarming with emergency vehicles.

"Stop here," Beckett ordered.

Jenkins pulled over to the side of the road. The café was about a hundred meters ahead on the opposite side of the street. A sizeable crowd had gathered, and the Carabinieri were unrolling yellow tape to cordon off the scene. Gabe reached for the door.

"Oh, no, you don't. You're not going anywhere," Beckett said. "Jenkins, circle the block and meet me here in five minutes. If I'm not back, go to the train station and wait for me. And Gabe, keep your freaking head down."

Beckett jumped out and crossed the street. Jenkins pulled back into traffic. Gabe instinctively checked his watch—3:13 p.m. They slowly drove past the café. Gabe scanned the premises for recognizable faces but found none. However, a well-dressed man in a dark suit caught Gabe's attention. He stood next to a black Mercedes and was talking on his cell phone.

The man stood out because his countenance was in sharp contrast to the horrified onlookers at the scene. Their faces expressed shock and disbelief. Two old women were crying. Many others were pacing, but this man's face was different. He looked calm and collected. He spoke and nodded his head in the affirmative. Gabe noticed a Grinch-like grin creep across his face.

The Carabinieri directed traffic. They waved Jenkins through, and he accelerated from the scene. Gabe watched the strange man until he disappeared.

They drove for a few minutes, circled the block, and approached the scene a second time. Five minutes had passed, and Beckett wasn't there. Under his orders, they were to abandon the café for a rendezvous at the train station.

They crept past the café a second time. They were slowed down by onlookers and the Carabinieri. Gabe kept his head low and scanned the horizon. Still no sign of Beckett, but he caught another glimpse of the man by the Mercedes. The man was still on the phone. He now had a broad smile on his face.

Jenkins cleared the roadblock and accelerated again. Gabe was watching the man out the back window when suddenly, the car careened to the right and stopped.

"Get in," Jenkins shouted.

Both doors on the passenger side flung open. Beckett ducked into the front. But to Gabe's amazement, Anna fell into the back.

"I thought you were dead!" Gabe said, wrapping his arms around her.

"Caruso's dead," Anna whispered slowly. She was in shock, her voice monotone.

41

"Get the hell out of here!" Beckett ordered.

Jenkins hit the accelerator. They circled the block and sped away in the direction of Amalfi.

"What happened to the others?" Gabe asked.

"I don't know," she replied. "Everyone scattered. Lorenzo left the scene. I saw him leave, but I couldn't find Uncle Paolo anywhere. It was chaos. Thank God you're alive." She lay her head against his shoulder.

Gabe tried to process what happened. Caruso was dead, but he and Anna had been spared. Lorenzo disappeared, and Paolo's whereabouts were unknown. The shooter must have had a specific target in mind—and he didn't miss. But why did they kill Caruso? It didn't make sense. And who was the man with the Mercedes?"

"Beckett, do any of your agents drive a black Mercedes?" Gabe asked.

"No, of course not. Do you think Uncle Sam would spring for a Benz?"

"What about an Audi?" Gabe asked.

"No. No Audis, either. Why?" Beckett asked.

"I know you have people watching us for our protection," Gabe said. "This morning, there was a guy waiting for us in the parking garage in Sorrento. He was driving an Audi—an A8."

"Did you get a good look at him?" Beckett asked.

"I did," Gabe said. "He followed us toward Amalfi but then turned off. I told myself I was being paranoid, but now I'm convinced otherwise."

Beckett picked up his phone. He hit speed dial and relayed what happened. He listened for a moment then said, "No, it'd be too easy to find us there. I had no trouble locating her apartment. They won't either. Rome is no longer safe." He again listened to the voice on the other end, eventually agreed, and snapped his phone shut.

"Who was that?" Gabe asked.

"Cardinal Bauer."

"You know Cardinal Bauer?" Gabe asked.

"His name was in John's contact records," Beckett said. "I spoke to him in Rome. We both agree it's too dangerous for you to return to the hotel. We need to hide you somewhere."

Beckett didn't elaborate. Instead, he addressed Jenkins, "Use the A3. We want to avoid the coastal road."

Gabe was frustrated by Beckett's evasiveness. He was also distracted by Anna. She remained tucked under his arm and wept quietly.

He thought about the carnage at the café. Caruso had attempted to warn him. Caruso implicated Beckett. Now, he was dead. Were Beckett and his agents really protecting them? Gabe worried. He'd been pulled out of the fire, and they did get Anna, but was this the trap he'd been warned about? *Maybe we're hostages,* he thought.

The men in the front seat remained silent while Gabe examined Beckett. He looked cold and calculating and appeared entirely unfazed by the tragedy.

"Caruso was suspicious of your NSA connections," Gabe said. "Now he's dead."

"When are you going to get it?" Beckett asked. "John was my friend and colleague."

"Yeah, and he's dead, too," Gabe said.

"That's right," Beckett replied, his tone edgy. "And I'm trying to protect you from the same fate."

"So why did Caruso get killed?"

"I don't know," Beckett answered.

There was a long pause. Finally, Anna blurted out, "Caruso thought you were after Mr. Roslo's diary."

Gabe was bewildered. He'd been so careful not to tell Beckett about the diary. *Why on Earth did she say that?* he wondered.

"Diary—what diary?" Beckett asked.

Gabe watched his face.

"You don't know about the diary, do you?" she pressed ahead.

Gabe was mortified. What was she doing?

"I don't know what you're talking about," Beckett answered.

Gabe couldn't interpret Beckett's response. Was he lying? Beckett was either unaware of the diary or an incredibly good actor.

"After Mr. Roslo passed away, Gabe found a diary in his grandfather's hotel room," Anna continued. Gabe tightened his grip on her, but she continued. "He showed it to my Uncle Paolo. That's how Gabe became involved in this mess."

"Where is it now? I need to see it," Beckett demanded.

Gabe was not about to hand it over. What if Caruso was right?

"Listen, Gabe, we're on the same side here," Beckett said pointedly. "We both want to know why your grandfather is dead. You've got a potential lead but little else without my help. I have resources to turn your clues into answers, but you need to trust me. You have no other choice, especially if you want to live long enough to find out what happened."

Beckett was right. Considering the threat in Capri, the death of Caruso, and his lack of resources, time had run out. Reluctantly, Gabe pulled the diary from his pocket and passed it over the front seat.

"Uncle Paolo recognized the diary and immediately suspected foul play," Anna continued. "That's why he sent Gabe to meet Cardinal Bauer. Didn't the cardinal mention it to you?"

"No, he did not," Beckett answered. He carefully eyed the diary, closed it, and tapped his fingers on the dash.

"Anna, your uncle's instincts were correct," Beckett continued. "John was murdered. We know that for a fact. The autopsy confirmed it."

She shot a confused look at Gabe.

He explained, "My grandfather was working for the NSA again, a subcontractor of sorts. By prior agreement, they were authorized to perform an autopsy on him without the approval of the family. He was poisoned," Gabe said.

She gasped. "How?"

"Injection—TTX," Beckett stated.

"TTX? What in the world is TTX?" she asked.

"Tetrodotoxin, TTX for short," Beckett replied. "It's an extremely potent neurotoxin found in pufferfish. In its purified form, two milligrams can be lethal. Our people estimate he had fifty milligrams in his system. TTX is very rare. It's mostly used as a concoction for voodoo rituals."

"Voodoo!" Gabe exclaimed. The diary contained many pages of information about the use of occult practices in Masonic rituals. Surely, this wasn't a coincidence. Perhaps it was even a statement. *Was this another warning?* Gabe wondered.

Beckett handed the diary back to Gabe. "We were as stunned as you are," Beckett said. "The use of TTX is very peculiar, and it's changed our scope of suspects entirely. We first suspected Islamic extremists or perhaps someone with a Cold War vendetta, but neither fits the profile. My people are cross-referencing the use of TTX to lists of known assassins as we speak, but so far, we've got nothing."

Anna's instincts had been right. Caruso had been lying. Zach Beckett was not the enemy. He was trying to help. Gabe breathed a sigh of relief.

Just then, Anna's cell phone rang. She answered it, listened for a moment, and hung up. Her lips were pressed tightly together. "More bad news," she said. "That was an associate from my office. Security just reported another break-in at Mr. Roslo's apartment. A neighbor discovered the door ajar."

"Is anything missing?" Gabe asked.

"It was a total ransack," she said. "They were looking for something."

Beckett's expression was grim. He handed his phone to Anna. "Please call them back and find out if the computer is gone. Use my phone. Yours contains a GPS unit. We've been using it to track your movements. It's time to switch it off and leave it that way. This one is completely untraceable."

Gabe looked at Anna. He raised an eyebrow. No wonder Beckett had been able to find them so easily. She shrugged and turned off her phone. She placed the call and waited for the report. A few minutes passed. She nodded several times then hung up.

"The CPU is gone, but they left the monitor and connection cables."

"Damn it!" Beckett growled. "It keeps getting worse."

"What's going on?" Gabe demanded.

"The day I was in your grandfather's flat, I dumped the contents of his hard drive to a zip disk and sent it to headquarters for analysis. Our technicians discovered residue from a missing file. It had been deleted a couple of days prior, most likely by John. To recover the file, I need the hard drive."

"And now they have it," Gabe said.

"Exactly," Beckett replied. "It might be the key to this entire mystery."

"Any idea what was in that file?" Gabe asked.

"None," said Beckett.

"What are you going to do?" Gabe asked.

"Read," Beckett grunted.

"Read what? The diary?"

"No, this," Beckett replied. His portfolio was tucked beneath the seat. He reached into it and pulled out a thumb drive.

42

Marco was parked in front of the Seaside Café. He stood next to his Mercedes and watched the frenetic commotion rage in front of him. He flipped open his cell phone and called the recording technician. The tech was driving east out of Salerno in the inconspicuous, white delivery van that housed his equipment.

He recognized Marco's number and anticipated his question. He calmly answered the phone and said, "It's at the hotel, locked in the room safe."

"Very good. We'll take care of it," Marco replied.

He hung up and dialed again. He waited for the international call to connect. Marco heard a familiar voice at the other end. "The job is done," Marco said. "As always, you were correct. Gino Caruso was a traitor. If he sold out to me, he'd be willing to sell out to anyone for the right price. It was absolutely necessary."

"The White Lodge is indebted to you."

"Grazie," Macro replied. He was pleased with himself.

"Who else was there?"

"Lorenzo Bonelli, Paolo Castriotti, his niece, and the young Roslo. Roslo and the girl have disappeared, but we're searching for them."

"Good. Keep me informed. What about the diary?"

"According to my source, it's at the hotel, locked in Roslo's room safe," Marco said.

"Hmm, Roslo is either incredibly stupid or extremely sly. Check the hotel. But get a tail on him as soon as you locate them. My bet is we'll find the diary with him. Relay my orders."

"Yes, sir," Marco replied. "One more thing: we also have the name of the NSA agent—Zach Beckett."

Marco was satisfied with the success of the Seaside Café operation. He got back in his car and made several more calls. Each member of his team now had their orders.

43

NSA HEADQUARTERS

Jason Hollingsworth arrived at his desk in Fort Meade, Maryland. When a flush-faced operative arrived, he was juggling an overfilled cup of coffee, a battered briefcase, and his daily copy of the *Washington Post*. "Classified, urgent," was all the operative said.

Hollingsworth put down his cup and spilled some coffee on his cluttered desk. He took the envelope, nodded, and sat down to open the file. NSA personnel had detected a series of related communiqués during the night. The coded messages were part of a pattern of rising chatter. The messages originated in Turkey and were bound for the United States and Italy. One particular communication had the staff hopping. A copy of it was attached to the memo in Hollingsworth's hand.

He flipped the page, glanced at it, then read the classified memo. It indicated a specific threat—an imminent terrorist attack against an undetermined US target. The quality of the intelligence was excellent. The threat was extremely serious. His eyes were transfixed on the single most important word on the page:

Nuclear

Hollingsworth finished reading the report and secretly wished Beckett was there. Under national security guidelines, this type of information had to be passed immediately to the National Security Advisor, who had the duty

THE AMALFI SECRET

of notifying the President and the Secretaries of Defense and Homeland Security.

Hollingsworth had never dealt directly with the National Security Advisor. That was Beckett's job. He picked up his phone and hit speed dial. It rang five times before rolling to voice mail. Beckett's phone was either out of range or turned off.

Hollingsworth flipped the page again and reread the intercepted communiqué. The last two sentences were the most disturbing.

> Our little darling has landed safely in the dragon's lair. Five days until show time.
>
> WSB

Hollingsworth reached for the *Far Side* calendar sitting on his desk. He flipped the page. It was September 6. *Is this a cruel hoax?* he wondered. Yet, the intelligence was credible. No, he concluded, it was authentic. He swallowed hard, picked up the phone, and asked his secretary to dial the office of the National Security Advisor.

He waited for the call to connect. He looked down and saw his leg spontaneously bouncing against his desk. More coffee was spilling over the edge. *Calm down,* he thought.

Hollingsworth was a longtime etymology buff. He mused over the word secretary as he waited for the call to clear. It was derived from the root word secret, *secretus* in Latin. Secretary—a person entrusted with secrets.

Ironic, he thought, *and fitting.* The American government was full of secretaries: the Secretary of Defense, the Secretary of State, and the Secretary of Homeland Security, to name a few. Hollingsworth looked down at the NSA insignia on his desk. He focused on the key in the eagle's talons, the key to security. It symbolized the mission of the NSA: to protect America by gaining access to secrets.

How will they deal with this secret? Hollingsworth wondered. Within a few hours, the President of the United States would be in secret meetings with his cabinet of secretaries and top advisors to discuss a very worrisome secret.

His thoughts were abruptly interrupted. "Go ahead, sir. You've been put through."

44

Agent Jenkins took the A3 expressway out of Salerno. The route connected it to Napoli and ran behind the coastal mountain range that formed the Amalfi Coast. Beckett ordered Jenkins to exit at Angri, an inconspicuous village that time forgot. Agriculture was the principal source of economic activity. Gabe saw a goat path over the highway that led to fields on either side. Gritty locals tended the herds. They also capitalized on tourism by selling travelers saint statues and other figurines. Little clearings appeared along the road filled with them. Saint Padre Pio was a favorite.

The exit at Angri was a twisted maze of tiny, two-lane roads. It led to SP1, or Strada Provinciale, meaning provincial road. SP1 rose up the back side of the mountain, traversed the top, and descended to the coastal road on the other side. Anna was familiar with the route.

The switchbacks were endless on both sides of the mountain. Gabe had seen plenty of switchbacks in the Canadian Rockies, but this was altogether different. The view of the sea was particularly stunning when they reached the top. They descended the other side to the coastal road just a few kilometers from Amalfi.

Jenkins turned right and shot through the roundabout in Amalfi. Beckett instructed Gabe and Anna to keep their heads down to avoid being spotted. They drove several kilometers and took the Agerola exit. Gabe recognized it. He and Paolo had used it the morning he left for Rome. Jenkins wasted no time. He ascended the nearly vertical rock face, and each successive switchback lifted them higher. No one spoke.

Beckett broke the silence. "Turn right," he ordered. The main route forked left. It led to San Michele, Castellamare, and eventually Napoli. A sign pointed to the right. It read "Pogerola." Jenkins swung right onto a local route, barely a single lane.

"There's a Franciscan monastery in Pogerola," Beckett explained. "Cardinal Bauer arranged for us to stay there."

Jenkins continued to speed up the mountain. He spun through a harrowing hairpin curve then hit the brakes behind a city bus. Plumes of exhaust billowed out the back as the bus chugged its way to the top.

"Go around him," Beckett demanded. Jenkins flashed a worried look. "I said, go around him!" Beckett demanded a second time. "I can't breathe."

Jenkins gritted his teeth and pulled out to pass. Suddenly, two motor scooters appeared out of nowhere. They were nearly sandwiched between the car, the bus, and the mountain. Neither scooter flinched as they calmly passed on the blind outside turn.

Gabe shook his head in amazement. "How do they do it?"

"It's just part of life here," Anna said. She mustered a grin.

Jenkins followed the bus through several switchbacks, then found a straight stretch long enough to pass. He gunned the accelerator and scorched the bus with seconds to spare. He quickly downshifted and wheeled around the next hairpin. The drive was intense, but Gabe was relieved to no longer choke on the thick, black exhaust.

They twisted their way farther up the mountain and finally reached Pogerola. The main route into the village led to Torre di Pogerola, an ancient Roman ruin perched thousands of feet above Amalfi that overlooked Saint Andrew's Cathedral. Gabe had seen it the day before when he and his grandmother left the cathedral.

Jenkins maneuvered through the village as they searched for the monastery. They traveled a few hundred meters beyond the castle entrance.

"That's it," Beckett said.

They found a driveway that dropped sharply to the right. Jenkins turned the wheel, and they drove over the edge. For an instant, it felt like they had driven off a cliff, but Gabe knew the disappearing act served another purpose: they were totally hidden from view.

Jenkins found a parking space and yanked up the parking brake.

There was a series of terraces lined with lemon trees and grape vines. Gabe also saw tomato plants, zucchini, and other local vegetables. Every available inch of the mountain was planted. Even so, the place looked deserted.

Beckett looked at Gabe and Anna. "Follow me," he directed.

Jenkins stayed with the car.

Gabe and Anna followed Beckett to the edge of the parking lot, where they descended a stone staircase with six flights of steps. Each flight led to a limestone landing and a new angle of descent. The stairs followed the slope of the mountain. Gabe checked his watch—6:28 p.m. The sun would soon disappear behind the peaks.

At the bottom of the staircase, a rock path was bordered by more lemon trees, which led to a tiny clearing and two buildings. One was a chapel. The other was a large, two-story residence built of stone with rough-hewn wooden doors and window encasements. Both buildings were ancient.

Beckett led them to the residence and rapped on the door. The sign above it read "San Pietro." Seconds later, the door opened, and they were greeted by a Franciscan monk with a warm demeanor.

"Good evening. I'm Father Fiore. Please come in." The monk spoke in accented English.

Gabe judged him to be about fifty years old. He had graying hair and was barely five feet tall. He gripped Gabe's hand in greeting. His hands bore well-formed calluses, and Gabe could tell by his firm handshake that Father Fiore was in excellent physical condition. *Anyone who tends to those terraced fields needs to be,* Gabe surmised. He'd noticed the same strength in the elderly women of Amalfi. They had incredible muscle definition in their calves and lower legs. Climbing the mountain walkways and getting around the village was an endless workout.

Father Fiore led them through a maze of darkened hallways until they came to his office. His name was etched into the smoked-glass window of the office door. He ushered them in, closed the door, and pulled up enough chairs for everyone.

"I'm the rector here," he explained. "We've been expecting you. Cardinal Bauer called me personally and asked that I offer you sanctuary for as long as you need."

He paused briefly. "The cardinal sounded distressed. I don't know what this is about, and I don't want to, but I can assure you that you'll be safe here. We're in a very remote location."

"Thank you, Padre," Beckett replied. "We won't be here long, but your hospitality is very much appreciated."

Gabe was surprised by Beckett's cordial deportment. He'd been so cold in their first meeting and downright demanding at their second, but now he showed another side.

"Although remote," Father Fiore continued, "I believe we can offer you suitable accommodations in the guest quarters. Please make yourselves at home. If you need anything to eat or drink, help yourselves to whatever you can find. Our kitchen is behind the double doors in the center of this hallway. Is there anything you need before I show you to your rooms?"

"As a matter of fact, yes," Beckett replied. He held up his portfolio. "I see you have a computer. May I use it to print something?"

"Yes, of course," Father Fiore replied.

"Thank you kindly," Beckett said. "Um, could you show Gabe and Anna to their rooms while I review this disk? They've endured a lot today."

"Certainly. Please make yourself comfortable, Mr. Beckett," Father Fiore responded. "I'll take them right away."

Beckett appeared concerned with their comfort, but he actually wanted privacy. Neither Gabe nor Anna had any security clearances, and he didn't want anyone looking over his shoulder.

Beckett turned to Gabe. "I'll find you when I'm finished."

Father Fiore extended his arm to guide them. He led Gabe and Anna out of his office and turned down a long hallway with marble flooring. Their footsteps resonated off the walls in a melancholic rhythm. The echo reminded Gabe of his grammar school days. They turned a corner and stopped at the last room on the right.

"Ms. Castriotti, this will be your room."

The rector pulled several keys from his pocket and found the one for her room. He unlocked the door and held it open while she entered to take a look. "It has its own bathroom and shower," he said, "as well as fresh towels and linens. If you need anything at all, please do not hesitate to ask." He handed her the key.

"Thank you for your hospitality. You are most gracious," she replied. Anna stepped back into the hall and pulled the door closed behind her.

Smiling, the rector led them further. They turned onto another long, marble corridor, where eight doors lined the left wall. The right wall had none. "The right wall backs up against the mountain," Father Fiore explained, "but the view out this side is impressive."

He unlocked the third door and pushed it open. Gabe and Anna stepped inside. He was right; the view of the sea was fabulous.

"I'm sorry, Mr. Roslo," he continued. "The views are nice, but these rooms don't have individual toilets. You'll find a toilet with showers at the end of the hall."

Gabe thanked Father Fiore and assured him the room was quite satisfactory.

"Remember, if you need anything at all, please ask." With that, Father Fiore bowed slightly, pulled the door closed, and left.

The room was austere but clean. It had a desk and chair in the far corner. There was a sofa along the wall in addition to a full-size bed. Anna took a seat on the bed while Gabe paced.

"What's on your mind?" she asked.

"Well, the truth is, I'm worried about my grandmother. I know Beckett said they're watching her, but I want to talk to her. I wish I could use your phone."

"Don't be ridiculous, Gabe. It could lead them straight here. It would be suicide."

"I know. I know. I just can't believe what happened today. I thought you were dead. Thank God you're okay."

"Caruso wasn't so lucky," she replied.

"How well did you know him?" he asked.

"He was just an acquaintance. He showed up at my uncle's wine time group from time to time. We were never close, though. I know he was self-serving, but I didn't think he was the type of guy to get assassinated in cold blood."

Gabe shuddered at the sound of her words. The ugly nightmare continued to worsen. Anna moved to the sofa, and Gabe took a seat beside her.

"I never thought I'd witness something like that, not in my wildest dreams," Gabe said. "I feel completely numb—worse than on 9/11."

The horrible feelings of that fateful day in 2001 still weighed heavily. Anna fully understood Gabe's sentiment.

Caruso was dead, and he'd been killed in Salerno. It was now clear that the letters SA referred to Salerno. Gabe wondered if those bullets had been intended for him. *When is it going to end,* he thought, *all the senseless tragedy that humanity inflicts upon itself?* Evil mushroomed everywhere.

Gabe looked into Anna's eyes. They revealed the same strength and resolve he admired in his grandmother. Surely, she was afraid, but it didn't show. He decided not to keep anything from her.

He glanced at her folded hands and began. "When we went to Capri, my grandmother mentioned something astonishing. She said my grandfather had acted strange before he died. He even went to Mass with her a couple of times. He never went to Mass. He wasn't religious, but it sounded like he was undergoing some type of change—a spiritual change. It was almost like he was preparing to die."

Anna reached out and placed her hand on Gabe's arm.

"It seems strange," he continued. "Matters of faith never played a role in his life. My grandmother was very devout—still is, but not my grandfather. She's a pious, holy woman, but her faith never rubbed off on him."

"Any idea why?" Anna asked.

"Until this week, I never gave it much thought. His lukewarm approach to religion was all I'd ever known. Religious conviction hasn't played a role in my life either. But my grandmother told me something else at Capri, and it's given me incredible new insight," Gabe said.

"What's that?" Anna asked.

"My grandfather had a twin sister—something I never knew. She entered a convent in Poland in the 1930s and remained there when the family moved to America. Evidently, she and several other nuns in her convent were murdered by the Nazis for hiding Jews."

Anna gasped.

"My grandfather was so bitter that he never mentioned it to me—or anyone else, for that matter. It was one of those family secrets that gets boxed up and filed away like it never happened. My grandmother thinks it caused a protective callous to form within him to hide the pain." His voice broke. Anna leaned forward and wrapped her arm around him.

"It's okay," she whispered into his ear.

He regained his composure, and she kissed him on the cheek.

"According to my grandmother, he compensated by immersing himself in worldly affairs. He had a favorite saying. 'All the important decisions are made by the people with the most money, the biggest guns, and the best information.' His philosophy left little need for prayer."

"Quite Masonic, too," Anna replied.

Gabe was offended by the comment but then remembered his great-grandfather's diary. It contained those exact same words. Evidently, his great-grandfather had passed them on to his son. A belief system that placed total reliance on power, money, and man's quest for knowledge—true Masonic ideals.

Gabe ran his hand through his hair. Maybe his grandfather had reconsidered this belief. *Maybe he came to a different understanding,* Gabe thought. It was certainly a possibility.

"What about your mother and father?" Anna asked.

He shrugged. "That's another story altogether. My father got drafted and did two tours of duty in Vietnam. He started drinking, got into drugs—the whole thing. When he came back, he was changed. My mother did the best she could under the circumstances but eventually divorced him. She never remarried. My grandparents treated her like a daughter, but you could say she was another silent casualty of the war. It left her bitter. Perhaps, as a result, she did little to develop my sense of faith."

Anna snuggled under Gabe's arm. "I'm really sorry. Do you have any kind of relationship with your father now?"

A deadpan demeanor replaced his sadness. "None at all. As I got older, I began to see the effects of my father's drug and alcohol abuse. He came home from Vietnam angry about America's involvement in the war. He despised our government. He couldn't hold a job. He lost his family and most of his friends. In truth, he really doesn't want anything to do with me."

"A casualty of the Huge Red Dragon," Anna whispered.

"Atheistic communism," Gabe replied. "At least according to the Gobbi messages."

"Revelation's first seven-headed monster," Anna said. "The red menace, foretold from the beginning, now revealed. It was the dominant nemesis of the twentieth century, particularly the second half, when the Western world sought to stop its spread. The Vietnam War was all about stopping the spread of communism. Yes, Gabe, your father was another victim of the red dragon—just like all the other men who lost their lives there."

The effects of atheistic communism had indeed hit close to home for the Roslos. Gabe's life, his father's life, his grandfather's life, his great-grandfather's life—they'd all been impacted by the rise of the red menace. In fact, their lives had been impacted by both of Revelation's seven-headed monsters. Gabe bit his lip as he absorbed the chilling reality.

He looked at Anna. "The Gobbi messages place the red dragon squarely in the twentieth century, right? But aren't there other interpretations?" he asked.

"Of course," she replied. "Scholars, theologians, historians, end-time pundits—they all have theories and interpretations. The early Christian martyrs, for instance, interpreted the seven-headed dragon as the Roman Caesars. The ruthless Caesars fed Christians to the lions for sport. Succeeding generations attached the distinction to the menace of their time. However, the ultimate meaning remained hidden until the twentieth century. The all-powerful Roman legions slaughtered people by the thousands, but their power was minuscule compared to the annihilation capability of the Soviet Union. The huge red dragon foretells the rise of a global superpower armed with nuclear weapons—an atheistic superpower capable of obliterating humanity! The rise of the Soviet Union produced an evil of truly Biblical proportions."

"And now the dragon's been slayed," Gabe said. "The Cold War is over."

Anna paused to choose her words carefully. "That's not entirely clear. Yes, everyone rejoiced when the Eastern Bloc collapsed, but we need to consider three undeniable facts before pronouncing the dragon dead."

"Which are?"

"First, North Korea. Its government is modeled after Stalinism, and it continues to pursue nuclear power. It already has long-range missiles, which gives countries like Japan plenty to think about. North Korea presents a tremendous challenge to both the region and the world.

"Second, look at China. It's rapidly becoming an economic superpower, and it already has nuclear weapons.

"And third, but certainly not least, there's Russia. The former Soviet Union is growing rich from oil sales, and Russia is moving backward on human rights. Russian journalists are being killed, as are political opponents. Anyone who investigates or criticizes the Russian government is especially vulnerable. Gabe, you must ask yourself: what's behind the steely eyes of Vladimir Putin?"

"Hmm, I see your point," Gabe said.

"The dragon lives—perhaps wounded, but not dead."

Someone rapped on the door.

45

Zach Beckett was holding a large stack of papers. "There's something you need to see," he said.

Gabe stepped back and motioned for him to enter. Beckett crossed the room and took a seat on the couch next to Anna. Gabe sat on the bed.

"This document was on John's computer. It's a treatise he wrote. It discusses all the major conflicts of the twentieth and twenty-first centuries. Specifically, he analyzes each event within the context of the work he was doing. Here, take a look."

Beckett handed a copy to Gabe. The report was thick, perhaps 150 single-spaced pages. Gabe scanned the table of contents.

There were sections on the First World War (1914–1918), the Bolshevik Revolution (October 1917), the rise of Hitler (1932–1933), and the Second World War (1939–1945). There were also sections on each presidential era of the Cold War, beginning with Truman and continuing through the first Bush presidency.

The presidential sections were divided into subtopics. Under Kennedy, there were sections on Castro, the Bay of Pigs, the Kennedy-Kruschev Summit of 1961, Garabandal, the Building of the Berlin Wall, and the Cuban Missile Crisis.

Under Reagan, there were sections on the Evil Empire, Gorbachev, Star Wars, Poland, and John Paul II.

There was also a section on Clinton with subtopics titled "The Collapse of Yugoslavia," "Medjugorje," and "Genocide in Rwanda." The Rwandan Genocide caught his attention because Cardinal Bauer had specifically mentioned it regarding apparitions.

The last section was titled "Osama bin Laden." It had two subsections: "Fatwa & Oil" and "WSB." Gabe slumped backward. His mind raced. He rubbed his hand through his hair. WSB—*unbelievable!* His grandfather knew about WSB? Gabe's heart rate accelerated.

Beckett spoke. "Three weeks ago, John sent me the section called 'Fatwa & Oil.' I didn't know it at the time, but there's a related section called 'WSB.' He included it in the table of contents," Beckett continued, "but it's not in the document. See for yourself." Gabe flipped to the end of the report. He was right. The report ended with "Fatwa & Oil."

"Maybe WSB is code for an organization," Beckett speculated. He tapped his fingers on the couch, "But what the hell is it?"

An organization—or a person, Gabe thought. Anna shot a worried glance at Gabe but remained quiet.

Gabe thought about the message on his pillow in Capri. He also thought about the cryptic message his grandfather left on the mirror. He debated whether to share these with Beckett. Suddenly, he was struck by an ominous thought. Did SA mean NSA? Had the N been smudged somehow? *Was my grandfather trying to warn me about Zach Beckett?*

Gabe decided to err on the side of caution. Maybe Beckett pulled him out of the fray to use him for information—or worse, to silence him. If Masonry's dark side was filled with deception, maybe Zach Beckett was part of it. Gabe swallowed hard. Beckett would have to prove himself before he'd disclose anything about Masonry, the Beast, or WSB. It was time to find out just which side Zach Beckett played for.

"Zach, what exactly was my grandfather doing for you?" Gabe asked.

"Some of John's work is classified, but here's what I can tell you. After 9/11, the NSA put me in charge of a newly formed task force called Never Again. It's a crack team of analysts and field operatives with a singular mission: to monitor all forms of religious fanaticism around the world. The whole thing is part of the NSA's broader plan to leave no stone unturned in the wake of 9/11. We won't be surprised again."

"How did that involve my grandfather?"

Beckett fidgeted with his pen. "My responsibilities include a mandate to research paranormal phenomena," he said. "You know, things like UFOs, crop circles, ESP, psychic phenomena, poltergeists, ghost sightings, apparitions—the whole gamut. The objective is to search for anything that could directly or indirectly present a threat to national security."

"That's a strange spectrum," Gabe said. "How would those things present a threat to national security?"

"Most of them don't, of course," Beckett replied. "The movie, *Independence Day*, was a great sci-fi flick, but the NSA's not particularly worried about an alien space invasion. We have plenty of real threats. On the other hand, these things can trigger indirect threats. Do either of you remember the comet, Hale Bop?"

"Sure, I remember," Gabe replied. "A bunch of people committed suicide when it passed by Earth."

"Bingo. Back in 1997, nearly forty people committed mass suicide in San Diego. They were part of an organization called Heaven's Gate. Their leader convinced them they'd arise to be with the comet in some sort of paranormal experience. Totally bizarre, I know, but to the people involved, it sounded perfectly reasonable—an extreme form of religious fanaticism."

"How awful," Anna gasped.

"It was awful and completely senseless," Beckett replied. "I sympathize with the families, but what if that bizarre event had translated into a national security threat? What if the leader of Heaven's Gate had convinced his followers to engage in domestic terrorism? Given their unwavering loyalty and distorted thinking, anything could happen."

"I see what you mean," Gabe said.

"So Never Again looks into all sorts of things—not just the obvious threats," Beckett said.

A huge challenge had been laid at Beckett's feet. The terror possibilities were vast, and spiritual fanaticism came in many shades.

"We don't give every paranormal phenomenon the same degree of review," Beckett continued, "but we have a duty to learn about these things and identify the associated risks to national security. As you might imagine, my team has been overwhelmed by the task. Our primary concern is radical Islam, but that's not the only place we find religious zealotry and fanaticism."

"You still haven't explained my grandfather's role," Gabe said. "What exactly was he doing for you?" Gabe demanded harshly.

"Your grandfather was a loyal and dedicated member of the intelligence service for many years," Beckett replied. "He served his country with distinction, and I always valued his input and discernment."

Beckett paused a moment to collect his thoughts. "During the Clinton Administration, John was forced out. He didn't want to retire, but the Cold War had ended, and the agency thought it was time for 'relics' like him to move on—budget constraints. I was angry about it, but there was nothing I could do, at least officially."

Beckett shook his head as he recalled the injustice. "After his retirement, we kept a standing lunch date every few weeks whenever I was in town," Beckett continued. "We discussed security concerns, political developments, and the like. John was stripped of his security clearances, so certain issues were off-limits, but we both benefited from the arrangement. After 9/11, my new duties mushroomed, as did the funding, which allowed me to tap every available resource. Never Again was a huge responsibility, and I needed help—lots of help. With most of my resources devoted to tracking and monitoring Islamic terror cells, I asked John if he'd investigate a phenomenon called apparitions."

Gabe and Anna exchanged anxious glances.

"John was enthusiastic. His only condition was that he needed full security clearance. As always, his analysis was incredibly thorough. He used our lunch dates to brief me on his findings. He told me he'd found a significant connection between apparitions and the Cold War. He said his final report would include an extensive section on the plight of Poland. His childhood home played a critical role in the collapse of the Soviet Union, especially regarding apparitions and the supernatural. His conclusions were incredibly lucid. This report contains his analysis."

Gabe shifted in his seat but said nothing.

"John didn't know anything about apparitions when I first asked him to do the investigation," Beckett continued, "but he was willing to do whatever he could in support of national security. Neither of us imagined his findings would amount to much. We were both skeptical of the supernatural. John intended to prove apparitions were nothing more than the wild delusions of well-meaning but otherwise harmless people. What he found instead was quite the opposite. Authentic apparitions were far from delusional."

Gabe was intrigued.

Beckett continued. "Spiritual matters were not John's bailiwick, so he asked Francesca what she knew about apparitions. She gave him a videotape called *Marian Apparitions of the 20th Century*."

He's telling the truth, Gabe thought. His grandmother told him the same story.

"John watched the video and was fascinated by the correlation between apparitions and the major geopolitical events of the twentieth century. He started to call them supernatural interventions. I think he found them profoundly moving. I would not have said this two years ago, but I believe there's something to this. So did John."

Gabe's confidence in Zach Beckett was growing.

"That initial videotape led John along a path of discovery," Beckett continued. "Each step shed new light on the present geopolitical landscape. He was still conducting the investigation when he was murdered."

Gabe thought back to the words of Cardinal Bauer. The cardinal told him that apparitions occur during times of difficulty in the world to help people through them. His grandfather lived through some of the most difficult history the world had ever known. Gabe refocused.

Beckett continued. "John uncovered things that totally defied reason yet were undeniably accurate. Our professional training taught us to be skeptical of the supernatural, but what he found was an unmistakable pattern of events. He discovered a stunning series of connections between the supernatural realm and the history of the twentieth century. He told me there was only one rational conclusion—to find meaning in it. And he did—lots of meaning."

Gabe looked at Anna. Her face was serious as Beckett spoke.

"Evidently, John's investigations led to Paolo Castriotti," Beckett continued, "which led to Cardinal Bauer. That's why we're here now." Beckett hesitated momentarily.

Gabe leaned back in his seat. Zach Beckett's story corroborated everything he knew to be true. For the first time since their paths crossed, he'd heard a completely consistent story from Zach Beckett. It also clarified the secrecy surrounding the autopsy.

"I couldn't tell you this in Rome," Beckett said, "but it was John who wanted me here in Italy. He told me he'd uncovered another piece of the mystery. He said it involved the highest levels of national security. I tried to pry the information from him, but he wouldn't budge. He was incredibly cautious. He demanded that I come here personally, so I did."

Beckett paused to straighten his sleeve. "John had arranged a secret meeting with Cardinal Bauer. The three of us were supposed to meet the night he died. I found the appointment in John's calendar. The cardinal confirmed it when I spoke to him.

"John had a plan. He asked me to check into a hotel in Sorrento and wait there, which I did. He wanted me to depart at 22:30, drive the coastal road, and meet him in the marina parking lot in Amalfi. Once there, he would tell me the location and purpose of the meeting. That's all he said. I still don't know what he planned to reveal at the meeting because he never came."

Beckett's face suddenly bore genuine emotion. "Gabe, I'm truly sorry I got your grandfather involved in this. He was a true friend. I regret my decision."

"No one holds you responsible," Gabe said. "He never wanted to retire in the first place. My grandmother said as much. He loved his work and took it seriously. He gave his life for the greater good and died for his country. My grandfather was a true patriot. He wouldn't have called you here unless it was important."

Gabe paused a moment to collect his thoughts. He decided it was time to put his trust in Zach Beckett.

"Yesterday, I found a threatening note in my room at the hotel in Capri," Gabe said. "It read, 'Gabriel Roslo, stop your search. Go back to America. There's nothing here for you but agony and heartache. You're being watched! WSB.' When our boat arrived in Sorrento, we were followed by the Audi I mentioned earlier. The note implies that WSB is a person. Any ideas?" Gabe asked.

"None," Beckett replied, "but I suspect your grandfather was going to tell me at the meeting with Cardinal Bauer." Beckett's face once again fell into the cold, expressionless demeanor of a national security agent.

"I wish I could tell you the Audi was one of mine," Beckett said. "I can't. As to the identity of WSB, that answer lies in John's report."

"And now you need to find it," Gabe said.

"Correction—we need to find it," Beckett replied. "John intentionally deleted 'WSB' from the report, but there must be a copy somewhere. Any chance you found a disk or thumb drive among your grandfather's things?"

"No—just the diary with the missing pages," Gabe answered. "When we found my grandfather's body, the diary was next to him in the bathroom. Some pages had been torn out. I assumed that whoever killed him has those pages."

"Doubtful. John wouldn't have been that careless," Beckett said. "If those pages contained incriminating information, he would've torn them out himself—and even flushed them—before he died."

"Do you think they're connected to WSB and the deleted file?" Gabe asked.

"That's a definite possibility," Beckett nodded. He held up the Roslo Report. "This document has serious implications for the times we live in, both now and in the days ahead. What do you know about apparitions?"

"Cardinal Bauer gave me a basic overview," Gabe replied. "Anna is familiar with them, too."

Beckett looked at her quizzically.

"I've learned a thing or two from my uncle," she explained. "I was a very good listener at his wine time gatherings."

Beckett frowned at her for a split second. He then divided his stack in two. "I've already read this part," he said, handing that portion to Anna. "This document is not yet classified. I want you to read it, but don't let it out of your sight. The more clues we can draw from it, the better. Let's get back together in an hour and compare notes."

He didn't wait for a response. Beckett abruptly stood and walked out of the room.

Anna turned to Gabe. "Where do you want to begin?" she asked.

46

Gabe looked down at the copy in his hands. He took a deep breath and let it out slowly. He looked at Anna. Her face was pensive. He joined her on the sofa and scanned the table of contents again. Under the Bolshevik Revolution, Gabe found a section titled "Masonry, Portugal, and the Rise & Fall of an Atheistic Superpower." The title caught his eye. He flipped open the document and read the title aloud.

"Let's start here," he said. Anna nodded and turned to the corresponding page in her copy. Both began to read.

In 1917, as staggering bloodshed poured out on the battlefields of Europe, three events occurred simultaneously that forever changed the course of human history:

1. Arabian tribal leaders banded together under British influence and attacked the Ottoman Empire, contributing to its downfall. The Ottoman Turks had ruled the Middle East for centuries. Their defeat in World War I resulted in one of the greatest wealth transfers in the history of the world. Oil was discovered in Arabia twenty years later, placing the greatest pool of natural resources known to man into Saudi hands. The Arabian victory also gave shape and purpose to the world's most volatile political climate as the newly formed nations of Iran, Iraq, Jordan, Syria, Lebanon, and Saudi Arabia emerged.

2. In Russia, the Bolshevik Revolution filled a power void that opened when Czar Nicholas II abdicated his throne. The rise of Soviet communism

brought to fulfillment the unforgettable opening sentence of Karl Marx's Communist Manifesto: "A specter is haunting Europe—the specter of communism." The rise of Soviet tyranny led to the slaughter of millions, yet it had a far worse consequence. Soviet totalitarianism challenged the Western democracies in every corner of the planet for global supremacy. Stalin's Iron Curtain defined East-West relations for half a century and was directly responsible for the most massive arms buildup in the history of the world. In truth, the haunting specter of communism is their nuclear stockpile, numbering in the thousands. Humanity will never be the same.

3. A spectacular series of supernatural apparitions took place in Fatima, Portugal. According to official Roman Catholic Church documents, the Virgin Mary appeared to three children on six separate occasions at the exact same time the Bolsheviks prepared for their revolution. The final apparition occurred in October 1917 and was accompanied by a dazzling public miracle witnessed by tens of thousands. According to historical accounts, the powerful miracle known as the Miracle of the Sun was offered as public evidence of the importance of the apparition's messages. The messages contained both spiritual and political warnings. After conducting my extensive research, I realized that the Fatima prophecies and the rise of Soviet communism were deeply intertwined. Furthermore, I believe the apparition prophecies have continuing relevance for the twenty-first century.

BECKETT RETURNED TO Father Fiore's office. He poured a cup of coffee and sat down to read. He searched for clues regarding the identity of WSB. After twenty minutes, his search produced little, but a section on Pakistan caught his attention. In particular, he noted a strange coincidence of dates.

> The US fostered an alliance with Pakistan after 9/11. The alliance arose out of necessity because Osama bin Laden was hiding somewhere along Pakistan's 1,400-mile border with Afghanistan.

Beckett knew that was true, but America courted Pakistan for a second reason. In 1998, Pakistan became the world's first Islamic nuclear state. By appeasing it with economic and military support, the US had hoped to curtail Pakistan's nuclear ambitions and prevent weapons of mass destruction from falling into the hands of Islamic terrorists.

The region's nuclear escalation began when India resumed nuclear tests in 1998. Pakistan immediately followed suit and declared itself the first Islamic nuclear power. Pakistan's General Pervez Musharraf seized control of those weapons the following year when he staged a successful military coup in October 1999. Beckett recalled the extraordinary danger of that period.

Pakistan and India fought three wars over the disputed Kashmir region during the prior half-century. Tensions mounted and finally spilled over when Islamic terrorists stormed the Indian parliament and killed nine people in December 2001. The massacre was orchestrated by Pakistanis and happened just three months after 9/11.

The defiant act threatened the US alliance with Pakistan and catapulted global security risks into the stratosphere. Both sides made strong overtures toward war. The world braced itself for a possible nuclear exchange as the two populous nations moved precariously close to the brink of catastrophe.

Beckett went back to the Roslo Report.

> The Bush Administration rushed in with diplomatic pressure to quell the uproar. War was averted because of an extraordinary piece of diplomacy, but security risks remained high. The chief concern: AQ Khan and Pakistan's nuclear secrets.
>
> AQ Khan, the architect of Pakistan's nuclear program, was at the center of a black-market conspiracy selling nuclear secrets to Iran, Libya, and North Korea. Evidence of his crimes surfaced, and he confessed publicly on Pakistani television. That was in February 2004.
>
> Iran and North Korea are known sponsors of state terrorism. Coupled with Iraq, they form President Bush's famous Axis of Evil. The proliferation of Pakistan's nuclear secrets to these countries is a major destabilization of global security. It also places Pakistan at the heart of the War on Terror.
>
> As I researched these unsettling developments, I discovered something even more disturbing. My work uncovered a link between these events, the Fatima apparitions, and the messages to Father Gobbi. India's nuclear tests were successfully concluded on May 13, 1998, exactly eighty-one years after the first Fatima apparition (May 13, 1917). My first inclination was to dismiss the coincidence, but then I discovered a dreadful and ominous warning given to Father Gobbi. It was of supernatural origin and delivered on May 13, 1993, precisely five years before the Indian nuclear tests.
>
> The mother of Jesus began by recapping the condition of the world. She indicated that sinister forces were now guiding and organizing human events and had triumphed in their grand design. They had seduced humanity into

a godless existence by offering dazzling and deceptive idols instead. People everywhere extolled the hedonistic pursuit of pleasure, possessed an insatiable hunger for wealth, and were filled with egoism and pride. Moral decay, blasphemy, and the ruthless domination of others were hallmarks of society. Hearts had grown cold, violence had taken root everywhere, wars were spreading across the earth, and hatred raged like an inferno.

Against this backdrop, she delivered an ominous warning to humanity. She indicated that we now live in danger of a new and catastrophic global conflict—a war so devastating it promised no victors.

The horrors of the twentieth century established the validity of Fatima's apparition warnings. Therefore, Never Again must ask itself a terrifying question. Is the date May 13 merely a coincidence or an indication that supernatural evil is advancing a new plan for the twenty-first century?

Beckett knew full well that Pakistan's nuclear secrets had passed into the wrong hands. It was a documented fact. *Have those secrets—or worse, weapons—made their way into the hands of terrorists?* he wondered. No doubt they'd be used against America if they had. Yet, oddly enough, America was now aligned with Pakistan in the War on Terror, the source of that threat. *Times of war make for strange bedfellows,* he thought.

Beckett looked back at the Roslo Report. The final sentence glared off the page: "a war so devastating it promised no victors." Beckett was pierced by a thought. *Had the Mother of God foretold the War on Terror?* If so, the consequences were chilling. It raised the question of whether the War on Terror was winnable at all. Perhaps violence and destruction would only spread and escalate. He gritted his teeth and tapped his fingers on the desk.

"1998—what a year," he muttered.

47

Back at NSA headquarters, Jason Hollingsworth also dissected the work of John Roslo. Beckett had received a copy of "Fatwa & Oil" two weeks earlier as a preview to the larger document. Stunned by its content, Beckett immediately convened the senior members of Never Again to debate its explosive ramifications. He grilled his task force on the details, including Hollingsworth, to ensure they analyzed it from every angle.

In a series of marathon meetings, they argued about the war in Iraq, the counterinsurgency, al-Qaeda, and the critical differences between Osama bin Laden's first fatwa in 1996 and his second in 1998. Both were treacherous, but John Roslo's discovery in the Gobbi messages cast a spine-chilling shadow over the agency's current crisis.

A month earlier, Beckett and the NSA learned that two nuclear devices were missing from the Russian arsenal. It was unclear where they were, who had them, or how they'd been stolen. Publicly, it was business as usual, but privately, the US and Russia were cooperating in a top-secret mission to locate the missing weapons. Both nations suspected Islamic extremists, and both were horror-stricken by the prospect of failing to locate them in time.

Tensions were already sky-high, but "Fatwa & Oil" launched them into the stratosphere. Hollingsworth picked up the document and read the words of John Roslo for the fourth time.

FATWA & OIL

Fatwa: An Islamic legal declaration rooted in the laws and teachings of Islam.

In 1996, Osama bin Laden issued a fatwa and declared war on the United States of America. The fatwa accused America of shameless aggression against all Islamic people and condemned it because of its oil policy and military presence in Saudi Arabia.

With the permission of the Saudi royal family, American military forces have been stationed in Saudi Arabia since 1990. They remained there after the Persian Gulf War to ensure the adequate flow of oil to world markets and to defend Saudi Arabia from invasion by Saddam Hussein. Bin Laden considered this a religious abomination and condemned the Saudi royal family for granting access to American infidels.

Bin Laden's 1996 fatwa was directed toward American military personnel stationed in Saudi. The raging terror of Osama bin Laden was made known that same summer by the bombing of an American Army barracks, killing nineteen soldiers.

Bin Laden referenced the Koran to powerfully convey the beliefs of his al-Qaeda network and to invoke the deepest seeds of religious zealotry.

Hollingsworth knew that Bin Laden and his al-Qaeda followers boasted an audacious brand of Islam, one that divided the world into two camps: the People of Heaven (themselves) and the People of Hell (everyone else). In their view, the sinful acts of the Saudi princes placed them squarely in the second camp, along with every other Muslim who disagreed with them. He continued reading.

Osama bin Laden's second fatwa was issued in February 1998. It expanded the declaration of war to include all Americans everywhere, including civilians, and was cosigned by the leaders of other holy war movements. Under the title World Islamic Front, they united their terror and extended the battlefield to the entire globe, spawning the 9/11 attacks on American soil. Bin Laden cited three reasons for expanding his holy war:

1. The United States still occupied Islam's holiest place, the Arabian Peninsula, home to Mecca and Medina. He accused America of plundering

Arabian riches, dictating to its rulers, humiliating its people, and terrorizing its neighbors.

2. Bin Laden claimed America would use its Saudi military bases to launch an attack on Iraq. President Bush validated that claim five years later when he launched the Iraqi invasion in 2003. (The fact America quietly pulled its troops out of Saudi Arabia before the invasion proved ineffective in diffusing the rage of Islamic extremists.)

3. Bin Laden cited America's support of Israel. He called it an American Crusader-Zionist alliance. He argued America had both economic and religious reasons for waging war in the Middle East. He declared that proof of the American-Zionist alliance was America's eagerness to destroy Iraq, Saudi Arabia's strongest neighbor. He claimed America would simultaneously serve its economic need for oil and advance Jewish religious objectives by diverting the world's attention away from the Israeli occupation of Jerusalem and its murder of Muslims. These claims were all made in 1998, well before 9/11 and long before the American invasion of Iraq.

Hollingsworth shook his head. Bin Laden wrote those statements five years before the 2003 US invasion of Iraq. Hollingsworth contemplated the violence. *Had America unwittingly played into the hands of radical Islam by invading Iraq?* he wondered. Would America succeed in keeping the destruction off American soil? For the moment, it made no difference. What mattered now were the two missing nuclear devices. He looked back at Roslo's work and continued reading.

The most chilling statements in the 1996 fatwa pertained to the recruitment of Islamic youth by al-Qaeda. Those statements were directed toward William Perry, President Clinton's Defense Secretary.

Bin Laden wrote, "Our youths believe in paradise after death. They believe in what has been said about the greatness of the reward of the Martyrs. They are in the highest level of paradise—married off to the beautiful ones, protected from the test in the grave, assured security on the day of judgment, wedded to seventy-two of the pure, beautiful ones of Paradise. These youths love death as you love life."

Iraqi insurgents quoted those exact words after beheading American hostages following the American invasion of Iraq. Those barbaric deeds, videotaped and placed on the Internet for all to see, were deliberately conducted in accordance with the ideas set forth by Osama bin Laden in his 1996 fatwa.

Hollingsworth was all too familiar with those haunting words. Bin Laden boasted about the Islamic youth. He said they fought among themselves for the right to kill Americans because the reward was eternal paradise. The bombing of two American embassies in Africa in 1998, the bombing of the USS Cole, and the events of 9/11 were all proof of Bin Laden's claim. Hollingsworth was convinced that the treachery of Islamic religious fanaticism was the greatest threat of all against American security.

He stood up, walked to the window, and looked in the direction of Washington, DC, twenty miles in the distance. His mind replayed that fateful day when Bin Laden's zealots crashed a commercial airliner into the Pentagon. He recalled the frenetic scramble, the confusion, and the immediate list of suspects.

He shook his head and exhaled hard. He sat back down, placed his elbows on the desk, and rested his forehead on his hands. He then reread John Roslo's stunning discovery. It directly linked Osama bin Laden to another Revelation symbol.

> Osama bin Laden and the World Islamic Front declared war on America in 1998, a truly fateful year. At the root of their declaration lies a brand of violent religious fanaticism that threatens the entire social and political stability of the planet.
>
> American intelligence agencies now recognize the religious aspects of the security threats facing the country. Never Again has taken a central role in this work. However, none of us was prepared for the discovery I made in Italy.
>
> The discovery was both frightening and surreal, but most of all, it…

The phone rang. Hollingsworth looked at the caller ID and picked it up. "Zach, where have you been?"

48

Gabe was still absorbed in his grandfather's treatise. He was fascinated by the connections between Fatima, the Cold War, and nuclear proliferation. The Fatima apparitions foretold the horrors of the twentieth century, and they were worse than anyone could have imagined. The Soviet Union and the United States launched an arms race, and nuclear confrontation seemed inevitable.

Amazingly, the Soviet red menace collapsed peacefully, but a new threat emerged. Raging Islamic militancy posed a threat to global peace and security. The Cold War was history. However, the War on Terror took its place, and religious zealotry fueled the hatred. If that weren't enough, an even darker secret was revealed in the Gobbi messages. The shadowy rise of Freemasonry, a worldwide organization steeped in secrecy, fulfilled the black beast of Revelation. Gabe bristled at the imagery.

Just then, the door burst open. Father Fiore stepped inside. "Come quickly. You must leave," he said. Beckett followed him into the room.

"What's wrong?" Gabe asked.

"Hurry!" Father Fiore answered without explaining.

"Grab the treatise," Beckett ordered. "We need to destroy it."

"I know a place," Father Fiore added. "This way."

Gabe and Anna grabbed the Roslo Report. They handed it to Beckett, and all three followed Father Fiori down the hall. Their quick footsteps reverberated as they moved through the darkened corridor. Gabe checked his watch—10:06 p.m.

"Where are we going?" Gabe demanded.

Beckett ignored the question.

"Where's Jenkins?" Gabe asked.

"Not here. I gave him a job to do," Beckett answered.

The rector turned right and exited the building through a set of double doors then descended a narrow staircase to a stone path. Without pausing, he bolted into the darkness. The others followed closely. The moon glistened in the cloudless sky. It offered just enough light to see the silhouette of the path. The chilly night air nipped at Gabe's cheeks.

"Over here," Father Fiore said. He led them to a large metal door. He unlocked and opened it.

Gabe saw the glow of a large furnace. Beckett stepped inside and pitched both copies of the Roslo Report into the flames. Within seconds, the pages disintegrated in the inferno.

"Let's move," Beckett ordered.

Father Fiore led them back into the darkness. They passed through a grove of lemon trees, crossed a narrow clearing, and moved along the backside of the chapel next to the abbey. They turned a corner and ascended a long, stone staircase into the blackness of night.

"What's happening?" Gabe demanded. "Where are we going?"

"Grotta Dello Smeraldo," Father Fiore answered.

"Where?" Gabe asked.

"The Emerald Grotto," Beckett clarified. "It's about four kilometers up the coast."

"What for?" Gabe inquired.

"To meet Cardinal Bauer," Beckett replied. "He's on his way there now. His driver just called. They're descending the mountain route from Castellamare."

"Why don't we just meet here?" Gabe asked.

"Too risky," Beckett said. "If someone tracked their location, it would lead them straight here. We can't put the monastery at risk."

"How do you know we haven't already been compromised?" Gabe asked.

"We don't. That's why we're getting the hell out," Beckett said.

At the top of the stone staircase, a young monk dressed in traditional Franciscan robes greeted them. Father Fiore introduced him. "This is Philippe. He'll take you to the arch bridge. From there, you'll be transported by boat to the grotto entrance. Cardinal Bauer will be waiting for you."

"Thank you, Padre," Beckett said as they exchanged a firm handshake. "We appreciate everything you've done."

"We'll pray for your success," Father Fiore replied. "Godspeed."

Philippe led them across the parking area to a brick, two-car garage. He hiked his robe to his knees and tucked it into the corded rope belt tied around his waist. He swung open the heavy wooden garage door, squeezed into the driver seat of a Volkswagen Polo, and backed out. The car jerked to a stop. Beckett grabbed the front seat. Gabe and Anna piled into the back. Gabe crammed his six-foot-three-inch frame into the seat behind the driver. Philippe pulled his seat forward as far as possible, but Gabe's knees were still smashed as he tried to keep them out of Anna's lap.

"It's not far," she said, giggling as she watched him struggle to get in.

The car lurched forward, and they were off. The mountain descent was protected by a ribbon of concrete that snaked along in the headlights. It created a hypnotic blur as they twisted around the steeply sloped switchbacks. *No doubt the protective wall has saved the lives of many drunks over the years,* Gabe thought. The only breaks in the wall were driveway access openings that led to hotels, bars, and residences built on the downside of the cliff. In the daylight, the driveways disappeared over the edge. At night, they disappeared into eternity.

Philippe was obviously an experienced Amalfi driver. He was completely calm as they blasted around each turn, clutching, breaking, and shifting in a series of fluid motions. He rounded one particularly tight hairpin turn, and Anna was thrown to Gabe's side of the car. They exchanged a slight chuckle as she retreated to her side. Gabe gave up trying to keep his legs behind the driver. They both readjusted, and his knees were pressed firmly against hers. She didn't seem to mind. He couldn't help but smell traces of her perfume.

Gabe's thoughts returned to the meeting with Cardinal Bauer. He'd learned so much since they first met. He wondered how the cardinal would react to the meaning of the message on the mirror. Perhaps he'd even be able to solve the final piece—SA. There were so many possibilities: Satan, Salerno, Saint Andrew's, maybe even NSA.

Beckett was his usual tight-lipped self. Suddenly, the vehicle screeched to a halt.

"We're here," Philippe announced. He parked between two cavernous walls and switched off the headlights. Everything went pitch black. "Follow me."

Philippe swung open his door and led them down a staircase into a deep canyon. Gabe's eyes had yet to adjust. It was far too dark to see the bottom, but Gabe heard waves crashing. The canyon walls towered above them on every side and glowed in the moonlight. Gabe saw the silhouette of a magnificent arched bridge that spanned the canyon walls. Beyond the arch, the moonlight reflected off the sea and glowed on the crashing waves' white foam.

They reached a landing where the walkway extended in two directions. One went toward the arched bridge, the other down another staircase. Philippe headed deeper into the gorge. Gabe's eyes adjusted to the darkness as they neared the bottom. He saw several small boats pulled up on a narrow beachhead. A larger boat was moored alongside the floating dock. It was a fishing rig. Immediately, Gabe recognized it. It was the same rig he'd seen the night he arrived in Amalfi.

"Buona sera," said the boat captain. Standing on the deck of the boat was Andre Gotto.

Gabe felt his pulse race. *What's Gotto doing here?* he thought. The last time Gabe saw Andre Gotto, he was leaving the Amalfi Hotel with Gino Caruso. Gotto was a no-show at the Salerno lunch. *A convenient coincidence?* Gabe wondered.

"Buona sera," Philippe said in return.

Gabe hadn't told Beckett or Anna about the boat he'd seen that night—Andre Gotto's boat. He looked up at the mammoth walls rising toward the sky. A sniper could be hiding anywhere in the canyon.

Gotto extended a hand to Anna and greeted her with a clumsy kiss on the cheek. Gabe saw a look of surprise flash across her face. She and Beckett climbed aboard, but Gabe hesitated. He wondered if Beckett knew what he was doing. He feared they were walking into another trap.

"Please, you must hurry," Gotto said. "We don't have much time."

Gabe ran his hand through his hair. He took one last look upward and stepped aboard. Philippe remained behind. "You're not going with us?" Gabe asked.

"No, this is as far as I go. I'll wait here for you," Philippe replied. "God be with you."

In an instant, the motor was running. Diesel engines chugged a low growl as they idled. Gotto backed away from the dock, turned his rig toward the sea, and eased forward the throttle. The boat inched ahead. He skillfully maneuvered around several large rock formations that guarded the entrance to the gorge. No one said a word.

Gotto stood in the boat's wheelhouse, a small cabin just large enough for two people. The wheelhouse had sliding metal doors on either side, and both were open. Gabe took a position at the portside door to keep an eye on Gotto. Anna sat near the deck rail a few feet away. Beckett stood in the bow and showed no emotion. Gabe suspected his stern demeanor belied the truth.

Gabe continued to search for snipers, but it was too dark, even in the moonlight. The craggy rock walls were filled with shadows. Pitch darkness

THE AMALFI SECRET

passed over them as they slid beneath the arched bridge. Finally, they were in open water.

Gotto shoved forward the throttles. The powerful diesels roared to life and lifted them higher in the surf. Their speed increased. They sailed across the surface and curved eastward toward the caped inlet known as the Emerald Grotto.

Gabe took advantage of the deafening roar to warn Beckett about what he knew. He kept an eye on Gotto and moved to the bow. Gabe leaned in so Beckett could hear him over the howl of the engines. "How did you make arrangements with Gotto?" he asked.

"I didn't," Beckett replied.

"Then who did?"

"Father Fiore," Beckett said. "He assured me Gotto was totally trustworthy."

"Zach, there's something you need to know. I saw this boat the night my grandfather was murdered."

"Where?" Beckett demanded.

"Outside the Amalfi Hotel, and not only that, I saw him signal his flashlight at the hotel three separate times."

Beckett flashed a worried look at Gabe. "Why didn't you tell me this earlier?"

"I didn't know," Gabe replied. "There was a party at the hotel that night. People were shouting at him. When he flashed the light, they thought he was signaling back. I thought so, too, but that was before I knew it was Andre Gotto. Paolo Castriotti said Gotto was opposed to calling the Carabinieri, and now he's taking us to meet Cardinal Bauer—it's too much of a coincidence."

Beckett did a quick sweep of their surroundings. They were far enough from shore to make a sniper shot difficult but not impossible. He was no longer stone-faced. It wasn't panic, but for the first time, Zach Beckett appeared disoriented.

"What should we do?" Gabe pressed. "We can't just let him drive us into another trap. Let's confront him. I'll take one side. You take the other. Let me take the lead."

Beckett nodded in agreement. They moved to opposite sides of the wheelhouse with Gotto pinned inside.

"Signore Gotto," Gabe shouted over the roar of the engines.

"Please, call me Andre."

"Very well. Andre, there's something I need to know," Gabe said.

"Yes," Gotto replied.

"Why were you opposed to calling the Carabinieri when you found out about my grandfather's death?" Gabe asked.

Gotto shot a nervous glance in Gabe's direction. "What do you mean?" he asked, evading the question.

"I mean, what was your reason?" Gabe demanded. "Why did you sway Gino Caruso when he wanted to call the Carabinieri?"

Andre Gotto stared straight ahead.

"Well?" Gabe demanded again.

Gotto began to fidget with the controls. He pointed to one of the gauges. "Gabriel, did you know the maritime compass was invented in Amalfi?"

"Yes, I read the brochure!" Gabe snapped. He was getting impatient.

Beckett discreetly slipped his hand into his breast pocket and felt for his trusty Glock.

"Nobody uses the compass anymore," Gotto continued. "Today, we all have GPS, much more accurate. Here, have a look."

"Turn off your GPS—*now*!" Beckett demanded. He pulled out his weapon and shoved it into Gotto's face.

"Don't shoot!" Gotto yelled. He panicked and thrust his hands in the air.

The boat swung wildly left and headed full throttle toward the rocky coastline. The sudden change of direction caused Gabe to stumble into the cabin and knock Gotto to the floor. Beckett kept his footing. His weapon was still trained on Gotto.

"I said turn off the GPS!" Beckett demanded.

Gotto's eyes darted back and forth between the controls and Beckett's gun. Gabe grabbed the wheel.

"*Now!*" Beckett barked.

Gotto scrambled to his feet and complied.

"No sudden moves," Beckett said.

"Please!" Gotto begged. He motioned toward the steering mechanism. Beckett nodded.

Gotto took the wheel from Gabe and eased back on the throttle. The deafening roar dropped to a low rumble. He turned the rig away from the coast. Gabe stepped back but stayed within striking distance. Anna was riveted to her seat. She clenched the rail with both hands, a look of horror on her face.

"Take us further out to sea," Beckett ordered.

Gotto accelerated. They reached a safe distance from shore, and Beckett directed him to idle the engines.

"We want some answers," Gabe demanded.

"It's not what you think. Let me explain," Gotto said.

"This better be good," Beckett snapped, his gun planted firmly into Gotto's side.

Gotto looked nervous. "Gabriel," he began with a serious tone, "there's something you must know—something I need to get off my chest. The night your grandfather died, I was hired to flash a signal light at the Amalfi Hotel. I was paid 250 euros to fish along the coast that night, something I would've done anyway. My only instruction was to flash a light at the hotel three times at 11:30."

"Who hired you?" Gabe demanded.

Gotto's foot tapped anxiously. "I don't know. I never saw him before," he said.

"Why didn't you tell me this earlier?" Gabe asked.

"I didn't give it much thought when he hired me. I needed the money," Gotto continued. "Only a fool would've turned it down. When I learned about your grandfather's passing," he said remorsefully, "I was afraid. I tried to console my conscience by convincing myself the events were unrelated. But now, I know for a fact that they were."

"How do you know that?" Gabe demanded.

"I was approached by another man this evening," Gotto said. "This time, it was someone I knew well. He came to me late in the afternoon to tell me about the murder of Gino Caruso. He was waiting at my slip when I returned from sea. It was Father Fiore, rector of the abbey."

Gabe felt his pulse race. "What did he want?" Gabe asked.

"I've known him for many years, but this was the first time he ever met me at the dock," Gotto continued slowly. "I greeted him, but his face bore a dire concern. He told me about Caruso's murder and the incredible circumstances of the past few days. He then apologized profusely."

"Apologized for what?" Gabe asked.

"For using me without my knowledge," Gotto replied. "I asked Father Fiore what he was talking about. He explained that he was the one who hired me to flash the light at John's window. He used an intermediary—someone I didn't know."

Beckett nudged Gotto's side with his weapon. It prompted him to continue. "Father Fiore told me the intermediary was Cardinal Bauer's driver. Cardinal Bauer used a stranger to maintain total secrecy."

"I still don't understand," Gabe protested.

Andre looked at Gabe. "Father Fiore said your grandfather had arranged a secret meeting between Cardinal Bauer and Mr. Beckett. He told me neither party knew who was going to be at the meeting. Only your grandfather did. Evidently, my flashlight was the signal to confirm the cardinal had arrived for the meeting."

With those words, Gabe and Beckett locked eyes. Andre Gotto was telling the truth. Anna's sentiments about the man had been correct. He was an ally and a good man. Beckett put his gun back into its holster.

"Please accept our apology," Beckett said. "We're all a little edgy right now."

Andre Gotto nodded humbly. He wiped his sweating brow with the back of his sleeve.

"Gabriel, I'm so very sorry about what happened. Tonight, I'm at your service," Andre said.

Gabe put a hand on Andre's shoulder, extending his own silent apology. The communication was clear and understood.

Andre checked his watch. "We need to hurry, with your permission."

Beckett nodded. Andre pushed forward on the throttles. Gabe took a seat next to Anna and placed an arm around her. She asked no questions and let her head drop to his shoulder. Andre slowed the engines ten minutes later and steered the craft into a caped inlet.

The boat maintained a course toward the far back corner. As they approached the cliffs, Gabe saw a cement, V-shaped dock in the moonlight. Andre killed the engines, and they drifted toward the dock. They'd reached the Emerald Grotto.

The place appeared deserted. It was perfectly quiet except for the sloshing of waves against the concrete. Andre moored the rig. For a moment, they stood silently and stared at the enormous rock walls surrounding the grotto entrance. Cardinal Bauer was nowhere to be seen.

"Where is he?" Gabe asked.

"I don't know," Andre replied. "He was supposed to be here when we arrived."

Gabe looked up. *More ideal locations for a sniper,* he thought.

"It looks like the perfect setup for an ambush," Gabe whispered under his breath to Beckett.

"Don't worry," Beckett replied. "The location is secure. I sent Jenkins and another agent to comb the area around the grotto. They secured the perimeter an hour ago."

"Where are they now?" Gabe asked.

"I ordered Jenkins to Ravello. He's providing security at Francesca's cousins. The other agent is watching from the road above."

The grotto entrance was on the other side of the dock. It was covered by a strong steel door. Gabe turned to Andre. "How do we get in?"

"Over there—the old entrance," Andre replied. He pointed to a narrow staircase that curved upward and around the rocky face. "It's covered by a gate of steel bars, but I have the key," he said slyly.

They disembarked and headed for the staircase. Andre pulled out a huge metal ring of keys, like those used by janitors or prison guards. He jostled them for a second then inserted the proper key. With a loud, metallic clank, the tumblers released. At that instant, another boat entered the harbor.

"That must be them," Andre whispered.

Gabe checked his watch—11:17 p.m.

The boat stopped, and two men disembarked. Both were dressed in black. It was impossible to recognize their faces in the darkness. The captain remained onboard. The engines hummed as the shadowy figures moved toward the grotto entrance. No one spoke. Beckett instinctively pulled out his weapon. Then the engines stopped. All was quiet except for the sloshing of waves. Gabe struggled to identify the two approaching men.

Suddenly, Anna cried out, "Uncle Paolo! Is that you?"

"*Si, il mio amore*," Paolo replied. "Thank God you're all right."

Anna rushed down the stairs and embraced him with a colossal hug. She kissed him on both cheeks and tucked her head into his shoulder. "Thank God you're safe. I'm so happy to see you," she said. She froze and then asked, "Lorenzo?"

"I don't know," Paolo answered. "We were separated in the chaos. I haven't seen him since, but thank God you're alive. I thought you were abducted."

"I'm safe. Thanks to Zach Beckett. He rescued me. Gabe, too," she said.

"Yes, that's what I was told," Paolo said. A broad smile formed on his face.

"Allow me to introduce you," Anna said. She turned and led Paolo up the stairs. "Uncle Paolo, this is Zach Beckett."

Beckett slid his Glock back into its holster and extended his hand. "It's good to meet you."

"Likewise," Paolo replied. Paolo then introduced his companion. "Zach Beckett, this is Cardinal Bauer."

"Cardinal," Beckett replied. "It's good to finally meet you in person."

The cardinal was dressed in street clothes, but Gabe saw the glint of the cardinal's ring reflect in the moonlight.

"Let's get inside," Andre insisted. "It is safer there."

49

Andre Gotto strapped on a headlamp and led the party of six into the Emerald Grotto. They descended a flight of steps to a boat dock where they found two flat-bottomed row boats used for tours. Each could seat twenty people.

Andre helped Cardinal Bauer into one of the boats, followed by Anna and the others. Gabe and Anna took seats at the front. Andre lit a lantern and handed it to Gabe. He climbed in the back, untied the tether, pushed away from the dock, and started rowing into the darkness.

The grotto was a huge cavern filled with water. Gabe saw faintly lit natural limestone walls in the lantern light. They rose majestically from the water and arched overhead to form a domed roof three stories high at the peak. The air was damp, and the only sound he heard was the splash of the oars.

Andre broke the silence and pointed to one of the grotto's manmade features. "There's a life-size nativity scene below the surface on the grotto floor. During the daytime, it's illuminated with lights."

Gabe couldn't see anything in the inky-black water. "How long has this place been here?" Gabe asked.

"Eons," Andre replied, "but it wasn't discovered until the 1930s. It's been a favorite of tourists ever since. Busloads come every day. Others arrive by boat from Sorrento and Amalfi."

"By boat?" Gabe asked. He was alarmed. "What if someone finds us here? We'd be trapped, and there's only one way out."

"Not true," Andre replied. He stopped rowing. "Look over there." Andre aimed his light at the right side of the grotto.

All Gabe saw was a rock wall rising from the water. "I don't see anything," he said.

Andre pointed again. "Below the surface. There's an underwater passage. If someone finds you here, there's another way out if you can swim."

"You're joking, right?" Gabe protested.

Andre's expression suggested otherwise. "The passage has a diameter of six meters," he said, "plenty of room to swim through. It's only fifteen meters long. During the day, sunlight reflects through the passage, giving the water its emerald color, hence the name."

Gabe was not amused. The passage had a guiding light during the daytime, but it was pitch black at night. It would be nearly impossible to find, and even if they did, Gabe had serious doubts the cardinal could swim the distance. According to Beckett, an agent was watching the road above, but what if someone arrived by boat? Gabe didn't like it at all.

Andre started rowing again. They made their way across the grotto to the far side, where there was a small natural landing area. It rose from the water's edge to the back corner of the grotto and was hidden from the entrance. Andre made one last strong pull on the oars, and the front of the boat scraped onto the rocky shore. He helped them all disembark but remained in the boat.

"You're not coming?" Gabe asked.

"I'm not," Andre replied. "Someone has to keep a lookout. I'll be outside." He handed Gabe a small, two-way radio. "This should have plenty of range, but we'll test it when I get back to my boat. If there's any trouble, I'll use it to signal you. Don't worry about me; I'm well protected. I keep a suitable cadre of firearms aboard."

Andre pushed back into the still, dark water. A moment later, he disappeared.

Gabe carried the lantern up the shallow slope to the back wall where the grade leveled off. There were some large rocks that they pushed into a circle. Each person found a place to sit. Gabe put the lantern in the middle near his feet. His gaze was deadly serious as he looked at each face. He turned toward Cardinal Bauer.

"Your Eminence," Gabe began, "I apologize for my abrupt manner, but today's events underscore the seriousness of the present situation. My acquaintance with Gino Caruso was brief, but his very public murder was a statement and a warning to all of us. Whoever killed him probably killed my grandfather, and they won't hesitate to kill every one of us to get us out of the way. The question is, who are they, and what are they trying to hide?

"We have several clues," Gabe continued. "First, we know that my grandfather arranged a secret meeting between you and Zach. That meeting never took place, of course. Second, we know that my grandfather prepared an extensive report for the NSA detailing his investigation into supernatural apparitions and religious fanaticism. The final section of that report, titled 'WSB,' has been hidden. Third, I received a death threat last night warning me to go home. It was also signed 'WSB'—certainly not a coincidence."

Gabe looked at Beckett then back at Cardinal Bauer. "Did you and my grandfather ever discuss WSB?" he asked.

The cardinal shook his head. "I'm afraid not," he said. "He never mentioned it. Tonight is the first time I've heard those initials."

"Damn," Beckett muttered under his breath. "I was really hoping you'd know. He didn't tell me either. Surely that was the reason for our meeting. He wanted to tell us at the same time. It leads me to think it has a bearing on the security of the Catholic Church—perhaps the Vatican itself."

"Perhaps," the cardinal replied.

At that, Gabe ran his hand through his hair. He turned to Beckett. "There's something I need to tell you. The morning my grandfather was murdered, I found a message written on the bathroom mirror. I have the distinct impression it was written for me—another clue."

Beckett's eyes locked on Gabe. "What kind of message?" he asked.

Gabe reached into his pocket and pulled out a piece of paper. He handed it to Beckett.

T H B S T
I S H R
S A

"What is this?" Beckett asked.

"Turn it over, and you'll see what I've deciphered so far," Gabe said. "I'm nearly certain the first part means 'the beast is here,' as in the beast of Revelation."

Cardinal Bauer's head snapped in Gabe's direction. "That's it! The beast is here!"

Paolo and Anna nodded.

Beckett flipped over the piece of paper and studied Gabe's translation of the message.

T H e   B e a S T
I S   H e R e
S A

"Have I missed something?" Beckett asked.

Gabe explained, "It's a reference to the black beast of Revelation. The Book of Revelation describes two seven-headed monsters. The first one is a huge red dragon. It foretells the rise of atheistic communism in Russia. It can be found in Chapter 12. The other is a black beast found in Chapter 13. It uses the symbolism of a black beast to foretell the rise of the Masonic secret societies—associations hidden in the shadows but very powerful and influential, nonetheless. The beast's animal form is a leopard because leopards hunt their prey under the cover of darkness, hidden in the shadows."

"So you're suggesting that John's murder had something to do with the Masons?" Beckett asked in a cautious tone.

"Exactly," Gabe replied.

"Why didn't you tell me this earlier?" Beckett asked.

"I didn't trust you," Gabe answered. "You gave me every reason to be suspicious. Until recently, it looked like you were playing both sides."

"Fair enough," Beckett said. He nodded his head. "I'm trained to keep secrets. What have you figured out about the letters SA?"

"I'm not sure about that part yet," Gabe responded. "There are several possibilities: Satan, Saint Andrew's, Salerno, even NSA."

Zach raised an eyebrow.

Gabe mistook Beckett's reaction as a response to NSA, but the mention of Salerno was what set off an alarm in Beckett's mind. In his haste to rescue Gabe, he hadn't made it to the shipyards, but he had a strong suspicion about what was unfolding there.

"Hell, it could be anything," Gabe continued. "It's not much to go on."

Beckett filed away each possibility for further investigation. He then looked at Cardinal Bauer. "Do you think he's right?"

"I do. I've always suspected a Masonic connection," the cardinal said.

"I'm not sure what to do with this information," Beckett said. "My team doesn't monitor Freemasonry. It's classified as a benevolent civic organization that accepts people of all religious backgrounds. It doesn't even fall under the umbrella of a religious organization—much less one that breeds religious fanaticism—so we haven't investigated it."

Cardinal Bauer raised his hand to interrupt. "I can assure you that's what the world believes because of Masonry's propaganda campaign. Even low-level members of the organization are misled about its religious dimension. Simply stated, Masonry is a religion of deception with global aims. That's what I told John when he asked me about the symbolism in Chapter 13."

"What symbolism?" Beckett asked.

"The systematic dismantling of Christianity," the cardinal continued. "Freemasonry wants to overthrow the entire religious and political order of the world—everything Christian teaching has produced. This has been evolving for centuries, all the way back to the French Revolution. At one time, the Catholic Church was far more involved in European governance than it is now, so an attack on the papacy also attacked Europe's political structures. However, today, the Masonic attack is primarily spiritual. Emboldened, it now cultivates its darker aims—the destruction of souls. The Masonic lodges, especially deep in their inner circles, embody the spirit of Satan. The true aim of Freemasonry is to herd the faithful into rebellion and lead them into perdition—in other words, hell. That's the supreme aim."

Beckett paused to think then said, "I don't see how this helps us. How does it relate to WSB?" He exhaled heavily. "We know John arranged a meeting with the two of us in absolute secrecy. I think he knew the identity of WSB and was concerned there was an overlapping security risk for the US and the Vatican. I believe that's why he arranged the meeting."

"Most likely," replied Cardinal Bauer.

"But the Masons got to him first," Gabe said. He lowered his head and felt the sting of his grief more acutely than he had at any time that week. The cold, damp surroundings magnified those feelings.

Beckett looked at Cardinal Bauer. "I appreciate your concern about spiritual matters, I truly do, but John insisted that I come here in person. He told me it was urgent. There must be something pressing and immediate—a reason he was focused on the Vatican specifically. Do you have any idea what that might be?" Beckett asked.

All eyes turned to Cardinal Bauer. "John started coming to see me after 9/11. As you know, John was investigating religious fanaticism. On his third visit, he showed me his father's diary and wanted to know more about apparitions."

Gabe reached under his coat. The diary was still safely inside.

"He was developing a treatise," Cardinal Bauer continued, "a report on his findings. He called it *Cold Darkness*. We consulted about it for over two years. More recently, he was concerned about Vatican security. He was worried about a direct terrorist attack on the Vatican. We discussed it at length in connection with his research."

"How so?" Beckett asked.

"John asked me about the symbols in Chapter 13 of the Book of Revelation," the cardinal continued. "As Gabe just explained, the black beast foretells the rise of Freemasonry. John asked me about other symbols as well.

Chapter 13 describes a second beast. Its animal form is a lamb with two horns that speaks like a dragon. The two-horned lamb is a direct reference to the place of liturgical sacrifice—in other words, the Catholic Church. John asked me a lot of questions about this symbol. He feared the Catholic Church was coming under attack because of what he'd read in the Gobbi messages."

Beckett reached into the breast pocket of his trench coat and pulled out a single sheet of paper. "Earlier tonight, I found this in John's report," Beckett said. "It's the first time I've seen it."

"What is it?" Gabe asked.

"A warning," Beckett replied. "It caught my attention because it caught your grandfather's attention. Evidently, in the Gobbi messages, the Virgin Mary explained the meaning of the second beast. Along with that explanation, she gave a stern warning. She pointed out the terrific dangers facing the Catholic Church at this time because of the numerous and diabolical assaults being organized and executed against it. The goal is to destroy it completely."

Beckett turned to Cardinal Bauer. "Have you seen this?"

"I have," replied the cardinal. "John and I discussed it at length, too. He wanted to know if I thought that meant an attack on the Catholic Church was imminent. He was specifically concerned about a terrorist attack against the Vatican, and he wanted to know if the pope knew about this warning."

"What did you tell him?" Beckett asked.

"First, I told him that the pope had, indeed, seen the warning. However, I explained that the symbolism of Chapter 13 does not point to a physical attack."

"Still, a terrorist attack is a possibility?" Beckett asked.

"Of course," replied Cardinal Bauer. "I told John he was missing the essential point. I explained that a physical attack on the Catholic Church was always a possibility. Nevertheless, the meaning behind the symbol signified something far darker."

"Go on," Beckett said.

"As a senior member of the Catholic clergy, it pains me to say this, but the Masonic agenda has secretly woven its way into the fabric of the Catholic clerical hierarchy—in other words, certain bishops and even cardinals. This infiltration was foretold since the beginning.

"According to the Virgin Mother of Christ, the first beast in Chapter 13 foretells the rise of the Masonic secret societies, and the second beast foretells its infiltration into the Catholic Church."

"Excuse me," Beckett interrupted. "I thought the first beast signified atheistic communism."

"Don't confuse these symbols with the ones from Chapter 12," Cardinal Bauer replied. "In Chapter 12, we see a huge red dragon with seven heads. That one foretold the rise of atheistic communism and the Soviet Union. Chapter 13 also has a seven-headed monster. It's described as a black beast and signifies the rise of Freemasonry. It's the first beast of Chapter 13. The second beast of Chapter 13 foretells the infiltration of Freemasonry into the Catholic Church."

"Got it," Beckett said.

"By infiltrating the hierarchy, Freemasonry has found traitors—clergy willing to compromise on the key issues of life," the cardinal continued. "We now see some Catholic theologians openly defying the most fundamental teachings, teachings that have been with us since the days of the apostles. They speak like dragons, deceivers willing to say anything people want to hear. Realizing it or not, their half-truths and confusing statements cause people to question and reject the authentic teachings of Christianity. Through indifference or outright rebellion, people are now abandoning ship, and they're cutting themselves off from the salvation of Christ. In this way, rogue clergy serve the objectives of Freemasonry, and the diabolical plan set forth by Lucifer is fulfilled."

Cardinal Bauer paused to let his statement sink in.

"We were warned of these developments as early as 1961 in Garabandal, Spain," he continued. "In a long series of supernatural apparitions that spanned four years, the Mother of Christ warned us the day was coming when priests would rise up against priests and bishops against bishops. Battles would rage around matters of faith and morals, sowing confusion everywhere. Masonic influences would coalesce to bring about a rejection of all things Catholic. That is now happening before our very eyes. Baptized Catholics become former Catholics. They proclaim it proudly. It's a badge of honor in Western Civilization.

"Today, a wide swath of humanity has abandoned their Christian faith," he continued. "They worship instead the gods of technology, progress, wealth, and pleasure, especially sexual gratification. The idea of self-sacrifice for the common good has been pushed aside. The culture encourages selfishness instead. Through the media, we are bombarded with images and messages that promote the unbridled satiation of all our passions. The notion of sin or sinfulness has been cast aside because it's considered passé. It's the cultural norm. People now exalt themselves above all else.

"This cultural development is the perverse fulfillment of what was foretold in scripture. It's come to fruition in our days. Jesus is scorned, the

Catholic Church is scorned, and both are publicly ridiculed. Pop culture has turned Jesus into a brand and brings contempt against His teachings. It's the blasphemy foretold in Revelation. To blaspheme is to ridicule God and make a mockery of all things sacred.

"On the surface, this all appears to be the normal functioning of society. However, this seismic shift in culture did not happen in a vacuum. Freemasonry, through its masterful use of the media, has worked in the shadows for decades to help bring this about. It's the Kingdom of Satan, using the words of Pope Leo XIII. Lucifer and his demon spirits have been unleashed to bring about the destruction of souls, and their chosen method is the abandonment of God and the glorification of self. It's so simple, yet so cunning.

"Today, we witness the rejection of Christian principles in favor of self-styled, self-governed lives in which each person defines right and wrong. It's a religious deception with widespread appeal. Christian piety is decimated. Catholic moral authority is ridiculed. Humanity rejects the salvation offered by Christ, and we do so freely without duress. That's what the beasts of Revelation have accomplished."

"The great apostasy," Anna said.

"Correct," Cardinal Bauer replied.

"So many of my peers have succumbed," she lamented. Her face expressed bona fide grief. Gabe reached out and took her hand.

For a moment, all was silent.

Cardinal Bauer paused for emphasis. "On a supernatural level," he said, "the Masonic infiltration into the Catholic Church is part of the mystery of evil. Some of the very men with the highest duty to shepherd the people have used their authority to confuse them and lead them astray. Mark my words, the clergy who deceive the faithful will be asked to give a full account of their duplicity on the Day of Judgment."

Gabe was stunned by the cardinal's directness and impressed by his authoritative command of the facts.

"John and I discussed this," Cardinal Bauer said. "He wanted me to sound the alarm, raise the red flag, notify the pontiff, that sort of thing. I assured him the pope was already very much aware of the Masonic infiltration."

Gabe swallowed hard. He wondered where this was leading.

"Those clergy still loyal to the doctrines of the Catholic Church speak with a unified voice of truth," the cardinal said. "The papacy is the essence of Christian unity, and unity is its natural state because the truth cannot be divided. Yet, division is the actual state of Christianity. Satan has labored to divide it for centuries. This is not new, and it's truly diabolical. Indeed, the word diabolical means to divide. The Masonic infiltration is diabolical—speaking like dragons, sowing division everywhere."

Beckett exhaled hard and sat quietly for a moment. Gabe heard a slow drip of water fall from the ceiling into the water below.

"Cardinal Bauer," Beckett said, "you used the word 'dragon' several times."

"That's correct."

"Normally, I wouldn't say what I'm about to tell you," Beckett said. "However, under present circumstances, I have no choice. I have a duty to my country and to yours. We need to do whatever we can to prevent a catastrophe.

"The NSA routinely monitors global communications," Beckett continued. "We search for secrets, patterns, and threats. A few months ago, my task force detected a smattering of disparate but disturbing indications of another terrorist plot by al-Qaeda against the American Homeland. The most worrisome chatter came from Pakistan and Turkey. It put my team on high alert.

"More recently, a report surfaced that two nuclear warheads are missing from the Russian arsenal, the suitcase variety. Officially, the Russian government refuses to acknowledge the report. They claim their nuclear stockpile is totally secure."

Beckett leaned forward for emphasis. The lantern cast a macabre glow on his face. "But that's not true. The Russian government has secretly requested our assistance in locating the devices. The request is shrouded in complete secrecy to avoid a public panic. John knew about the missing nukes."

Gabe shot a look at Anna.

"No wonder he was so concerned about Vatican security," the cardinal said.

"There's more," Beckett continued. "Earlier this evening, I spoke to one of my associates in Washington. We intercepted another communication. It indicated at least one of the devices is now in position."

"Where?" Cardinal Bauer asked.

"We're not sure, but the message said it was in the dragon's lair. It was signed 'WSB.'"

Anna gasped.

This time, it was Cardinal Bauer who exhaled loudly.

Beckett's steely demeanor returned. "Are you certain about the symbolism?" he asked the cardinal. "Because it sounds like it's pointing in your direction."

The cardinal bit his bottom lip and let out another long exhale. "To be sure, violence is spreading everywhere," he began, "but the fundamental meaning of the symbolism is clear. It's dark and concerns the destruction of souls—not the destruction of property. Still, a direct terrorist attack on the Vatican cannot be ruled out. As horrific as that might be, it's always a possibility. However, consider this: Lucifer is cunning and sinister. He wants people to abandon their salvation freely without duress. He wants them to reject their inheritance and reject Christ by their free choosing. A direct, powerful, and spectacular attack on the Vatican might have the opposite effect. People all over the world would sympathize with the Catholic Church. An event like that might even reawaken their hearts. It could cause them to amend their lives and reattach to their Christian roots, much like the response after 9/11. Think about it."

Beckett leaned back to consider his hypothesis. "I hope you're right," he said. "Still, religious fanaticism, especially militant Islam, has shown a willingness to commit the spectacular."

All was quiet. Gabe again heard the slow drip of water falling from the ceiling. Each drop made a tiny splash below. *Plop, plop, plop.*

Finally, Cardinal Bauer spoke. "I share your concern, Mr. Beckett. The world has become a very dangerous place. I pray constantly for the safety and security of our planet, but I also pray for souls. The meaning of the two beasts was revealed by the Holy Mother of God. Their essential meaning is clear. They foretell the era we live in. It's the time of the great apostasy—the widespread rejection and abandonment of the Christian faith. It's happening before our very eyes, especially in Western civilization. John and I discussed it extensively."

"There must be a current significance to all of this," Zach lamented. "Why else would John have placed so much emphasis on it? Where's the connection?"

"I think I might have the answer," Cardinal Bauer replied. "Recently, John came to me and asked my opinion. He wanted to know whether it was possible that Osama bin Laden was the lawless one, the one foretold by Saint Paul."

"I don't follow," Beckett said. "What do you mean?"

"I'll explain," said the cardinal. "In the first century, the gospel was spread throughout the Roman Empire, and communities of Christian believers formed. One such place was Thessaloniki in Greece. The people of that era were awaiting the return of Christ, just as they are now, but they began to die. The believers were fearful they'd miss it because they were dead.

"In response, Saint Paul wrote his second letter to the Thessalonians. He reassured them that those who died before the return of Christ would still be united with Him. He then gave two signs to watch for as precursors to Christ's return. The first is the great apostasy, which we're now experiencing. The second is the rise of the lawless one—in other words, the Antichrist. John asked me if it was possible that Osama bin Laden was the lawless one, the Antichrist foretold by Saint Paul."

"What did you say?" Gabe asked.

"I told him it didn't matter what I thought. I told him that people of every age have attempted to pin that distinction on the menace of their time, but every one of them has passed into eternity."

"And that satisfied him?" Beckett asked.

"Well, no, it didn't," said the cardinal. "John pointed out that we now live in a different world—one filled with weapons of mass destruction, thanks to the arms race. There can be no doubt that in the hands of a religious fanatic like Osama bin Laden, the devastation of a nuclear attack would make 9/11 look like a tea party. I didn't know about the missing nukes, of course, but reluctantly, I conceded it was a possibility. We then previewed his latest findings. He called it 'Fatwa & Oil.'"

"You know about 'Fatwa & Oil'?" Beckett asked.

The cardinal nodded. "John had read the Gobbi messages and was distressed by his findings," he said. "In fact, he discovered something downright terrifying. His discovery was both sobering and deadly. I must admit, it gave me pause. We met so he could confirm that he understood the prophetic symbolism correctly."

"And what was that?" Beckett asked.

"Nearly everyone is familiar with this," said the cardinal. "In Chapter 13 of Revelation, we find these words: 'Wisdom is needed here; one who understands can calculate the number of the beast, for it is a number that stands for a person. His number is six hundred and sixty-six.' The infamous number 666. He read the explanation of this number in the Gobbi messages and wanted to know if the calculation pointed to Osama bin Laden."

"Did it?" Gabe asked.

All eyes were focused on Cardinal Bauer. Just then, Gabe's radio crackled.

"Gabriel, this is Andre. Do you read me? Over."

Gabe pulled the radio from his pocket. "I read you, loud and clear, over," Gabe replied.

"Everything is calm out here," Andre said. "We're still alone. Over."

"Thanks, Andre. Over and out." Gabe answered. He put the radio back in his pocket and turned to Cardinal Bauer.

"I read that message, too," Gabe said. "I think I understand the calculation, but how does that relate to Osama bin Laden and the present crisis?"

All eyes refocused on Cardinal Bauer. He began slowly. "People have tried to decipher this calculation since the earliest days of Christianity but inevitably failed. You could say the time had not yet come, but now that's changed. The sealed book has been opened."

50

AMALFI: 11:49 P.M.

Lorenzo Bonelli sat on his faux leather sofa in the parlor of his residence. Well into his second bottle of merlot, he was finally feeling its relaxing effects. The parlor, adjacent to the lobby of the Amalfi Hotel, was separated by a heavy, blue-green velveteen curtain draped across the doorway. According to the guest registry, one more patron was expected to check in. After the day's events, he was anxious to lock out the world for the night.

He poured himself another glass and heard the bell chime and the lobby door open. He stumbled slightly as he pushed aside the curtain. A well-dressed, perfectly groomed Italian man in his thirties stood in the lobby. His dark hair, dark clothes, and black gloves were a perfect contrast to the rumpled appearance of Lorenzo Bonelli.

"*Buona sera*, Signore Bolino," Lorenzo said. He peeked at the name on the guest registry. "I've been expecting you."

"*Buona sera*. I apologize for my late arrival," said the guest.

"No problem. No problem," Lorenzo replied with customary hospitality. He laid a registration card on the counter with a pen. The guest scratched some information on the card and slid it back. "And how will you settle your account?" Lorenzo asked.

The guest reached into his pocket, pulled out a money clip, and peeled 150 euros from the thick pile of neatly folded bills.

"Grazie," Lorenzo replied. He marked the account as paid. "I'll need some identification."

The guest grabbed his driver's license and handed it to Lorenzo, who quickly scribbled down the guest's name and driver's license number. He barely glanced at the photo. Under official procedures, Lorenzo should have photocopied it, but he often dispensed with formalities. It wasn't intentional, but he was careless whenever the wine settled into his veins.

While Lorenzo was writing, the guest looked across the counter and scanned the registry. He read upside down and found what he was looking for: "Room 5C, Gabriel Roslo."

"And your bags?" Lorenzo inquired.

"Still in the car," said the guest.

Lorenzo nodded. He hadn't seen the black Audi A8 pull into the parking lot. "This way," he said.

It was Lorenzo's custom to assist guests with their bags. He grabbed the room key, handed it to the guest, and led him toward the door. The instant Lorenzo stepped into the night air, he was grabbed from behind. The guest had him in a chokehold. Lorenzo was no match for the much younger and stronger man. He felt a knife press against his Adam's apple.

"5C," the man said. Lorenzo was paralyzed with fear. "I said, 5C."

"What about it?" Lorenzo demanded, struggling to get the words out.

"Take me there, or tomorrow, your poor wife will find you in a pool of blood—not nearly as clean as the good Mr. Roslo."

Lorenzo panicked. He struggled to free himself, but the arm around his throat tightened, cutting off his air.

"You can make this easy, or you can make it difficult, but you're going to give me what I want," the man said. Lorenzo realized it was hopeless. He was outmatched. He gasped for air and nodded his head. The assassin loosened his grip slightly. "Move!"

Lorenzo started down the stairs, his assailant close behind. He reached 5C, pulled out the master key, and slid it into the keyhole. Lorenzo turned the deadbolt and pushed open the door. The assassin shoved him inside. He flipped on the light and closed the door behind them.

"Open the room safe!" the assassin demanded.

Lorenzo's mind was clouded by the alcohol. He had trouble remembering the combination. Nervously, he approached the box and punched in a series of numbers. He pulled the handle. Nothing. He tried a second time. He pulled the handle again. Still nothing. Sweat formed above his thick eyebrows.

"I can't remember the combination," he said finally.

"I don't have time for games," the man warned. "You have one minute. Don't make it your last."

Lorenzo closed his eyes and tried to recall the code.

"You're testing my patience," the man said.

Lorenzo steadied himself and punched in a series of numbers again. The knife pressed into the back of his neck. He reached for the lever and prayed it would open. He pulled down. Nothing.

"Do you think I'm bluffing?" the assassin said angrily.

The knife dug into Lorenzo's neck and drew blood. "I'm sorry. I'm sorry," Lorenzo said in a panic.

"You have one more chance. You have exactly fifteen seconds."

Lorenzo's hand shook. All the terrible thoughts of the past few days flashed through his mind. Was he next? He struggled to remember the pattern of numbers. Then it hit him. He pushed the buttons again: one, nine, nine, eight, six, six, six. *Click.* The door swung open.

The assassin shoved Lorenzo aside. "Damn it! The Master was right. The bastard has it with him." The man swung around and faced Lorenzo. "Or do you have it?"

"Have what?" Lorenzo asked.

"The diary."

Lorenzo was terrified. He shook his head. "I don't have it. I don't know where it is." He was telling the truth. He knew Gabe took it with him. However, Gabe was being marshaled out of the Seaside Café the last time he saw him.

The assassin took a moment to survey the room. He checked all the drawers, under the bed, between the mattresses, and in the closets. He found nothing. Gabe Roslo had lied. He had the diary with him.

The assassin turned back toward Lorenzo. "Where's Roslo now?"

"I don't know. I haven't seen him since this afternoon."

"What about the Castriottis?"

"I haven't seen them either," Lorenzo answered.

"Have you spoken to them?"

Lorenzo shook his head.

"They haven't called?" the assassin asked.

Lorenzo again shook his head.

The assassin paused a moment to think. Tails had been assigned to track the Castriottis, but both eluded their grasp. The girl had disappeared from the scene without a trace, and Paolo Castriotti evaded his tail with a slick piece of mountain driving.

The assassin raised his knife and pushed the tip into Lorenzo's throat. "I'll give you one chance to get this right. If you want to see the light of day, you better give me the right answer. Paolo Castriotti did not go home tonight. Where is he?"

Lorenzo trembled, fear in his eyes. He truly didn't know.

"Well?" the assassin demanded.

Lorenzo hesitated for just a second. "I don't know where he is at this moment, but I can tell you he's a very faithful man."

"What does that mean?" the assassin asked.

"It means you can find him at Saint Andrew's just about every morning. He goes to daily Mass."

"What time?"

"8:00," Lorenzo replied.

In one swift, effortless move, the assassin shoved the blade through Lorenzo's esophagus. He retrieved the knife, shoved Lorenzo to the floor, wiped the blade on the bedspread, and calmly walked out the door.

The assassin had been sent to get the diary in the unlikely event it was still in the room. It wasn't. However, he didn't leave empty-handed, thanks to Signore Lorenzo Bonelli. Bonelli provided a useful piece of information. The assassin returned to his car, flipped open his cell phone, and made a call.

LORENZO FOUGHT FOR BREATH as he drowned in his own blood. He groped for the phone and dialed Paolo Castriotti's cell number. He had to warn him. The phone rang several times and then rolled to voicemail. Lorenzo expired before he heard the recording: "The phone you have called is either turned off or the user has moved outside the service area."

51

GROTTO

Cardinal Bauer's expression was serious, his voice monotone. He made eye contact with each person then continued.

"Thanks to the Gobbi messages and the supernatural insights of the Holy Mother of God, we might very well have the definitive formula. Her message in 1989 provided a long explanation about why Satan chose the number 666. He did so to pridefully supersede the number 333, which signifies the mystery of the Holy Trinity.

"She explained how the number 666 expresses three eras, three periods of 666 years each. These eras point to the years 666, 1332, and 1998, respectively. Each era manifests a new development of anti-Christianity. The third era opens the door for the actual person of Antichrist to appear. That's the calculation."

He continued, "The first era points to the year 666. In that period of history, the Antichrist was manifested through the birth of Islam. Islam directly denied the divinity of Jesus and the existence of the Trinity, which is precisely why Islam is antichristian. It denied that Jesus was *the* Christ. Moreover, the Koran claims God has no son and that Jesus was not even crucified—much less resurrected from the dead. To fit the calculation, Islam was born in the Arabian Peninsula in the year 620 AD, and by 660 AD, it conquered Jerusalem. Eventually, it destroyed all the ancient Christian communities of the Middle East."

"So the calculation specifically points to Islam?" Beckett asked.

"John had the same question," the cardinal replied. "It's one of the reasons he asked about Osama bin Laden, but there's more. The second era points to the year 1332," he said.

"In that period of history, the Antichrist was manifested through a radical attack on Christian belief by philosophers. They claimed science and reason were the sole sources of truth. Revealed truth—that which comes from God Himself—was suppressed. It was the beginning of the Enlightenment, and everything needed to be proved to be worthy of belief.

"Disagreements arose even among Christians about what to believe. It created a massive fissure within Christianity, one that was never intended. Wide variances of belief developed within the Christian world, even though the truth cannot be divided. Christianity was divided against itself.

"It was also the era of the Black Death. It killed as much as half of Europe's population in five years. War was incessant. Starting in 1337, the French and English battled a Hundred Years' War. Ultimately, God raised up a new prophet, Saint Joan of Arc, as a catalyst to bring about its conclusion. However, even that ended in darkness when corrupt clergy condemned her and burned her at the stake."

Cardinal Bauer paused briefly. His face glowed in the lamplight.

"The calculation has a third part," he said. "The third era points to the year 1998, the modern era. Freemasonry succeeded in its great design in that era by establishing alternatives to Christ and Christianity. It was everything we've just talked about, including its infiltration into the Catholic Church. Baptized Christians everywhere are throwing off traditional Christian beliefs to idolize the world around us instead. It's the great apostasy foretold by the apostle Paul. These markers are all in place."

Gabe looked at Anna then Cardinal Bauer. "But the calculation points to a certain man. Why did my grandfather ask about Osama bin Laden?

"I know the answer," Beckett interrupted. "We all know what happened on September 11, 2001, but what John zeroed in on happened three and half years earlier. Few people realized it at the time, but that's when the United States entered the War on Terror. That's the year that got John's attention."

Gabe ran his hand through his hair, puzzled. "What happened in 1998?" he asked.

"Osama bin Laden published his second fatwa. It declared a global holy war on all Americans everywhere, including civilians. It spawned the 9/11 attacks and led to the present global War on Terror. It was published on February 23, 1998."

"God help us!" exclaimed Anna. She instinctively made the sign of the cross.

Gabe couldn't believe his ears. "Are you sure?" he asked.

"We're sure," Beckett replied. "It's true. That was when Bin Laden and his followers declared their global holy war. Of course, the American public barely noticed because 1998 was the year of Monica Lewinsky. Bin Laden and the World Islamic Front declared war on the United States, but the media virtually ignored it. There was too much frenzy over Monica and Bill. While our Commander-in-Chief was headed for impeachment, Bin Laden bombed two of our African embassies.

"Clinton ordered reprisals, so the US bombed known terror camps in Afghanistan. The reprisal bombings came just days after Clinton gave his grand jury testimony that led to his eventual impeachment. The media criticized him roundly. They accused him of conducting a wag-the-dog response to turn the spotlight away from the hearings. Consequently, he hesitated later that year when the CIA discovered Bin Laden's precise location. Clinton had the opportunity to chop off the monster's head but withheld the order. The rest is history."

Beckett motioned for the cardinal to continue.

"So, you see, Gabe," said Cardinal Bauer, "it was your grandfather who connected the number 666 to Osama bin Laden and the monstrous events of 9/11. He wrote 'Fatwa & Oil' after making this connection, and he asked me if Osama bin Laden was the actual person of Antichrist."

"Is he?" Gabe asked.

"Probably not, but it cannot be ruled out," the cardinal answered. "Bin Laden's mystique is elevated by the fact the American government cannot find him. However, we must remember something very important. Antichristian influence develops in all three layers. Those influences pile up like a sedimentary rock and become intertwined with each other. They form a labyrinth of confusion and push the truth of the resurrected Jesus Christ deeper and deeper into the past."

Beckett interjected, "But aren't Bin Laden and his militant followers motivated by a unifying theme? Don't they believe they're the Kingdom of Heaven? They're willing to use absolute force to impose those beliefs on everyone, even Muslims who disagree with them. That certainly sounds like a monster to me."

"I share your concern," replied the cardinal. "I haven't been able to push the thought out of my mind since John shared his discovery, but I asked him a question: what would happen if focusing on Osama bin Laden caused the world to miss something else, perhaps something worse?"

Beckett fidgeted with his shirt sleeve. He thought back to the warning he'd read earlier that evening: the possibility of a new world war so devastating that no one would emerge victorious. Cardinal Bauer had a point. What if Osama bin Laden's actions were creating a distraction for something even more terrible, something brewing but not yet revealed?

"The person of Antichrist could come from anywhere," the cardinal said. "And we shouldn't overlook the role of Freemasonry. If Freemasonry is truly the beast of Revelation, then perhaps it will be instrumental in bringing forth the person of Antichrist."

Gabe swallowed hard.

"Here's what we know," the cardinal said. "We now see the forces behind all three layers of the calculation coming together. We see the spread of militant Islam. We see relentless attacks on the divinity of Jesus, especially in pop culture and the media, and we see Freemasonry's victory taking shape as the world rejects Christianity in favor of the New Age movement. It's on these foundations that the world braces for the emergence of the Antichrist. That's why John's work was so serious."

Gabe felt the cool, damp air settle into his bones as he listened to the cardinal. His grandfather had indeed made a shocking discovery. Gabe turned to Beckett. "What can we do?" he asked. "The full force of the American government hasn't been able to find Bin Laden. How can we find someone darker and more hidden, assuming he already exists?"

Beckett shrugged, but the cardinal offered an answer.

"The Antichrist will eventually show himself. In the meantime, you need to find your grandfather's file. The "WSB" file is the key to your present crisis, is it not? Find it, and perhaps it will shed light on the bigger one to come."

Gabe pondered the cardinal's words. The initials WSB were the key to the whole mystery. *Are the diary and missing pages the source of that mystery?* he wondered. If so, it was more precious than ever. He instinctively felt for the diary under his coat.

Suddenly, he thought about his grandmother. His adversaries would surely be looking for her in their quest to get their hands on the diary. He spoke up.

"Zach, none of us knows the meaning of WSB or where to find the "WSB" file. However, there's one more person to ask—the person closest to my grandfather for the past sixty years."

"Francesca?" Beckett asked.

"Exactly," Gabe replied. "It's time to tell her what's going on, and we need to get her out of Amalfi."

At that instant, Gabe's radio crackled, followed by voices and, finally, the explosion of three gunshots. The sound ricocheted off the walls of the grotto. Then all fell silent.

Beckett instinctively jumped to his feet. He extinguished the lantern. Gabe held the radio in his hand. "Don't say a word," Beckett said in a low whisper.

Silence.

Gabe swiftly gauged the distance to the underwater opening. From memory, he judged it to be seventy-five meters, an easy swim but impossible to find in the total darkness.

Still silence.

Gabe heard Anna breathe. He didn't want to leave her behind, but he also needed to get the diary out and reach his grandmother.

Still, there was silence.

It was unclear if anyone had entered the grotto. All Gabe could see was the blue, iridescent face of his watch. It glowed brightly in the pitch-black darkness. He cupped his hand over it.

Still silence.

Three minutes passed, and Gabe's eyes began to adjust. He looked out over the murky water and noticed faint traces of light along the far side of the grotto. Moonlight seeped in through the underwater passage. *Thank God for a cloudless night,* Gabe thought.

"Look," he whispered. He grabbed Anna's hand, "The way out."

52

PARIS: 12:19 A.M.

Claude Arneau was sitting at his desk in the Paris financial district when the phone rang. He picked up the headset and placed it to his ear. It was the call he'd been waiting for all evening.

"It's here," said the caller.

"Excellent. You know what I'm looking for. Tear it apart. Call me the instant you find it."

With that, Arneau hung up. He looked out his window to see the Eiffel Tower in the distance. It was an important night, indeed.

At the other end of the line was a brilliant, young computer wizard—Syrian-born but working in Copenhagen. He sat at his desk in his employer's cramped, third-floor office, the Danish division of Allbritton Enterprises.

Earlier that evening, he'd received word from Arneau to expect a package and was told to make it his top priority. He cleared his desk and awaited its arrival. John Roslo's computer, stolen from his apartment, was being flown by private jet from Rome to Copenhagen.

An empty brown cardboard box now sat on the floor with its contents spread out on the desk. He performed a cursory inspection and connected Roslo's computer to an intricate set of diagnostic tools.

Despite his young age, the Syrian was Arneau's confidant. He proved completely trustworthy, and Arneau liked using him on important projects, especially those requiring discretion.

Arneau sounded edgy when he'd assigned the task. He described the project as urgent—top priority. The Syrian knew better than to ask why. It wasn't his concern. He just wanted to keep the massive paychecks rolling in.

When he hit the power button, the fan motor kicked in, and the hum of the hard drive worked its way through the boot-up routine. He reached the home screen. "Naturally, password protected," he sneered to himself. "No problem."

He typed a few keystrokes and hit enter. The machine restarted, but this time, it bypassed the home screen. His sophisticated software seized the operating system and gave him unlimited access to Roslo's computer. He controlled it through random access memory technology hardware attribution or RAMTHA.

RAMTHA had served him well more times than he could remember. He named his creation after the mythical god of the same name, the powerful warrior ram. His software was powerful indeed. He liked the name for a second reason. The arrogant, young Syrian was a graduate of Ramtha's School of Enlightenment.

He scrolled through the list of files and put them in reverse date order. The most recent was a document called *Cold Darkness*. He ran it through one of his diagnostic tools and searched for matches against an established database of proper names, aliases, addresses, phone numbers, and email addresses. There was only one match: "WSB." He opened the file and examined it closely. He found "WSB" in the table of contents, but the corresponding section did not exist.

He considered two or three alternative possibilities and instinctively engaged in another diagnostic. A few seconds later, it produced a three-dimensional spectrograph showing hard disk usage, activity, content, and residue. As suspected, a file was deleted on the same day *Cold Darkness* was last saved.

He punched a few more keys and reached for his cup of coffee. He was pleased with himself as he listened to the familiar cadence of his diagnostic equipment. He slurped a few gulps, but before the cup was empty, RAMTHA recovered the file he was looking for—the all-important file. It had a simple, three-letter title: "WSB."

He quickly read it. Raising an eyebrow, he reached for the phone to call Arneau.

"You need to see this," he told the Frenchman.

"Transmit immediately. Use the secured line."

Arneau tapped his fingers nervously as he waited for the file to appear on his computer screen. A few seconds later, the file was displayed. "Roslo, that son of a bitch!" he muttered aloud as he read it. "He knew more than we thought."

Arneau picked up the phone to dial Istanbul. A bank of clocks across his wall showed the time in New York, Paris, Tokyo, and Istanbul. It was 3:15 a.m. in Istanbul. Regardless, the call needed to be made. He punched in the number. The Master of the Royal Secret answered on the first ring.

"Report!"

Does he ever sleep? Arneau wondered. "Sir, we have Roslo's computer. RAMTHA recovered a deleted file from the hard disk. The file contained a name," Arneau went on to explain. When he finished, the line went dead. The Master had heard enough.

53

Marco slowly sipped his third Macallan single malt scotch. He was particularly fond of the soothing, thirty-year-old sherry oak variety. Earlier in the evening, he ate an exquisite dinner prepared and served by his personal chef. The dishes had been cleared away, and he savored his favorite liquor. The butler delivered a box of fine Cuban cigars. He retained a three-person staff to cater to such needs. The butler left the room and clicked the door shut.

Marco scanned his lavishly decorated office. He surveyed the fine leather and mahogany furniture, fabulous oil paintings, and the eighteenth-century Persian rug underfoot. The lights were dimmed to create the perfect ambiance. The serenity of his office was enhanced by the sound of classical music, which played softly in the background. His office was truly his oasis.

He lit a cigar and stepped to the window to observe the steady stream of activity in the shipyard below. A team of workers had been methodically loading cargo onto the *Ruse of the Sea* all night.

He returned to his leather easy chair, picked up the phone, and called the loading dock foreman.

"*Quanto tiempo?*" he asked.

"Ten or eleven more hours, sir," the voice replied in Italian. "She should be ready to set sail by noon at the latest."

"Keep me posted," Marco said and hung up.

His crystal inlaid clock read 12:56 a.m. He relaxed in his easy chair and took another sip of scotch. He reflected on the trust the Master placed in him. He'd been chosen from among the twelve for this all-important task—to facilitate and deliver their "little darlings." He'd traveled to Istanbul seven times during the past year to meet with the Master and report on progress. All was now ready.

Marco knew he'd assumed the greatest risk but was also positioned to reap the greatest benefits. The Master of the Royal Secret had put to rest any lingering doubts, and Marco firmly believed the Master was right. He envisioned the backlash against the Islamic countries trying to develop nuclear weapons once the full weight of the American war machine descended on the Middle East. It would spell the end of radical Islam and its interference with the free flow of oil forever, and few people made more money shipping oil around the globe than Marco Sorrentino.

Everything had come together perfectly, just as the Master predicted. Other than an old man's nosiness and an over-eager politician's nuisance, the plan had evolved flawlessly.

He pressed the call button. In an instant, his butler poured another scotch. The butler bowed and disappeared as quickly as he arrived. Marco lifted his glass and took an unusually long drink. The flavor elicited great pleasure. He felt his eyes get heavy, and he slowly faded to the edge of consciousness.

Suddenly, the phone rang. He snapped back to life.

"Marco here."

It was the Master. "You have a problem. Roslo knew more than you realized. We extracted a deleted file from his computer. I've seen its contents. He titled it 'WSB!' You'll be on an island if that file finds its way into the wrong hands. I'll cut you off, and you'll face governmental retribution all alone. Am I clear?"

"Yes, sir," Marco replied.

"It's time to clear up the loose ends," the Master continued. "I want you to find that missing file, destroy it, and eliminate the grandson. He didn't take the hint in Capri. He's a risk. For all we know, he's already seen the file. Then systematically liquidate every person connected to him but make them look like accidents—no more Salernos. Before you do anything, get your hands on that diary. It wasn't in the room safe, was it?" the Master inquired. He had more than a hint of sarcasm in his voice.

"No, it wasn't," Marco replied. "You were right. You're always right. The grandson has it. My agent called a couple of hours ago. He searched the safe and found nothing. But he didn't come away empty-handed, either. I think we can eliminate one of our problems in the morning."

"Namely?" the Master asked.

"Castriotti," Marco replied. "Evidently, he's a visitor to Saint Andrew's every morning around 8:00."

"That sounds like progress—and I want progress. Don't disappoint me," the Master demanded calmly. With that, the line went dead.

Marco slumped in his chair. A file titled "WSB"? John Roslo was smarter than he realized. *That bastard!* he thought. Marco begrudgingly admitted he should've taken him out much earlier.

He set his glass on the table, picked up the phone, and hit speed dial. It rang seven or eight times, no answer. The driver of the Audi A8 was preoccupied.

54

GROTTO

Gabe strained to make out the faint silhouettes illuminated by the moonlit water. He saw that Beckett was standing. No one else had moved a muscle.

"We need to split up," Beckett said quietly.

"I think I can make it to the opening," Gabe whispered in reply.

"Me too," said Anna.

Gabe didn't like the idea of trying to make it out with a second person, but he wasn't leaving Anna behind again.

"Are you sure?" Gabe asked.

"I'm sure. I'm a good swimmer. Don't worry about me. Just take care of yourself," she said.

"I'll stay with Paolo and Cardinal Bauer," Beckett said. "I'm armed." He sounded confident as he said those words, but he knew it would be difficult to defend himself, much less two others. Still, he had little choice. He gave Gabe a final instruction. "We'll rendezvous at the monastery."

"I'll be there," Gabe said.

"Don't make me wait," Beckett replied as he shook Gabe's hand.

Gabe grinned slightly and nodded in the darkness. He then handed the radio and diary to Beckett. "You better hold this for safekeeping," he said.

"I'll keep it safe," Beckett replied.

Gabe took Anna's hand and led her to the water. She stumbled over a rock as they crept along in the darkness. She maintained her balance, and Gabe tightened his grip on her. He felt for the water's edge with each step. At last, one of his shoes splashed into the water. It was a lot colder than it had been a few days earlier when he went for a swim in the warm sunlight.

He pulled off his shoes, tied the laces together, and hung them around his neck.

"You better do the same," he whispered to Anna.

"I can't," she said. "Mine don't have laces." He held her steady as she unzipped her boots and tossed them to the side.

"I'm ready," she said.

Gabe braced himself for the chill and waded up to his waist into the water. The cold water tightened his muscles. Anna followed, and a small gasp escaped as the cold water shocked her.

Once they started swimming, there would be no place to stop and catch their breath. They had to cross the grotto, dive into the underwater passage, and swim through. Easier said than done, even for Gabe.

"Ready?" he whispered.

"Ready," she said.

Gabe sunk to his neck and pushed off toward the faint moonlight. He swam the breaststroke to keep his head above water. It had become more difficult to locate the underwater passage because the moonlight was diffused by the newly created waves. Anna waded in to her waist, prepared to follow.

Just then, the radio crackled. "Do you read me? Over."

Gabe heard the radio and stopped swimming. Anna froze. He turned around and did a few strokes until his feet touched the bottom again.

"Don't say a word," Beckett whispered.

The radio crackled again.

"Gabriel, do you read me? Over." It sounded like Andre.

Beckett cautiously pressed the talk button. "Andre, this is Zach Beckett. I read you loud and clear. I've maintained my position. I'm still up here on the coastal road, but I can't see you down there."

Beckett pretended to be outside the grotto, looking down from the coastal road. *A brilliant ruse,* Gabe thought.

"What's your location?" Beckett asked.

"We have a visitor," Andre replied.

Again silence.

No one spoke. Gabe was in limbo. He'd need to move soon because hypothermia was a real possibility. Everyone held their breath. Still no sound.

Finally, the radio crackled again.

"Zach, let me correct that," Andre said. "We had a visitor, and I'm pretty sure he won't bother us again. He'll need a fitting burial at sea."

Beckett chuckled, which relieved the tension. "Are you okay, Andre?" he asked.

"I'm fine," Andre said, "but I'm a little confused. How did you get to the road?"

Muted laughter followed.

"We're still in the grotto," Beckett replied. "It was just a ploy. Could you please come and get us?"

"Right away," Andre said.

Beckett reached into his pocket, pulled out a lighter, and relit the lantern. Gabe and Anna climbed from the water, shivering. They struggled back into their footwear. The cardinal offered Anna his jacket. She gladly accepted and snuggled close to Gabe to keep him warm. Gabe wrapped his arm around her and kissed her on the forehead. She drew closer.

As they waited for Andre's arrival, Beckett laid out the plan. "Your Eminence, we need to ensure your safety. You should leave with Paolo the same way you arrived. Is your driver still waiting for you?"

"Yes, he's at the dock in Positano. He'll drive me back to Rome," the cardinal replied.

"And you?" Beckett asked, looking at Paolo.

"Anna's car is parked there, too," Paolo replied. "I drove it from Salerno."

"Good," said Beckett. "When Cardinal Bauer is safely on his way, meet us at the monastery. How long will it take you to get there?"

"This time of night, no more than thirty minutes," Paolo replied.

"Perfect," Beckett said. "Be careful. If anyone follows you, keep driving. Go to Amalfi. Don't lead them to the monastery—and whatever you do, don't stop at home. Surely, your house is being watched."

"I'll be fine," Paolo said.

Beckett turned to Gabe. "We need to get to Francesca," he said. "We must interview her. She'll need to be told about John's murder. I'm sorry, but it's the only way. Then we need to send her home for her safety. We'll arrange for her to get to Fiumicino and then on to Dulles."

"I understand," Gabe nodded.

Anna gave Gabe a reassuring squeeze.

"We need to find out if she's heard of WSB," Beckett continued, "and whether she can shed light on the meaning of the letters SA. Let's hope so. A lot of lives depend on it."

Gabe heard the slosh of the oars. Andre rowed toward them.

"Thank God, you're all right!" Anna exclaimed as he came into view.

"I'm fine," he said. He turned to Cardinal Bauer. "So is your boat driver, but I can't say as much for our intruder. I was hiding in the shadows and saw him approach from the road above. He was armed and had his gun drawn. When he reached the bottom of the stairs, I shot him in the chest. I couldn't call you right away because I had to make sure he was alone."

Gabe exhaled hard. "How do you think he found us?" he asked.

"No telling," Beckett replied, "but let's get going before someone else does." Beckett wondered what had happened to his agent. He'd been posted up there to keep a lookout.

"I have blankets on board," Andre said. He helped Anna into the boat. She wrapped one around herself and handed one to Gabe. The others piled in.

Andre pushed back and started to row. In minutes, they reached the other side of the grotto, exited, and walked around the V-shaped dock.

Cardinal Bauer shared a final thought before they boarded their respective boats. "Zach, I offer my blessing. A possible cataclysm is at the world's doorstep. You and your government need to do whatever you can to stop it. I pray for your success. Humanity is at a precarious point, and the possibility of a nuclear confrontation is all too real. One of the Gobbi messages warns that the world is now worse than at the time of the great flood—indeed, a thousand times worse. I wish I could do more, but I offer you this metaphor for hope and encouragement: *Don't be afraid to climb into the ark of Mary's protection.* It's her natural role to protect her children." Cardinal Bauer then made the sign of the cross in the air.

The cardinal turned to Gabe. He shook his hand and whispered something in Gabe's ear.

"Thank you. I understand," Gabe replied. "I will tell her."

With that, they boarded and headed their separate ways. Andre guided his boat out of the inlet into open water and pushed the throttles forward. The engines surged, and they were back at the arch bridge in no time. The GPS remained off. Philippe, the young monk, was there to meet them. He led Anna and Gabe to the car, but Beckett stayed onboard. "I'll catch up to you in a minute," he said. Once the others were out of earshot, he asked Andre what he'd done with the body.

"I told you—a burial at sea," Andre replied. He lifted the lid to his fishing hold, normally reserved for the daily catch. The corpse was inside with a hole through his chest.

"Nice shot," Beckett said. He checked for ID. None found. No surprise. "We need to identify him, but we can't get the local authorities involved at this point," Beckett continued. "Can you pack him on ice for now?"

"No problem. My boat has an ice machine to preserve the catch. I'll keep him fresh until I hear from you," Andre answered.

"Perfect," Beckett said. They shook hands.

Beckett jumped ashore and took the stairs three at a time to catch up with the others. He arrived at the car just as Philippe turned it around. They loaded and were off. The sound of gravel crunched under the tires.

Gabe again felt exposed. Moonlight reflected off the mountains, highlighting an endless supply of hiding places in the craggy shadows. Still, there were no suspicious cars or anyone following them. The drive to the monastery was brief, and Paolo pulled up in Anna's car a few minutes later.

"I need dry clothes," Gabe said. Paolo unlocked the trunk, and Gabe grabbed his travel bag. It had been there since he returned from Capri.

"Change quickly," Beckett ordered with the finesse of a drill sergeant. They hustled toward the monastery. "Meet me in the foyer in five minutes. We'll go from there."

Father Fiore was waiting for them. Beckett ducked into his office and placed a call. When the line was answered, Beckett's instructions were short and direct. "Unable to investigate *Ruse of the Sea*. Stop. Have port authority detain ship if departure attempted. Stop. Might have a live one. Stop. Priority. Stop. Code name: Signal Fire."

The message was encrypted and delivered to the office in Washington.

Paolo took a seat on the couch in the foyer. Gabe and Anna rushed to her room. She unlocked the door. Gabe threw his suitcase on the bed. He opened it, rooted through the bag, and pulled out some clothes.

"These are clean," he said and handed them to Anna. She went into the bathroom and changed into Gabe's sweatpants and a black sweater. He quickly changed as well.

When she came out, she had a sheepish grin. The clothes were obviously a touch too big. Gabe walked toward her. He leaned in and kissed her full on the mouth. The embrace sent a jolt of excitement through her. Neither wanted to pull back. Gabe finally straightened and pulled her head toward his chest. He cupped her thick black hair in his hand as she rested her cheek against him.

"I'm glad you're here," he said.

"Me too, Gabe."

After several moments, he said they'd better get moving. He picked up his bag and closed it, and they hurried out the door. Many things had changed for him that day, and he knew his life was on a new course.

55

Gabe and Anna hurried back to the foyer, where they found Beckett looking at his watch—2:10 a.m. Gabe was wearing a navy shirt, a light jacket, and the jeans he'd worn in Capri. Anna hastily put her hair in a ponytail as Beckett spoke.

"Let's get going," he said.

Father Fiore stood at the door. "If you need anything else, I would be pleased to help," he said.

They thanked him, headed up the hill, and piled into Anna's BMW. Paolo drove with Beckett in the passenger seat. Gabe and Anna squeezed into the back, which was only slightly larger than the Volkswagen Polo. Thirty minutes later, they entered Ravello.

Jenkins was parked at the end of the street, keeping watch. Beckett called him for a report. All was clear.

Gabe checked his watch as the cousins' home came into view. It was exactly 2:43 a.m. He felt a sudden rush of anxiety. How would he tell his grandmother about the murder? How would she react to news of the autopsy? And how would they find out what they needed to know? The car pulled into the driveway and rolled to a stop. *It's now or never,* Gabe thought.

Beckett motioned to Agent Mallon, who had been posted just off the front porch. Mallon was discreetly obscured from view by a large oleander bush. Beckett received an all-clear, so he and Gabe went to the door. Gabe knocked softly to no avail. He tried again. This time, three loud raps brought one of the elderly cousins to the door.

"Gabriel, Gabriel," she said with a look of concern. She invited Gabe inside. He pointed to the others behind him. "*Si, Si,*" she said. She held the door open and waved them all into the parlor. Once inside, she patted at the pin curl beneath her hair net and made gestures to apologize for her appearance.

She motioned for them to sit and excused herself. She called, "Francesca!" as she headed down the hall. Gabe heard her voice echo off the slate floor as she awoke his grandmother.

Moments later, Francesca appeared in her robe and slippers. "Gabriel, I've been so worried about you," she said. "I tried to call Lorenzo when I didn't hear from you but couldn't reach him. Is everything all right?"

She passed through the doorway and caught sight of Beckett, Paolo, and Anna. "No, I guess it isn't," she corrected herself. She saw their grim expressions and took Gabe's hands into hers. "Tell me, *amoré,* what's the matter? What's happened?"

"Gram, please sit down," he said. He led her across the room to the worn sofa. Paolo and Anna sat in the armchairs, and Beckett was standing near the front window, which gave him an unobstructed view of the driveway.

"What's going on?" she insisted. "Is this related to what you told me on Capri?"

"Many things have surfaced these past few days," Gabe said. "I have some terrible news." He choked on his words. "It's about Grandfather. His death was not from natural causes."

"What do you mean?" she asked.

"He was killed—murdered," Gabe said in a low voice, barely able to say it out loud.

Francesca gasped. She maintained her composure, but tears welled in her eyes and rolled down her cheeks.

"Murdered?" she asked in a near whisper.

Gabe reached over to embrace her. "I'm so sorry," he said as he held her. She gave him a tight squeeze, sat back, and wiped the tears from her face.

"What happened?" she asked. "How do you know this?"

Gabe looked to Beckett for support.

He came over and squatted down beside her. "Francesca, I dread this conversation. You know how much John meant to me," Beckett said, "but we're in a tight spot right now. We need your help."

She nodded.

"As you know, John was doing some investigative work for me," Beckett explained. "I was already in Rome when Gabe called me about John's death.

John and I were scheduled to meet the night he died, but he never made the rendezvous. I immediately suspected a connection between his death and the urgency he expressed when he arranged the meeting. I was concerned enough to order an autopsy."

"An autopsy—but how?" she asked. "I thought he was being prepared for the trip home."

"I know that's what you thought, but we had to know how he died for sure because of his work," Beckett said.

"Where is he now?" Francesca asked.

"I had him transported to Rome, so our people could do the work," Beckett answered. "He's still there. I hope you can forgive me, Francesca, but it had to be done without your knowledge. The situation is extremely serious."

Francesca gave a single nod. She waited for Beckett to continue.

Gabe heard dishes clanking in the kitchen. He was grateful the cousins didn't speak English. As if on cue, Paolo rose from his seat and touched Anna on the shoulder. She stood, and the two of them headed down the hall without saying a word. Both cousins were in the kitchen, and from the sound of the commotion, Gabe figured they were preparing a tray of food, even at that early hour. He heard muted Italian and knew Anna would keep them busy.

Beckett pulled up a chair and sat down in front of Francesca. "The autopsy results showed that John was poisoned," he said slowly.

A tiny gasp escaped from Francesca. She regained her composure. "But why? Who would do this?" she asked.

"That's what we've been working on for the last few days," Beckett said. "I suspect that John lost his life because he was closing in on something very dark. I can't share the details with you, Francesca, as you well know, to keep you safe."

She nodded and understood. "I knew something was wrong," she said finally. "He was so agitated before we came to Italy this time."

Gabe and Beckett glanced at each other. Beckett then turned back to Francesca. "We need to ask you some important questions about what John was working on."

"Go ahead," she said.

Beckett passed his handkerchief to her. "Have you ever heard the initials WSB?" he asked.

She shook her head no.

"John never mentioned anything like that?" he asked.

She again shook her head.

"Can you tell us what happened from the time you arrived in Italy until his death?" Beckett asked.

She nodded and dabbed at the tears on her cheeks. "We arrived in Rome on Sunday morning, rented a car, and went to the Vatican. I went to Mass at Saint Peter's while John took a stroll to pass the time. He liked to walk around the Vatican wall for exercise, that sort of thing."

Gabe and Beckett made eye contact again. Gabe didn't have the heart to tell her he was working at his apartment across the street.

"After Mass, we left Rome and drove down here," she continued. "We arrived late and went straight to bed. The next day was Monday, the day Gabe arrived."

"What happened on Monday?" Beckett asked. "We need to know every detail about what you did that day."

"I understand," she said.

"Assume nothing is irrelevant," Beckett added. "Start with when you woke up that day. Did he make any phone calls, go anywhere without you, leave you alone at any time?"

"Well, let me think a moment," she replied softly. She looked down at her hands and neatly refolded the handkerchief.

She closed her eyes and began. "Our day started early. It's hard to sleep when you're our age. I was in the bathroom getting ready for morning Mass. I was combing my hair when John came in and said he wanted to go with me."

She opened her eyes and looked at Beckett. "He wasn't much of a church-goer, you know, but he seemed to be changing. It's difficult to explain. I attributed it to answered prayers. Or maybe it was because you begin to think about what comes next at our age."

Beckett nodded sympathetically but pressed on. "John went to Mass with you. Where?"

"At the cathedral—Saint Andrew's in Amalfi. The same place Gabe and I went the other morning."

Gabe's eyes widened. He looked at Beckett. "Do you still have that piece of paper I gave you?"

Beckett reached into his pocket and pulled it out. "Right here."

"Look at it again," Gabe said. "Remember the last line?"

Beckett remembered full well. He glanced at the letters SA, the final two letters of the puzzle. He then looked back at Francesca. "Think. Did anything unusual happen that morning, perhaps at church?"

Francesca squinted as she tried to recall the details. "No, nothing unusual. We just strolled down the hill from the hotel and went to Mass in the crypt.

The same ladies who are always there were there. When Mass ended, I said my morning prayers, and we went upstairs. A few local women were visiting in the courtyard, so I joined in. After greeting John, they updated me on the local gossip."

Francesca's eyes widened suddenly.

"Wait a minute!" she exclaimed. "John did leave me at one point that morning—while I visited with the ladies. Maria was telling us about her granddaughter's upcoming wedding when John whispered that he'd be right back. I saw him go in the door and head down the stairs."

"Where do those stairs lead?" Beckett asked with an edge in his voice.

"To the crypt," Gabe replied.

"He was only gone a few minutes," she added. "When he returned, we said goodbye to my friends and left. We went back to the hotel, ate breakfast, and relaxed on the veranda. Lorenzo joined us. We visited with him for quite a while. We're very old friends."

"Lorenzo?" Beckett asked, feigning ignorance.

"Lorenzo Bonelli, owner of the Amalfi Hotel," Gabe replied.

Beckett nodded. He knew full well who Bonelli was. "Go on," he urged her. "What else happened that day?"

"Nothing much to speak of. We had lunch in our room and napped in the afternoon. I did some reading. I tried to convince John to go into town, but he seemed preoccupied. He said he wanted to stay near the hotel in case we heard from Gabe. I thought he was worried about your drive here from Rome," she said, looking at Gabe.

"Then what?" Beckett asked.

"We relaxed until dinner, which we ate at the hotel. Then Gabe arrived. We sat on the terrace and talked until 10:00 or 10:30. After that, Gabe went to his room, and I went to bed. John couldn't sleep. He spent some time on the balcony, then came in and said he was going for a walk."

Her voice faltered. "That's the last time I saw him alive," she said, weeping again.

Gabe moved closer and took hold of her hands. "Gram, Lorenzo and I discovered something written on the bathroom mirror the morning we found him. It was a cryptic message. I think it was directed at me. We've been trying to solve it, but the last two letters, SA, are a mystery. We have several theories, but nothing is certain. Do you have any ideas? Did anything else happen, something that might explain what they mean?"

Francesca lowered her head to concentrate.

"I was awfully tired that night," she began. "I was already in bed. I was almost asleep when John decided to take his stroll. I asked him not to be gone too long."

She paused a moment to savor the memory. "He then came over to the bed, kissed me on the cheek, and said, 'Remember me to Saint Andrew.' Those words were so comforting to me the next morning when I found him—gone. It was almost like he knew."

Gabe and Beckett's eyes locked.

"We need to get into that crypt!" Beckett exclaimed. He bolted out of his chair. "Now!"

At that instant, Paolo, Anna, and the two cousins entered the hall. One of the cousins carried a tray of coffee, juice, and pastries.

Beckett pulled Paolo aside as they laid out the serving tray. "We have a lead," he said. "I think the file might be hidden in the crypt at Saint Andrew's. How do we get in there?"

"I know the rector—very well, in fact. I can get him to let us in even at this hour," Paolo offered.

"Do it," Beckett replied.

Paolo went to the kitchen and made the call.

Beckett sat back down in front of Francesca. "There's something else you need to know," he said. "It's too dangerous for you to be here. You need to get back to the States immediately. I'm sending you to a safe house. John's already dead, and yesterday, Gino Caruso was shot in a very public execution. I'll have an agent escort you. We'll make the necessary arrangements to have John's body transported back home."

Beckett awaited her response.

"I'll go," she answered solemnly, "but what about Gabe?"

"I need him here," Beckett replied.

She nodded, suddenly looking very much alone. Gabe wanted to escort her home, but his work in Amalfi was unfinished. She needed him, but so did Beckett. After all, his grandfather had chosen him for this mission. He was torn. Gabe was about to speak, but Anna jumped in ahead of him. "What if I go with her?"

Gabe looked at Anna's face. It was so warm. She crouched down next to Francesca. "I would be pleased to go with you to the airport in Rome. That way, Gabe can stay here to help."

Gabe began to protest, but Francesca interrupted him.

"My sweet Gabriel, I'll be fine and would be delighted if you honored John's good name by finishing what he started. I never interfered with his work and always supported him the best I could. John did many important things over the decades to protect us all. He was a good man and a great American patriot. Gabe, you're the son he always wanted. Now, I want to support you." She turned to Anna and added, "I'll get my things together immediately."

Gabe wasn't sure how to respond, but his grandmother's sense of purpose inspired him. She was, indeed, a woman of great courage.

He looked at Anna. She smiled confidently. "We'll be fine," she said. "We'll keep each other company."

Francesca rose to collect her things, and Beckett took her by the hand. "I know this has been very difficult for you," he said. "Is there anything at all I can do for you at this time?"

She thought for a moment then responded. "Yes, there is. I want to tell Alex about his father's death, but I haven't heard from him in years. I have no idea where he is. I would be so grateful if there is a way to find him."

Beckett looked at Francesca sympathetically. "I'll see what I can do."

She nodded her appreciation. A gentle smile formed on her face. "Thank you, I'll get my things."

As she packed, Gabe heard a flurry of Italian exchanged between his grandmother and her cousins. He had no idea what they were saying, but when they returned to the parlor, they appeared convinced, if not completely satisfied, that she was leaving.

"I'm ready," Francesca said solemnly.

Gabe embraced his grandmother. "I'll find you as soon as I get back to the States." He could see tears in her eyes, and they hugged a second time. Beckett picked up Francesca's bag and carried it to Anna's car. He pulled Gabe's bag from the trunk and replaced it with Francesca's.

Gabe escorted his grandmother to the car. He helped her into the passenger seat, looked into her eyes, and smiled. "Gram, there's one more thing I need to tell you. I met a man named Cardinal Bauer. Have you heard of him?"

She looked at him, puzzled. "Cardinal Bauer? *The* Cardinal Bauer?"

"I think so," Gabe replied. "He's a fascinating man. He was also an acquaintance of Grandfather's—a confidante, actually. He was helping him with his work."

"Your grandfather never ceases to amaze me," she replied. "Cardinal Bauer has a very high office in the Vatican. He's close to the pontiff."

"That's what I've come to understand," Gabe said. "I saw him earlier tonight, just an hour ago."

Francesca was stunned but knew better than to ask why.

"He asked me to pass along a message to you," Gabe continued. "He thought you would find it comforting. Evidently, he witnessed a change in Grandfather, too. He said Grandfather was working hard to purge his bitterness and hatred of the Nazis; then he said something truly amazing. He told me that recently, Grandfather asked him to hear his confession."

Francesca let a deep sigh escape and clasped her hands over her heart. She closed her eyes and embraced the sound of those words. A smile spread over her face. She reopened her eyes.

"Cardinal Bauer happily complied," Gabe continued. "It was the first time he'd gone to confession in over fifty years."

She took Gabe's hand into both of hers. "I'm so proud of you," she said. "Your effort gives meaning to John's sacrifice. Be careful."

"I will," he nodded.

Anna got in behind the wheel and started the car. Agent Mallon took a seat in the back.

Gabe bent down and looked past his grandmother toward Anna. "I'll see you again in Rome—if you don't mind, that is," he said.

"I won't mind," she replied. An affectionate grin beamed across her face.

Gabe then turned to the agent in the back. "Take care of them." Agent Mallon patted his gun.

Beckett gave them a series of instructions about what to do and where to go when they reached the airport in Rome. "Don't stop anywhere until you get there. Above all, keep your phone off," he said to Anna. She nodded, put the car in gear, and backed out of the driveway. Gabe waved one last time as they drove away and disappeared into the darkness.

"I hope I made the right decision to stay here," Gabe said.

"So do I," Beckett replied. "So do I."

Paolo rejoined them. "We're all set. The rector will meet us at the side door of Saint Andrew's in thirty minutes."

Beckett pulled out his phone, called Jenkins, and barked a series of instructions. A few seconds later, his car appeared at the end of the driveway. Paolo, Gabe, and Beckett jumped in. Gabe checked his watch—3:27 a.m.

"Amalfi," Beckett said. "We're going to Saint Andrew's." Jenkins released the clutch, and the car shot forward, kicking up gravel.

Beckett tucked his phone into his coat pocket and adjusted his pant cuff. *I hope we're right,* he thought. He let out a huge sigh. More importantly, he hoped John was right.

56

Marco was still in his penthouse office. The clock read 3:41 a.m. He reached for his phone. He'd been trying to reach the driver of the Audi A8 for a couple of hours. Marco knew the man had a penchant for the ladies. In fact, women were his Achilles heel, the one thing that distracted him from business. Marco dialed, and the driver answered on the third ring this time.

"Where have you been?" Marco demanded. "I've been trying to reach you!"

"Must've been in a dead zone," the assassin replied. He unceremoniously pushed the sleeping woman's body away.

"Where are you now?" Marco asked.

"In my car," he lied. He pulled on his pants. In truth, he'd stopped at a local pub after killing Lorenzo Bonelli. He wanted a drink and to find some companionship. He'd succeeded on both accounts. Now, he was with the anonymous woman in her apartment twenty kilometers up the coast. She'd mentioned her name, but he'd already forgotten. "Where do you need me?" the assassin asked.

"Saint Andrew's Cathedral," Marco replied. "I already have a man watching the entrance, but I need you there when Castriotti arrives. How fast can you get there?"

"Thirty minutes."

"Good. Check the perimeter and call me with a report when you get there."

As the assassin put on his black coat and gloves, the beautiful woman rolled over lazily. "*Cos'e caduto?*" He didn't bother to reply. He let the door slam behind him.

JENKINS BLAZED DOWN the mountain toward Amalfi. Gabe noticed the sky was now partly cloudy. The moon backlit the clouds and cast an eerie glow over the Mediterranean. Beckett ordered Jenkins to make a hard left into the marina parking lot when they reached Amalfi. They drove toward the main pier and pulled into a parking space.

A series of buildings and restaurants hid them from view.

"Which way to the side entrance?" Beckett asked.

"Back there," Paolo answered. He pointed to an opening on the edge of the village. "That road leads to a parking lot behind the cathedral. It's only a few hundred meters from there to the side entrance. That's where the rector will meet us."

Beckett surveyed the setting. Four of them together might draw attention. "We'd better split up," he said. "I'll take Gabe. Jenkins, you go with Paolo. Are there other entrances to the crypt?"

"On the other side of the cathedral," Paolo replied.

"How do you get there?" Beckett asked.

Paolo turned to Gabe. "You've been to the cathedral. From Piazza Duomo, take the main stairs up to the colonnade. Look left. At the end of the colonnade, you'll see an iron gate. Go through it, and you'll find yourself in a courtyard area called the Paradise Cloister. There's a set of bronze doors on the right side. I'll let you in there."

Gabe nodded.

Beckett looked around the car. "Any questions before we split up?" he asked.

"We're good," Jenkins assured him.

"One more thing," Paolo said. "Once we're inside, we only have thirty minutes. After that, the custodial staff arrives, and the rector wants us to keep him in the dark about our activities. After he lets us in, we're on our own."

"I'm good with that," Beckett said. "Let's go."

Gabe and Beckett jumped out of the car and hustled across the road. They disappeared through an archway onto a darkened side street leading to the piazza.

Beckett pulled out his Glock. "Do you know how to use one of these?" he asked.

"No problem," Gabe replied as they entered the piazza. "I pack a gun when I'm on the trail. I've killed mountain lions, cougars, even snakes."

Beckett pulled a second weapon from his ankle holster and handed it to Gabe. It was a smaller Glock, a subcompact G26, 9mm. "Just point and shoot," he said. "Stay hidden as best you can. Someone could be lurking in the shadows."

The cold night air nipped at Gabe through his thin jacket. Beckett's words sent a shiver down his spine. Gabe thrust the gun into his jacket pocket and kept his hand on the stock. He was ready.

JENKINS WATCHED BECKETT and Gabe disappear into the piazza. He turned the wheel over to Paolo and climbed into the passenger seat. Paolo drove two blocks, pulled into the parking lot behind the cathedral, and found a parking space. Four-story flats, a market, and a pensioner hotel surrounded the lot. It was full of motor scooters and small cars, but no signs of life. Jenkins checked his watch—3:55 a.m.

"Back there," Paolo said. He pointed to the far corner of the lot. "That walkway leads to a tunnel. The side entrance to the cathedral is at the other end."

Paolo led them toward the walkway. Twice, Jenkins thought he heard footsteps. Each time, he stopped and backtracked, gun drawn. He checked around the corner but saw no one. Confident they were alone, they made a series of quick turns through the winding maze of buildings. They moved through the tunnel and arrived at the side entrance. Paolo reached up to knock when Jenkins's cell phone vibrated. It was Beckett.

"All clear on this side, too," Jenkins whispered. "We're about to go in."

Paolo knocked three times to signal their arrival. They heard the clank of the deadbolt, and the door swung open. A diminutive, elderly priest stood inside. Paolo and Jenkins stepped in, and the rector closed the door and locked it.

"*Buona sera*, Don Rossi," Paolo said.

"*Buona sera*, Paolo," the priest replied.

"We have two others at the door to the Paradise Cloister," Paolo said.

The rector nodded without comment. He led them down the marble staircase to the crypt. The entrance was covered with a heavy, floor-to-ceiling iron gate. The rector unlocked it and pushed it open. The three of them squeezed through, and he relocked it behind them. Jenkins immediately began searching for the file.

Paolo followed the rector through the crypt and up the opposite staircase. They entered the original cathedral built in the ninth century, the Basilica of the Crucifix. It now served as a museum and was filled with glassed-in cases of artifacts. They made their way to an exterior door. It opened to the

Paradise Cloister courtyard, where Gabe and Beckett were waiting on the other side.

"Right on time," Beckett said.

The rector pulled the door closed and addressed them. "I don't want to be an accomplice in these matters, so I'll leave you to your work. Let yourselves out through this door. It will automatically lock behind you."

"Understood," said Beckett.

The rector reminded them to be out before the custodial staff arrived. With that, he disappeared into the private elevator the clergy used to move between the crypt and their residence two floors above. Gabe heard the door slide shut, followed by the hum of the elevator motor as it lifted him higher.

Gabe, Beckett, and Paolo descended into the crypt to join Jenkins. Working at a feverish pace, they checked under pews, behind pictures, and in each of the alcoves. There were literally hundreds of possible hiding places, given all the treasures on display there. Jenkins looked inside the wall sconces while Paolo searched the priest's sacristy in the back of the crypt.

Beckett squatted to search the area under the altar where the bones of Saint Andrew were entombed. He found nothing behind the gold metal grate. He circled behind the altar to a tiny prayer alcove in the rear—again, nothing.

Gabe ran his finger behind a series of saint pictures on the far wall but came up empty. He moved to the other side. As he passed the altar, he glanced up at the imposing statue of Saint Andrew. Suddenly, his grandfather's words echoed in his mind: "Remember me to Saint Andrew." Gabe scanned the huge bronze statue from head to foot. He noticed a small gap beneath the base.

The larger-than-life statue was slightly uneven at the bottom. It created a narrow gap between the base and the marble stand on which it stood. Gabe peered into the gap but saw nothing. The lighting in the crypt was too dim. He noticed the gap widened on the left side. It was just big enough for Gabe to slide his fingers inside. He felt around—still nothing.

"I need some light," Gabe whispered.

"What've you got?" Beckett asked, his voice inflected with anticipation.

"Just a hunch, but take a look," Gabe said. "There's a gap under this statue."

Beckett saw it and immediately handed him a pen light. "Try this," he said.

Gabe flipped on the light and peered into the crevice. He swept it back and forth and saw something reflected in the light. It appeared to be the edge of a thumb drive.

"I think I've found it!" Gabe exclaimed. He pulled the light back and crammed his hand into the gap as far as he could reach. He felt the corner of the drive with his index finger but couldn't get hold of it. He pulled his hand back and flashed the light into the crack a second time. "That's got to be it, but I can't reach it."

"Get it out," Beckett demanded.

Gabe tried again but still couldn't reach it. "I need something longer to grab it," he said. Beckett pulled out a pen and handed it to him. Gabe held the light in one hand and the pen in the other. He slid the pen inside and fished for the drive.

Just then, a thud echoed down the marble staircase, followed by a clicking sound. Someone was at the side entrance.

Zach motioned to Jenkins. Jenkins swiftly circled the crypt and took a position by the iron gate. He found a spot concealed by a large column. With his back pressed against the wall, Jenkins readied himself, Glock drawn.

Gabe tried several more times to reach the drive, but each attempt failed. The pen kept slipping off the edge because of the angle. The clicking stopped and was replaced by the whir of a drill. A few seconds later, they heard the door swing open and the sound of footsteps. Someone was descending the staircase. Gabe's hand shook nervously. He made yet another attempt. Another failure. Two more attempts. Two more failures.

"He's coming," Beckett whispered sharply. Gabe and Beckett ducked behind the statue.

The footsteps reached the bottom of the staircase and then stopped. The intruder was at the iron gate.

As Gabe crouched behind the statue, he noticed the gap widened even further along the back side. He quietly reached up and slid his finger into the opening. He touched the drive. Extending his index finger, he carefully slid it to the edge and drew it out completely. "I've got it," he mouthed excitedly. "Let's get out of here."

Beckett nodded. He peered around the corner of the statue. The path to the exit was fully exposed, and the intruder was armed. They were trapped. It was completely silent.

Paolo saw their predicament from the sacristy. He looked for a diversion. *Perhaps I can distract the intruder by engaging the elevator,* he thought. He silently moved to the elevator and hit the call button. The elevator came to life. The hum of the motor reverberated throughout the crypt. *Bing!* The intruder instinctively stepped back into the darkened stairwell.

The diversion gave Beckett and Gabe just enough time to reach the other staircase. They bounded up the steps to the museum with Paolo close behind.

"We need to get the drive out of here and find out what's on it," Beckett said.

"I know a place," Paolo offered. "There's a paper mill museum further up the gorge, about a kilometer from here. There's a computer in the office. I'm on the board of trustees. I have a key."

There was an explosion in the crypt. Beckett's head jerked in that direction. "I need to help Jenkins. I'll meet you there. You're still armed, right?" Beckett asked.

Gabe pulled the gun from his coat.

"Good. Go, now!" Beckett barked. He pulled out his powerful G18. "Don't go near the car. They're probably watching it."

Gabe and Paolo bolted for the exit but paused at the door. Gabe signaled for Paolo to wait. Gabe crashed open the door, gun drawn. He methodically pointed his weapon in each direction. The Paradise Cloister courtyard was empty. The area was secure.

"All clear," he said. "Let's go."

Paolo ran out, and they rushed across the courtyard. They bypassed Piazza Duomo, turned right onto a covered walkway, and picked up the village road toward the paper mill. Gabe recalled it well. He'd taken the same route on his run the morning his grandfather died.

57

Marco, still in his penthouse office, savored the smooth flavor of yet another cigar. He was confident one of his loose ends would soon be eliminated. The clock read 4:42 a.m. He reviewed the chain of events in his mind.

Just before midnight, he'd received a call from two of his thugs. They saw Andre Gotto ship out from the Amalfi marina. He ordered them to track the boat, which they did. They followed it to the Emerald Grotto and quietly parked out of sight. Once there, they surprised Beckett's agent and killed him.

However, their encounter with Andre Gotto proved deadly. One of the thugs now had a bullet in his chest. His whereabouts were unknown

The other thug managed to escape unnoticed. He was now parked behind Saint Andrew's Cathedral in a small, inconspicuous car. Marco ordered him to wait for Paolo Castriotti's arrival. He knew to expect him shortly before 8:00 a.m., thanks to Lorenzo Bonelli's final slip of the tongue.

Just then, the phone rang. It was his thug.

"Marco, a car just arrived. The driver fits the description of Paolo Castriotti, and there's someone with him. They're headed toward the cathedral."

"Already? We weren't expecting him until morning," Marco replied.

"My orders?" the thug asked.

"Follow them, but don't kill Castriotti. We're looking for a computer file. We think it's probably hidden somewhere. Let him lead you to it. Once you have it, kill both of them and get rid of the bodies. Report back to me as soon as the job is done. Help is on the way."

Marco calmly hung up. He sat for a moment to think then placed another call.

MARCO'S ASSASSIN PULLED his Audi A8 into Piazza Duomo. He was parked in the shadows with the engine turned off. Just then, his phone vibrated. It was Marco. He explained the situation and delivered a new set of orders.

"I understand," the assassin replied. "As you wish." With that, he hung up.

The assassin watched the cathedral intently for several minutes as he formed a strategy. He scanned the piazza. It was deserted. The assassin locked the car, pocketed the keys, and set out on foot.

He stayed in the shadows and worked his way toward the cathedral's main staircase. He momentarily exposed himself as he climbed the stairs in full view. Still nothing. He concealed himself once again, turned left into the shadows, and made his way along the facade of the cathedral. At the north end of the colonnade, he noticed an open gate that led to a courtyard: the Paradise Cloister. He entered, circled the perimeter, and tried each set of doors. All were locked. It was still quiet.

Where the hell are they? he thought. *They must be close.* He exited the courtyard and entered a tunnel. It curved around two private residences with flowerpots on the stoops. Fifty meters ahead, the tunnel angled left and led back to the main village road. At the end of the tunnel, he found a bakery with a corner window. That's when he heard voices.

GABE AND PAOLO hustled deeper into the village. They passed beneath a large residence that bridged over the street. As they approached, the assassin pressed himself against the wall to hide. He watched them go by and then called Marco.

"Castriotti is headed up the main road, and guess who's with him— young Roslo," said the assassin.

"Roslo? Perfect," replied Marco. "It's time to kill two birds with one stone. Follow them and get the diary. They're also looking for a computer file. Get that, too. Then finish it—no witnesses."

The assassin flipped his phone shut and peered through the corner window of the bakery. He watched Gabe and Paolo disappear around a curve in the road.

"HERE WE ARE," Paolo said quietly.

An ancient stone structure was built into an incline on the left side of the street. It had an ominous, haunting appearance in the dark.

"The mill machinery is down there," Paolo explained as they crossed the street. He pointed to a submerged entrance to the building. A waterwheel was built near the entrance. It was fed by an endless source of energy: the Canneto River. "The office is this way."

Paolo led them around the right edge of the building and up a flight of stairs to the main entrance. He pulled out his key and unlocked the door. They entered the pitch darkness.

"This is the upper portion of the mill," Paolo explained. "It has an office and an exhibition area to display the paper made downstairs." Gabe recalled reading about Amalfi's ancient paper mills and their collection of antique machinery.

They entered the exhibition area. It was lined with plate glass windows and had no privacy shades. Paolo closed the door and locked it behind them but did not switch on the light. When their eyes adjusted, the dim, red glow of the exit sign provided just enough light to cross the exhibition space and enter the office. Once inside, Paolo closed the door and switched on the light. Gabe handed him the drive. Paolo logged onto the computer and slid it into the port. A few seconds later, the contents were displayed on the screen. Before their eyes was the file titled "WSB."

58

Paolo stepped aside. Gabe sat down and clicked on "WSB," the final chapter of his grandfather's treatise. He began to read. Paolo looked over his shoulder. The front page was a scanned copy of a handwritten note.

> Gabriel, if you're reading this file, it means I'm already dead, and you've followed the trail of clues. They were sending me threats, and I knew they were closing in on me. You must now protect your grandmother. Give her my love and keep her safe. These people will stop at nothing to achieve what they want.
>
> I have a secret meeting with Zach Beckett and Cardinal Bauer tonight. I plan to show them what I found in my father's diary. I made this file as a precaution. It's a copy of what I plan to show them. It's the only one. If you're reading this file, it's now your duty to get it to them.

Paolo flipped off the overhead light. The office faded into an eerie, bluish glow from the computer monitor. Gabe paged forward and read the final chapter of his grandfather's treatise: "WSB."

> In February 1979, just four months after John Paul II was elected pope, Ayatollah Ruhollah Khomeini returned to Iran as the triumphant leader of the Iranian Revolution. His adoring subjects saw him as the Islamic Mahdi, the divinely guided one who would come in the Last Days to restore Islam to its original perfection. Khomeini did not claim a divine title, but he

embraced the messianic charisma of the Mahdi when he fused Iranian law, politics, and religion into a single person—himself.

Khomeini fostered a highly militant brand of Islam, a foretaste of the one promoted by Osama bin Laden. The harsh reality of Khomeini's regime shocked the world when an angry mob stormed the American embassy and took fifty-two hostages in November 1979. That very same year, my father attended a covert power rally for another type of messiah, as I will explain below.

Initially, I theorized that Osama bin Laden was the Antichrist. However, I now realize Islam represents only one layer in the calculation. I believe that someone else is looming on the horizon. I found clues about this danger in my father's diary, clues that were hidden many years ago.

My father, Ivan Roslovsky, was a high-ranking Freemason. He kept a private diary of his innermost thoughts. I found this diary in 2003 among a collection of his books stored in my attic. They were placed there after his death in 1986.

Certain entries represent a significant betrayal of the Masonic Brotherhood. The most damaging were written in 1979 after he attended the power rally. According to his diary, a bitter disagreement developed afterward between my father and one of his highly motivated Masonic brothers, a much younger man named Robert Durand.

"Here it is!" Gabe exclaimed. "A name—Robert Durand—does it mean anything to you?"

Paolo rubbed his chin. "Not a thing, but it might to Zach." They kept reading.

To recruit my father, Durand invited him to hear the Master of the Royal Secret speak. My father was a respected elder within the Brotherhood. Durand coveted his support because it lent credibility to the Master's radical new plan to build something called the Great White Lodge.

However, my father had misgivings about Durand and his ideology, so he decided to secretly record the rally speech. He later transcribed it into his diary. That alone was reason enough to keep the diary hidden until after his death. Even today, it is a dangerous mission to possess it.

My father's handwritten entries have been scanned and appended to the end of this file. The following is the text of the speech delivered by the Master of the Royal Secret on the night of December 8, 1979.

MASTER OF THE ROYAL SECRET

Throughout history, Freemasonry has progressed from its Operative roots into Speculative inquiry. This change propelled forward the enlightenment of humanity and helped throw off the restraining shackles of Judeo-Christian belief. Today, Christian belief is in decline, especially in Europe and the Americas. That achievement alone attests to the greatness of Masonry. However, Freemasonry has an even more glorious future.

The confining beliefs of Christianity restrain humankind and keep it from achieving its full potential. Christians cling to the outdated notion of suffering. Human progress has never been based on suffering. Human progress is best served by alleviating suffering. Therefore, the time has come for Masonry to evolve yet again and ascend to its ultimate purpose. It's now time for Freemasonry to evolve from Speculative inquiry into Spiritual mastery. (Cheers!)

This evolution is accomplished every day as we build the Great White Lodge of Spiritual Masonry. The Great White Lodge is the place of man's ultimate destiny—the realm of supreme consciousness. In the Great White Lodge, a person recognizes that he alone is in control of his destiny. He rejects once and for all the notion that his assent to the next life depends upon Jesus, Allah, Yahweh, or any other supposed deity. (Applause)

The Great White Lodge is not an actual place, of course, but rather a pathway to the spirit realm. It's where the mind is totally free. The human body acts like an anchor in mortal life. It traps the spirit and holds it tightly in place on planet Earth. But when the body dies, the mind is released from this trap forever, no longer bound by the limits of space and time.

By following this path, people overcome the weakness of their mortal bodies, and the promise made to Eve is fulfilled: "You certainly will not die! No, God knows well that the moment you eat of its fruit, your eyes shall be opened, and you will be like God!" That is the destiny of those who reach the Great White Lodge! (Thunderous applause)

When people seek the Great White Lodge, they learn the beautiful truth about Freemasonry. However, this knowledge must be learned gradually and in stages. In the formative degrees of Masonry, the Masonic initiates are taught to believe they are free to bow down and worship their respective gods. Christians, Jews, and Muslims are encouraged to worship in communal brotherhood, each respecting the beliefs of the other.

Of course, those of us in possession of the secret know this is done deliberately. It's a necessary part of our program. If history has taught us anything, it is this: when threatened, human beings hold onto their spiritual beliefs like a pit bull holds onto a piece of steak. Both defend themselves at all costs, even to the point of death. The magnitude of the great unknown is so vast that the attempt to rip these beliefs from their hearts by force is defended viciously.

Therefore, it is necessary that people discard their beliefs willingly. For that, we offer more attractive alternatives. If you want a pit bull to drop his steak, throw him a bigger, more beautiful piece of meat. We do the same within the lodge. Encouraging communal worship allows our initiates to think their spiritual beliefs are secure. We claim all religions are equal and appeal to their sense of respect for mankind. We point to the conflicts and hatred produced by religious differences and offer up the Masonic Lodge as a place of harmony. Then, just like the pit bull, they willingly let go of their beliefs and latch onto ours. We've used this secret technique for centuries. Our Masonic brothers slowly reject their spiritual convictions by adopting alternatives. (Wild applause)

The Masonic master plan has evolved for centuries. It has acted in the shadows to prepare for this day. To the credit of our predecessors, the plan is achieving spectacular success during the second half of the twentieth century. In the modern world, Speculative Masonry grants worship to many deities, which is good. It is, nevertheless, a man-made enterprise that lacks the perfection of Spiritual Masonry. True perfection can only be attained by following the Ascended Masters of Light into the Great White Lodge.

History has provided these Masters—great teachers like Buddha, Zoroaster, Moses, Jesus, Muhammad, and Lucifer, to name a few. These Masters pave the way for other men to follow. They are our guiding lights. Among them, Lucifer's light shines the brightest! (Wild cheering and applause)

Lucifer, whose very name means light-bearer, reigns supreme. His guiding presence is the brightest, and he alone owns the title of Most Highly

Ascended Master. Only Lucifer has evolved to the seventh degree of initiation. He exceeds even Buddha, who reached the sixth degree, and Jesus, who reached the fourth.

At one time, it was thought Jesus had ascended to the fifth degree of initiation, thereby releasing him from further reincarnation. However, his fraudulent credentials prevented that. He lacked the power to come down from that cross. He failed at the time of his trial. He regressed in his journey and holds the ugly distinction of being the only Ascended Master to get downgraded. Happily, people now recognize this defect. So, they choose to follow Lucifer—a Higher Master, a brighter light. (Applause, hushed murmurs)

"Diabolical!" Paolo exclaimed angrily. He arched his back.

Gabe looked at him, speechless, then directed his eyes back to the monitor. Paolo leaned forward. They continued to read.

Gentlemen, we are now on the precipice of a new astrological age. Thanks to the precession of the equinoxes, the zodiac is leaving the Age of Pisces and entering the Age of Aquarius.

The two fishes of Pisces symbolize Christianity. However, just as Judaism gave way to Christianity during the last zodiacal shift, it's now time for Christianity to give way to the New Age of technology, knowledge, and progress. The Age of Pisces was characterized by Christian myth and the words "I Believe." The Age of Aquarius is characterized by scientific proof and the words "I Know." Never again will the world live in the darkness of its mythological past! The Great White Lodge will put an end to those myths forever as our knowledge expands to the infinite! (Standing ovation, wild cheering)

Gentlemen, the duty to build the Great White Lodge has been laid upon our backs. We accept this duty with enthusiasm and attendant care. Very soon, the remaining impediments to our progress will be vanquished. The Black Lodge, also known as Judeo-Christianity, has darkened the hearts and minds of humanity for too many centuries. It has enslaved too many generations with its false teachings. At the zenith of those lies is the teaching that Jesus is the only truth and the only way to eternal life. Preposterous! Life is much too complex. The cosmos is far too vast. Our destiny cannot be defined by one single path!

Therefore, it's time we put an end to this. Speculative Masonry has already made tremendous progress in that regard. It has neutralized the Black Lodge by infiltrating its institutions of higher learning. It has made spectacular use of the media to chisel away at its core beliefs, and it has undermined the message of the Black Lodge by offering a wide array of spiritual alternatives. (Applause)

My favorites include transcendental meditation, Tarot cards, Kundalini yoga, chakras, spiritual elements of the martial arts, auras, UFO belief, vampire energy, witchcraft, the redefinition of Kabbalah, black magic, white magic, psychic powers, guided imagery, dream interpretation, shamanism, astrology, Scientology, EST, psychological rebirthing, Jungian psychology, blood sacrifice, pagan ritual, animal and tree worship, alternative lifestyles, mind-altering drugs, sex orgies, and black masses. (Applause and cheers)

These spiritual pathways yield much fruit. They breathe life into the New Age movement. We encourage people to expand their spiritual journeys by selecting the spirituality most suitable to their needs. That is how people gain the fullest knowledge of themselves. They elevate their minds without boundaries or limits. They depend only on themselves to choose their path of destiny. Free choice, therefore, is the defining characteristic. The Great White Lodge always advances the cause of free choice. There is no victory unless people choose their spiritual path freely! (Sustained applause)

Still, some members of the Black Lodge are hopelessly attached to their inverted beliefs. They promote the reprehensible idea that all human beings have dignity, a supposed royal character. Such utter nonsense flies in the face of evolution and enlightened truth! Can there be any doubt that inferior classes of people are holding back human progress? Weak people are nothing more than products of their bad karma—sad reminders of the great balancing force within Nature! (Applause)

"Ridiculous!" Paolo complained. "We do have dignity in the eyes of our Creator—all of us. Human frailty is a fact of life, but faith in God overcomes all weakness."

Gabe turned his eyes back to the rally speech.

We all know Christianity is harmful. Fortunately, our purpose is served by the division among Christians, especially when they argue over the meaning of Holy Scripture. This division creates confusion and casts doubt upon the Christian message. It pushes lukewarm believers away from the Christian myth and allows them to choose one of our spiritual pathways instead. Division is useful!

These divisions have expanded within Protestantism, which is good. However, our real enemy is the Roman Catholic Church. It has maintained steadfast opposition to our cause for centuries. It's a formidable foe. Neither we nor Soviet communism have been able to defeat the Roman Church through direct attack. Therefore, we've adopted a new approach that bears wonderful fruit. We've cultivated initiates among the clergy to infiltrate the Vatican and other prominent positions. We've convinced these leaders to betray the Roman Catholic Church's teachings and speak out against its pope and his rules. To that end, we've succeeded greatly in fostering the same confusion and disagreements we see within Protestantism. Nothing is more pleasing to my ears than to hear a Catholic theologian raise an exception to Catholic doctrine and its teachings. (Snickers, a few claps)

This method is reaping a great harvest. Millions and millions of Catholic people are rejecting the Catholic Church to follow us. Millions of others are following nothing at all. That is also a beautiful outcome. It signifies contentment. They are neither hot nor cold. Their Catholic beliefs simply melt away in the lukewarm waters. (Pause for emphasis)

Still, not everyone is rejecting the Black Lodge. Some adherents stubbornly hold onto their convictions. One of them is the newly elected Polish pope. John Paul II is an anti-communist. He's also rigidly attached to the myth that Jesus was the Christ, the so-called chosen one. This stubbornness indicates a defective intellect. Worst of all, his message poisons our youth. It convinces them to hold onto these convictions. It's disgusting! (Roaring cheer)

If that weren't bad enough, the pope's youthful vigor is energizing the people of Poland. It gives them hope that the Iron Curtain will soon fall. The Soviets are alarmed by this development and share our concerns. They worry his young age will lead to a long pontificate. Fear not! The Soviets are already looking for a way to eliminate him. I'm confident they'll soon solve both our problems. (More hushed murmurs)

The Roman Pontiff preaches many falsehoods about the next life. We know that souls are neither created nor destroyed. We know that souls remain ever pure and always white, and we know that souls rejoin the mighty Universal Soul from which they came when our mortal bodies die. From there, our souls either ascend to glory like the Ascended Masters or begin anew in freshly reincarnated bodies—innocent babes, pure and regenerated. I tell you the truth. *There is no entrapment of souls! There is no hell!* (Loud sustained applause, standing ovation)

Hell is a weapon used by the Black Lodge to cast fear into the hearts of men. It's superstition. There is no hell, and there are no rules. I find no greater joy than watching a person recognize this fact and freely choose to follow one of our paths to *enlightened glory!* (Thunderous sustained applause, taking nearly a minute to subside—the Master waited for the room to become perfectly silent before proceeding in a slow, measured tone.)

Yet, not everyone will be capable of taking the journey to enlightenment. They are simply too far down the human chain to make the leap. Their deluded minds possess the same debilitating characteristics as the Roman Pontiff. They suffer from faith—blind faith in the unseen, in the unproven. It is a faith that prevents them from throwing off their Christian superstitions. They are humanity's weakest link!

This faith—this obvious character flaw—is particularly prevalent at the very bottom of the human chain. That's where we find the most stubborn adherents to Christian belief. Fortunately, Nature provides a way of cleansing the Earth and eliminating weakness. That day has now arrived! The time has come for us to deal with these inferior, obstinate minds! It's time to drive these reprobates into extinction! (Wild applause and cheering)

However. . .
(Pause, room goes silent)

However, we must be realistic about the task ahead of us. Blind faith should not be underestimated. It is a powerful, motivating force. Because of it, some have held onto their convictions no matter what the circumstances. (Hushed murmurs)

Yes, we must break their attachments! (Cheering)

For some, simple coercion will be sufficient; for others, it will be detention and isolation. However, even that won't be enough for those who prove to be the most defective. For them, more aggressive measures will be required. (More cheering)

Rest assured, we will enact whatever measures are necessary because we abide by a single truism. The Law of Human Ascendancy demands the elimination of the weak to allow for the emergence of a truly enlightened Master Race! (Prolonged thunderous ovation)

In this respect, we draw our inspiration from Margaret Sanger. Her pioneering work in eugenics serves as our model. Her prescient ideas inspired many—even Adolf Hitler, a man of vision. Hitler's near-perfect philosophy was guided by two overriding principles: first, if you tell a lie, tell a colossal lie, and second, if you cannot change a person's spirit, use absolute force! (More hushed murmurs)

These principles served him well. Nevertheless, he made two mistakes. First, he used state-controlled fascism to run his propaganda machine. That approach no longer works. Society is too sophisticated. Modern society demands a free press, so we've learned from his mistake. We allow the media to maintain their freedom. In doing so, we guarantee the credibility of our message, no matter how polarizing or conflicting it sounds. The free press acts as our mouthpiece. Then, when our message is delivered to the masses, it's devoured like a satisfying meal. That message is changing the spirit of humanity! (Long sustained applause)

Second, Hitler used too much force to implement his policies. His forceful actions gave the eugenics movement a bad name. His actions undermined its essential purpose: the elimination of the weak and undesirable. Fortunately, the principles of eugenics have been revived. They're now promoted under warmer titles, such as Planned Parenthood. It's both natural and effective to let the agencies execute their mission with the protection of the law and the consent of the people!

Earlier this decade, we triumphed with the success of *Roe v. Wade*. We'll build upon that success by defending free choice and encouraging voluntary abortions among the poor, the culturally inferior, and, most especially, among Christians. To that end, we give special thanks to Catholic politicians who promote our free choice agenda! (Applause)

Roe v. Wade represents a major victory in our quest to eliminate the inferior, but we also need a victory at the other end of life. We must implement legal freedoms for end-of-life decisions. We must promote laws that support the termination of unproductive lives, especially the infirmed, the destitute, and the aged. Our economic development demands it!

To be sure, there's work left to do. A further shift in cultural norms will be necessary for these ideas to gain universal acceptance. However, cultural change is tilting in favor of our ideas. We've assured it by fostering a public narrative—a narrative that focuses on the alleviation of suffering! Eliminating suffering is both expedient and cost-effective. (Cheering, wild applause)

Still, we must be prepared for the possibility that our liberating message will fail to achieve 100 percent success. Pockets of resistance could hold out no matter what we do. We must be prepared to do whatever is necessary to rid the world of the inferior human rot holding back progress! The vilest are those unwilling to come out of the darkness of the Black Lodge!

However, we also face another enemy. We cannot overlook the radical, militant Islamic uprising taking place in Iran. The Ayatollah Khomeini is spearheading an Islamic revival within Shia Islam that calls for world dominance. His movement has religious underpinnings and the zeal of prophets. If the day arises and the need becomes evident, we'll foment a clash between cultures.

We'll counter any attempt to usurp our supremacy and the supremacy of our message, whether that attempt is Christian or Muslim. Therefore, when the time comes, we'll pit those two forces against each other to bring about a cleansing of the earth! We will eliminate the holdouts, and we will reign supreme. That is our destiny! (Standing ovation, wild cheering, end of speech)

Gabe felt a sharp and renewed sense of rage. "It's no wonder my great-grandfather kept this hidden. He's talking about extreme ethnic and religious cleansing—like a new Hitler figure."

Paolo fumbled through the desk drawer. He pulled out a second thumb drive and shoved it at Gabe. "You better make a copy," he said.

Gabe switched the drives and clicked save. He then pulled out the duplicate and handed it to Paolo. "Hold on to this," he said.

Gabe scrolled forward and found a commentary from his grandfather in the next section. John Roslo wrote:

> My father, Ivan Roslovsky, was repulsed by Adolf Hitler and his ideology. Hitler tried to establish a Master Race by eradicating Jews, Gypsies, intellectuals, and anyone else considered inferior or a threat to the Aryans, including many Catholics. His entire regime was built on a foundation of hatred. Modern social scientists have attempted to characterize Hitler

as insane, but evil and insanity are not always linked. Unadulterated evil sometimes hides under the veil of insanity, but it's nothing more than a cold, calculating lack of humanity.

Hitler and his followers adopted their ideology with full knowledge. They were driven by an evil that poured straight out of hell. Indeed, Hitler and his inner circle were involved in the same occult practices that underlie Freemasonry.

My father was a Mason, but he was a man of liberty and justice. His very daughter perished at the hands of the Nazis, and he found their policies abhorrent and reprehensible. Nothing could have made him angrier than a rallying speech linked to Adolf Hitler.

Robert Durand attempted to recruit my father into the Master's inner circle. Durand was disgusted at my father's rejection. He saw it as a weakness. My father rebuked him, which became the basis of their dispute.

Durand contended the Master of the Royal Secret possessed a special knowledge of the mysteries of life. He believed the Master was the true personification of wisdom, strength, and beauty—the divine attributes. Durand believed the Master of the Royal Secret knew the true path. However, my father disagreed with Durand and left his diary behind as a warning to the world.

Durand conveyed his affection for the Master by referring to him using the English translation WSB, which expresses the Masonic god. My father provided the translation. Through a convoluted series of interpretations, the words *dabar*, *oz*, and *gomer* signify wisdom, strength, and beauty in Masonic instruction. Taking the first letter of each word, we get the acronym D.O.G., which Freemasonry then reverses to further shroud the meaning in mystery. Hence, the esoteric Masonic symbol: G.O.D.

Dabar	=	**W**isdom		
Oz	=	**S**trength	=	G.O.D.
Gomer	=	**B**eauty		

Gabe turned to Paolo. "WSB means god!" Gabe exclaimed. "Anna told me about the bizarre interpretation Masonry attached to Christian symbols. I didn't understand at first. Then she said, 'Think of it this way. If the devil had a language…' That's when it clicked. Here it is again."

Gabe and Paolo continued reading.

I've completed my analysis of the relationship between geopolitics and religious fanaticism. My task was to investigate the security implications associated with Christian apparitions, if any.

My findings evolved along two clear lines—natural and supernatural. When I started this project, I was skeptical and intended to prove that they were unrelated. What I found instead was something altogether different.

No matter how hard I tried, I encountered an inescapable conclusion. I found a vast, interlocking relationship between the natural order and the supernatural realm. I found links in every theory, observation, and event I investigated. Consequently, I've come to recognize a deeper connection between religion and politics, one that extends beyond the terrestrial realm. It is evident. I now believe that human endeavor is intertwined with the realm of God, and mankind is being aided by the protection of Christ and His mother.

It is also clear that supernatural evil exists. I'm now convinced of that beyond any shadow of a doubt. The horrors of the twentieth century defined that evil. Still, supernatural evil does not act directly. It requires cooperation. On 9/11, the world witnessed firsthand this cooperation.

On that sunny morning, monstrous acts of evil were perpetrated by Islamic terrorists on an unsuspecting America. Osama bin Laden and his band of religious fanatics attacked innocent people in cold blood. They did so with a firm belief they were acting in accordance with the will of God. Something else happened that day. It launched the global War on Terror. Osama bin Laden and Islamic terrorists became the number one enemy of the United States. They must be stopped. That fact exists and is true.

There is a striking coincidence between the meaning of the three sixes and Bin Laden's declaration of war in 1998. It is impossible to avoid speculation about a link to supernatural evil. The War on Terror, the rise of Islamic militancy, and the secret societies of Freemasonry have now coalesced into a crescendo of human tragedy. This I firmly believe.

Gabe noticed a handwritten note appended to the end. It was from his grandfather.

Gabe, a week ago, I was surreptitiously contacted by a man who claimed to be in the inner circle of a secret cohort. He would not divulge his identity, but he knew things about their charismatic leader that only a confidant could know. He told me that my father was familiar with their leader. He was the very same person my father heard speak, the so-called Master of the Royal Secret.

The man explained that he'd been an ardent disciple of the Master but now had misgivings. He said there was a plot set in motion a year ago that would soon come to fruition. They're planning to enflame rage against militant Islam by using a nuclear weapon against an American city. It would look like the work of al-Qaeda but was intentionally designed to draw unsuspecting people into armed conflict. He told me the Master said the conflict would bleed the world into purification while ensuring the Master and his followers rose to prominence. He also told me the Master now claims to have divine guidance.

This man approached me in secret. Evidently, his conscience has given way to doubt. He's concerned the conflict might spiral out of control with no one emerging victorious. He also dropped a bombshell. It's the reason that I insisted my meeting with Zach Beckett and Cardinal Bauer occur in person. He said one member of the Master's inner circle worked for...

The sound of breaking glass reverberated throughout the building.

59

The breaking glass had come from the basement. Paolo switched off the computer. They each had a copy of the file. Gabe felt horribly exposed. *Should we run, hide, or challenge the intruder head-on?* he thought and then made his decision.

"We need to split up," Gabe whispered quickly. "I'm going down there."

"Are you crazy?" Paolo said. "We'd be better off making a run for it."

"No," Gabe protested. "You make a run for it. I'll slow the guy down. It'll improve our chances of getting one of these disks to Zach."

"It's dark down there," Paolo said.

"True, but I'll have the element of surprise," Gabe said. "Don't worry about me. I'm well armed but need a quick lay of the land."

"There's a doorway at the bottom of the stairs," Paolo replied. "The basement is rectangular, ten by fifteen meters. There's a huge vat of water on the left. Just beyond that is a line of wooden mallets that beat rags into pulp. On the right is a large press and three drying racks. In the far-left corner is the hydraulic wheel that powers it all. Be careful. The equipment's extremely dangerous."

Gabe placed the diary in Paolo's hand. "If anything happens, get this to Zach through the embassy in Rome."

Paolo squeezed his arm. "You have my word on it, but we'll take it together."

"Let's go," Gabe said. He drew his weapon and eased open the office door. The room was empty. He waited for Paolo to make it to the exit. Paolo clicked the latch and was gone a second later. Gabe crept toward the staircase and hoped like hell Beckett was not far behind. He entered the stairwell and placed his back flat against the wall. All was silent.

He quietly started down the stairs. He rounded a curve in the staircase and saw broken glass illuminated by the moonlight. The wooden entrance door was still ajar. He couldn't see the intruder in the darkness.

Gabe fished through his pocket and pulled out a pair of sunglasses. He descended two more steps, reached around the corner, and tossed them across the room. They made a clean hit on the wooden door.

Whap, whap, whap. Shots from a silencer sent splinters flying. He instantly pulled his hand back. *Where the hell is Beckett?* he thought.

Gabe couldn't tell where the shots came from, but he knew the intruder now had his sight trained on the entrance. He could take one more step without exposing himself. After that, he would need to make a dive for it.

Gabe steadied his weapon and slowly stepped onto the bottom stair. His jacket caught on something. He felt the wall. It was a switch box with two switches. One was a light switch. The other was a large toggle. Paolo said it was a working mill. *Perhaps the toggle will start the equipment and create a distraction,* Gabe thought. He reached for it and pushed it down.

The basement suddenly came to life in a magnificent and terrifying way. In the darkness, the sound of rushing water flooded into the basement, immediately followed by the screech of grinding metal gears and the pounding of gigantic wooden mallets. The noise was deafening. He could no longer listen for the intruder, but the assassin had the same disadvantage.

Gabe dove into the basement and ducked behind the wooden vat. His diversion was successful. He squinted in the darkness—no sign of the intruder. He worked his way around the perimeter of the room, hoping to force the assassin to move among the machinery. Then he would have the advantage, but he needed to stay alive long enough to flush him out.

Gabe crept around the back side of the vat. He inched closer to the huge wooden mallets, hammering out an alternating pattern. The crushing blows were ear-splitting as the mallets pounded against the empty planks. Cotton, hemp, and linen rags normally muffled the sound.

Still on his knees and using the mallet machine as cover, he slowly made his way to the far corner of the basement. He found a narrow gap between the mallet machine and a massive hydraulic wheel tank adjacent to the wall. A wooden flume spanned the gap at shoulder height. Gabe had to cross the gap to reach the large press located at the other end of the room.

He still couldn't find his adversary, but his eyes had adjusted to the dark. He looked up and saw the outline of an old hand lever attached to the wheel tank. Presumably, it closed off water access to the wheel.

He peered around the edge of the last mallet. Water now poured from several newly created holes in the flume—shots from the assassin. There was no way forward. Gabe was pinned down. He peered around the corner and saw something perched on top of the paper press. It was the assassin's weapon silhouetted in moonlight, but he still couldn't see the intruder.

Gabe retreated and bumped into a storage bin filled with rags. The rags were torn into strips for papermaking. Suddenly, he had an idea. He grabbed a handful of strips, tied them end-to-end, and formed a four-foot rope. He then pulled Beckett's penlight from his pocket and tied it to the end of the rope. He wedged the light into a crevice in the flume and aimed it toward the paper press. The light switch pressed against the side of the crevice.

During the commotion, Beckett slipped unnoticed into the basement. He slid behind the drying racks and tucked himself between large sheets of heavy paper. He had an unobstructed view of the room. His eyes adjusted, and he saw the figure of a man crouched behind the paper press. He leveled his G18 and prepared to fire but then paused. How could he be sure it wasn't Gabe?

Gabe was still pinned behind the mallet machine. Sweat poured from his forehead. He wiped it on his sleeve and checked the position of the penlight a second time. He then took the rag rope in his left hand, crawled to the opposite edge of the mallet machine, and positioned himself. He pulled the rope taut. He could now activate the light and create a visible target without being seen. He lifted his right hand and aimed his Glock toward the paper press. Moonlight still silhouetted the weapon. He would only get one shot.

Gabe pulled on the rag rope with his left hand. The penlight snapped to life. The assassin instinctively recoiled and fired his weapon. His silencer made the shots inaudible, but the blast of Gabe's Glock rang out over the machinery.

Beckett watched what happened and dove for the hand lever on the waterwheel. He shoved it upward and closed the water source. Everything came to a slow, grinding halt in the darkness.

Then silence.

"Are you okay?" Beckett asked finally.

"Yes," Gabe replied.

"What about the shooter?" Beckett asked.

"He's down," Gabe said. "I think I killed him."

Beckett lifted his gun and made his way to the paper press. A dark-haired man was lying in a pool of blood. He was in his early thirties, well-dressed, and had a hole through his chest. His weapon lay beside him, and Beckett kicked it out of reach. "That's some aim," he said. "You're quite a marksman."

Gabe appeared from behind the mallet machine. "My grandfather taught me."

60

Gabe and Beckett were standing over the body when they heard the basement door creak. Paolo Castriotti and Agent Jenkins filled the doorway. Jenkins shut the door and sent shards of broken glass tinkling to the floor.

"Gabe's been busy down here," Beckett said, "and the body count's building." His understated comment hung in the air.

"What happened after we left the cathedral?" Gabe asked.

"Nothing to worry about," Beckett replied. "Jenkins knocked him silly and cuffed him to the handrail in the elevator. He'll get reported in the morning when the rector finds him. Right now, he's cooling his heels and going nowhere. We ran into Paolo on our way here. I told him to stay with Jenkins, and I came in after you." He looked at the body and grinned. "But obviously, you didn't need my help. Jenkins, check him for identification."

Jenkins quickly rifled through his coat pockets. They were empty. He rolled him over and found a money clip in his left pants pocket. It contained a wad of Euros. Tucked into the crease was a driver's license. Jenkins pulled it out and compared it to the body. "An obvious fake," Jenkins complained. "We've got nothing. The other guy was clean, too."

Beckett turned to Gabe. "What about the disk? Did you find the file?"

Gabe nodded, his expression serious. "We did, and we read it," he said. "It contained a name: Robert Durand."

"Is he connected to WSB?" Beckett asked.

"Yes, and he knew my great-grandfather," Gabe answered. Gabe handed the thumb drive to Beckett and quickly summarized what they found.

Beckett was floored. "I need to dispatch his name to Washington immediately," he said. Beckett pulled out his phone and called Jason Hollingsworth. Hollingsworth's voice was on the other end of the line within seconds.

"I have a name for you," Beckett said. "Robert Durand. He's directly connected to WSB. Run his name through the databank. Give me everything you have. I'll give you fifteen minutes."

"Fifteen minutes?" Hollingsworth complained. "It's almost midnight here."

"Make it ten minutes, dammit. Do you understand?" Beckett said sharply.

"Got it," Hollingsworth acknowledged and hung up.

Beckett had no doubt he'd get answers back in the prescribed time. Jason Hollingsworth was completely reliable. As predicted, his phone rang eight minutes later.

"We've run the name through our database," Hollingsworth said. "Durand is the chief operating officer of Allbritton Enterprises. Does the name ring a bell?"

"Allbritton Enterprises—as in Jack Allbritton?" Beckett asked.

"Exactly!" Hollingsworth replied.

"As in *Ruse of the Sea,* Jack Allbritton?" Beckett asked.

"One and the same," Hollingsworth reported.

Zach Beckett knew the name well. His prior NSA duties involved the close monitoring of certain people moving in and out of Eastern Europe. Spy games were common in those days, and his role was to identify Soviet double agents. It was part of the Cold War effort. Jack Allbritton's name was added to the NSA watch list in 1978. The NSA monitored him closely for years but was unable to produce anything tangible against him. Eventually, his name faded from the radar, and when the Soviet empire collapsed, monitoring activity ceased altogether.

Beckett explained the current situation to Hollingsworth. He ordered him to arrange for tactical support in Salerno. The letters SA clearly meant Saint Andrew's, but it looked like they now meant Salerno, too. He wasn't taking any chances. "Give me everything you can on the *Ruse of the Sea,*" Beckett demanded. "I want to know where it's been, where it's headed, and why it was suspicious in the first place."

"Right away," Hollingsworth replied. "Anything else?" he asked.

"As a matter of fact, yes," Beckett said. "Try to confirm if Durand is a Mason."

"Will do," Hollingsworth said. "Zach, there's one more thing. I'm getting a lot of heat about your whereabouts. Even the President has asked about you. The National Security Advisor told me directly. I hope you know what you're doing."

"Just send backup," Beckett demanded. "I have a feeling about this." With that, he hung up without waiting for Hollingsworth's response.

Beckett looked at Gabe. "It's out of our hands now," he said. "Let's get out of here."

"What about the body?" Gabe asked.

"I have an idea," Paolo said. "The Canneto River runs beneath the street and flows out to sea. There's a large storm sewer fifty meters down the road. We can dump the body there. After that, it's all underground."

"Does it have enough flow?" Beckett asked.

"With certainty," Paolo replied. "It's poured down the mountain for millions of years to create the gorge where Amalfi sits."

"Perfect," Beckett said. "Jenkins, mark him."

Jenkins pulled a small vile from his coat and took a blood sample. He capped it and placed it back in his coat. He then pulled out a fingerprint kit, marked both hands, and closed the lid. Lastly, he reached into his breast pocket, retrieved a miniature camera, and took a photo. When he finished, Gabe and Jenkins dragged the body up the stairs. Paolo cleaned up the blood as best he could with rags from the stock bin and pitched them into the river with the body. The four men watched it disappear and then hustled down the road toward Piazza Duomo.

"Where's the diary?" Gabe asked as they moved.

"Right here," Paolo said. He handed it to Gabe.

Just then, Beckett's phone rang. It was Hollingsworth. "Zach, your instincts about Salerno were on target. Satellite imagery indicates the ship is still in port. I've already notified our agents. A team is headed there now."

"Who's involved?" Beckett asked.

"Homeland Security and Defense," Hollingsworth replied. "A raid is being planned for late morning. The Pentagon has control of the operation."

"Got it," Beckett said. "I'm headed to Salerno now. I want to be there when it goes down. I'll coordinate a rendezvous, but I have a few loose ends to tie up."

"Ten-four," Hollingsworth replied.

Beckett hung up and tucked the phone back in his coat pocket. When they reached the piazza, Beckett turned to Paolo. "You have offered invaluable service, but I have one more thing to ask of you. I need to get Gabe out of Italy—and fast. Can you drive him to Rome for me?"

"I would be honored," Paolo answered.

"I want to go with you," Gabe protested.

"You've done enough," Beckett said.

"I have a duty. I owe it to my grandfather," Gabe insisted.

"I'm sorry, but no. I need to get you out of here," Beckett said flatly.

"You can't stop me," Gabe argued.

"Oh, yes, I can," Beckett insisted. He reached for his Glock. "How's that kneecap?"

"This isn't right," Gabe complained. His eyes darted back and forth between Beckett and Paolo. He ran his hand through his hair. "So this is it?"

"Gabe, this is as far as you go. I owe your grandfather a debt of gratitude, too. Part of my payment is to ensure your grandmother's safety. I think we've found our missing weapons. A team of agents is headed to Salerno now. Jenkins and I need to get down there, but I can't put you in any more danger. You're already a marked man."

Gabe didn't like it at all, but he was in no position to argue. *Perhaps Zach is right,* he thought. *Maybe it is time to head home.*

"Don't go to the airport," Beckett said. "They'll be looking for you there. I want you to take the train to Zurich and catch a flight to the States from there. Call this number." He handed Gabe a business card. "They'll arrange everything."

Gabe looked at it and slipped it into his pocket. The card contained a phone number.

"It's our secure travel desk," Beckett said.

Gabe looked at him and nodded his head. "Okay. I'll get out of here. I don't want anyone to say I was a liability."

"That will never be said—ever," Beckett responded. "You've done great things here for your grandfather and your country. I'm proud of you."

"I appreciate your words," Gabe said. He was briefly overcome with emotion. He had exposed the Amalfi secret and was proud of his contribution. His grandfather would have been proud, too. He extended his hand, and they exchanged a firm handshake. Gabe composed himself and then said, "All right, let's go."

Beckett pointed to Jenkins. "Hand over the keys. They can take the rental."

"How will we get to Salerno?" Jenkins asked.

Beckett grinned and flashed a set of Audi keys. "A donation from our floating friend. I'm sure he won't mind."

"Perfect," Paolo replied. "Travel in style. The A8 is a fabulous ride."

Jenkins tossed the rental keys to Paolo.

"Ready?" Gabe asked. "Let's go."

Gabe and Paolo beat a hasty retreat through the tunnel maze to the parking lot behind the cathedral. They found the rental car, jumped in, and fired up the engine. Paolo was behind the wheel.

The faint light of daybreak crept into the eastern sky. Paolo looked at Gabe. "Next stop, Rome."

61

High above the Port of Salerno, Marco observed the steady progress on the docks below. He calmly watched as he saw one crate after another get loaded onto the *Ruse of the Sea*, and not even he was sure which of the steel containers was the one. Nevertheless, he was completely confident their little darling was moving into position as planned.

He checked the clock on his desk. Nearly an hour had passed since he spoke to either of his men. His instructions were clear: find the disk, get the diary, kill them, and report. He'd heard nothing from either and contemplated his next move.

Then the phone rang. It was an informant, a local police inspector. The informant had dipped into the Marco slush fund for years. "Sir, I thought you might be interested in some information."

"I might be," Marco replied.

"I'm standing in the parking lot of the Amalfi Hotel. The proprietor was found murdered in one of the guest rooms," said the police inspector.

"Why is that my concern?" Marco asked.

"A security camera captured the image of a black Audi in the vicinity of the hotel. Judging from the body temp, it was here around the time of the murder," said the inspector.

"I see. Why are you telling me this?" Marco asked.

"We ran the tag number. The vehicle is registered to one of your corporations in Salerno," the inspector replied.

"And you're looking for this vehicle?" Marco asked.

"We already know where it is," the police inspector replied. "One of my junior officers just spotted it driving past the hotel. The plate number matched. We know it's the same car. He said there were two suits inside—one in his fifties, the other, perhaps in his mid-thirties. They weren't tourists, and it was much too early for a meeting. They were headed in the direction of Salerno."

"Has this vehicle been implicated in your investigation in some other way?" Marco asked.

"Not at this point, but we'll want them for questioning. I thought you should know."

"Thank you, inspector. I appreciate your diligence in this matter," Marco said. "Rest assured, my people will cooperate fully with the investigation. No doubt there's a perfectly reasonable explanation."

"Would you like me to have them picked up as they pass through Erchie?" the inspector asked.

"That won't be necessary," Marco replied. "We'll arrange to have them questioned by your people in Salerno. Thank you again for the notice. Please give your wife my best."

"I will, sir," the inspector said.

Marco hung up. He needed to find them first. Something was wrong. Neither of his men had called. More than enough time had passed to do their jobs, and now two guys in suits were driving the Audi.

Marco picked up the phone again. He dialed both his men. Neither answered. Their phones rolled to voicemail. He held the phone in his hand and thought about his options. A gentle smile formed across his face. He was pretty sure he knew who drove the Audi.

He hit speed dial to call his most reliable assets, the sniper from Salerno and his recording technician. They had completed their job at the Seaside Café and were awaiting further instruction at a ragged, little hotel outside Salerno. The recording tech answered on the second ring.

Marco had no need to identify himself. "I have another job for you, and this one's urgent." He provided detailed instructions and then hung up.

One more call, Marco thought. He picked up the phone and pushed a single button. The Master answered.

"Report," the mysterious Master of the Royal Secret demanded in a calm tone.

"There's been a development," Marco explained. "Two NSA agents are headed toward Salerno. They're driving my hire's Audi. He was sent to kill Castriotti, but he hasn't reported. I can't reach him. He must be dead."

"And the disk?" the Master asked.

"I don't know," Marco replied.

The Master became impatient. "What about Roslo and the diary?" he asked.

"We spotted him in Amalfi, but no sign of him since," Marco answered. "Don't worry. Things are under control. The loose ends will be eliminated."

"I see," the Master replied. His response was slow and deliberate. The Master swiveled his chair toward the window to admire the glistening city of Istanbul. The rising sun reflected off his mahogany desktop. "Obviously, these developments represent a serious deviation from the plan," the Master added.

"Should we abort?" Marco asked.

"No. Initiate Phase II." With that, the Master hung up.

Marco resumed his position at the window to watch the loading docks below.

62

Gabe and Paolo climbed the switchbacks. The car was silent. Gabe reflected on everything that had happened. He'd planned to go rock climbing, but circumstances traded the serenity of nature for the bizarre world of secret societies. It was the strangest week of his life.

He thought about the magnificence of the Canadian Rockies. He'd always loved nature and marveled at its existence, but for the first time in his life, he also experienced a profound appreciation for the Creator.

He also thought about his grandparents. They were together for over sixty years and lived a fascinating journey. They'd witnessed firsthand the great struggles of humanity during the twentieth century—his grandmother with her resilience and faith and his grandfather with his pragmatic self-reliance. In the end, even his grandfather saw the deep and mysterious connections between God and man.

His grandfather battled evil just like his twin sister had before him; like her, he was consumed by it in the end. Gabe felt pain in his heart but took consolation that his grandfather's tragic ending was for a noble cause. John Roslo had been a true patriot.

Then there was Anna. Gabe looked at his watch and estimated that she and his grandmother were nearing Rome. He would be greatly relieved when he knew they'd made it safely. He had confidence in Anna. What an amazing woman. She was intelligent but compassionate, confident yet hopeful. Her view of the greater existence was solidly rooted. He admired that, too. She was also beautiful and vivacious. He would miss her.

His mind then turned to Zach Beckett, an enigma. He was cold, calculating, and deliberate, but for all the right reasons. Beckett carried a gigantic weight on his shoulders and was headed straight into the hornet's nest. *Will Zach find what he's looking for?* he wondered. *And if he does, what will he do about it?*

Gabe stared out the window as the road wound around curve after curve. The eastern sky was now light blue. The setting moon had disappeared behind the mountains, and the morning star glowed brightly. He loved Venus, a source of fascination for everyone who ever walked the earth. Still, he doubted Beckett noticed its beauty at that moment.

Gabe still felt the sting of being sent away. He did his best to mask it, but he really wanted to be with Beckett in Salerno. He watched the scenery drift by for another ten minutes and became even more anxious. Finally, he could stand it no longer. "Paolo, I need to go to Salerno," he said.

"That's not a good idea," Paolo replied. "Let Beckett do his job. He has a team of agents on the way."

"I know, but I want to help him. I want to be there. I want to do something," Gabe lamented.

Paolo rubbed his mustache. "Haven't you had enough?"

"I need to go. I have a feeling about this," Gabe said.

Paolo exhaled hard. He pulled to the side of the road and thought for a moment. Then, suddenly, he spun a U-turn. "The fastest way there is along the coastal road," he said. He gunned the engine. "I don't like it, but I understand."

Gabe and Paolo descended to the coast, turned left, and sped along the coast toward Salerno. They passed through the turnabout in Amalfi. The village was still asleep in the early morning dawn. Gabe looked at this watch—5:47 a.m. Paolo negotiated the twists and turns swiftly, but their progress ground to a halt at the Amalfi Hotel. The road was partially blocked by an emergency vehicle. Two Carabinieri stood in the parking lot.

"Oh, no!" Paolo exclaimed as they approached. "Something's happened."

"Should we stop?" Gabe asked.

Paolo shook his head. Gabe looked at him and could tell he was visibly shaken. "No. Let's keep going. We need to get these bastards!" Paolo exclaimed.

63

Gabe and Paolo sped toward Salerno amidst an endless series of clutching, breaking, shifting, and accelerating. Traffic was light at that hour. They made excellent time.

Gabe read a road sign: "VIETRI 2 KM." Vietri sul Mare was a scenic gem. It was the last truly enchanting town on the Amalfi Coast before the industrial hub of Salerno.

They wound around a few more turns and made a sweeping arc to the left. In the distance and far below, Gabe saw the beaches of Vietri in the dawning light. He was still looking out the passenger side window when the rental car screeched to a halt.

"Oh, no, not them too!" Paolo lamented.

Gabe looked forward. He saw the black Audi A8 parked at the side of the road. Paolo advanced a few meters and stopped directly behind it. The front windshield was cracked like a spider web. Gabe jumped out and approached the driver's side door. Jenkins was slumped over in the front seat, a bullet through his head. Glass fragments and blood were everywhere. Gabe felt for a pulse—nothing. "Jenkins is dead," he said.

"Get back in the car," Paolo demanded. "We need to get out of here now."

Gabe did a quick 360 sweep. Beckett was nowhere to be seen. "You're right," he said. He lunged back in the car.

Paolo slammed it into gear. They flew down the mountain. Paolo crossed the centerline as they rounded each curve. Suddenly, Gabe noticed a white van parked in a small pullout used by tourists.

"Slow down," Gabe demanded. "Why is that van there?"

Paolo clutched and downshifted.

"Stop here," Gabe said. He pointed to a rock outcropping, a large slab of limestone perched on top of the seawall.

Paolo parked fifteen meters from the van. Their car was shielded by the mountain on one side and the slab of limestone on the other. Gabe reached for his Glock and got out. He slowly approached the van. The back doors were solid, with no windows. He reached the back of the van and peered around the driver's side. The side mirror gave him a clear view of the passenger cabin. There was no one behind the wheel.

He listened but heard nothing, then he checked the passenger side. It was empty. He moved toward the front of the van and noticed a partial handprint on the sliding side door. It was red. Gabe ran his finger through it. Blood—and it was fresh. He eased toward the cabin and carefully peered into the window. Nobody inside, just a bunch of electrical gadgets.

Gabe stepped back and motioned to Paolo. He pulled the car forward, and Gabe leaned in. "I found blood," he said.

He made another 360-degree sweep. The place was deserted, but he noticed a rock staircase a few meters ahead. He ran to the landing and peered over the edge. Stairs descended the side of the cliff. He traced the zigzag pattern down the side of the mountain. That's when he saw Beckett being shoved along by two men.

Gabe quickly pulled his head back and ran to the car. "I've found him. Zach is being forced down those stairs at gunpoint."

"What are you going to do?" Paolo asked.

"I don't know," Gabe replied, "but we need to help him. Where does that staircase lead?"

"All the way to the sea," Paolo answered. "It ends at the beach, but that's a long way down."

"Can you get there by car?" Gabe asked.

Paolo nodded.

"How long?"

"Maybe five minutes," Paolo answered. "Ten at the most."

Gabe jumped back in the car. "Let's do it," he said. "Hopefully, they won't see me coming up from the bottom."

They were off in a flash. Seven minutes later, they were at the bottom of the seawall. Paolo pulled into a secluded parking place. They were obscured from view by a weathered shack.

Gabe reached into his pocket when the car stopped. "Here. Take this in case I don't make it back," he said. He handed Paolo the diary for the second time. "Wait here."

Paolo stayed in the car.

Gabe jumped out and charged up the side of the cliff. He was concealed from sight for the first hundred steps but was in full view when the staircase curved around a bend. He ducked and crouched against the rock face. Careful to stay out of sight, he paused to listen. He heard the muffled voices of the men above and the thud of fists on flesh.

Gabe assessed his surroundings. The stairs were no longer an option. He'd have to scale the vertical rock face. It was jagged but full of clefts. He judged it was perhaps fifty feet up to where Beckett was being interrogated and beaten. Gabe tucked his weapon back in his jacket and reached for the first handhold.

The first twenty feet were easy, but the next thirty proved harder. Gabe abhorred climbing without a safety rope, and the sounds from above had his adrenalin rushing. *Focus,* he thought. He concentrated on his handholds and footholds rather than what might be happening to Beckett.

The final fifteen feet changed again. Instead of a vertical rock face, he found a crevice in the limestone. Large enough to climb into, it was angled in such a way that it protected him from the men above. He placed his back against one side and his feet against the other and quietly shimmied toward the top. Progress was painfully slow.

He advanced to within a few feet of a concrete observation deck built on the side of the mountain. He paused to listen. It sounded like the men were at the other end. From what Gabe could tell, they already had the disk and were demanding the diary.

"Mr. Beckett, you test my patience," he heard the sniper say in accented English.

"I told you. I don't know," Beckett said.

Smack. Gabe heard a sharp slap across Beckett's face.

"Yes, you do, Mr. Beckett," the sniper said. "I will give you one more chance to improve your memory."

"Even if I knew, I wouldn't tell you," Beckett said defiantly. "I know who you work for."

Gabe heard another sickening thud and a loud exhale. He climbed the final few feet in the commotion and found a solid foothold. He peered over the edge. Beckett and two other men stood at the far end of the observation deck. The deck was served by two staircases—one to the road above and the other to the rocks and beach below. It was surrounded by a waist-high rock wall that ran around the perimeter. Beckett was doubled over and pressed up against it. He faced away from Gabe, a gun pointed at the back of his head. The two men were forcing Beckett to climb onto the rock wall.

"Get on the wall, Beckett," the second man demanded. Gabe was stunned. *That's an American accent,* he thought. The first man sounded Italian, but this one was clearly an American.

"Now!" the American demanded.

Beckett didn't move. He said nothing.

There was a long pause. Gabe heard the screech of a hawk in the distance.

"Shoot him," the American said finally. "He'll be one less problem."

The Italian man simply nodded. At that second, a shot rang out.

The Italian slumped forward. His gun dropped to the ground. Beckett spun around. The American dove for the weapon, but Beckett's knee shot upward into his jaw. With a rocket-like movement, he broke it in two places. The American fell sideways, barely conscious. Beckett quickly picked up the gun and set himself, both hands on the stock. He looked across the observation deck at Gabe then down at the man lying at his feet in a pool of blood. Beckett felt for a pulse. Nothing. The American was curled into a fetal position and groaning in agony. Beckett held his gaze for a few seconds then looked back at Gabe. A sarcastic grin spread across his face.

"Good thing I sent you home," he said finally.

The rental car crested a hill, and Gabe caught his first glimpse of Salerno in the distance. The vessels in the harbor glowed yellow in the early morning sunlight. Gabe checked his watch—7:08 a.m.

"Pull over," Beckett barked. He hung up his phone.

Paolo pulled to the side of the road, the engine idling.

"We have a fleet of Apache and Blackhawk helicopters on the way," Beckett said. "They're less than forty minutes out. We also have a team of thirty agents and more than twice that many riot police assembled a few kilometers from here."

Beckett turned toward Gabe. He had a serious look on his face. "Once everything's in position, we're going in," he said. "This time, there's nothing you can do to help. I sent you home once. This time, I mean it. I'm being direct. Don't take it the wrong way. I'm deeply grateful for your courageous rescue, but you need to get out of here."

"Stop," Gabe said. He held up his hand. "You're right. Just tell us where to take you."

"We'll wait right here," Beckett replied. "My ride's on the way."

A few moments later, Gabe heard a chopper approach from the south. It slowed, descended in front of them, and set down on the roadway. It had an Interpol insignia on the side. Beckett opened the car door and stepped out. Gabe jumped out, too.

"This is it," Beckett shouted over the noise.

"Godspeed," Gabe shouted back.

They shook hands, and Beckett climbed into the chopper. It lifted off and disappeared behind the mountain a moment later.

Gabe got back into the car. Paolo looked at him. "Did you mean it? Are you ready to get out of here?" Paolo asked.

Gabe pursed his lips and looked at the harbor in the distance. "We have a pretty good view from here, don't we? It ought to be quite a show."

Paolo laughed. "I suppose you're right." He shut off the engine, and they watched quietly.

The harbor was business as usual. Shipping crates were being loaded onto three separate cargo ships. One particular ship sat prominently in the harbor. Its reddish color glowed orange in the morning light. The *Ruse of the Sea* was being stacked five high with shipping containers. A half-hour passed, and the activity in the harbor continued undisturbed.

Suddenly, Gabe saw seven Apache and five Blackhawk helicopters appear on the horizon. They flew in from the west. They descended on the harbor, machine guns ready. Simultaneously, a swarm of armored trucks and emergency vehicles burst through the port's main gate and fanned out in every direction. At least a hundred police officers in riot gear jumped out to secure the perimeter. A few seconds later, American soldiers started dropping from the Blackhawks. They rappelled into position for a massive, coordinated assault. Armed soldiers boarded each of the ships. The largest contingent flooded onto the *Ruse of the Sea*. Dockworkers and shipmates were herded together at gunpoint.

Finally, Gabe turned to Paolo. "I think it's time to go. We've done all we can."

Paolo nodded. Before he started the car, he reached under the seat. "I almost forgot. These are yours," he said. He pulled out the thumb drive and the diary. "Make sure you get a copy of that file to Cardinal Bauer."

Gabe tucked them into the breast pocket of his coat. Paolo fired up the engine, and they headed for the A3.

64

Gabe had been asleep for over three hours. The exhaustion of the previous forty-eight hours finally caught up with him. The radio was on and Italian music played softly in the background.

Eventually, Gabe stirred. "Where are we?" he asked.

"About an hour from Rome," Paolo replied.

The sun was now high in the sky. "Any sign of trouble?" Gabe asked.

"None," Paolo replied. "No one's tailing us, and we're making great time."

Gabe looked at the speedometer: 160 km/h. *So that's where Anna gets it*, he thought. "Have you heard from Anna?" he asked.

Paolo shook his head. "I don't expect to. My phone's shut off."

Gabe understood. "Do you think we could stop somewhere and use a landline?" he asked.

Paolo thought for a second. "I don't see any harm in that. I'll leave a message at her office," he said. He eased off the accelerator, moved to the right lane, and pulled over at one of the many Autostops along the highway. It bustled with people filling their cars and bellies.

They found a pay phone, and Paolo placed the call. He spoke in Italian. Three minutes later, he said, "Ciao," and hung up.

"Was she there?" Gabe asked.

"No, but I have great news," Paolo replied. "She called and said your grandmother made it safely to the airport. Her flight took off an hour ago. Agent Mallon is with her. He's been assigned to protect her when they arrive at Dulles. She also reported seeing a casket being loaded into the cargo hold."

Gabe felt an enormous sense of relief.

They bought some sandwiches and water bottles and got back in the car. Gabe took a bite of his sandwich, but his mind was preoccupied as they entered the Autostrade. He couldn't shake the images that formed in his brain when he read the "WSB" file. He saw visions of the Hitler rallies and the Master of the Royal Secret whipping his devoted followers into a frenzy of outbursts with his talk of a master race—wisdom, strength, and beauty, G.O.D. The Master sounded like a madman. He raved on about the glory of the Great White Lodge. *Surely it would never happen,* Gabe thought. Then again, few people took Adolf Hitler seriously before his rise to power.

Gabe pondered the possibilities. Various scenarios ran through his mind. Then there was the most intriguing possibility of all. Was this man the Antichrist? Would he succeed where all others had failed, even Hitler?

He turned to Paolo. "What did you make of that business about the Great White Lodge?" he asked. "I've never heard of it before. It sounds bizarre."

Paolo rubbed his chin to contemplate his reply. "Your grandfather asked me the same question."

"He did?" Gabe asked. He was surprised.

"Indeed, he did," Paolo said.

"What did you tell him?" Gabe asked.

"To tell you the truth, I hadn't heard of it either," Paolo replied. "That's what I told him. However, it made me curious, so I did some research."

"What did you find out?" Gabe asked.

"It turns out that in the nineteenth century," Paolo said, "the Great White Lodge was written about extensively by a Russian woman named Madame Helena Petrova Blavatsky and her protégé, a Brit named Alice Bailey. They were two of the original founders of the New Age movement. They also claimed to have spirit guides from the 'other side' helping them usher in the glorious New Age of Aquarius. The Age of Pisces had come to an end, an age symbolized by fish—in other words, the age of Christianity. In the New Age, the words 'I believe' were to be replaced with the words 'I know.' In the New Age, faith is dead, and human knowledge reigns supreme. Many of the ideas professed by the Master of the Royal Secret originated with them—or should I say their spirit guides."

"You're kidding," Gabe said.

"I wish I were," Paolo answered. "There's something else. Some of Hitler's inner circle were students of this same Satanic philosophy. Many people reject the notion of spirit guides as New Age crap, but rest assured, these demonic spirits are as real as the nose on your face. Just read Second Thessalonians. Their arrival was prophesied. Is it any wonder their influence began in the nineteenth century? Humanity was on a collision course with 1998, and the horrifying cataclysms of the twentieth century were all part of the carnage preparing the way."

"Do you think the Master of the Royal Secret is the Antichrist?" Gabe asked.

"I'm not sure what to think," Paolo replied, "but you can be certain the conditions are ripe for his arrival."

"How will we know?" Gabe asked.

"That's not entirely clear, but here's something we do know: as the world sinks deeper into chaos, the Antichrist will offer humanity an apparent solution to its problems, one that humanity will soak up blindly. But it's a trap. Vast numbers of people are falling into it."

"With all this deception, how do we know what to believe?" Gabe asked.

"Here's the test of truth. Does the proposed solution stand on the name of Jesus Christ or not? Is Jesus held up as the Christ of history, humanity's savior and hope, or is He presented as just one of many guiding lights that have come and gone? That's the test. All truth rests on the name of Jesus as divinity. Every lie diminishes Jesus or exalts man. The Great White Lodge is the essence of that lie. The Master of the Royal Secret said it himself when he quoted the serpent, 'No, you shall not die, for God knows that when you eat of it, your eyes will be opened, and you will be like God!' The disguise of the messenger may change, but the lie remains the same."

Gabe thought for a moment. "But this deception is perpetrated on the entire globe," he responded.

"True, but don't despair, Gabe. God makes all things new. He has a plan. It was foretold in the beginning. It includes things that even Lucifer can't stop."

"Like what?" Gabe asked.

"Like the apparitions of Mary in Fatima and Medjugorje, for example. Like Stefano Gobbi and his messages of warning and hope. Like the magnificent pontificate of John Paul II, Mary's spiritual son. John Paul was sent by Jesus to guide the world at that moment in history. His teaching and example of Christian love fortified the entire world. He built a massive barrier of defense against the lies and deceptions. Even assassination attempts on his life couldn't stop him. He survived to fulfill his duties. Even if Freemasonry has infiltrated the Catholic Church to confuse the faithful, John Paul II has produced the *Catechism of the Catholic Church*. It's a complete and definitive statement of Catholic belief, Catholic teaching, and Catholic faith. He has passed on to the next life, but his document remains to shine forth as a sure guide for all. The Blessed Virgin Mary even called it his last will and testament. God has not abandoned us!"

"I see what you mean," Gabe said.

Paolo nodded. "God is in control. The putrid White Lodge may culminate in the religious deception of the Antichrist, but never forget the words of Jesus: 'Upon this rock, I will build my church, and the gates of hell shall not prevail against it!' That promise was made to Peter and, by inference, to all his successors until the end of time."

Gabe found great solace in those words. It was the same thing he'd read in the Gobbi messages. He sat back and contemplated the cosmic battle between good and evil that played out on the stage of earthly existence. He closed his eyes. He rested his head against the seat as the music continued to play softly. He thought, *I'm just one little player in one small scene of a major epic*. Yet his choices impacted the whole. He hoped he'd played his role well.

THEY PULLED THROUGH the ancient wall surrounding Rome, and traffic picked up substantially. It was 12:16 p.m. Paolo wove through the maze of vehicles as they made their way to the train terminal. They pulled onto Via Giovanni Giolitti, and Gabe recognized the mammoth building that loomed ahead. It was where he'd first met Anna.

He felt the way any traveler does when he recognizes a place in a foreign country, like he'd arrived home. Only this time, Gabe really was headed home, and his stomach was in knots. He couldn't get his mind off Anna.

Tragedy brings people together in unexpected ways, but the return to daily life often pulls them apart. He'd developed a relationship with Anna that he didn't want to lose. He also knew that wanting to be with her was beyond a temporary rush of emotion. Deep inside, he secretly hoped she'd be at the station. Yet, Gabe was a realist—not because of everything they'd been through the past few days but despite it.

Paolo double-parked and jumped out of the car. He retrieved Gabe's bag from the trunk. They started toward the main entrance, and Gabe checked his coat pocket. The diary and disk were still there.

"Do you still have your weapon?" Paolo asked.

Gabe nodded. "Do you think I'll need it?"

"You never know," Paolo replied.

Once inside, they checked the departure monitors for Zurich and purchased a ticket. His train was leaving in nineteen minutes from Bin 16.

As they hustled to the loading platform, Gabe scanned the crowded terminal for potential danger. They reached the train. Everything appeared normal. No one paid any attention to them. It offered both a sense of relief and a sense of anxiety at the same time. He turned his back to the train and extended his hand to Paolo. "Well, I guess this is it. Give Anna my best," he said.

Paolo grabbed his shoulder and pointed. "Why don't you, my friend?" Paolo beamed.

Gabe turned around and saw Anna. She stood in the doorway of the train and held a suitcase. She had a hesitant smile on her face. Gabe leaped onto the step and quickly embraced her.

"Going somewhere?" he asked.

"I'm thinking about a holiday in America. That is if I can find a place to stay," she said.

"I believe something could be arranged," Gabe replied. He smiled broadly.

"Oh, I almost forgot," Anna raised her finger and reached into her purse. She pulled out a small envelope and handed it to Gabe. "It's a gift from Cardinal Bauer. He had it delivered to my office for you."

Gabe glanced at it and slipped it into his jacket pocket. There was something heavy inside. It felt like a coin of some sort. He then turned to Paolo. "You knew about Anna, didn't you?"

Paolo nodded.

"Thank you, sir, for everything," he said, reaching out again to shake Paolo's hand. "I'll never forget all you've done for my family and me."

"Come back one day and join us for wine time," Paolo replied.

Gabe paused. "I will. We'll have some great stories to recount, won't we?"

Paolo then leaned in and kissed Anna. "Take care of her, Gabriel."

"You have my word," Gabe said.

They shook hands a second time. Gabe took Anna by the hand and led her into the passenger compartment, Zurich-bound.

65

The train reached the Alps after a stopover in Milan. Gabe awoke to find Anna still asleep in his arms. He held her tightly as they wound through the picturesque mountain passes. It was Gabe's first time in the Alps, and they were every bit as beautiful as the Canadian Rockies. He stared out the window and thought about this fantastic woman, Anna Castriotti. He gently stroked her silky black hair. He also thought about the future. Someday, he'd return here and complete the climbing adventure he'd originally planned. He checked the time. Another three hours until they arrived in Zurich.

Gabe silently rode until Anna awoke an hour later. He briefed her on everything that had happened since they last saw each other. When he finished, Anna asked him what he received from Cardinal Bauer.

He retrieved it from his pocket and read the words Cardinal Bauer had written on the outside of the envelope:

> Gabe, this is for you. No soldier goes into battle unarmed.
> Never let your guard down.

He unfastened the clasp and opened it. As he peered inside, the train jerked and began to slow. Instinctively, they glanced out the window. "We've reached the border," Anna said. "Get your passport ready."

Gabe refastened the clasp and slid it back into his coat pocket. They pulled to a stop. Dozens of armed soldiers lined the platform on both sides of the train. A moment later, the train was crawling with Italian military police.

"Passaporti! Pässe! Passeports! Passports!"

Gabe looked at Anna, her face white as a sheet. "What's going on?" he asked.

"I don't know," she said. "This is highly unusual. I've never seen this before. Just relax, act like a tourist."

Soldiers swept into their compartment accompanied by civil authorities. An agent and two armed soldiers approached. They questioned Gabe first.

"What was your business in Italy?" the agent asked in English.

"Vacation. I was here on holiday," Gabe said.

"Final destination?"

"Zurich," Gabe answered. "From there, we're flying back to the US."

"Are you together?" the agent asked.

"We are," Gabe replied.

The agent carefully compared Gabe's passport photo to the sheet of paper he was holding. "How do you know each other?" he asked. He pointed to Anna.

"We met in Rome," she answered.

He eyed her suspiciously. "Papers!" he demanded.

The agent handed Gabe's passport back and reached for Anna's. He examined it for a moment then asked her a question in Italian. She nodded. He asked her another question. She nodded a second time. Gabe could see the agent stiffen. "Come with me," he said in English. He grabbed Anna by the arm.

Gabe was paralyzed as he stared down the barrel of two Israeli-made Uzis. One soldier remained with Gabe while Anna, the agent, and the other soldier disappeared out the back of the carriage.

Gabe's mind spun. He felt completely helpless. Several minutes passed. He tried to speak, but the soldier ordered him to remain silent. Other people were being questioned, too, but no one else was taken from the train. The regiment of military police remained posted outside.

Finally, the rear door opened. Gabe's heart exploded with relief as he saw Anna being escorted back to her seat. The agent bowed slightly, said something in Italian, and disappeared along with his military escort.

A few minutes later, the train was underway, but only for a few seconds. It moved slowly forward then stopped a second time. Once again, agents passed through the train, but they looked like official border personnel this time. They were now on the Swiss side of the border and had to pass through customs. Both were silent as they produced their passports without incident.

The second stop was brief. Gabe was still puzzled as the train pulled away. He leaned over and whispered into her ear, "What happened?"

Anna shook her head no and remained completely silent, clearly for a reason. Gabe was confused but followed her cue and did the same. Neither said a word for the next half hour. The train meandered through the Alps, but the majesty of the mountains was far from his mind. Finally, Gabe leaned over and asked again, "What happened back there?"

Anna did a quick sweep of the carriage with her eyes. "My name surfaced in connection with a murder at the Amalfi Hotel," she answered. Tears filled her eyes. "Lorenzo is dead, stabbed through the throat."

"Oh my God!" Gabe exclaimed in a horrified whisper. "That explains the police vehicles we saw there this morning. How did your name come up?"

"They wouldn't say at first. They just peppered me with questions. I finally convinced them I didn't know anything, which was true. That's when they told me the police traced a call from the hotel to Uncle Paolo's cell phone. It linked the Castriotti name to the murder. When they saw my passport, they wanted to know why I was leaving the country."

Tears spilled onto her cheeks. "I told them I had no idea what they were talking about or who Paolo Castriotti was. I was simply a girl from Rome headed on holiday with my boyfriend from Canada. They eventually agreed to release me."

Gabe squeezed her hand. "It's all right, Anna. You did what Paolo would have wanted you to do. He'll be fine," Gabe added. "Beckett will see to that."

She wiped away the tears with her other hand.

Gabe didn't believe his own words. Lorenzo was dead, and the police were searching for Paolo. That last piece of news cast an even darker pall over the train.

The remainder of the ride was quiet. A couple of hours later, they reached the train station in Zurich. Gabe scanned the platform as they pulled into the station. He saw nothing out of the ordinary. When the train stopped, they gathered their bags and beat a hasty retreat through the concourse to the cab stand outside, where Gabe hailed a taxi. A few minutes later, they were on their way to the airport.

The cab driver spilled over both sides of his narrow seat. His thick, gray hair bristled out the sides of his knit cap. The sour smell of pungent cheese wafted from his lunch. He hadn't finished it, and the remainder sat on the front passenger seat next to him. But he was an amiable fellow.

"Good day to be alive," he said. He pulled back the napkin covering his lunch. The odor in the cab grew stronger.

"Sure is," Gabe replied. He smiled at Anna and cracked the window to let in a little fresh air.

"Especially given today's news from Salerno," the driver went on.

"What did you say?" Gabe asked.

"Didn't you hear the news? Oh, I guess not," he said, "being on the train. It all happened this morning."

Gabe and Anna exchanged a wary glance. "What happened?" Gabe asked.

"It's all over the news. A nuclear bomb was discovered in a packing container on a ship headed for America."

"Unbelievable," Gabe replied. He laid his head against the seat and exhaled a deep, satisfying sigh.

"Where are you arriving from?" the driver asked.

"Rome," Gabe answered.

The driver looked in the mirror at Gabe. "Rome? You're lucky you got out of Italy."

"Why?" Gabe asked, surprised.

"They sealed the borders less than an hour ago. The whole country is under a massive manhunt for the perpetrators," the driver said.

Gabe put his arm around Anna. She laid her head on his shoulder. They rode in silence the remainder of the way, listening to the sounds of road noise and an endless stream of dispatch chatter from the cab's two-way radio. Early evening traffic was relatively light. They made excellent time.

"Which airline?" the driver asked as they turned into the airport.

"KLM," Anna replied. She had already arranged their itinerary through the NSA's secure travel desk. Beckett's agent had given her the phone number. They were scheduled to fly to Amsterdam, followed by a connection to Washington.

The driver pulled up to the terminal and helped them unload. Gabe handed him a twenty-euro bill. "Keep it," he said.

"Thanks," the driver replied.

They sensed a notable excitement in the air as they checked their bags. People were discussing the day's news. They heard conversations in various languages. Anna overheard snippets of the events in Spanish and German.

"This is huge!" she whispered as they checked in.

They passed through the concourse and saw pockets of people clustered around the television monitors throughout the terminal. Gabe read his watch—6:56 p.m. They still had more than an hour before departure. "Let's get a drink," he said.

"I didn't think you were a drinker," Anna teased.

"We're celebrating," he replied with a grin.

Gabe took her by the hand and led her into a pub near their gate. It was jammed with people crowded around a giant plasma screen. Gabe and Anna found an empty table along the window that offered an excellent vantage point to catch the news. They ordered drinks and took their seats just in time for the top-of-the-hour news cycle.

CNN blared. "We're now going live to Salerno, Italy, for an update on today's breaking top story."

Gabe and Anna were mesmerized as the correspondent explained the raid that happened earlier in the day.

"Approximately 9:00 a.m. local time, Interpol and a coordinated team of federal agents from several US governmental agencies, along with Italian authorities, descended on this port city and raided a cargo freighter, the *Ruse of the Sea*, sailing under the Danish flag. Authorities acting on a tip secured the ship and launched a massive search, culminating in the discovery of what is being called a fully functional nuclear warhead. The device was concealed inside a shipping container. We are receiving conflicting reports, but one undisclosed source indicated the container originated from an unspecified manufacturing facility in Turkey, where it was packed and sealed. We have not been able to confirm. Authorities have confirmed the freighter was headed to the United States but would not disclose its specific destination."

The correspondent suddenly leaned forward. He strained to hear the voice in his earpiece. Straightening himself, he looked into the camera.

"CNN has just received an unconfirmed report that the device is suspected to be of Russian origin. The Russian government has flatly denied the report, restating its position that its nuclear arsenal is completely secure. Bill Higgins reporting live from Salerno, Italy. Back to you, Ted."

"Thank you, Bill. We're waiting for a news conference to begin in just a few minutes when we'll hear from today's hero, the man who uncovered this terrorist plot and led authorities to Salerno."

The CNN background screen flashed the words "Holocaust Averted." It then broke to a commercial.

Gabe and Anna were on the edge of their seats, awaiting the appearance of Zach Beckett. The music cued up. The CNN anchor reappeared.

"We're now ready to go live in Washington, where we will hear from the chief operating officer of Allbritton Enterprises, Mr. Robert Durand."

Gabe dropped his beer glass. "My God, that's him!" he exclaimed. Anna grabbed his arm.

The scene flashed to the US headquarters of the international conglomerate Allbritton Enterprises. Robert Durand stood at a podium behind a bank of microphones with the corporate logo of Allbritton Enterprises plastered on the wall behind him.

Durand began to speak. "Acting on the information we received through our corporate affiliate in Istanbul, Turkey, the internal security forces of Allbritton Enterprises made a heroic discovery today in Salerno, Italy. Earlier this week, our alert security team investigated a discrepancy in the tracking number of a particular shipping container. Evidently, it had been modified without authorization after leaving its point of origin. The container in question was packed and sealed at a Turkish textile manufacturing facility and then transported by truck to Italy. We traced the container to one of our ocean freighters, the *Ruse of the Sea*, which was being loaded with cargo in the port city of Salerno, Italy. Internal security confirmed the discrepancy and notified my office."

He paused and looked straight into the cameras.

"My office became extremely concerned when we learned late last night that the body of a Turkish truck driver was discovered shot to death in Amalfi, Italy, approximately twenty-five kilometers from Salerno. His remains were found floating in the Amalfi harbor by authorities at the mouth of an underground river. In accordance with our corporate risk management procedures, my office contacted Interpol late last night, Washington time. In a joint operation between Italian and American authorities, a team of agents was dispatched to Salerno to secure the ship. We granted full access to the *Ruse of the Sea* so authorities could search for the container in question. At approximately 10:30 this morning, Salerno time, the carton was located and opened. Inside, authorities found what they are calling a fully functional nuclear warhead."

Durand surveyed the press corps standing before him.

"We were shocked by this discovery but are thankful today for the cooperation of the American, Italian, and Turkish governments. Through their efforts, we have averted a catastrophe. I can assure you that Allbritton Enterprises is fully prepared to assist with the investigation. We will not stop until those responsible are arrested and prosecuted to the fullest extent of the law."

He delivered that last statement with earnestness. His demeanor belied his false humility. Robert Durand loved his position of power. He pretended to dodge the spotlight but, in fact, glowed in it.

"I will now take your questions," Durand said.

A female reporter asked, "What can you tell us about the Turkish textile manufacturing company?"

"Let me begin by saying the company in question is not owned by Allbritton Enterprises," Durand began. "Our affiliation with that company is limited to shipping their products to the world market. All I know at this time is what I've learned from our people in Turkey. There are conflicting reports, but evidence has surfaced linking the Turkish firm to a highly concealed operation for Islamic extremists funded by al-Qaeda. That will be for the authorities of Homeland Security to determine. Investigators are at the scene now. Next question."

"What about Salerno? Do you think the terrorists chose Salerno because of a breach in security procedures there?" a male reporter asked.

"We have no way of knowing why Islamic terrorists do what they do," Durand answered. "Our company has transported shipments in and out of Salerno for decades. The Salerno port has some of the most thorough security measures in the industry."

"What about Marco Sorrentino?" a different reporter asked. "We understand he's been detained in Salerno. Can you tell us what you know about that?"

"Detained is a mischaracterization," Durand replied. "Sorrentino's corporation controls over 80 percent of the shipping traffic through Salerno, so naturally, he's being questioned. The authorities say his company and the port authority followed all appropriate security procedures. They are cooperating fully with the investigation. The security breach was in Turkey. That fact is clear."

"What about rumors the device was stolen from the Russian arsenal?" another reporter asked.

"I have no such information," Durand answered.

"Where was the *Ruse of the Sea* headed?"

"That information has been classified by Homeland Security pending their investigation," Durand said. "Thank you. That's all for now." He turned and walked away from the podium.

The CNN anchor reappeared. "Both the President and Secretary of Homeland Security are hailing the heroic efforts of Robert Durand and Allbritton Enterprises today," the anchor began.

Gabe's face went completely pale. Anna was speechless. The news anchor droned on.

"We've been double-crossed," Gabe said defiantly. "Zach Beckett betrayed us—and all of America, too. The only people who knew the name Robert Durand were Zach, Paolo, and me. Neither Paolo nor I had anything to do with this. We drove from Amalfi to Rome after the raid started. It had to be Zach. Don't you see, Anna? He tipped off Durand. That bastard!"

Gabe was fuming and disoriented. He couldn't believe he'd been played by Zach Beckett. He even helped him accomplish his duplicitous act of treachery. Images of all the events from the past few days flashed through his mind. *Never let your guard down,* had been the warning from Cardinal Bauer. He ran his hand through his hair.

"What are we going to do?" she asked.

"I don't know… I don't know," Gabe said. His mind reeled. If he couldn't trust the NSA, who could he trust? "But I'm glad I have these," he added. He patted his jacket pocket.

"What?" she asked.

"The diary and the 'WSB' file," he answered. "We made a copy when Paolo and I read it in Amalfi. Beckett doesn't know I have it."

"That's a relief," she said, "but what will you do? You'll be a hunted man, and what about Uncle Paolo?"

"I have no idea," he said grimly, shaking his head in disbelief.

Suddenly, he froze. Gabe slowly turned his head to make sure no one was listening. The crowd still gaped at the television. "I just realized something," he said. He leaned over to whisper in her ear. "According to the news report, they only found one device in Salerno. It's not over."

66

Zach Beckett shoved his way down the crowded dock. It was jammed with Interpol agents, bomb squad vehicles, and security officers from both the United States and Italy. Stacks of shipping containers littered the pier, and helicopters flew overhead. The noise was deafening. A security zone had been created around the *Ruse of the Sea*. The gathering of international press crowding around the perimeter steadily increased throughout the day.

Beckett pushed his way through the crowd and caught sight of a television monitor. He stopped dead in his tracks. "Who the hell is that?" he shouted. It drew the attention of those within earshot. He inched closer and saw the face of a well-groomed corporate executive. He was giving a press conference.

The wall behind the man was filled with images of the Allbritton Enterprises corporate logo. The tagline at the bottom of the screen caused his jaw to drop:

Allbritton Enterprises Thwarts Terrorist Plot
Robert Durand, COO, Comments on the Day's Events

Beckett manhandled his way through the throng of reporters and entered the security zone surrounding the freighter. He flashed his identification at the armed Interpol officers guarding the area. He started to board the freighter but thought better of it. Instead, he turned and bolted toward the port authority offices. Once inside, he searched for privacy. The first-floor offices were brimming with people. He found the stairs and ducked into a vacant office on the second floor. He pulled out his phone and dialed headquarters.

"Signal Fire," was all he said. He seethed.

The call was answered in Washington. "One moment, please."

A few seconds later, Jason Hollingsworth picked up the line.

"How the hell did this happen?" Beckett demanded.

"Sorry, Zach. We don't get credit for the kill," Hollingsworth answered. "Apparently, the internal security department of Allbritton Enterprises had already contacted Interpol. Allbritton traced the device to a Turkish textile plant, a front operation for al-Qaeda. The warhead was trucked in from Turkey. The truck driver was found floating in an underground river."

"Damn it, Jason. We killed that guy. Something's completely screwed up," Beckett said.

"What're you talking about? We dodged a bullet on this one, Zach," Hollingsworth replied.

"Why was Robert Durand on television?" Beckett asked.

"Evidently, he reported the warhead," Hollingsworth answered. "Interpol said he made the call personally. We just got word that twenty Pakistanis were picked up in a raid on the plant. They're being interrogated now. It has all the markings of Islamic extremists."

Beckett slammed his phone shut. *Someone tipped off Durand*, he thought. And there was now an elaborate deception pinning the blame on Islamic extremists. Who would believe it to be any different? He burst out of the office and ran back outside. He was outraged.

HOLLINGSWORTH HUNG UP when the line went dead. He was nonplussed by Beckett's reaction. He flipped the page on his *Far Side* calendar and read the cartoon with amusement: "A new day in the nation's capital." He chuckled to himself.

He reached for his lunch and looked out the window. The morning sky was perfectly clear. The sun shone brightly. It was going to be a glorious autumn day. He savored the view for several minutes while his mind drifted. He felt a powerful sense of satisfaction. He'd done his job well, and he knew it. Reason and common sense had prevailed over his earlier doubts.

He slowly drew himself back to the task at hand. He took a deep breath and reached for the secure phone line. He picked up the handset and dialed. When the other party answered, he heard a single word.

"Report!"

67

"Mission accomplished," Hollingsworth replied.

The Master of the Royal Secret reached for the remote and muted the news reports. When the phone rang, he had been watching Istanbul's skyline glisten in the sunset.

"Beckett took the bait, and so did the media," Hollingsworth continued. "Beckett was especially pissed off about Durand taking credit for the discovery. Now everyone believes Islamic terror is behind the shipment, just as you predicted."

"It worked flawlessly," the Master replied.

"When do you want me to leak the intended destination?" Hollingsworth asked.

"Give it a couple of days," the Master answered. "Public opinion has already shifted in our direction. The media are doing a fine job sowing fear among the masses."

"Have you decided where?" Hollingsworth asked.

"New York is the obvious choice," the Master said. "It has the most to lose. We'll let Americans think that terrorists were about to rip out the heart of the Big Apple. That kind of fear galvanizes people. It will push the administration toward our higher objectives. No one will ever know that Salerno was just a decoy to sow fear."

"What about the other weapon? When do you want that leaked?" Hollingsworth asked.

"Soon. It's a powerful instrument of control," the Master answered. "As long as we have it in reserve, we hold all the cards. It allows us to squeeze our grip on power. We'll amplify fear and confusion through the media. It's always worked in the past.

"We'll choreograph our intended outcome through strategic security breaches," the Master continued. "Remember, our goal is to unify the Western powers in their battle against Islamic terror. We need that to happen with the full backing of the American people. It's an essential element of my plan. Leaking news that the weapon is moving here or there is a very powerful means of control, and we'll have that control until the day we use it. Of course, when and where we use it is a secret only I know."

"What about Beckett?" Hollingsworth asked. "He's going to be asking a lot of questions."

"Don't worry about him," the Master replied. "He's already been discredited. Can you imagine the response he'll get from the administration when he tries to assert that Americans were involved instead of foreign terrorists? The media are hailing Durand as a hero. If Beckett tries to say otherwise, he'll be crucified in the court of public opinion."

"And Roslo?" Hollingsworth inquired.

"Leave him alone for the time being. He might prove useful to us. Besides, I'm having him watched—closely."

ANNA LOOKED AT GABE. Her eyes were sympathetic. Gabe was still in shock.

"How could Beckett have double-crossed us?" he asked. "He was my grandfather's friend and colleague." Gabe was still lamenting when he felt the envelope from Cardinal Bauer rumple in his coat pocket. He pulled it out and read the words written on the outside a second time.

> Gabe, this is for you. No soldier goes into battle unarmed.
> Never let your guard down.

"Never let your guard down, never let your guard down," Gabe repeated out loud. He unfastened the clasp and examined the contents. It contained a note and a round metal medallion. He dumped the medallion into his hand. "What's this?" he asked. He held it up for Anna to see.

"A Benedictine medal," she replied.

Gabe inspected it closely. The front of the medallion contained the image of a man. He held a cross in his right hand. To the right of the man was the image of a cup. On his left was a raven. The back of the medallion showed a cross covered with letters. "What does this mean?" he asked. Gabe pointed to the Latin inscriptions.

"They translate roughly, 'Holy Cross, be my light,'" Anna replied.
"And these?" he asked.
"That's a prayer for protection against the forces of evil. Something to the effect, 'Be gone, Satan, drink your own poison,'" she answered.

Gabe turned the medallion back over. "I suppose this is Saint Benedict?"

Anna nodded. "Benedict is credited with almost single-handedly saving Christianity from disappearing from the face of the earth as invading barbarians overran Europe," she said. "He built his monastery at Montecassino to preserve the Christian faith during the fall of the Roman Empire. He used these prayers against the forces of evil. It explains why sixteen Roman Pontiffs have chosen him as their namesake."

Gabe recalled their conversation about Montecassino. *Never let your guard down,* he thought.

"What does the note say?" she asked.

Gabe unfolded the sheet of paper and laid it out so they could both read it. The letter was typed, single-spaced, and signed by Cardinal Bauer.

Dear Gabe,

Now you know the truth. Satan and the principalities of evil are waging a war of hatred throughout the world. Above all, it is a war of blasphemy against God. Blasphemous attacks on Christ and Christianity are now the norm. Attacks against the Catholic Church are particularly virulent. No longer does Satan deny God's existence. That was last century's atheistic battle. The new battle, the final battle, is a war on truth.

Today, the Adversary sows hatred throughout the world to bring about division, discord, and violence everywhere. Many have fallen victim to terrorism, and blood flows in the streets. The Adversary has seduced the world with the poisonous venom of neo-paganism. How many souls have fallen victim to this deception? How many have been overcome by vice in their quest for pleasures of every kind? Immorality spreads everywhere, claiming the souls of God's children. Neo-paganism is a manifestation of Masonic influence. Tragically, many have succumbed without even realizing it. Others have rejected the truth with full knowledge.

The twin evils of terrorism and paganism are part of the final battle against truth—a war Christ foretold in the Book of Revelation. The pagan, Masonic attacks on Christianity and the rise of Islamic terrorism are real. They serve as calling cards for the kingdom of Satan, which has arisen in our midst.

This battle is also being waged at the level of the spirits between Saint Michael the Archangel and Lucifer himself, who will appear very soon with all the powers of the Antichrist.

But take courage! The crushing defeat of Satan has also been foretold. A great cohort of faithful Christians has formed. They are prepared to battle for the triumph of Jesus, which is the triumph of love, goodness, and truth.

For this reason, I entrust you to the powerful protection of the archangels, your guardian angel, and Saint Benedict so you may be guided and defended in the epic struggle being waged between heaven and hell. I also give thanks because, in the end, the battle will be decided by the power of love. In God's plan for the world, the power of love will triumph. It will overwhelm and quench the fires of hatred, and all things will be renewed.

There is much need for faith! There is much need for hope! Gabe, be a beacon of light and watch for the great sign that announces the supreme victory. When the time is at hand, the sign of the Son of Man will appear in the sky. The bloody cross of Christ's crucifixion will be transformed into a glorious, radiant sign for all to see.

That great sign will announce the return of Jesus in glory. It will be transformed into a throne of triumph because Jesus will come upon it to establish His glorious reign in the world. It will become the door that opens to lead humanity into a new reign of life. Jesus will bring this new life with him at the time of His glorious return. Never give up hope! Never succumb to the deception!

Peace of Christ Be with You,
Cardinal Bauer

    Gabe folded the sheet of paper and slipped it back into the envelope. He took a deep breath. He picked up the Benedictine medal and studied it carefully. With a solemn look, he pointed to the words written on the front of the envelope: "No soldier goes into battle unarmed."
    Anna opened her purse and fished around for something. She pulled out a thin green ribbon and reached for the medallion. Gabe handed it to her. She took the ribbon and threaded it through the small clasp attached to the top of the medallion, formed a loop, and tied the ends together.

"Here," she said as she raised it up. She leaned forward and placed it around Gabe's neck. She then tucked it inside his shirt collar. "Now you understand why Cardinal Bauer gave this to you. The great battle has begun. The cross is your armor."

Gabe nodded his head slowly. He felt a renewed sense of resolve. He was ready.

He looked at his watch. It was time to go. "Come on, Anna," he said. "We have a plane to catch."

THE AUTHORS

Dean and Catherine Reineking have been collaborating on writing projects and life for decades. Dean was an investment and financial consultant for over thirty years and is now writing full-time with Catherine, while managing the family's small resort near Glacier National Park. Catherine is a retired creative writing teacher and a trained marriage and family counselor. She and Dean are both students of history and enjoy traveling the world in pursuit of a good story. They are bicycling enthusiasts and live in Memphis, Tennessee where they raised three children and enjoy a vibrant life in the community. They can be reached at www.theamalfisecret.com.